Child-Sized History

Child-Sized History

Fictions of the Past in U.S. Classrooms

Sara L. Schwebel

Vanderbilt University Press / Nashville

Library of Congress Cataloging-in-Publication Data

Schwebel, Sara L.
Child-sized history : fictions of the past in
U.S. classrooms / Sara L. Schwebel.
p. cm.
Includes bibliographical references and index.
ISBN 978-0-8265-1792-0 (cloth edition : alk. paper)
ISBN 978-0-8265-1793-7 (pbk. edition : alk. paper)
1. United States—History—Study and teaching.
2. Historical fiction, American—Study and
teaching. 3. Literature and history—Study
and teaching—United States. 4. Children—
Books and reading—United States. I. Title.
E175.8.S375 2011
973.007—dc22
2011003010

For my mother, Carol Schwebel

Contents

Acknowledgments

■ It is a great pleasure to thank the many people who traveled with me during the journey of this book's creation. Julie Reuben and John Stauffer have been superb mentors; their approach to scholarship, advising, teaching, and community building continue to inspire me. During my years at Harvard, I received considerable nurture from outstanding scholars including Lizabeth Cohen, Nancy F. Cott, Evelyn Brooks Higginbotham, Jill Lepore, and Laurel Thatcher Ulrich. Along with members of the History of Education reading group at Harvard's Graduate School of Education, they have been critical to this work.

Erin Royston Battat, Judy Kertész, Sonia Lee, and Margot Minardi enveloped me in a supportive, creative, and intellectually stimulating community in graduate school. For listening to countless summaries of ideas-in-formation, reading multiple chapter drafts, and sharing hopes, dreams, and joys, I am extremely grateful. Scott Gelber, historian, teacher-educator, and former high school history teacher, read parts of this research in its earliest forms and provided important feedback on Chapter 5. Others at Harvard enriched my thinking in myriad ways; thanks to Michael Cohen, Carrie Endries, Yonatan Eyal, Carey Reeve, and Abby Williamson. Beyond the campus walls, friends from the Riverway Project challenged me to consider the many ways we interact with and teach pivotal texts; special thanks to Laura Abrasely, Jason Brown, Julie Childers, Beth Cousens, Staci Eisenberg, Seth Kosto, Bethie Miller, Molly Schmidt, Aaron Schwartz, and above all, Jeremy Morrison. The Knopovs provided a second home in Boston and, through Anita and David, a window into the daily lives of middle school students and their books. Conversations with Marisa Tabizon Thompson, Kristin Harris Walsh, and Kim Cary Warren took place primarily by phone and e-mail, but their questions and wisdom have been indispensable to this project and to my development as a scholar.

As I moved from Cambridge to Carolina, friends and colleagues supported me in important ways: thanks to faculty and staff in the departments of English, history, and Jewish studies, and especially to Bob Brinkmeyer, Emily Brock, Saskia Coenen-Snyder, Elaine Chun, Federica Clementi, Stan Dubinsky, Christy Friend, Brian Glavey, Chris Holcomb, Dianne Johnson, Catherine Keyser, Nina Levine, Tara Powell, David Riesman, Bill Rivers, and David Snyder. Anne Gulick not only read multiple chapters but also cheered me through the process with sage advice and immense enthusiasm. Katja Vehlow joined me in searching conversations about history, historiography, and teaching, helping me move toward manuscript completion.

My students—seventh and eighth graders in Virginia and Connecticut, undergraduates at the University of South Carolina, and doctoral and MAT candidates at the Harvard Graduate School of Education and USC—have helped clarify my thinking about reading, teaching, and learning from children's historical fiction. I am grateful to the many preservice teachers and adolescent readers who enthusiastically shared their thoughts about the texts discussed within these pages.

I am indebted to the novelists and their children, as well to the actors and directors in movie adaptations of *Sounder*, who shared books, personal papers, and family stories: Christopher (Kip) Armstrong, Joseph Bruchac, Mary Speare Carey, Christopher Collier, Suzzanne Douglas, Linwood Erskine, and Kevin Hooks. Brent Colley took me on an unforgettable tour of Redding, Connecticut, setting of *My Brother Sam Is Dead*. Librarians at the Schomburg Center for Research in Black Culture, the Howard Gotlieb Archival Center at Boston University, the Department of Rare Books and Special Collections at Princeton University, and the Kerlan Collection at the University of Minnesota (especially Karen Nelson Hoyle) were incredibly helpful, as was the staff at Harvard's Widener Library and the University of South Carolina's Thomas Cooper Library (especially Jeffrey Makala, Mark Volmer, and Greg Wilsbacher). For financial support, I thank the Mellon Foundation, the Humanities Center at Harvard, the Children's Literature Association, the Charles Warren Center for Studies in American History, and the University of South Carolina.

Michael Ames's enthusiasm for and belief in this book made working with Vanderbilt University Press a joy; his eye for clarity and exceptional editing sharpened the manuscript as a whole. For expert assistance steering the book through production, I thank Ed Huddleston and Jessie Hunnicutt.

The most important thanks go to my family, which has sustained me from the time I first became captivated by historical fiction. My mother, Carol, to whom this book is dedicated, has long been a champion of children's literature. While other adults pushed avid young readers to tackle Austen and Brontë, she gave me permission to linger over L. M. Montgomery and Louisa May Alcott, to read and reread *All-of-a-Kind-Family* and *Witch of Blackbird Pond*. I benefited enormously from this childhood pleasure. If my mother shaped me as a reader, it was my father, Andy, who helped me envision myself as a writer. I know how much he would have enjoyed discussing this book with me. My brother, David, the best mentor a little sister could have, and my grandfather, Milt, my role model for an intellectual life well lived, have been present from the start, watching me devour historical novels as both a grade-schooler and a doctoral student. Memories of my grandmothers echo in these pages: Bunky's love of nursery rhymes, picture books, and imagination expanded my world, while Ruth's gorgeously knitted doll blankets and carefully selected antiques brightened years of "old-fashioned" play. My uncles Bob and Len, aunts Claudia and Marian, sister-in-law Yikun, Boston cousins Robin Hodus and Geoffrey King, great aunts and uncles, and three generations of extended family showered me with love. Rosa and Andy, my niece and nephew, have given me the joy of sharing books and make-believe play with childlike wonder once again.

Child-Sized History

Introduction

■ I started first grade in 1982, a moment when the "whole language" and "authentic literature" movements began sweeping across U.S. schools, transforming the way teachers and librarians conceived of how children read. The new scholarship around literacy placed books, not reading instruction, at its center. Educators argued that if children could be hooked on the magic of story, they would develop into confident, capable readers. The key was matching each child to the right book at the right time. When a budding reader had access to high-interest, high-quality literature aimed at an appropriate level, motivation would take over, helping the beginning reader derive meaning from familiar words, colorful illustrations, and other cues both textual and extratextual.

The leading advocate of this authentic literature approach was Charlotte Huck, professor of education at Ohio State University. Her textbook *Children's Literature in the Elementary School* went through eight editions between 1961 and 2003, influencing hundreds of thousands of classroom teachers and helping to position Ohio State, the first university to endow a chair in children's literature, as a national leader in reading instruction and applied educational research.[1] Citing the capacity high-quality children's books had to improve reader fluency, comprehension, and vocabulary, advocates of authentic literature like Huck pressed for trade books—that is, literature written for children's pleasure rather than for their edification and marketed to individuals rather than to textbook committees—to be integrated throughout the curriculum.

Practically speaking, this push for "real books" had the largest effect in the areas of English language arts and social studies. Informational books about science and math existed, but they were often a difficult instructional fit, especially in teacher-centered classrooms. By contrast, historical fiction seemed ready-made for literature-based programs. Not only had it long been a popular genre in children's literature, but historical fiction also provided a convenient means for teachers to address the historical experiences of women and racial minorities, stories frequently

1

absent from textbooks. As the politics of multiculturalism entered K–12 schools in the 1980s, this became increasingly important. Ultimately, the dual influences of authentic literature and multiculturalism helped forge a classroom canon of middle-grade historical novels that were set in the United States and used to satisfy a range of educational aims. As these political and pedagogical trends merged with the growth of the middle school—an institution that emphasized interdisciplinarity, making it distinct from the high school in both its "junior" and "senior" capacities—historical novels became a common point of reference in many young people's knowledge of U.S. history.[2]

Born and raised a stone's throw away from Ohio State, I attended schools that adopted the authentic literature approach early and enthusiastically. Children's trade books appeared everywhere. Visits to the school library, "Sustained Silent Reading" (SSR) periods, and creative, artistic responses to literature were commonplace, as was the daily ritual of teachers reading aloud in the classroom. Novels, picture books, biographies, and informational texts crowded out textbooks' time in the limelight. Between the third and eighth grade, I read countless books in the middle-grade canon of historical fiction: novels and novellas that are regularly assigned to students who can independently tackle chapter books but who are not yet ready for canonical adult fiction. In doing so, I participated in a nationwide trend. Statistics testify to the pervasiveness of trade books in Generation X and Y childhoods: U.S. sales of children's books doubled between 1986 and 1990, crossing the $1 billion mark for the first time. By the 1990s, thanks in part to an authentic literature movement that convinced parents of the benefit of daily reading, children's books had become the fastest-growing segment of the American publishing industry.[3] Historical fiction was an important player in this trend. In fact, during the years in which children's book sales doubled, three out of five books winning the Newbery Medal—the top prize in American children's literature and an award that greatly increases a book's circulation—were historical fiction; a fourth was Russell Freedman's *Lincoln: A Photobiography*.[4] Not surprisingly, historical fiction entered school curricula with force; novels served as teacher read-alouds, independent reading selections, classroom-wide language arts texts, and supplements to the social studies textbook.

What does it mean for elementary and middle school students to learn U.S. history through trade books, and more specifically, through the historical novels that were widely adopted by schools in the 1980s and continue to circulate briskly today? When I first read from this classroom canon of historical fiction in elementary school, my teachers

guided me and my classmates in discussions about character development, literary themes, and historical settings. This last feature, setting,
was emphasized through a variety of extension projects that included
cooking food from the historical era, building models of period trans-
portation, and dressing up like the book's "old-fashioned" characters. For
me and many of my peers, the history embedded in the novels became
real. After being introduced to Laura Ingalls Wilder's series as a third-
grade read-aloud, I spent weeks reenacting parts of *The Long Winter*
with friends. We gathered berries on the school playground and tied
bundles of pine needles together to approximate the hay Pa used to heat
the family's Dakota Territory cabin. As historian Anita Clair Fellman has
documented, neither my school's extension projects nor my childhood
impulse to turn the Little House books into play is unique.[5] Although I
doubt my teachers knew of my elaborate recess reenactments, the school
curriculum actually encouraged it.

The fact that my classmates and I inserted ourselves into the Ingalls
family, vicariously experiencing their hardships and learning their lessons (the McGuffey Readers were habitually checked out of the school library), points to the way historical fiction works at one level: it stimulates
young people's interest in history by enabling them to imagine themselves in, and as part of, the past. The process of acting out historical
behaviors also triggers a degree of critical thinking. As students metaphorically travel back in time, they ask questions in an effort to imagine
how their lives may have differed had they been born in another time
and place. These questions build understanding about the relationship
between historical events (political and economic history) and people's
day-to-day realities (social history). Students might wonder, for example,
how the development of new technologies changed daily tasks like cooking and bathing, or how the kind of work adults engaged in affected the
kind of education they deemed appropriate for their children. Given that
high school students, who invariably study history from textbooks, consistently rank the subject among their least favorites, the use of historical
fiction in upper elementary and middle school seems to work a small
miracle. Proponents of the approach have made this claim forcefully.[6]

But there is also something thorny about children playing Laura Ingalls or adolescents engaging in novel extension activities that have them
reenacting the national past. Historical novels are always products of a
particular historical context. As a result, their characters and historical
arguments reflect the knowledge, politics, and worldview of authors at
a particular moment in time. Typically, children's historical novels invite reader identification with the protagonist and his or her immediate

family. This enables an intimate, visceral connection with the past, but it is also limiting. Throughout the colonial period and early republic, indigenous peoples were forcibly displaced to create "free" western lands for pioneers to settle. These characters—as well as their compulsory removal—have traditionally been minimized in fictional narratives of western settlement written for children. If a reader empathizes with a frontier protagonist, can she comprehend the experience of that woman's Native contemporaries?

When my classmates and I listened to our teacher read the Little House books and then became Laura Ingalls on the playground, we absorbed a celebratory narrative of the nation-state and inserted ourselves into an American myth: the settlement of western lands was part of the nation's Manifest Destiny; pioneers were heroic, self-sufficient individuals who tamed the wilderness single-handedly; and this story of westward expansion, self-sufficiency, and rural democracy is the shared heritage of all Americans, regardless of their ancestry. The argument of the Little House books, like those of children's historical novels more generally, is implicit rather than explicit. Neatly bound up in the confines of book covers, the polemic of the narrative and its interpretation of history are difficult to resist, especially when educators encourage children to become lost in books that are beautifully rendered.

The reenacting of historical events, experiences, and myths raises another troublesome issue: can twenty-first century moderns know and understand people remote in time, culture, and worldview? When today's students, far removed from the reality of personal danger, display empathy for historical peoples, at what point does their declaration of knowing and understanding become problematic, or even offensive? Historical novelists use their deep knowledge of the past, gleaned from the study of historical documents and secondary scholarship, to imagine the thoughts, feelings, and actions of three-dimensional historical figures. They do so attuned to the constraints of time and place, striving to create fictional and fictionalized characters appropriate to their setting and range of available worldviews. They self-consciously straddle the divide between fiction and history, balancing literature's belief in the ability to access universal truths of the human condition with history's guardedness about the possibility of accessing that which is distant, foreign, and irrevocably past. Despite their best efforts, individual novelists sometimes fail.

Fiction writers start with research and move from historical sources to analysis to creative art. In describing this process, Elizabeth George Speare, author of three children's novels set in colonial New England, wrote, "I began to read, carrying home armloads of books from the library. This, incidentally, is called research and I have said many times that it is the fun part of writing historical stories. . . . At last I could begin my story with some confidence, though many questions could never be answered with certainty. Sometimes, I had to choose from contradictory sources." Joseph Bruchac, author of numerous books set in Native North America, stresses the importance of oral as well as written historical sources. "I haven't mentioned academic research because that is what everyone mentions first," he said in describing his process of writing historical fiction. "In most cases, each story I've heard, I've also been able to find recorded in various texts. So I do make comparisons and do a scholarly study of those stories."[7] Speare and Bruchac describe similar research processes, but the novels they have written about the colonial American past often interpret the same historical events quite differently. The discrepancies between their interpretations of the past demand analysis, yet this need is rarely recognized in K–12 classroom practice.

The historical novels taught in schools today span more than a half century in creation. Older titles like Speare's *The Witch of Blackbird Pond* (1958) and *The Sign of the Beaver* (1983) circulate side by side with newer books like Joseph Bruchac's *Sacajawea: The Story of Bird Woman and the Lewis and Clark Expedition* (2000) and *The Winter People* (2002), novels that have expanded the characters, topics, and authorial backgrounds represented. The endurance of trade book titles contrasts starkly with the ephemerality of history textbooks, which are updated by publishers and replaced by schools on a regular basis. Unlike history textbooks, historical novels figure as both literary classics (infrequently replaced and rarely edited for language) *and* social studies curricula. As historical scholarship shifts, the historical arguments embedded in middle-grade fiction endure, frozen in time. This complicates the already complex issues embedded in the sanctioned and spontaneous historical play the books spawn. One of the oldest novels in the classroom canon is *Johnny Tremain*, Esther Forbes's story of the American Revolution. First published in 1943, *Johnny Tremain* includes the fleeting but unflattering appearance of a stereotypical "empty-headed" slave. Twenty-first century students would never encounter such a character in their history textbooks; the idea is unthinkable. But in a novel of more than eighty-two thousand words, the scene goes unnoticed.

It is precisely within this silence that promising pedagogical opportunities rest. The cyclical replacement of school textbooks obscures the fact that while the past itself is static, history—the interpretation of that past—continually evolves. History textbooks' authoritative tone masks this mediation of analysis, presenting their accounts of the past as definitive. Students who learn history from a textbook therefore understand its narrative as presenting the objective truth of "what really happened."[8] Historical novels trouble this notion of a master narrative even when they echo aspects of its logic, as do the fiction of Laura Ingalls Wilder, Elizabeth George Speare, and Esther Forbes. Because no single work of historical fiction covers the breadth of time and space encompassed by a history textbook, a novel must be paired with other works (often written by different authors at different moments in time) in order to tell a complete story of the nation-state. By creating space for incongruity, this juxtaposition of narratives invites questions, investigation, and analysis. A range of historical novels read collectively thus has the capacity to offer a kind of "people's history," a span of interpretative voices that vary across time and space.[9] Students and teachers who explore the commonalities and discrepancies among texts thus not only learn history but also gain the skills to participate in the larger debates about knowledge, truth, and perspective that color history discourse today.

Child-Sized History looks closely at historical fiction that has entered school curricula since the 1980s, books that continue to maintain their place in classroom lessons today even as recent education policy has emphasized accountability, basic skills, and standardized tests. Specifically, this book examines those novels in the middle-grade canon that are concerned with the history of the United States as a nation, a topic often taught in the fourth, fifth, and eighth grades.[10] These widely assigned novels share in common the ability to negotiate turbulent political waters, frequently by pairing traditional American social values with representations of diverse American peoples. Reading the books as a group reveals that the authentic literature and multicultural movements have proved mutually reinforcing, generating surprising consensus among the political left and right—and among school reading lists nationwide.

Today's classroom teachers retain considerable influence over the selection of day-to-day teaching materials, even amid a nationwide movement to centralize curricula by means of standardized tests, state textbook adoption, and core achievement goals shared across the United States.[11] This continued local independence makes it impossible to measure with precision the reach of any given historical novel in today's schools. Nonetheless, it is feasible to track nationwide trends. The adoption of a book by a populous state or by many large school districts triggers a cycle that all but ensures its adoption elsewhere in the country. Publishers respond to educators' demand by printing inexpensive paperbacks that can be purchased through school and trade book markets, a process that makes the books affordable to all. As more educators use the texts, teacher-created lesson plans appear on the Internet and in bookstores, and student study aids materialize in the form of SparkNotes and other reading guides. Paper mill sites provide another sure sign that a book is being read in school, as book reports and student essays clustered around a particular novel begin to appear for purchase. As a result, it is possible to gauge nationwide curricular trends through repeated searches for middle-grade titles on high-traffic websites, by regularly monitoring display tables for summer reading and other school assignments in bookstores and libraries, and by following online booksellers' up-to-the-minute sales rankings.

These measures, which fluctuate daily, can be juxtaposed with harder and more stable numbers. In 2010, 12 percent of U.S. states published on their Department of Education website lists of fiction titles (or in the case of Massachusetts, authors) that the state endorsed or that classroom teachers within the state recommended. Additionally, the Common Core State Standards Initiative created a language arts framework that includes a list of approximately ten trade book titles for every grade-level category. Renaissance Learning, producer of a widely adopted commercial literacy program, tracks annually which children's trade books its 6.2 million users read at each grade level. Data from *Publishers Weekly*, which regularly publishes a list of the 101 all-time best-selling children's paperbacks, complement online booksellers' real-time sales ranking by capturing long-term trends. Of the novels in the classroom canon of historical fiction discussed in this book, ten figure on *Publishers Weekly*'s most recent list, published in 2001.[12] Other documentable factors help assess a novel's overall popularity, including the creation of a sequel, movie adaptation, Spanish-language edition, audiobook recording, or school-group museum program designed to enhance students' study of the book.

Not all texts examined in *Child-Sized History* have qualified for inclusion in the canon. In some cases, analysis of award-winning novels not (yet) widely taught helps illustrate trends likely to influence school curricula in the future.[13] In other instances, analysis of an older award-winning historical novel that was never widely assigned illuminates the boundaries of the canon, which has been characterized since its inception by its ability to satisfy both the political left and right.[14]

Historical fiction figures in students' academic lives in interdisciplinary ways; similarly, this book approaches the place of historical fiction in U.S. classrooms through historical, literary, and pedagogical lenses. Chapter 1 traces the way three different but related developments—the

War on Poverty, multiculturalism, and the rise of the authentic literature movement—fused to bring historical novels into U.S. classrooms during the 1980s. Historical fiction has been written about a dizzying array of topics, but children's books set in the United States and widely taught in U.S. schools develop the themes of indigeneity, war, and race with singular frequency. Together, these topics outline the myth of the U.S. nation-state: Europeans arrived in the New World, tamed the wilderness, and replaced "primitive" tribes; war established Anglo-Americans as an independent people, forged a common culture and purpose, and solidified the national values of freedom and democracy; and the eradication of slavery enabled the nation to embrace diversity and recognize, at last, the common bond shared by all Americans. Chapters 2–4 explore each of these themes in turn, offering close readings of narratives grouped thematically and presented chronologically.

By weaving together literary analysis, author biography, and cultural and intellectual history, I demonstrate how historical novels should be conceptualized as both literature and history, and as both primary sources and historiographical markers. In tracing the protean nature of literary representations of the past, Chapters 2–4 also model the kind of deep, contextualized reading of children's literature that could transform the teaching and learning of history in middle and high school classrooms. Historical novelists do not write in isolation. Rather, their books reflect engagement with contemporary politics, evolving academic scholarship, and current trends in children's book publishing. Probing the nature of that complex relationship is central to critically reading an author's historical fiction.

Chapter 5 shifts the focus from historical novels and novelists to educational research, training, and practice. Teachers and administrators operate under federal and state policy that has accelerated standardized testing, privileged reading and mathematics over history, and called for "scientifically based" literacy research that in practice construes reading narrowly, thus ignoring the complexity of skills needed to interpret historical writing. Chapter 5 traces the history of recent policy changes and examines the effect that the educational research, teacher training, and standardized testing generated by those changes has had on historical fiction's classroom use. Additionally, this chapter highlights existing challenges to transforming conversations about historical fiction—and history—in today's K–12 classrooms. Unsurprisingly, the obstacles are global in nature, requiring new priorities in academic research, school assessment, children's book publishing, and the education and professional development of teachers. Yet, there is much a single teacher, and even more a team of teachers, can do to tap the rich pedagogical potential of historical novels already present in classrooms. Dedicated classroom teachers and teacher educators need not wait for wholesale change to take action.

The afterword is written with teachers and teacher educators in mind. In this final section of the book, I offer a vision for a powerful new way to engage students with historical fiction. As teachers have long known, historical novels capture students' interest in the past. The many historical novels set in the United States and taught in today's schools, however, have the capacity to do much more. Historical novels can be taught in ways that both develop students' understanding of history as a discipline and help students to understand the nation as a means of organizing society and an entity that engages in political action, including telling stories about itself. When students and teachers interact with historical fiction in this way, the books they read can become catalysts to cultivating thoughtful, engaged citizens.

Chapter 1

Classroom Entry

■ In a middle school classroom in Iowa, students who have just finished reading William H. Armstrong's Newbery Medal–winning novel, *Sounder*, turn to a teacher-created assignment to extend their learning. The story of an African American boy and his sharecropping family, *Sounder* is a poignant tale of oppression, hardship, and individual triumph over meager circumstances. Written by a white southerner transplanted to New England, the book—first published in 1969—is very much a product of its time. The Iowa teenagers studying the novel, however, read it without regard to the historical context of its creation. Their teacher instructs them to compare and contrast three aspects of African American life in the late nineteenth-century and early twenty-first-century South: "folk medicine vs. modern medicine, Bible stories as literature vs. newspaper articles, chain gangs vs. modern criminal punishment." In Nashville, Tennessee, ninth-grade students reading *Sounder* complete a similar exercise. Their teacher-created assignment asks, "How does rural life in the early part of this century differ from the life we live today?"[1] Other classroom activities might engage students in considering character development, narration, and symbolism—literary entrées into the text—but the questions above, which consider change over time, indicate that teachers are using the novel to explore history.

In these lessons based on *Sounder*, students are encouraged to conceive of U.S. history as a tale of progress. Teachers prompt students to consider two time periods, that of the novel's setting and that of the present day, and guide them to view the contemporary period as superior. Moreover, students are discouraged from considering the intervening period, the years between the past of the novel's setting and the present of today; there is no room to imagine that change could have taken another form or that the present was not inevitable. The predetermined line of inquiry differs starkly from the approach of professional historians, who seek to understand the past on its own terms. By treating change as inevitable and a positive good, the teachers' questions foster a heritage-based, as opposed to history-based, relationship to the past.[2] Students are directed to view historical figures as role models whose virtuous attributes—in *Sounder*, a connection to the land and its natural rhythms, a personal relationship to the Bible, and strong families and faith—constitute the common heritage of the nation. Negative aspects of the past—in *Sounder*, ignorance, cruelty, and racism—are understood as deviations from national culture that have been corrected over time. That a heritage-based approach tied to authentic literature can embrace African American history illustrates the success of the multicultural initiative in schools as well as the limitations that success entails. Emphasizing the similarities of the American experience across race, class, religion, and gender can obscure the *differences* Jim Crow and other racist practices maintained—and the continuing legacy of those practices in the present. A heritage-based approach to the past sees its purpose as serving the present; it deters questioning of the way either the past or the present is conceptualized.

Importantly, the teachers' heritage-based questions about *Sounder* privilege text over context and subtext. Students are asked to cull details from the novel, regard them (uncritically) as evidence of how people lived, worked, and thought at the dawn of the twentieth century, and then draw comparisons to the present. The novel stands as a reliable source of historical information about the past rather than as a historical narrative that has been constructed by a particular person at a particular moment in time. Notably, the questions do not ask students to look at the novel's publication date and consider how the complex civil rights movement that gave birth to the tale might have shaped its interpretation of both the problems of the postbellum South and the potential solutions it offered for addressing racial inequality in its present (the late 1960s). The questions, moreover, do not ask students to articulate the novel's argument about how racial uplift is achieved—by means of individual, rather than societal, change—or to consider how this figures in the political debates of the 1960s and 1970s. Nor do the questions ask students to move beyond the text to research the author's life and politics or to consider the relationship between his identity, his message, and the book's reception across racial and political communities, then and now.[3]

Of course, the teacher-created questions presented at the beginning of this chapter are but a fraction of the many questions teachers might pose during the course of studying *Sounder* with students; absent of in-depth qualitative research, it is impossible to know the complete nature of instruction. Nonetheless, analysis of these published questions is instructive; they capture qualities common to many lessons on historical novels outlined in commercial curriculum guides and available on teacher- and publisher-produced Internet lesson plans.

How did books like *Sounder* and the range of teachers' questions associated with them come to dominate school curricula at the end of the twentieth century? A number of factors came together during the 1980s to set the course for this trend: publishing houses became increasingly concerned with the bottom line and aware of children's books as a profitable commodity, educators sought to balance multicultural initiatives with a deep commitment to the social studies as a means of citizenship education, and schools nationwide embraced the use of trade books as well as textbooks as core curricular tools.

Children's Librarians, Children's Editors, and the Literati Ideal

The classroom canon that includes *Sounder* coalesced during the 1980s; its shape, therefore, reflects even today the range of historical novels available for adoption at that time. Well into the 1960s, public libraries were the central purchaser of children's books in the United States and children's librarians the primary reviewers of these texts.[4] During the inter- and postwar period, children's librarians were a fairly homogeneous group of well-educated, well-heeled, white women. They held tremendous sway over the content and scope of children's trade publishing, often consulting directly with those of similar race, social class, and aesthetic bent who ran the children's literature desks at New York, Philadelphia, and Boston publishing houses. The intertwining personal and professional relationships between librarians and editors—what some have termed a "benign conspiracy"—influenced the imaginative range of manuscripts accepted for publication and the "feel" of a children's book, both literally in terms of paper quality and literarily in terms of subject and form, for much of the twentieth century.[5] Children's literature scholar Kenneth Kidd has used the term "edubrow" to describe the middlebrow aesthetic shared by twentieth-century librarians, public school teachers, and children's book editors.[6] Midcentury "juvenile" historical novels capture this style and value system perfectly. Literary trends rose and fell throughout the century, but children's librarians returned to praise historical fiction again and again, awarding historical novels the industry's highest prize, the Newbery Medal, with disproportionate frequency.[7] Teachers seeking books for curricular adoption in the 1980s thus had an abundance of award-winning historical novels to choose from.

Despite the homogeneity of the mid-twentieth-century world of children's books, the diversity of texts produced and available for canonization was less limited than one might suppose. As historian Julia Mickenberg has demonstrated, the reputation of the founding generation of children's editors as conservative, elitist, and staid is somewhat misplaced. All had been trained with the idea that books and their guardians were "apostles of culture," but as public-spirited reformers, some were also attracted to progressive and even leftist messages.[8] These interests are reflected in the attention children's books show to matters of race, civil rights, and free speech, particularly in the postwar period. During the Cold War, two important trends emerged: left-leaning children's authors who had previously published with small, communist presses began seeking mainstream publishing houses, and adult writers like Meridel Le Sueur and Helen Kay, who had been blacklisted for leftist political activity, reinvented themselves as juvenile authors and found safe havens in the children's division of mainstream presses. The influx of both categories of writers affected picture books—generating, for example, Syd Hoff's *Danny and the Dinosaur* (1958) and William Steig's Caldecott Medal–winning *Sylvester and the Magic Pebble* (1969)—and nonfiction, particularly biographies and science books for elementary and middle school readers. Left-leaning writers had far less influence on historical novels; books were produced, but they neither won the Newbery nor made inroads into classrooms. Le Sueur's *Sparrow Hawk*, for example, was published by Alfred A. Knopf in 1950 but soon went out of print.[9] By contrast, Elizabeth Yates's *Amos Fortune, Free Man*, a white apologist narrative for slavery published the same year, won the Newbery and continues to appear on the state-recommended reading lists of California, New York, and Alaska. Elizabeth George Speare's book *The Sign of the Beaver* (1983), which is thematically similar to Le Sueur's *Sparrow Hawk* in that it features a friendship between a European American boy and a Native boy, won the Newbery Honor (awarded to runners-up) and has similarly enjoyed an exalted status. Despite vocal criticism by indigenous peoples beginning in the 1980s, it remains widely taught in today's classrooms even as *Sparrow Hawk*, which was reissued in 1987 with a foreword by prominent Native scholar Vine Deloria Jr. (Standing Rock Sioux), languishes out of print.[10]

Racial and ethnic diversity appeared first in public libraries, then in publishing houses, but in both cases, change came slowly. In the 1930s, Charlemae Hill Rollins became the first African American to rise to a position of influence in the field when she was named head of children's services in a Chicago Public Library branch; from this position, which she held into the early 1960s, she launched a letter-writing campaign aimed at publishers to raise awareness about the dearth of appropriate books for the predominantly African American children her library served. Both she and Augusta Baker, whose career followed a similar trajectory in New York City, published guides to literature for African American children. Librarians from other minority groups made similar efforts but faced even greater challenges. Best known is Pura Teresa Belpré, the first Puerto Rican employed by the New York Public Library system.[11]

The persistence of barriers to the kind of change sought by librarians such as Rollins, Baker, and Belpré can be seen in the work of the 1958 Newbery Medal committee, which Rollins chaired. Harold Keith's *Rifles for Watie*, a reconciliationist—and therefore arguably racist—bildungsroman narrative in which Union soldier Jefferson Davis Bussey marries a slaveholding Cherokee belle, was selected as the winning text. Knowing that demand for a Newbery-winning book increases to such an extent that reprinting is routine after announcement of the award, Rollins approached Keith seeking changes to the language describing slave characters. Although Keith was open to multiple alterations, only a select few were made. Of course, editorial changes would not reverse the reconciliationist assumptions of the novel—its naturalization of North and South's postwar reunion and simultaneous erasure of racial conflict as both trigger and outcome of the Civil War—but Rollins's failure to secure even this small concession is telling.[12] Focused almost exclusively on what was termed literary quality in identifying "the most distinguished contribution to American literature for children," neither librarians selecting Newbery winners nor publishers cultivating contenders for the prize were yet attuned to subtexts.

But change was afoot. In 1965, politicized by the civil rights movement, like-minded librarians of varied racial and ethnic backgrounds joined with activists outside librarianship to form the Council on Interracial Books for Children (CIBC). Influenced by the feminist, Black Power, and personal liberation movements, the CIBC was committed to raising awareness about stereotypes, distortions, and racialized representations in children's literature. Moreover, it was committed to fostering publication of minority-authored children's books. The manuscript contests the CIBC launched to attract minority authors would eventually lead the American Library Association (ALA) to establish book prizes, including the Pura Belpré Award and Coretta Scott King Award, specifically for literature authored and illustrated by people of color. Long before the ALA began its top-down transformation, however, librarians frustrated with the professional organization's inattention to the needs of African American constituencies formed a black caucus.[13]

As the diverse voices of public librarians began to be heard, shifts also occurred in the publishing industry. Children's books became big business: in 1964, juvenile sales totaled $112 million, a figure comparable to that of hardcover adult trade books. Yet at the time, fewer than three thousand children's books—10 percent of the publishing industry's output—were produced annually.[14] To meet rapidly increasing market demand, children's desks expanded even as publishing houses consolidated and the old way of doing business—the personal relationships developed between a single children's editor and her authors and between an editor and her (East Coast) librarian advocates—eroded. The new corporate climate that materialized made a focus on the bottom line paramount.

The emergence of the public school as a market rivaling that of public libraries for middle-grade trade books played an important role in shaping production in this new era. Librarians continued to write the majority of children's book reviews and select the recipients of the most important literary prizes, but increasingly, teachers' enthusiasm for a title affected sales. The lackluster performance of *Rifles for Watie*, the ALA's 1958 Newbery pick, is instructive. The novel's 105,000-plus word count made it impractical for classroom use even as its racist character descriptions rapidly dated the book in the era following *Brown v. Board of Education* (1954).[15] In the next decade, the distance between librarians and teachers would decrease as ALA committees chose titles such as *Island of the Blue Dolphins*, *A Wrinkle in Time*, *Mrs. Frisby and the Rats of NIMH*, and *Julie of the Wolves* as Newbery winners; these were books that upper elementary and middle school teachers warmly embraced.[16] Publishers had courted K–12 teachers as consumers since at least the 1920s, but during the postwar period, new realities made schools especially open to publishers' offerings. Fearful that the Soviet Union would surpass the United States in military capacity and scientific advancement, Congress passed the National Defense Education Act (NDEA) in 1958, granting funds to schools for the purchase of math and science books. The federal money gave publishers the opening they had long craved; they scrambled to produce informational books on everything from the Milky Way to the human heart, and educators joyfully restocked their library shelves. In the process, publishers learned key lessons about marketing trade books to public schools, knowledge that they would use when antipoverty legislation passed in the next decade generated more funds for educators to use for purchasing books.

Desegregating Textbooks and Trade Books

The Elementary and Secondary Education Act (ESEA) of 1965 proved transformative for children's literature. The ESEA married Lyndon Johnson's Great Society to both school desegregation and federal aid for K–12 schools, providing significant market demand for racially diverse children's books. Title II of the ESEA not only increased the amount of federal funding available to schools but also made $400 million available *specifically* for book purchases.[17] This funding, moreover, came with federal oversight; under the Civil Rights Act of 1964, the federal government could withhold what were now considerable funds from any school districts refusing to desegregate. Additionally, it could stipulate that when federal money was spent, it be used in ways that furthered the administration's larger agenda of eradicating poverty and advancing racial equality.

As the national press had reported earlier that year, American textbook publishers were producing two versions of standard texts, one for the northern market (in which African Americans appeared) and one for the southern market (in which they did not). Given that testimony for *Brown* had included findings demonstrating the psychological damage that school segregation wrought on black children, it followed that monocultural textbooks that segregated the black experience could inflict similar damage. Therefore, the Congressional Committee on Education and Labor formed an ad hoc subcommittee on de facto school segregation in 1965 to investigate, among other issues, "the role of the publishing industry in producing books suitable for the needs of the educationally disadvantaged, low income, and what is variously referred to as culturally deprived schoolchildren [and] the treatment of minority groups and their role in American society in the basic reading texts used in all schools."[18] As federal oversight of book purchases became a reality in every school district receiving federal money—that is, any district enrolling children from low-income families—trade book publishers discovered that racially and culturally diverse books sold. Textbook publishers, meanwhile, learned they had better adjust to a new market if they hoped to stay in business.

Forced to negotiate the demands of diverse constituencies, textbook publishers found themselves on the defensive, asking how they could satisfy—or at least not offend—the greatest possible number of customers on both sides of the Mason-Dixon Line.[19] U.S. history and social studies texts proved especially tricky for reasons both practical and political. When minority actors were added to the narrative, it became more difficult to tell a story about core American values present from the nation's birth. It also became more challenging to tell a story of relentless progress. A stated aim of teaching U.S. history, however, was to cultivate patriotism; how could one confront the nation's failings, particularly with regard to race, and still fulfill that goal? If psychological damage could result from school curricula, how could slavery and racial oppression be addressed in a classroom without causing harm to either the descendants of slaves or the descendants of slaveholders? How could a book be mild enough to offend no one and still interesting enough to hold teachers' and students' interests?

Textbook writers tackled the challenge of rewriting school histories for new times and new markets. Taking their lead from disciplinary shifts in the academy, some addressed the issue of inclusion by abandoning the "great-man" approach to storytelling and embracing the new social history with its arguments that social forces, as well as people, shaped action in the past.[20] By eliminating heroes and villains, these texts created an illusion of scientific objectivity and political neutrality, making them safe for a national market and acceptable to readers of various backgrounds and identities. The strategy backfired, however, because in the process of striving for objectivity, the textbooks obscured individual responsibility for historical actions. Critics disparaged the books as morally ambiguous and thus anathema to school history instruction.[21]

In addition to failing in their role of citizen building, these textbooks proved difficult for children to read. Because the texts lacked storylike elements and characters with whom children could identify, young readers struggled to insert themselves within them, to see their lives as part of the nation's story. Yet authors who chose to retain a great-man approach, expanding definitions to include *more* great men (and women), fared little better. Minority actors appeared as afterthoughts, great men and women whose stories didn't fit the superficially revised narrative and were therefore relegated to sidebars.[22] The fundamental disconnect between the central narrative and these add-ons led to predictable results: most students skipped over the "additional" information. Regardless of whether authors abandoned or retained in modified form the great-man approach, post-*Brown* textbooks were held to new standards of diction in the wake of the ESEA's federal oversight. Groups from the left, best represented by the CIBC, succeeded in establishing antiracist, antisexist standards for publishers. Editors' attempts to dance around controversy by omitting divisive words, events, and images, however, frequently displeased the left as well as the right, since the narratives that resulted were less interesting, less cohesive, and substantively—that is, in terms of historical argument—unchanged.[23] No one was happy.

As separate northern and southern editions disappeared and bias and sensitivity guidelines became industry standards, a new textbook landscape emerged. States seeking to monitor the issues, ideas, and images presented to students strengthened or created textbook adoption policies; committees then approved a set list of texts that they determined met state instructional goals. So-called adoption states gained disproportionate influence over the textbook market as publishers sought inclusion on approval lists. Twenty-two states, most in the Sunbelt with growing school-age populations, have adoption policies today.[24] Texas and California are the biggest, and to a degree, the states' curricular priorities balance each other out: the Texas Board of Education has advanced a conservative agenda while the California Board has advanced a liberal one. But as Joan DelFattore argues in *What Johnny Shouldn't Read: Textbook Censorship in America* (1992), balance is not necessarily a good thing: "Publishers aiming for the approved lists in both states have responded by producing books designed, as far as possible, not to offend anyone. In order to increase minority representation in textbooks, for example, publishers include Martin Luther King's 'I Have a Dream' speech in high school literature anthologies—but only after removing references to racism in various Southern states, making the speech sound bland."[25] The result of more than a decade of such compromises, one historian wryly observed, was that "the market for texts held together, but the story they told began to fall apart."[26] Again, no one was happy.

Given widespread dissatisfaction with history textbooks, many educators sought an alternative. Passage of the ESEA made trade books a viable option by providing funding that enabled schools, sometimes for the first time, to purchase curricular "extras," including historical novels, biographies, and nonfiction reference books that could supplement or replace less-than-satisfactory textbooks.[27] The ESEA did not close the achievement gap, but it did, in a roundabout way, diversify the curricular materials available to disadvantaged children.[28] Just as federal money and federal oversight had influenced the production of textbooks, they now influenced the offerings of trade book publishers. The ESEA created an unprecedented market for children's literature in the first five years of its implementation, and it stimulated interest in books reflective of American society as a whole, including the populations constituting the "educationally disadvantaged."[29] In this regard, it differed radically from the NDEA of 1958, which also influenced trade book publishers' offerings but was aimed at and primarily benefited "gifted" students (largely white and middle class). Passage of the ESEA, by contrast, created demand for trade books exploring the black experience.[30] Numbers tell the story: whereas black characters appeared in 6.7 percent of all children's literature in 1965, the year of the ESEA's passage, black characters appeared in 14.4 percent of all children's books ten years later. More dramatically, 60 percent of black characters in children's books circulating in 1965 appeared in settings outside of the United States, while only 20 percent of black characters in 1975 were depicted as non-American.[31]

The year 1965 proved critical for other reasons. A decade after *Brown*, it was painfully obvious how little had changed. In what would prove to be a widely cited and frequently replicated study, Nancy Larrick—former associate children's editor at Random House and founder of the International Reading Association—investigated the presence or absence of African Americans in recently released children's books, publishing her results in the *Saturday Review of Books*. Her article, "The All-White World of Children's Literature," directly addressed the gap between stated federal goals and the reality market-produced books showed: "Integration may be the law of the land, but most of the books children see are all white."[32] The missive provided further stimulus to an already-primed-for-profit publishing industry. So, too, did the formation of the CIBC, which, beginning in 1966, began awarding annual prizes to the best children's manuscripts by previously unpublished African Americans (and in subsequent years, members of other minority groups). Hand-delivered to mainstream publishers, a number of these manuscripts found their way into print, and then into libraries and classrooms.

The period of expansion was short-lived. Federal money began to evaporate by the early 1970s, as Richard Nixon replaced Lyndon Johnson in the White House, and had shrunk considerably by the Reagan-Bush era of the 1980s. Nonetheless, trade book publishers, eager to sustain market growth, continued publishing the now-established minority authors as well as fiction that tackled racial themes; they also began experimenting with the production of "literary" or "edubrow" children's books in paperback.[33] Prior to the 1970s, 85 percent of all children's books were sold for use in public or school libraries. During that era, as the *New York Times* reported in 1972, "so few children's books of quality were available to the ordinary bookbuyer in paper cover that the question 'where does a parent or a child of any age start in selecting a good paperback?' would have been pointless."[34] Retail stores initially eschewed children's paperbacks, but soft-cover books entered the school market through the efforts of the children's book publisher Scholastic, which sponsored book clubs and book fairs that targeted parent (and child) consumers. Even more important, paperbacks entered classrooms through direct bulk orders from schools choosing to adopt novels for instruction.[35] It was this latter trend in particular that created a classroom canon dotted with historical fiction titles.

Issued in paperback, historical novels addressed the problems of expensive, narratively bland history textbooks and the continued sidelining of nonwhite, nonmale actors in traditional narratives. For many teachers, these were driving motivations for introducing novels like *Sounder* into the curriculum. An unrelated development in literacy research, however, was equally if not more important. In fact, it was the confluence of three trends that crystallized in the 1960s, reached maturity in the 1980s, and continue to spawn innovation, criticism, and study today that created a classroom niche for middle-grade historical novels: the authentic literature movement, multiculturalism, and the rise of the middle school as distinct from the junior high and K–8 primary.

Authentic Literature, the Middle School, and the Trade Book as Text

During the decades coinciding with court-ordered desegregation and its aftermath, a staggering 80 percent of American children were learning how to read using Scott, Foresman's basal reader series, which featured the characters Dick and Jane.[36] Methodologically, the readers were rooted in a "whole language" approach to literacy acquisition; the textbooks aimed to build fluency and confidence by means of repetition and gradual, strategic exposure to new words within a familiar narrative context. The whole language approach differs from phonics instruction, which initiates children into the world of literacy through step-by-step mastery of alphabetic letters and blended pairs; in a strict phonics approach, children learn to "sound out" words before they begin reading books.[37] In 1955, readability expert Rudolf Flesch attacked the dominance of whole language pedagogy in a provocatively titled book aimed at a popular audience, *Why Johnny Can't Read and What You Can Do about It*.[38] The book, which advocated a return to phonics, sold half a million copies and spent thirty weeks on the best-seller list. Many elementary schools responded to the critique articulated by Flesch (and others in the field) by bolstering phonics instruction as a supplement to the look-and-say approach used in primary grades. Publishing houses, however, responded in a different way. Attuned to complaints about the numbingly dull Dick and Jane "adventures," editors sought out authors who could write enticing stories for beginning readers using the same controlled vocabulary found in whole language textbooks like Dick and Jane. Dr. Seuss and the I Can Read series were among the best results.

As the debate raged over how best to teach reading, a new element gained prominence: *what* rather than *how* to teach. In many ways, it proved less controversial and more influential in shaping late twentieth- and early twenty-first-century curriculum, despite the fact that it became entangled in the politics of race and power. During the 1980s, following a period in which phonics had regained ascendancy in the wake of Flesch's and others' critiques, the whole language approach once again gained dominance.[39] This time around, however, whole language (the "how") was tied to a rejection of basal readers (the "what"), whose fate mirrored that of social studies texts: their attempt to please all—Dick and Jane were joined by a group of middle-class black characters in the 1965 edition—ended in their pleasing none.[40] Whole language advocates pressed for the replacement of basal readers with authentic literature, books written for children rather than for instructional purposes. Because effective literacy instruction ensures that children become fluent readers by second or third grade, the association of whole language instruction and trade books initially affected elementary schools exclusively. But the logic of using high-interest, authentic literature to aid in learning easily translated into the middle grades. If books like *The Cat and the Hat* could help young children become readers, it made sense that high-interest titles like *Sounder* could similarly aid competent readers in moving to the next stages of literacy development: reading for pleasure, information, and point of view.

The rise of the middle school and its distinctive philosophy of organizing curriculum and preparing teachers gave further impetus to the logic of incorporating authentic literature in general and historical fiction in particular into the middle-grade classroom. The middle school movement from its inception emphasized interdisciplinarity and the privileging of students and their interests over school subjects narrowly construed. If high school teachers and their junior high counterparts were viewed as teaching *disciplines*—physics, Latin, history—middle school teachers prided themselves on teaching *students*. Founded in 1973, the National Middle School Association (NMSA) has remained committed to this ideal over the course of almost four decades. NMSA's 2002 position statement on curriculum integration, for example, reads, "We must encourage middle level educators to push themselves beyond the conventional, separate subject format and to expand their use of integrated curriculum formats."[41] The rationale for interdisciplinarity presented in middle-education publications parallels in some ways the argument unfolding in higher education that artificial disciplinary divides frustrate creative thinking around problems that demand knowledge and research skills rooted in multiple disciplines. But the movement for interdisciplinarity among middle-grade educators is less about frontiers of knowledge than about processes of learning and developmental stages.

Middle-level educators link interdisciplinarity to their belief that teachers' focus should be on students and their ideas rather than on academic subjects and students' mastery thereof. According to the NMSA, the ideal middle school curriculum should be general, exploratory, and student centered as opposed to specialized, rigid, and teacher directed. This line of argumentation complements earlier critiques of basal readers and textbooks that pointed to the way prepackaged curriculum thwarted both student-centered learning and teacher creativity. In a series of articles and an influential book, education professor Patrick Shannon argued that the system of teaching reading by means of basal readers and their didactic teacher editions "deskilled" classroom educators by transforming the art of teaching into a series of mechanized steps that divorced knowledge of children from knowledge of literacy.[42] As Shannon explained in his 1989 book, "Administrators sought to control teachers' use of the teachers' guidebook and materials in order to limit the choices they had to make before and during lessons."[43] Shannon's recommendations for reinvigorating literacy instruction by replacing "scientific" basal readers with authentic children's literature thus served purposes both pedagogical and political. Authentic literature empowered teachers to use their expertise, including knowledge of the specific students in their classroom, to select books best suited for instructional purposes. This logic matched that espoused by the NMSA: the magic of education lay in what teachers knew about their students and adolescent development, not in foolproof lesson plans designed for all teachers to use with all students.

In order to facilitate its vision for middle-level education, the NMSA advocated differential training for pre-service teachers preparing for careers in the middle grades. Pre-service high school teachers are trained as specialists prepared to teach one academic discipline at advanced levels.

Pre-service elementary school teachers, by contrast, are trained as generalists prepared to teach all core subjects at the primary level. Where middle-level certification programs exist (in twenty-three states and the District of Columbia), however, pre-service teachers must demonstrate mastery of two academic subjects, a stipulation designed to foster interdisciplinary thinking.[44] By encouraging interdisciplinarity in teacher training, professional development, and academic research, the NMSA primes middle school teachers to embrace the use of historical novels. Historical fiction's inherent blending of social studies content and literary form fits beautifully into the middle school curriculum concept even as its diverse historical actors address persistent issues of underrepresentation in school textbooks.

Ultimately, what made authentic literature and use of historical novels in middle grades pervasive was that both left-leaning *and* right-leaning states championed the idea. In 1987, California, a textbook adoption state, established whole language (K–3) and literature-based (4–8) curricula for all its elementary and middle schools.[45] Solidly Democratic since the end of the Reagan years, California has advanced an educational agenda dominated—if not entirely controlled—by liberals; the state's literacy programs are no exception. And because of California's large school-age population, its curricular decisions affect the rest of the country as well. When the Golden State assembled a list of recommended trade book titles for all grades K–8, book publishers took note. California's stamp of approval guaranteed sales, meaning that publishers could reissue and market modern, affordable editions of California-recommended titles for wide distribution both within and outside the state. The reading list has been updated and expanded regularly since its inception, creating a steady market for titles now frequently released in special school editions.[46]

Trade books appeared equally attractive to states dominated by political conservatives; although few followed California in developing a list of recommended trade books, authentic literature nonetheless moved into classrooms in these states. Unlike textbooks published by large corporations in the politically correct era of the 1980s and 1990s, trade books were written by private citizens who used whatever diction they wished. True, textbooks and their teacher guides provided a surer means of shaping curriculum and controlling teacher initiative than did trade books, which were not published with step-by-step teacher guides. But the language policing and self-censorship practiced by textbook publishers frustrated conservatives as much as, if not more than, the continued ghettoizing of minority concerns exasperated liberals. As textbook companies poured more and more money into eye-catching graphics and computer technology in the hopes that adoption committees would overlook bland narratives and PC language, many on both sides of the political spectrum refused to be persuaded. "By the end of the 1980s," historian and social critic Diane Ravitch wrote,

> every publisher had complied with the demands of the critics, both from left and right. Publishers had established bias guidelines with which they could impose self-censorship and head off the outside censors, as well as satisfy state adoption reviews. Achieving demographic balance and excluding sensitive topics had become more important to their success than teaching children to read or to appreciate good literature. . . . So long as books and stories continue to be strained through a sieve of political correctness, fashioned by partisans of both left and right, all that is left for students to read will be thin gruel.[47]

Trade books, by contrast, presented themselves as a hearty bowl of oatmeal. Written by an individual rather than assembled by a committee, and marketed to independent consumers rather than to state adoption agencies, novels neither self-censored nor participated in political hoop-jumping. And they frequently contained rich vocabulary and memorable characters to boot.

Pleasing Left and Right Alike

Teachers who turned to trade books in the 1980s found historical novels particularly attractive choices. Historical fiction fulfilled the interdisciplinary aims prized by the middle-grade concept, featured minority characters with frequency, and boasted a disproportionate number of Newbery Medals and starred reviews. More important, they seemed "safe" at a time when the taboos of 1950s children's literature (sex, violence, bad language, disobedience absent of consequences) were crumbling, particularly in realistic fiction. Consider, for example, two adolescent novels about teenage love. Elizabeth George Speare's *The Witch of Blackbird Pond*, published in 1958, features chaste flirtation between the protagonist and a young man; it ends in a church wedding. By contrast, the teenage romance depicted in Judy Blume's *Forever*, published in 1975, culminates in sex and the realization that teenage love is not, in fact, "forever"—and that's a good thing. So-called problem novels like Judy Blume's, which focused on protagonists' struggles with personal and societal issues, ultimately developed into a new category of children's literature called "young adult" (YA). As this subgenre grew in the 1970s, historical fiction continued to evolve in ways largely removed from its trends.[48]

The relative tameness of historical fiction had important consequences for classroom adoption. Books like *The Witch of Blackbird Pond* and *Sounder* granted agency to historically underrepresented groups (women in colonial New England, African Americans in the Jim Crow South) and broached tough political issues (political witch-hunting, structural racism), but because they eschewed sex, violence, bad language, and punishment-free disobedience, they passed as "conservative." The pairing of traditional family values with moderate political critique enabled a selection of historical novels published between the 1940s and 1980s to coalesce into a classroom canon. The state superintendent largely responsible for California's adoption of authentic literature captured the cross-political appeal of well-regarded trade books in an article explaining the state's reading initiative. Combining the language of Matthew Arnold with a message about access for all, he concluded with the assertion that "our reform movement [can] unlock the doors of language to discover the best that human beings have thought, written, and spoken. These are the doors that must be opened if we are to achieve the goals we have set for ourselves and our children." He took for granted that everyone could agree on both "the values and ethics" that must be transmitted to children and the qualities, mainly the inclusion of such values, that made certain children's books "good."[49] Today, the trade book titles listed on California's recommended reading list—books categorized not only by genre and grade but also by the ethnicity and race of the books' characters—also appear with high frequency in the catalogs of Christian homeschool companies.[50] Clearly, the most widely taught historical novels succeed where textbooks failed: they negotiate the political waters of the left and right without seeming to descend into platitudes.

A close reading of William Armstrong's *Sounder*—the novel from which the lesson plans beginning this chapter were drawn—beautifully illustrates the phenomenon. As a book, *Sounder* engages with American racism in nuanced ways. But when *Sounder* is examined not only as a text but also as the product of a particular author—a white man writing in the late 1960s—analyzing its representations of and messages about race becomes even more intricate. In its very complexity, *Sounder* epitomizes an aspect that all widely taught historical novels share to some degree. It is their openness to multiple readings as well as their high literary quality that enable the books to enter and retain a place in school classrooms.

Sounder tells the story of an African American family living somewhere in the South at some unspecified time between the end of the Civil War and the beginning of the civil rights movement. Both the father and mother work at the "big house" down the road while the boy protagonist and his three younger siblings, who remain nameless and ageless, struggle to maintain youthful optimism in the absence of sufficient sustenance. The oldest boy's overwhelming desire for learning is frustrated by a prohibitively long walk to school; the mother attempts to fill his intellectual and spiritual hunger with Bible stories. The father, desperate to put *actual* food on the table, steals a pig. A torn piece of clothing and the smell of ham give the family away, and the father pays for his transgression through forced labor that ultimately leads to his death.

Spare in language but rich in detail, *Sounder* is a beautiful, moving story. A black adolescent, his family, and their dog dominate the narrative. White people appear only as flat characters, jealous wielders of power. And unlike history textbooks that focus on railroads, immigration, expanding industry, and the North when discussing turn-of-the-century America, *Sounder* tells of daily life among ordinary, rural black sharecroppers. Race is mentioned at only two points in the narrative: when the father is apprehended for stealing a pig, and when the boy goes to the town jail and confronts a "red-faced" guard who informs him that visiting hours are over.[51] At all other times, readers see as the boy does; the distinction between black and white is so obvious in a world shaped by structural racism that it goes unsaid.[52]

Armstrong wrote the manuscript for *Sounder* during an era when many civil rights advocates held colorblindness as the highest ideal; he said in a 1974 interview, "I go back to Diogenes, who said there's no difference between Greek or barbarian, there's no difference between black and white, there's no difference between slave and free, except as to the degree of goodness, or badness, in the heart of the man."[53] The author spoke of his experiences as a white boy growing up in rural Virginia during the 1920s. His father developed a friendship with Charlie Jones, an African American who taught the segregated school and who worked on Armstrong's family farm during the summer, and with Isaac

Wineburg, a white storekeeper whose name suggests that he was another type of outsider, a Jew. As an adolescent, Armstrong began to discern the uniqueness of his father's friendships at a time when blacks and whites, employers and hired men, did not associate socially: "My father and this black man sat down and ate together always, always. . . . And they went places together. . . . And they also had a great friend who ran the clothing store in the town. He used to always stand around philosophizing—a man named Isaac Wineburg, a great person. They were a great trio. They enjoyed each other. And even as a little boy I came to appreciate them tremendously."[54] Jones ultimately became Armstrong's tutor, supplying him with books such as the *Nicene Fathers* from his own library. The author talked about the lessons—and black teacher—for the rest of his life.

Just as Armstrong, a poor, white boy, learned to empathize with outsiders as a child, he hoped to teach young people to identify with and have compassion for the oppressed. *Sounder* invites readers to connect with its black protagonist, experiencing his hardships and sharing his ambitions. Those reviewing *Sounder* at the time of its publication saw the novel's potential to engage readers in honest reflection about race. Teachers and students ready to wrestle with tough questions about inequalities in their own day could look to William Armstrong, white author of a humanizing tale about the black experience, as a role model.

Sounder's success in schools, however, depended on its simultaneous appeal to politically conservative teachers and educators. The novel depicts a nuclear family who reveres the Bible and rejects bitterness, however bleak its fate. It also presents a problem (structural racism) and narrative solution (individual escape and self-invention) that are fundamentally at odds. In a line often highlighted by antiracist critics, the mother in *Sounder* tells the boy, "Some people is born to keep. Some is born to lose. We was born to lose, I reckon" (53). Armstrong saw tremendous strength and dignity in such acceptance of the inevitable.[55] But *Sounder* does not linger on bad fortune or passive acceptance. The boy protagonist, unlike his mother, is unwilling to accept resignation. He continues to search for both his dog, Sounder, and his incarcerated father, and he continues, against all odds, to hope for a better future. He is sustained by faith: "In Bible-story journeys, ain't no journey hopeless. Everybody finds what they suppose to find" (78). The words prove prophetic. As a consequence of his wanderings, the boy meets a black teacher who takes him under his wing. The message to readers is clear: individual effort combined with a degree of chance—the classic "luck and pluck" formula of Horatio Alger stories—enables one to rise above even the worst circumstances.[56]

Just as *Sounder* can be championed by the political left and the political right, so too can its author. Widowed early, he raised three children—and a flock of Corriedale sheep—on land he cleared himself. In a Random House filmstrip made a few years after the novel's release, Armstrong's image is carefully constructed as that of a farmer-pioneer who draws inspiration from the Hebrews. The viewer hears the squeals of sheep waiting to be sheared as the narration begins, describing Armstrong's daily rounds mending fences and cleaning the barn. It notes that *Sounder's* author routinely rises before four, writing each morning before waking his children and walking to his high school classroom. Armstrong taught at a New England prep school, but the filmstrip's biographical sketch roots him firmly in the South. Onscreen Armstrong describes his childhood home as being in the midst of battlefields from the "War between the States" and his church as the site of Confederate general Stonewall Jackson's Sunday school lessons. As the filmstrip suggests, Armstrong can be seen in different ways, as a New England don spreading the message of racial liberalism to the nation's elite or as a southerner rooted in Bible-belt soil, a practical farmer who knows the value of hard physical labor, a good day's work, and "respectable" distance between the races. Armstrong and *Sounder* are not unique among widely taught children's novels: they have the ability to be read in disparate ways, to cross ideological lines.

History as Citizenship Education: School Consensus

Historical fiction's appeal to language arts teachers and interdisciplinary middle school teams comes as no surprise given the multiplicity of issues surrounding children's literature and the education of young adolescents in the 1980s: the rise of realism and the erosion of literary taboos in books for youth, diversity as a pressing curricular concern, bias and sensitivity guidelines in textbooks and basal readers, interdisciplinarity as an ideal, and authentic literature's embrace by both the left and right. Using historical fiction as a replacement for social studies textbooks, however, would at first glance seem controversial, and problematic, for history teachers. After all, historical fiction is *fiction*; its first responsibility is to tell a good story, not to adhere to the historical record. Research has shown that middle-grade students who study history through literature sometimes conflate the "historical" and "fictional" aspects of a novel, placing Johnny Tremain, for example, on a list of leaders of the American Revolution.[57] Yet, among the most important players in K–12 debates about history education—classroom teachers, university teacher educators, state curriculum committees, and researchers with an interest in history pedagogy—none has objected to historical novels.

Reasons for embracing historical fiction differ, but a key factor for both classroom teachers and university educators is a shared belief that history instruction's primary function in schools is to inculcate citizenship, and that to do that well, the subject must be interesting, relevant, and comprehensible to adolescent learners.[58] This consensus and its translation into support for fiction extends to groups one might expect to be strongly wedded to more traditional—that is, fact-based and patriotism-infused—history instruction. The web-based Christian homeschool organization Sonlight tells its families, "On the surface, of course, the idea that you can use fiction to teach real history sounds ridiculous. But when you think about it, there is a lot of common sense to the notion. First, good historical fiction is based on solid research. . . . Second, keep in mind that neither textbooks nor great literature are entirely free from error." But most important, "the textbook lists many names and dates, but provides almost no *context*. There's no *story* in which to anchor the information . . . no *drama* to make the information memorable."[59]

Literacy research and the belief that students need to both understand and appreciate historical content in order to derive citizenship benefits has been central to the widespread adoption of historical novels in schools. In a study of textbooks and trade books written for young adolescents, Carl M. Tomlinson and his colleagues, teacher educators in language arts and children's literature, found textbooks' "text structure," the organizational pattern used to present ideas in a text, to be characterized by "shallow coverage and language restraints [that] result in lack of cohesion and clarity," while that of trade books was characterized by "connected, sequential ideas, focus on topic, and multi-idea-unit sentences [that] result in clear, cohesive passages."[60] In other words, trade books containing more complex sentences and more sophisticated vocabulary proved easier for children to comprehend than did textbooks adhering to publishers' readability formulas. Qualitative research conducted by others interested in reading processes and comprehension yielded similar conclusions: middle-grade readers struggled to draw meaning—defined narrowly as content and idea comprehension—from grade-level history textbooks.[61] This research was then linked, both in professional journals and their popular dissemination in teacher publications, to students' aversion to history as a school subject.

Researchers and practitioners advocating for historical fiction's classroom use have repeatedly emphasized its ability to capture student interest and thus improve comprehension. In stark contrast to textbooks, advocates argue, historical novels paint three-dimensional historical figures (real and imagined) that enable students to relate to and care about people removed from them by time and space and, depending on the characters featured, by gender, class, race, and religion. A teacher-education professor writing in *Language Arts* in 1981 explained, "Those of us who have worked with children and young adults have learned that they tend to live in the present. A historical story can enable the reader to view the past as a reality, experience it vicariously but personally thus giving it significance and relevance." A decade later, a teacher-scholar team echoed the same theme in *Social Studies*: "The protagonist's perspective helps the reader feel the poignancy of the character's thoughts and feelings, confusion and frustration, fears and hopes."[62]

Historical novels' empathetic capacity was initially championed by the left and tied to calls for combating racism; by the 1980s, however, this empathetic capacity was viewed as a strength by all once it become clear that multiculturalism as practiced in schools was not a radical, particularist movement but rather a politically moderate assertion of the American Dream, recast in pluralistic terms.[63] In other words, cultivating qualities of good citizenship through identification with a protagonist of color was no different from the traditional curricular practice of cultivating identification with American heroes such as George Washington.[64] The nonwhite characters appearing at the center of widely taught historical novels—the boy protagonist in *Sounder*, for example—were unobjectionable role models who elicited empathy and invited identification in part because they embodied mainstream values and reinforced dominant myths about the American past—and present.

In addition to praising historical novels' empathetic capacities, resources published for teachers in education journals like *Language Arts* and *Social Studies* and in books (for example, *U.S. History through Children's Literature* and *America as Story: Historical Fiction for Secondary Schools*) laud award-winning historical novels for their historical "accuracy."[65] The authors of these publications are primarily librarians, classroom teachers, and literacy and language arts specialists. As a group, they tend to be much more confident of both the knowability of the past and the possibility of objective history than are today's professional historians. In contrast to the public at large, historians emphasize the foreignness of the past, and hence the difficulty of understanding—even when equipped with deep contextual knowledge—the behavior, motivation, and feelings of people removed from them by time, space, and worldview. As cultural historian David Lowenthal has written, "I suspect few take historians' cautions to heart; so alien a past is too hard to bear, especially when we treasure it as our own possession."[66] Classroom teachers frequently view U.S. history as just that, a treasure to be passed on to the next generation.

Importantly, discussions of accuracy have extended to and become intertwined with notions of empathy. A 1987 article by Nancy Anderson in *Social Studies* demonstrates the trend: "Children's literature affords an exceptional resource to present a true perspective of the lifestyle of blacks before the civil rights era. Because literature has the potential for appealing to the affective as well as to the cognitive domains of the learner, it offers a perspective that is not often found in textbooks."[67] Anderson, an associate professor of education at the University of South Florida, is likely drawing on scholarship that understands empathy as both the cognitive task of reconstructing historical subjects' thoughts, ideas, and feelings by drawing on historical evidence and the affective task of imagining, from historical subjects' own perspective, how a given person might feel at a specific moment in time. In doing so, however, she associates fictional historical narrative with "truth" (historical accuracy), reinforcing the idea that "objective" history is a given.[68]

The widely held understanding of historical novels as accurate helps account for their acceptance as social studies curriculum. Despite their radical potential, historical novels have, in most cases, simply replaced textbooks as a form of delivery. Educators in the 1980s saw novels as modernizing the curriculum, not challenging cultural norms or fundamentally transforming the lessons taught; this explains why they were deemed acceptable by both the political left and political right. Liberals and conservatives expressed different frustrations with the history textbooks of the 1980s—the left sought increased attention to women and minorities and the cultivation of empathy, while the right sought more coverage of traditional American heroes and the cultivation of patriotism—but *both* desired lessons that inspired children and shaped citizens committed to the nation-state and its founding principles. It is around this shared belief in history's power to enlighten, purify, and improve that educators clustered.

The consensus about history education's purpose in the K–12 arena contrasts sharply with the contentious debates unfolding simultaneously in the academy. As knowledge came to be seen as contextual, perspective bound, and evanescent, a growing skepticism of the master narrative led to profound questioning of the defining purpose of humanities instruction in American universities. But as debates about the canon—not only what it should contain but also whether the very idea of a collection of books somehow encapsulating "truth" was tenable in an age of post-structuralist theory—raged in the academy, middle schools skirted epistemological questions. Those involved with the daily education of ten- to fourteen-year-olds were more interested in questions of self-esteem and social development than in questions about the nature of knowledge.[69] In the past three decades, research in history pedagogy has demonstrated that textbooks fail to produce historical understanding and to teach students about the constructed and contested nature of historical narrative. But this is not the reason educators have turned to historical fiction as an alternative.[70] Rather, teachers and curriculum experts have embraced historical fiction with diverse protagonists as a means of "opening up" the history curriculum to represent and academically motivate all. Historical novels are seen as an effective tool for cultivating democratic citizenship in a modern, multicultural nation.

■ As the educational tides have shifted from whole language to phonics, desegregation to multiculturalism, and student access to student accountability, historical fiction has held its place in the curriculum.[71] Widely taught historical novels have publication dates spanning more than sixty years, from the 1940s to 2000s, but they share in common literary quality, student appeal, and the ability to negotiate national political waters. Individually, each novel tells a powerful story about the United States and its past—that's what drew the books to the attention of librarians, who recognized them with the Newbery and other awards, and of teachers, who embraced the books as curricular aids. But the novels also tell a collective story: a story about what publishers, librarians, and educators have valued for children during more than three decades, as each of the professional fields has undergone significant change.

In the next three chapters, I explore recurring themes in the classroom canon: the role of war in shaping American identity, the place slavery and its legacy hold within the American story, and the relationship between white settlers and Native inhabitants in the forging of an American nation and American identity. In reading individual texts and tracing the development of central themes over the past sixty years, my aim is threefold. First, I model the kind of contextualized reading of historical novels that would facilitate classroom use of the books in ways that develop sophisticated understandings of history as a discipline. Second, I illustrate how both liberals and conservatives found ways to read the novels that reinforced their ideas of past and present while simultaneously serving the prerogatives they deemed central to citizenship and character education. Last, I suggest that children's historical fiction can be read as a challenge to the very master narrative it currently serves.

Chapter 2

Indians Mythic and Human

■ Cherokee editor Mary Gloyne Byler wrote in the early 1970s that in contrast to other minority groups in the United States, who "have been, and are still, largely ignored by the nation's major publishing houses— particularly in the field of children's books," Native Americans "contend with a mass of material about themselves. If anything, there are too many children's books about American Indians."[1] Native people play essential if supporting roles in the heroic children's tales of nation-building that ultimately demand their "disappearance." For that reason, when adults recall childhood experiences with classics like Laura Ingalls Wilder's Little House books (1932–1943) or Carol Ryrie Brink's *Caddie Woodlawn* (1935), they tend to forget that Indians were even present in the texts. Native characters lurk in the corners, serving as literary devices that highlight the warmth and safety of the nuclear Anglo-American family and the suppressed desires of white, tomboyish girls and liberty-loving boys who wish to be freed from the civilizing influence of domesticated women.

Indians have long been present in American adult literature too, but the abundance of indigenous characters in American children's books stems in part from nineteenth-century social Darwinist thinking that equated Indians with children. Psychologist G. Stanley Hall, best known for developing the concept of adolescence, argued that if Indians were permanently childlike, then it stood to reason that children must also be like Indians. Drawing on romantic conceptions of children being in a state of nature, Hall argued that child development mirrored the evolutionary process of the human—or more accurately, the Anglo-Saxon—at large. In their path to adulthood, children "recapitulated" the evolutionary stages of man. By mimicking the "primitive" activities and pursuits of Native peoples, white children smoothed the process of advancing to the next stage of social and intellectual development. Hall's theory ultimately informed the creation and programming of youth organizations such as the YMCA's Indian Guides and Princesses, Camp Fire Girls, Boy Scouts, and Girl Scouts.[2] But the association of non-Native children and Indians continued long after Hall's theory—and social Darwinist thinking more broadly—lost credibility.

As a genre, the western reached its heyday in the 1950s, precisely the time when the inevitable result of social Darwinist thinking—virulent, racist nationalism—was revealed in the defeat of Nazi ideology. The postwar popularity of American westerns invigorated children's cowboy-and-Indian fantasies, as did toy guns, Daniel Boone hats, juvenile frontier biographies, and summer camp activities. The trend continued well into the next decades, with the wildly popular television series *Little House on the Prairie* airing in the 1970s and early 1980s. In 1980, the year former western actor Ronald Reagan was elected president, British author Lynne Reid Banks published what was to become the best-selling children's book in recent U.S. history, the Harry Potter series excluded.[3] Banks's *The Indian in the Cupboard* (1980), a fantasy about cowboy-and-Indian play turned real, enthralled American children and their teachers, quickly becoming an elementary school read-aloud. When the boy protagonist Omri places a toy Indian and, later, a toy cowboy in a medicine cabinet and turns the key, he transforms his white, middle-class London bedroom into his very own American frontier.[4] As he explains to a friend, "Little Bear isn't a toy. He's a real man. He really lived. Maybe he's still— I don't know—he's in the middle of his life—somewhere in America in seventeen-something-or-other. He's from the *past*."[5]

Once alive, the miniature cowboy and Indian behave exactly the way their brightly colored bodies would suggest: as caricatures from an unspecified time and place. Antiracist critics have objected to the manner in which the novel's Indian speaks, pointing out that Little Bear identifies himself as an eighteenth-century Iroquois but talks like a 1950s movie Indian: "Now! You make magic. Deer for Little Bear hunt. Fire for cook. Good meat!" (59). Such racist dialogue, critics argue, is inexcusably ignorant.[6] Worse yet, Little Bear, who was originally a mass-produced plastic toy, can literally be possessed. Omri's reference to him as "my Indian" makes obvious the colonial perspective from which the novel is told. If the word "Indian" was replaced with that of another minority group, some educators argued, the racism would be instantly apparent. This recognition eventually drove *Indian in the Cupboard* from school curricula, particularly after Paramount Pictures' release of a movie adaptation. Many of the same states, school districts, and teachers that banished *Indian in the Cupboard*, however, continue to recommend and teach other books with equally mythic Indians.

Unlike Omri's Little Bear, the Indians peopling the widely taught historical novels published in the postwar period do not engage in time travel. Their rootedness in the past has made it more difficult for readers to recognize that they embody the same mythic tropes as *Indian in the Cupboard*. Considering the Native characters alongside their historical backdrop, critics have instead hailed them as authentic. Their "noble savage" qualities are read as "positive" and "historically accurate" rather than offensive and stereotypical. In addition, multiculturalism's demand for texts featuring all minority groups and the significant absence, prior to the twenty-first century, of commercially successful children's books authored by Native Americans have contributed to the endurance of such books in the curriculum. Beginning in the 1980s, these novels, once valued for their literary quality, survival themes, and links to frontier history, began to take on new cultural work as books with "multicultural" content. Ironically, they did so even as the Indian characters in the texts reinforced myths and facilitated triumphal historical narratives of the nation-state that discounted Native perspectives.

The circuitous route by which the most widely taught children's books with Indian characters became multicultural texts that celebrated difference has produced intriguing contradictions. The novelistic portrayal of Indians began to change following the end of World War II as non-Native children's authors attempted to position fictional Indians within contemporary political discourses of feminism and anticolonialism. Even as these non-Native authors moved away from essentialist ideas of race and gender that informed earlier representations of Indians, however, they continued to create Native characters that were mythic rather than historical. In short, the purpose of their fictional Indians centered on efforts to understand white people's place in America, not on a commitment to explore Native history, culture, identity, and power on their own terms. The books, then, are utterly at odds with contemporary indigenous people's efforts to establish tribal sovereignty, a process that defines Native people as politically outside of and separate from the nation-state.

Postwar Consensus and Nostalgia

During the 1950s, the American Indian as idea, image, and icon dominated American culture. As white Americans settled into tract housing, GIs returned to school and work, and heterosexual couples welcomed children into the world, all appeared calm. But suburban serenity masked anxieties bubbling under the surface: racial tension that would spark the civil rights movement, strained gender roles that would generate second-wave feminism, and the ominous threat of atomic weapons and Soviet infiltration that would pave the way for McCarthyism. In this age of fearful uncertainty, the nuclear family and its product-filled home was touted as a safe retreat from communism, the atom bomb, and Organization Man's malaise.[7] Frontier tales on television and in popular literature celebrated American dominance while simultaneously idolizing individuality, open land, and freedom from social constraints—precisely what the era of consensus, conformity, and anticommunism denied.

When Pulitzer Prize–winning author Conrad Richter decided to write a book that would sell big rather than win him prestigious medals, he turned to Indians and the frontier as the obvious subject. Richter "chafed" at this distraction from more serious literary endeavors, but the process produced his most enduring, if not his most acclaimed, work, *The Light in the Forest* (1953).[8] Born in Pine Grove, Pennsylvania, in 1890, Richter was descended from Revolutionary War soldiers who settled the Ohio Valley, a region in which Natives mounted robust resistance to Anglo-American incursions well into the nineteenth century. *Light in the Forest* draws on this local history and reflects the frontier values Richter absorbed traveling through small mining towns as a youth. Skeptical of technological progress and protective of the natural world, Richter became convinced that great men surfaced only through stints of adversity. "By thinking out in his work how the pioneers developed into a breed of heroically proportioned men and women," biographer Marvin J. LaHood wrote, "he hoped to devise a life style for modern man to make him strong and selfless. . . . He mourned the passing of the frontier precisely because he . . . saw it as a challenge that produced a race of giants."[9] In Richter's view, the heroes of the American past included both triumphant Anglo settlers and tragic Indian inhabitants who fought, futilely, for their land and lifestyle.

Richter's fiction makes clear that he idealized Indian life even as he dismissed it as incompatible with and anathema to modern America. The preface to *Light in the Forest* reveals the conflicted nature of these feelings; Richter suggests that by examining the United States from the perspective of outsiders like the Delaware, readers might appreciate the modern "perverted" view of "some African, European, and Asian peoples" toward the United States.[10] The march of progress and need for governmental order could appear threatening to such "primitives." But knowledge of this should not engender caution. Writing to the newly elected president John F. Kennedy, Richter lectured, "Our founding fathers pledged their lives and fortunes, and you must pledge ours. A cowardly nation incurs only contempt trying to buy respect from its fellow

nations with money and retreat. A brave man or nation requires neither."[11] It was necessary, Richter asserted, to display power in order to
protect American freedoms. Yet Richter had his doubts about both the
young president's and the current generation's ability to strike the right
balance between protecting personal freedoms and sacrificing them in
the name of a national effort to preserve and extend American liberties.
Light in the Forest participates in a long literary tradition of praising
"pure," "primitive" Indian ways as a means of scrutinizing the price paid
for progress.[12] The novel relies on nineteenth-century sources—accounts
written by white men who knew Indians well—that employ the same
technique. *Light in the Forest* thus provides a meeting of mid-twentieth-
and mid-nineteenth-century nostalgia.

Conrad Richter's *The Light in the Forest* (1953)

Light in the Forest opens during the aftermath of the French and Indian
War, a hopeful moment for Scots-Irish settlers who moved into the rich
Ohio Valley but a desperate one for Indians, already displaced from their
ancestral homelands to the east, occupying the same territory. Aware
that they faced further encroachment, local Indians refused to accept the
ceasefire made in their name by battling French and English troops. Violence erupted as Anglo-American settlers' hunger for land clashed with
Indians' determination to retain it. Both historically and in the novel, the
Delaware attacked isolated settlements, killed Anglo settlers, and took
captives. When governor John Penn and his assembly failed to provide
settlements with a militia, frontier residents took matters into their own
hands. The extralegal "Paxton boys"—a posse that in the novel includes
the protagonist's white relatives—expelled their anger on an easy target,
the peaceful Moravian Indians.[13] Horrified by the settlers' unauthorized
revenge, the governor sent Colonel Henry Bouquet deep into Indian
Country with an order to reclaim all white captives, some of whom had
been within Native communities for decades. Bouquet and his militia's
historical march into the forest—an attempt to appease settlers and prevent further retaliation against Indians—triggers the fictional events
that entrap Richter's protagonist, a thoroughly Indianized captive living
among the Delaware.

Light in the Forest opens as fifteen-year-old True Son, born John Butler but raised as a Lenni Lenape (Delaware) since age four, learns that he
must leave the only family he knows to live with the enemy, white people
who claim him as their son. While True Son fights the military order
for his return with Bouquet, his Indian father recognizes and accepts

the inevitable: with the English army in the forest, the Delaware have no choice but to concede. True Son returns to Paxton, the settlement of his birth, and for the next six months struggles against the constraints of Christian civilization, ultimately collapsing into a mysterious sickness. While the white doctor shakes his head in despair, a cure soon arrives in the form of True Son's Indian cousin Half Arrow. Spying his friend in the bushes, True Son's strength is instantly restored. He sneaks out of the house and into the forest, but not before attempting—unsuccessfully— to avenge the murder of his friend Little Crane, a Lenni Lenape whose white wife and child had been returned to Paxton as redeemed captives at the same time as he. Because True Son hears men approaching while he is scalping Little Crane's murderer—an infamous "Paxton boy" and his own biological uncle—he leaves the job unfinished.

Richter's mythic reading of True Son's destiny becomes clear in the scenes that follow. After escaping Paxton, the boys seize a canoe and row into Indian Country. Passing Fort Pitt, the European building marking the edge of the frontier, the boys relax and finally permit themselves to sleep. Later, they awaken to "[feast] on the passing richness of the Indian forest. Mile after mile it stood, untouched as the Great One had made it" (93).[14] In describing a "virgin land," Richter construes Indians as "natural" and indistinguishable from the landscape, the kind of scenic prop figuring in the nineteenth-century landscape paintings of romantics like Thomas Cole.[15] This mythic understanding of the Lenni Lenape relationship to the land obscures the ways in which Delaware fishing, hunting, and agricultural practices transformed the ecosystem of the Ohio Valley. Placing the boys alone on the water, moreover, associates Indian boyhood with what Richter describes as "a kind of primitive deliciousness" removed from time (95).

The water's current eventually propels the boys home, where, given their failure to secure the scalp of True Son's uncle, they must face the community's wrath. In a plot sequence that says more about Richter's understanding of Native-Anglo relations than about the historical practices of eighteenth-century Lenni Lenape, Little Crane's relatives test True Son's loyalty and find it wanting. As in the work of James Fenimore Cooper, who in his Leatherstocking tales describes Indians and Anglo-Americans as having racially determined "gifts," bloodlines determine fate in *Light in the Forest*. As much as True Son longs for the freedom of the forest, Richter argues that his "white blood" makes such a fate impossible. Just as he was unable to scalp his uncle in Paxton, he is incapable of playing the avenging Indian in the Delaware woods. In a critical scene, True Son spots a child's scalp among the spoils of his Delaware war party and becomes powerless to decoy a boat of unsuspecting white passengers.[16] Without grasping the significance of his decision, True Son warns away the boat, forgetting, the narrator states, "who and where he was" (109). But True Son didn't *really* forget. Paralleling the argument made a century earlier in Cooper's *Deerslayer* (1841), Richter suggests that True Son's blood stopped him from engaging in acts of violent treachery permissible only to Indians. True Son learns he is destined to live *in* the forest but not be *of* the forest.[17] "Your heart is Indian. Your head is Indian. But your blood is still thin like the whites," his Delaware father tells him. "It can be joined only with the thin blood of the white people" (115). Heartbroken, True Son, who never "felt more Indian than at this moment," eventually accepts the truth: he is white (172).

Historically, the Lenni Lenape privileged socially constructed kinship ties over biologically determined genes when deciding identity; they welcomed adopted captives wholeheartedly as fully integrated members of the community. White captives, then, routinely joined their "blood" with Native partners and raised children as Delaware. Richter, however, reinterpreted historical practice in order to formulate a narrative in which blood determines outcome. For example, True Son's Delaware father delivers the following speech before carrying out the community's banishment:

> From your early days you were not neglected. You were taught the
> kinds and signs of game. You were taught their habits and where
> to find them. You were taught to hunt and shoot. You gave me no
> shame as a hunter. I told myself that when I am old, you, my son, will
> support me. When my bones creak, you will keep me in bear's oil and
> venison. When the ashes of life cool, you will be the fire to warm my
> old age. Never did I think that you would turn against me and that
> I would have to send you back to your white people. All this time I
> looked on you as Indian. I leaned on you as a staff. Now it is broken.
> (114)

The speech facilitates Richter's larger argument: while the future lies with American civilization, national progress also brings with it sacrifices and lost freedoms. True Son *must* become John Butler, but he will never stop mourning the liberty of the forest.

In both theme and diction, the passage above echoes the writing of John Brickell, a white boy taken captive by the Delaware in 1791. In an article written years after his "redemption," Brickell recalled his Indian father's parting words:

You have lived a long time with us. I call on you to say if I have not been a father to you? If I have not used you as a father would use a son? . . . I have raised you—I have learned you to hunt. You are a good hunter—you have been better to me than my own sons. I am now getting old and I cannot hunt. I thought you would be a support to my age. I leaned on you as on a staff. Now it is broken—you are going to leave me and I have no right to say a word, but I am ruined.[18]

The similarity of the speeches is obvious, but their difference is also striking. In *Light in the Forest*, the oration is delivered after True Son violated the Delaware community's trust: "Never did I think that you would turn against me and that I would have to send you back" (115). In Brickell's narrative, the speech expresses paternal resignation: "You are going to leave me." Unlike True Son, John Brickell *chose* to return to white kin. What explains the difference? A straightforward explanation is that Brickell was nine rather than four when he was taken captive, and he remained with the Delaware for four rather than eleven years. But more intriguing is the possibility that Brickell's nonfictional narrative is every bit as carefully fashioned as Richter's fictional one.

Historians have documented Anglo-American captives' reluctance to return to the white families of their birth; those who remained within Native communities for life eventually lost their ability to communicate in English and, as a result, left few records.[19] Those who were redeemed, however, left plentiful accounts of their ordeal; they had to make sense of their experience and justify their "purity," "civility," and "whiteness" in order to reintegrate into Christian society. Did Brickell exaggerate the ease with which he parted from his Native parents, his only family during four formative years? In the absence of other sources, it is impossible to know. But what is clear is that Brickell's retrospective narrative is a genre piece. Like countless captivity narratives, it performs cultural work, closing with a public declaration of faith that "proves" that captivity did not endanger, but rather strengthened, his Christian convictions.

The contrast between Brickell's happy return to Christian civilization and True Son's resistance highlights the shock brought about by Richter's narrative decision. To readers in the 1950s, True Son's behavior would have seemed utterly remarkable, even fantastic: how could he choose to be Indian rather than white, to reject his "real" family?[20] Richter renders the choice believable by employing an omniscient narrator who probes the internal lives of several characters but lingers longest with True Son. Richter illustrates how True Son thinks fluently (and poetically) in the Delaware dialect of Algonquian but haltingly (and pragmatically) in

English, a distinction captured textually by means of dropped articles and missing conjunctions. The Lenni Lenape perspective is privileged throughout, making actions non-Native readers might deem cruel or abusive seem instead intelligible and appropriate because they are described in True Son's Algonquian voice.[21] Richter's narrative strategies and historical argument are noteworthy because it was not until the 1980s that professional historians began documenting Indianized captives' refusal to return home when "redeemed." *Light in the Forest* predated this scholarship by decades and, indeed, predated serious scholarly attention to Indians and the phenomenon of captivity, period. Only three articles about Indians appeared in *American Historical Review* between 1895 and 1920, while the long stretch between 1920 and 1960 saw even fewer, four in as many decades.[22]

In fact, accounts rivaling the ethnographical detail of Richter's novel had not appeared since the nineteenth century, before the rise of professional historians. Francis Parkman, the great narrative historian, had been the master in that era, writing about Indians prodigiously even as he took their "savagery" as given. When Alfred A. Knopf received the manuscript for Richter's *Light in the Forest*, he turned to Harvard historian Samuel Eliot Morison—a man epitomizing the professional establishment at midcentury—for advice. Morison gushed: "No writer since Parkman has made so moving and accurate a description of the great hardwood forests of the Old West."[23] The comment was more perceptive than contemporaries could recognize. Not only did Richter's cultural details and empathetic portrayal of Indians rival Parkman's, so too did his beliefs about Indians' fate: Richter assumed that the march of progress would beget Indian cultures' disappearance. Thus, while *Light in the Forest* provides startlingly lifelike portrayals of both Delawares and Anglo-Americans in the eighteenth-century Ohio Valley, it does so within a narrative argument shaped by mythic understanding of the past, an understanding forged in the nineteenth century and transformed in and by the first half of the twentieth.

Sales records indicate that *Light in the Forest* spoke powerfully to Richter's original audience of adult readers during the postwar period. Its romanticized picture of Indian childhood resonated with 1950s youth as well, a factor Richter anticipated by forcefully advocating for a young people's edition. He was aided by receipt of letters from teachers, such as one who wrote in 1953, "It occurred to me that the boys and girls in my seventh grade home room might enjoy [*Light in the Forest*] since Indians are always a favorite subject to children and True Son was so near their own years of age."[24] The teacher's comments echo Hall's recapitulation theory, but he was right; not only did his students beg for more, but fifty years later, the book continues to be assigned to seventh, eighth, and ninth graders. *Light in the Forest*'s presence in school curricula today speaks to a generalized nostalgia for a childhood free from modern technology and abounding in opportunities for youth to prove their mettle, but also to the book's seeming potential for multicultural positioning. Yet the book perpetuates mythic understandings of history, essentialist notions of race, and rigidly defined gender roles.[25] The novels of the next decade would explicitly tackle these shortcomings even as they reinscribed the mythic understanding of Native history evident in Richter's writing.

Civil Rights Movements and the Survival Story Reformed

Postwar Americans placed high value on social conformity as they confronted the terrors of the Cold War and embraced the possibilities of mass consumption. Even as suburban communities and network television helped shape a common, white, middle-class culture, however, the civil rights movement gained momentum. In drawing attention to fundamental biases of the American legal system, activists and intellectuals also highlighted the flaws of a normative culture rooted in whiteness, masculinity, heterosexuality, and middle-class status. During the second half of the century, cultural productions for children began to respond to the insights generated, and Native characters in children's books were put in service of feminism and anticolonialism. Even as they entered new discourses, however, they remained mythic: less Indian than Western *imagining* of the Indian. The civil rights movement's radical message of social justice was thus subverted as books continued to privilege Anglo-American perspectives.

Two giants of twentieth-century children's literature, Scott O'Dell and Elizabeth George Speare, best represent this historical phenomenon. Their literary awards—three Newbery Medals and four Newbery Honors between them—are but one indication of the tremendous reach of their historical fiction. The lives of O'Dell (1898–1989) and Speare (1908–1994) spanned the twentieth century, and their stories of early America reflect the complexity of historical interpretations that attempted to ask and answer new questions generated from civil rights activism and the rise of "bottom-up" social history in the academy. In book after book, O'Dell and Speare created strong female characters and peopled their texts with Indians. Even as they sought to overturn assumptions rooted in patriarchy and conquest, however, they reified Western perspectives and perpetuated the myth of the vanishing Indian.[26] The authors' efforts at innovation and their interpretative limits are visible in their attempts to rewrite Daniel Defoe's classic tale of adventure, survival, and empire: *Robinson Crusoe* (1719).

Scott O'Dell's *Island of the Blue Dolphins* (1960)

Scott O'Dell's first children's novel, *Island of the Blue Dolphins*, was also his most influential. In fact, few American children's books written for any age have made a larger impact. *Island* ranks as the sixth-best-selling children's paperback of all times, surpassing all other historical novels *and* all other Newbery Medal winners.[27] It has spawned a sequel, a made-for-TV movie, a presence in SparkNotes, and countless commercial lesson plans. The adventure story opens in 1835 on what is now called San Nicolas, a small link in the Channel Islands chain that sits just off the coast of California. Borrowing language from the Chumash, who populated the northern Channel Islands, Scott O'Dell calls the San Nicolas people Ghalas-at; he renames their homeland the "Island of the Blue Dolphins."

Twelve-year-old Karana, daughter of Chief Chowig, narrates *Island of the Blue Dolphins*. Through her voice readers learn that however idyllic the lush island setting may seem, the Ghalas-at have already begun to feel the strain of European contact. A number of years previous, Russian traders accompanied by Aleut hunters arrived on shore and tricked the unsuspecting community into hunting sea otters for them day and night. When Russian boats arrive at the beginning of the novel, therefore, the community knows it must protect itself by negotiating terms, establishing a watch, and claiming ownership of not only the island but also the waters surrounding it—knowledge that illustrates the degree to which the islanders have already adapted to capitalist realities.

Despite precaution, disaster strikes. When the hunters attempt to leave without paying, the Ghalas-at attack and twenty-seven Native men fall, the chief included, leaving only eight able-bodied males standing. In a desperate move to ensure survival, the newly appointed chief flouts gender taboos, ordering women to complete traditional male tasks essential to group survival. The social tensions that result, however, convince the chief that another solution is necessary; he leaves the island in search of an alternative. Nearly a year later, a European ship arrives, captained by a man who informs the crowd that their chief has sent for them. The community hurriedly climbs aboard, pulling anchor before a storm materializes. Noticing that her brother is missing, however, Karana dives overboard, expecting the ship to return within weeks. It never does. Long before this reality hits, Karana's brother, Ramo, is killed by dogs, leaving Karana alone on the island. By mastering the traditional labor of men, relying on her strength as a Ghalas-at woman, and domesticating animals to satisfy her need for companionship, Karana survives. Eighteen years later, a white man's ship again appears, and the lonely Ghalas-at allows herself to be "discovered," "rescued," and "saved" as she is brought to Father Gonzales, Santa Barbara Mission's priest.

Karana's story—the saga of a real historical woman who, neglected and forgotten, survived alone on San Nicolas between 1835 and 1853—has intrigued readers since it was first published more than a hundred years ago. During the late nineteenth and early twentieth centuries, a host of popular periodicals, including *Scribner's Monthly* (1880), *Harper's Magazine* (1898), and the *Pacific Monthly* (1907), published stories about the "lone (or lost) woman of San Nicolas." Critics have cited *Harper's* as O'Dell's source, but as the popularity of the story suggests, O'Dell read multiple accounts.[28] The tellings differ in detail but share a single, problematic source. As O'Dell wrote in his author's note, "Father Gonzales . . . learned that [the lone woman's] brother had been killed by wild dogs. He learned little else, for she spoke to him only in signs; neither he nor the many Indians at the mission could understand her strange language. The Indians of Ghalas-at had long since disappeared."[29] The Native woman's story was conveyed to her rescuers entirely in makeshift hand motions and oral language they could not comprehend.

Reading the accounts of colonizers for information about indigenous experiences is always challenging, given the power differentials and worldviews separating interviewer from interviewee. When the evidence drawn from the exchange stems entirely from interpretation of "signs," however, conclusions become even more suspect. Perhaps those interviewing the lone woman in California were so eager to understand her extraordinary trial that they convinced themselves of their ability to comprehend. As the frontiersman who transported her from the island asserted, "She expressed a great many ideas by signs, so plainly that we readily understood them."[30] Moreover, European listeners believed they "knew" what Karana experienced in part because they were familiar with romanticized tales of shipwrecks such as *Robinson Crusoe*. Inherent in their confidence, however, was the imposition of a European worldview on both the experience of isolation and survival and the "nature" of the Native.

This self-assurance pervading nineteenth-century sources is transmitted to modern readers encountering Karana in *Island of the Blue Dolphins*. Archeologist Steven Schwartz, who studies the Channel Islands today, has said that "professional people who think they know all there is to know about the [Channel] islands think the 'Blue Dolphin' story is true. I've gone on the Web . . . and you can get all kinds of things about how that book is how it happened. It is so untrue. A lot of information we know came out after the book."[31] More important, both the novel and the sources on which O'Dell relied are steeped in literary tropes that, because of their familiarity, discourage reader scrutiny. Contemporary readers of *Island*, like late nineteenth-century readers of popular magazines and early nineteenth-century recorders of the lone woman's tale, believe they understand just how Karana felt.

In his author's note, O'Dell describes his protagonist as a "girl Robinson Crusoe," and his descriptions of Karana's daily activities, creative adaptations of the landscape, and moral development mirror those of Defoe.[32] At the level of plot, both Karana and Crusoe domesticate animals, build homes on either side of the island, encounter frightening enemies, and cross gender norms in order to live with some degree of comfort on an uninhabited island. In addition, both Defoe and O'Dell interpret the experience of solitary living as instructive for their protagonist's soul. Crusoe's misfortune leads him to Christ. Karana's moral development leads her to eschew violence and vow never again to kill mammals or birds: "If [my sister] Ulape and my father had come back and laughed, and all the others had come back and laughed," Karana narrates, "still I would have felt the same way, for animals and birds are like people" (156).[33] In linking Karana to Crusoe, O'Dell imagined her island existence as both adventure and test, a character-strengthening experience like those of the fearless explorers and adventurers who appear in American history books.

Like his nineteenth-century sources and twentieth-century reviewers, O'Dell missed the irony of an indigenous woman figuring as Crusoe. Defoe's protagonist is an Englishman who owns a Brazilian plantation and embarks on an ocean journey in order to purchase slaves. When his ship sinks en route to Africa, Crusoe drifts to a South Pacific island. Here, he does little to encourage rescue; instead, he busies himself "improving" the island, of which he imagines himself "king." When Crusoe finally sails for Europe, he does so with Friday, a devoted Native servant rescued from cannibals, by his side. Mutinied sailors, protected by Crusoe and now his loyal subjects, are left behind to found a colony. Thus, despite the similarities of their isolation on deserted islands, the significance of Crusoe's and Karana's solitude couldn't be more different. Karana sees her relationship to the island and its inhabitants in nonpossessive ways, as her dramatic and culturally improbable vow to abstain from killing animals for food or clothing demonstrates.[34] When Karana leaves the island with white trappers and sailors, she gazes across the ocean wistfully: "For a long time I stood and looked back. . . . I thought . . . of all the happy days" (181). Unlike Crusoe, who is returning home with money in his pocket, servant by his side, and land in his possession, Karana is leaving home empty-handed, sacrificing both her island's material wealth and its nonquantifiable riches to her acknowledged conquerors. Both Crusoe and Karana are stranded on islands by European imperialism, but whereas Crusoe is a perpetrator and beneficiary, Karana is a victim.

In an important article, Susan Naramore Maher argues that O'Dell connects Karana with Crusoe in order to force a "revaluation of frontier myth." In defiance of a tradition that associates the survival tale with empire building, O'Dell writes against imperialist logic that celebrates violence, subjugation, masculinity, and expansion-induced mobility. *Island*, Maher contends, argues that "it is also adventure to face the conquerors, to suffer loss, to endure, and to resist." Maher captures O'Dell's intention "to turn the adventure genre . . . on its head" and the revolutionary nature of that goal in the early 1960s. Her claim that O'Dell penned "counterwesterns" nonetheless demands qualification.[35] Even as O'Dell reverses, inverts, and substitutes, he shapes Karana according to Anglo-American myth. As a nineteenth-century Native, Karana would not have understood solitary suffering as "adventure," but rather as a living nightmare. Because she defined herself through kinship ties, the notion of extended isolation as a test of *individual* strength yielding "happy days," in O'Dell's words, would have been utterly foreign (181).

Moreover, given the reality of her rescue by hunters and removal to a mission where no one understood her, "survival" would be fraught with ambivalence. In fact, after the historical lone woman reached Santa Barbara Mission, she lived only seven weeks. Her tribal name still unknown, she was buried as "Juana María" by Catholic priests.[36] Karana's death does not figure in *Island*, an omission that enables the "survival story" to cohere, but O'Dell uses her living presence to suggest the larger death of her people. Before leaving Ghalas-at, Karana adorns herself with tribal signs of maidenhood. She smiles inwardly as she does so, for she is "no longer a girl" (177). Karana's people had vanished and Karana herself would never bear children, making her the last of her tribe.[37] *Island* thus reinforces a myth central to American nationhood: that Indians "vanished" in the nineteenth century, making room for American expansion.

Like *Light in the Forest*'s author, Conrad Richter, who was born eight years before him, Scott O'Dell lived through a period of tremendous change. Los Angeles was a frontier town when he was born in 1898; by 1930, it ranked as the fourth-largest city in the nation. The year after his 1989 death, it ranked second only to New York. Perhaps inevitably given the transformation he witnessed, O'Dell was prone to nostalgia. "I would like to have it all go back to the farm, where children grew up knowing how to use a hoe and milk a cow. To live out in the country and raise a lot of the things that you use—that to me is the ideal life. It may be impossible, but it's still ideal," O'Dell mused in a 1974 interview.[38] The Native subjects of his historical fiction reflect a longing for the frontier past, while the books' themes reveal the blend of conservative populism he embraced: rugged individualism, rural self-sufficiency, and the "right to work" (anti-union) mixed with tolerance for long hair, marijuana, and teenage sexuality.[39]

O'Dell pointed to Joseph Conrad, author of *Heart of Darkness* (1889), as a central inspiration for his writing, and the reference is helpful in understanding O'Dell's work.[40] Like the masterpiece of his literary mentor, O'Dell's novels reveal the cruelties of imperialism by detailing the damage wreaked by colonizers on occupied lands, peoples, and cultures. Just as Conrad's classic story of Africa is ultimately more concerned with the English than with the African, however, *Island* is more interested in American society than it is in Ghalas-at community. In *Island* and other O'Dell books, Native characters function as mediums for exploring moral themes and social practices; having served that purpose, they are then dismissed, folded into Anglo-American myths of tragic disappearance.[41]

When asked why he wrote "so sympathetically" about indigenous peoples, O'Dell responded,

> I think it is accidental in the sense that I've lived in a country of Indians. The story of an Indian girl who lives eighteen years on an island alone is a dramatic idea, so I used it as a vehicle for what I wanted to say. If she had been a girl from Iowa or the Mayflower I still would have done it, because of the situation. . . . I think of all this as just an accident, that I was born out here. . . . They are people I've grown up with, people I do know. I have Indian friends, just as I have

Spanish and Mexican friends. There's quite a difference between the Spanish and the Mexicans, who are really Indians, or who have Indian blood in them. There are also a lot of different tribes in Mexico.[42]

O'Dell's repeated use of the word "accident" reveals more than he intended. To imply that the historical figure on whom *Island*'s protagonist was based was "accidentally" subjected to nearly two decades of solitude obscures the historical processes by which the event occurred. The island-dwelling Ghalas-at experienced severe population decline due to European diseases and warfare, followed by relocation to the mainland as part of the Spanish policy of *reducción* (forcible resettlement to facilitate conversion and clear lands for resource gathering).[43] Neither Karana's solitude on a once-populated island nor the concentration of Native peoples on the western mainland is accidental. Rather, the Spanish policy of gathering in Natives and the American laws that moved eastern tribes west while simultaneously ensuring that those Indians who remained in the East "disappeared" from census records *created* the concentrated population of Native Americans in the twentieth-century West.

During the turn of the twenty-first century, as educators and literary critics have devoted increased scrutiny to representations of Native as well as African American, Asian American, and Latino peoples in children's literature, O'Dell's opus has come under scrutiny. An outsider to the communities about whom he wrote, O'Dell did not foster relationships with tribal leaders and failed to seek permission to share their stories, an omission that leaves him open to attack. What is fascinating about the criticism that has emerged, however, is the degree to which *Island*, O'Dell's acknowledged masterpiece, has been exempted. C. Anita Tarr, for example, has argued that many of O'Dell's novels provide skeletal outlines of central Native characters, forcing readers to "fill in the gaps" of their character by relying on what they "know" about Indians—stereotypes. The article claims, however, that whereas this tactic fails in his later novels, it works in *Island*: "The more O'Dell wrote, it seems, the less careful he was. . . . We must realize that the very reasons that make this first novel good, make his subsequent novels less so. *Island of the Blue Dolphins* was, so to speak, a phenomenon in itself."[44] *Island*'s success *is* singular—more than 6.5 million paperback copies have sold—but its elevation to the status of modern classic stems in large part from the fact that its mythic framing of American Indians' place in U.S. history is anything but unique.[45]

Elizabeth George Speare's *The Sign of the Beaver* (1983)

Elizabeth George Speare's Robinsonade tale, *The Sign of the Beaver*, opens with twelve-year-old Matthew Hallowell standing at the edge of the Maine land he and his father have recently cleared; the year is 1769, and Matt is now "alone, with miles of wilderness stretching on every side."[46] His father has left the northern frontier earlier that day for Massachusetts, where he will collect the rest of the family, including the newborn whose arrival is imminent. Matt is to "hold down the fort," protecting the claim during the six- to seven-week journey. Like any Anglo-American boy on the brink of adulthood, Matt at first relishes the adventure his father's absence brings. After several weeks of only his dad's pocket watch for company, however, he begins to grow bored and lonely. At this unfortunate moment, a middle-aged trapper who has been living among the Indians and who "got away from that town just in time" arrives, asking for supper (14). Reminding himself of the rules of hospitality, Matt lets down his guard in spite of his suspicions; the next morning, he awakens to find the visitor—and his father's rifle—gone. Fresh meat is now out of the question, and when a bear visits the cabin during his absence, Matt's food supply is ravished. The boy's attempt to assuage his hardship by gathering honey goes sadly awry. Luckily, the local Indians thought to have abandoned the area return and discover a delirious Matt in time to nurse him back to health. Sensing the Anglo child's vulnerability, an elder arranges for his grandson to provide the boy with meat in exchange for reading lessons. Cautiously, the adolescents forge a friendship. After nearly two months, the tribe prepares for its seasonal migration, which this year will take the form of a permanent move west. Once again, Matt faces the prospect of being utterly alone in the wilderness. Although he begins to doubt his family will ever return, he refuses the Indians' offer of companionship and promise of adoption: "You've been very good to me. But I have to stay here" (112).

Young Matt, left alone in the forests of Maine, must provide himself with food, defend his property against animals, and stave off loneliness. As the days of waiting stretch into weeks and the weeks exceed the number projected for his father's return, Matt's confidence in reunion diminishes. Like *Island of the Blue Dolphin*'s Karana, he is offered the opportunity of rescue by a racial other, but unlike the Native woman, he refuses, preferring to risk continued solitude in order to retain his natal identity. Matt's decision is rewarded when his family arrives at the cabin just in time for Christmas.

In discussing the plot sequence of *Sign of the Beaver*, Speare told an interviewer, "It is somewhat surprising for me to discover that . . . I have written a survival story. That was never my intention, and I was still naïve enough when I reached the last page not to realize what had happened to my story, even though my publisher and the first reviewers recognized it at once."[47] Although unaware of her actions, Speare instinctively read *Robinson Crusoe* into the account of a historical fourteen-year-old boy she discovered in the histories of Maine. Local narratives tell the remarkable story of Benjamin and Theophilus Sargent, who arrived in what was still the Maine wilderness in 1802 to clear land and build a home. When the cabin was erected and the garden planted, Benjamin left his son to retrieve the womenfolk. When he arrived at the family home in Massachusetts, however, he found the family sick with typhus fever; the return trip was significantly delayed as a result. Back in Maine, Theophilus successfully fended for himself until a bear forced its way into the cabin and devastated his food supply. Fortunately, a "friendly tribe of (Penobscot) Indians" happened to be gathering bark nearby, and the chief, "on learning the serious condition in which the white boy was left, took pity on him." The Native leader provided food for the boy and commissioned his own son, Ateon Oseon, to keep Theophilus company until his family arrived from Massachusetts, "just before the river froze."[48]

This fragmentary historical account, which provides the scaffold for *Sign of the Beaver*, was written by town boosters at a time when white ownership of Maine's landscape was secure. Similar to Conrad Richter's source for *Light in the Forest*, Speare's sources were participating in a larger project of creating (vanished) noble savages. Writings about Indians in the late nineteenth and early twentieth centuries (the era of Speare's sources) were quite distinct from late eighteenth-century encounters with Indians (the subject of Speare's narrative). At the end of the eighteenth century, New England settlers hotly contested Indian claims to land on the frontiers; while engaged in this bitter power struggle, they emphasized the *differences* between themselves and the Native population. Efforts to link indigenous settlers to a noble past took place before this time period (in the sixteenth century, when writers were engaged in a project of selling the Americas to Englishmen) and after this time period (in the mid-nineteenth century, when Indians, safely "removed" from the New England landscape, could be glorified as noble savages).[49] And of course, narratives emphasizing the similarities between all cultures emerged with new force in the late twentieth century, when the rise of multiculturalism led writers such as Speare to create stories designed to foster empathy for the racial other. *Sign of the Beaver*'s origin lies in a nineteenth-century text, but Speare's twentieth-century adaptation actually deepens rather than corrects the mythic understanding of white-Indian contact implicit in the story of the Anglo-American and Penobscot boys.

When his father set forth for Massachusetts, the historical Theophilus Sargent had his basic needs—food, shelter, and protection—met. Yet by the time his parents reached Maine, historical sources indicated that he was enmeshed in the Native community. "There had to be some misfortune great enough so that the boy's need would overcome the suspicion and aloofness of the Indians," Speare reasoned; in other words, the white boy had to both elicit Indian sympathy and be reduced to a state in which he would accept it.[50] The historical account provided a marauding bear that destroyed his food supply, but Speare dismissed this as "not really an insurmountable loss, not for a boy with two strong legs and a rifle." To provide additional incentive for the boy to accept Indian companionship, Speare eliminated both legs and weapon. Head-to-toe bee stings cripple the body while a technique borrowed from James Fenimore Cooper—bringing a thieving white trapper onstage—eliminates the rifle. Matt fears Indians more than disreputable whites (he "could not entirely forget all those horrid tales," 9), but the Penobscot prove both peaceful and humanitarian. Speare encourages comparison between the Indians and the white trapper by having the Penobscot elder, Saknis, enter Matt's cabin unbidden, exactly the way the trapper had. Like the white man, Saknis notes the absence of adults and begins asking questions, but "it did not occur to [Matt] to lie to this old man as he had to Ben" (27). Just as Matt recognizes Saknis as "safe," skilled readers recognize him as a noble savage, a figure destined to vanish. Matt thanks the man for nursing him back to health by offering a gift; his clumsy selection of a novel that in Speare's telling Saknis cannot read (historical Penobscot were often literate in either French or English) facilitates the introduction of Matt's "man Friday."

Seeing in the book an opportunity to educate his grandson for changing political realities, Saknis asks Matt to teach Attean to read. When Matt agrees, his Crusoe-like isolation gives way to a Crusoe-like project of "civilizing" a "savage." Matt begins Attean's reading lessons with the only book other than the Bible that he owns, *Robinson Crusoe*. The reference to Defoe's novel is direct but complex: Speare uses the book to scrutinize the assumptions of colonial setters. As the reading lessons begin, Matt finds himself learning as much about narrative perspective as his pupil is learning about English prose. After listening unmoved for pages, Attean reacts, suddenly and forcefully, to Friday's obeisance to Crusoe:

> *"Nda!"* [Attean] shouted. "Him never do that!"
> "Never do what?"
> "Kneel down to white man!"
> "But Crusoe had saved his life."
> "Not kneel down," Attean repeated fiercely. "Not be slave. Better die."
>
> Now he'll never come back, Matt thought. He sat slowly turning over the pages. He had never questioned that story. Like Robinson Crusoe, he had thought it natural and right that the wild man should be the white man's slave. Was there perhaps another possibility? The thought was new and troubling. (43)[51]

The next day, Attean returns, and a wiser Matt begins to edit Defoe's words as he reads aloud. Attean's critique of the novel, as well as the Native boy's demonstrated superiority in trapping, fishing, and negotiating the woods, had forced Matt to see the favorite text of his childhood in new ways: "It would have been better perhaps if Friday hadn't been quite so thickheaded. After all, there must have been a thing or two about that desert island that a native who had lived there all his life could have taught Robinson Crusoe" (45). As Matt teaches Attean the alphabet, Attean teaches Matt to set snares and catch fish without metal hooks; before doing so, though, he forces Matt to confront his ignorance, to humble himself before a Native. Matt wonders whether "this [was] Attean's answer, in case [Matt] had any idea in his head about being a Robinson Crusoe" (47).

Speare clearly intended to have both Matt and the readers who identify with him confront the arrogance of colonialism, a goal that distinguishes *Sign of the Beaver* from the author's previous books set in early America, which were written in the 1950s and position primitive Indians as foils to learned white protagonists. In *Sign of the Beaver*, Matt's increased cultural awareness and subsequent moral growth hinges on two realizations. First, Matt learns that Europeans bring disease, warfare, and disruption to the ecosystem that cripple indigenous communities: "Matt thought of the village they had just left, how very poor it seemed, how few possessions the Indians could boast. For the first time Matt glimpsed how it might be for them, watching their old hunting grounds taken over by white settlers and by white traders demanding more skins than the woods could provide" (87). Second, Matt recognizes that perspective is everything. When Attean explains that his father was killed while avenging his mother's murder at the hands of white men, Matt realizes that the haunting fear of his childhood—being orphaned as a result of Indian war—could just as easily be reversed. In the same way that Defoe's *Crusoe* encodes European perspective, so too do the tales of violence Matt has heard on the village green in Massachusetts. In the final chapter of *Sign of the Beaver*, when Matt's mother announces that neighbors will soon arrive in Maine, Matt's happiness at family reunion is tinged with sadness that the forest he has learned to negotiate like an Indian will disappear along with Attean. He hopes that Attean and his people have found new hunting grounds to the west, but when he bows his head for grace, he admits to himself that he's not at all confident about their prospects.

Through Matt's internal dialogue, *Sign of the Beaver* asks readers to view the process of transforming virgin forests into New England townships from the perspective of displaced Indians. This view is compromised, however, by the novel's adherence to Anglo-American myth, particularly that of "regeneration through violence." As cultural historian Richard Slotkin has demonstrated, American narratives of conquest and rebirth typically hinge on an understanding of Indians as savages whose presence on American soil prevents the formation of a perfect Christian republic; Indians and Anglos cannot coexist, making an all-out fight for survival inevitable. In this understanding, European perfectibility in the New World wilderness required that white Christians regress to primitive Indian ways in order to both purge their own culture of false values and acquire "savage" skills and strengths that ultimately enabled them to destroy Native culture on its own turf. The trial of living among Indians—whether induced by war, captivity, or in Matt's case, accidental abandonment—was therefore necessary and desirable.[52] Each of Speare's novels set in early America incorporates the logic of regeneration through violence, and despite its attempt to highlight and celebrate Native perspectives, *Sign of the Beaver* is no exception.

Sign of the Beaver details Matt's journey from naive and inexperienced landholder to candidate for Indian adoption to savvy, founding American citizen. Saknis asks Matt to teach Attean to read, but the Indian's learning in the settlers' cabin pales in comparison to the white boy's growth in the Penobscot woods. Attean succeeds as a teacher whereas Matt fails, and white America is the beneficiary. Saknis initiates Matt's "regeneration" and Indianization by giving him moccasins. Once properly shod, Matt learns to follow Attean through the woods in silence, a feat rewarded by Attean teaching him "another secret of the forest," how to detect an Indian trail (58). Matt learns quickly and surprises the Penobscot boy with his ability to assist when a bear threatens their safety: "'You move quick,' [Attean] said. 'Like Indian'" (74). This final display of competence earns Matt an invitation to the village, where for the first time he is treated like an Indian, an equal.[53] All the while that Matt is gaining valuable skills, Attean continues to resist Matt's instruction. The reading lessons were "going badly" (51) because according to Attean, "the white man's signs on paper were *piz wat*—good for nothing" (66).

When Saknis approaches the cabin late in autumn, Matt fears that the old man, having discovered how little Matt has *taught*, comes in anger. Instead, Saknis conveys his pleasure with how much Matt has *learned*. Given that Matt's family still has not appeared and the time for the Indians' permanent departure west has arrived, Saknis extends an invitation for Matt to join the Beaver people, as family. Matt's pride at receiving the offer is tempered by distinct feelings of superiority. For all Matt jokes that "he and Attean had sure enough turned that [*Robinson Crusoe*] story right round about," he still sees himself as Crusoe and Attean and his people as Friday (57):

> He was proud that they had wanted him to live with them. But he
> knew that he could never be really proud, as Attean was proud, of
> being a hunter. He belonged to his own people. He was bound to
> his own family, as Attean was bound to his grandfather. The thought
> that he might never see his mother again was sharper than hunger or
> loneliness. This was the land his father had cleared to make a home for
> them all. It was his own land, too. He could not run away. (114)[54]

Soon after the Indians leave, Matt's family arrives. "You've done a grown man's job, son," Matt's father says. "I'm right proud of you" (133). Coming immediately after Matt has told his horrified mother that the Indians kept him company, his father's praise takes on additional meaning. Matt demonstrated maturity not only by surviving "alone" but also by using the Native population appropriately. Matt's mastery of Indian ways—the acquisition of forest skills, physical strength, and sharpened senses— makes him a better colonizer. His parents' praise causes Matt a twinge of guilt because he believes he came close to choosing degeneration over regeneration. As he tells his mother when she remarks that he is as brown as an Indian, "'I almost was one.'. . . He hoped she'd never know how true it was" (134). Matt may believe that he could have "gone Native," as many of his historical counterparts in similar circumstances did, but Speare never intended her protagonist to seriously consider this an option.

Matt's connection to the soil—a connection Attean fostered—enables him to become a founding citizen of Maine. Matt's historical prototype, in fact, is recorded as the first resident of the city of Milo.[55] The rise of such men to positions of leadership and prominence in frontier communities is intimately connected to the "vanishing" of local indigenous people. Through a complex political and cultural process, nineteenth-century New Englanders re-created themselves as indigenous to the land by removing—both physically through forced Indian removal and metaphorically through the declaration of Indians' "vanishing"—the people who were actually native to the northeastern landscape.[56] Matt's becoming a founding citizen of Maine hinges on Attean's disappearance. And yet, the historical Penobscot did *not* disappear; they remained in Maine. Today they are a federally recognized sovereign nation, and they achieved this legal status by acting in ways directly opposite to Speare's fictional Attean: they stayed on their homelands, mastered written and spoken English, and used their understanding of American diplomacy to demand land rights. Even as they did so, however, American arts and letters metaphorically made them "disappear"; through literature, Anglo-Americans transformed the Penobscot into relics of the past. *Sign of the Beaver*'s historical interpretation of vanishing, then, is far from anomalous.

Henry David Thoreau's *The Maine Woods* (1864), an account of the transcendentalist's exploration of northern forests about fifty years after the setting of Speare's novel, both demonstrates the narrative efforts of white New Englanders to erase Native peoples from Maine's landscape and captures Penobscot efforts to assert themselves as the rightful inhabitants and inheritors of the land. In an essay titled "Ktaadn," Thoreau describes the "shabby, forlorn and cheerless look" of Indian buildings, remarking that "these were once a powerful tribe."[57] Thoreau's language and his inclusion of a population count convey his dim outlook of the Penobscot future. But as literary scholar Lisa Brooks has argued, Thoreau's writings also document the way nineteenth-century Penobscot leaders were using American law to ensure continued access to land for hunting and fishing; Thoreau notes that the Penobscot spoke in an Algonquian language that had "not yet died away" and whose vocabulary was "still copious" enough to carry them into modernity.[58] His ambiguous treatment of Maine's Indians as both a disappearing race and a living people cognizant of the rights granted them by the American legal system is important because *The Maine Woods* seems a likely source for Speare's *Sign of the Beaver*. A man named Joe Aitteon served as Thoreau's guide for the second of his three trips into Maine, and according to Thoreau, this historical Aitteon, "though he was a [tribal] Governor's son . . . had not learned to read."[59] Thoreau characterizes this young Penobscot as playing with the English language in much the same way Speare's fictional Attean toys with Defoe's diction.

Speare set *Sign of the Beaver* in 1769. *The Maine Woods* documents the Penobscot presence in New England fifty years after the close of the novel, which has Attean's family moving west. Speare knew that her book's ending deviated from the historical record. "I don't remember at what point, or why, I realized that the Indians, too, had to go. That was not part of the original anecdote," Speare wrote. "But having introduced an English boy to an alternate way of life, and a very appealing way, it seemed to me important that he must make a choice."[60] In crafting her narrative, Speare responded to a literary tradition in which an Anglo-American's rise to leading citizen was always subtly linked to an Indian people's tragic vanishing.

Sign of the Beaver commands a healthy classroom presence today. But the book is also unique among widely taught historical novels featuring Indians in that it has sustained censure in both scholarly and popular forums. Even more noteworthy, antiracist criticism has begun to penetrate teacher-education materials. The University of Maine's Hudson Museum, for example, provides teacher lessons plans for *Sign of the Beaver* that draw on material objects from its collection. While continuing to encourage the book's classroom use, the museum alerts educators to antiracist critiques and recommends that teachers discuss with students the derogatory connotations of the word "squaw" and illustrate, by means of eighteenth-century documents, that Maine's Indians spoke and wrote proper English during the early republic. Finally, the novel's ending, the museum cautions, suggests that Maine's Indians were part of "a culture in decline and disappearing"; it recommends that teachers familiarize students with tribal websites and other resources demonstrating the community's vitality today.[61] Some teachers are beginning to ask students to explore the historical distortions in *Sign of the Beaver*, particularly the Penobscot use of language. But most stop short of exploring the complexity of the novel's layered meaning. In the 1980s, Speare was newly attuned to Native perspectives on American history, and she used *Robinson Crusoe* as a means to critique European imperialism throughout *Sign of the Beaver*. In doing so, however, she reinscribed colonialism in its potent American form: Indians still disappear.

Like *Indian in the Cupboard*, which also appeared in the early 1980s, *Sign of the Beaver* entered the curriculum at a time when dramatic changes were unfolding in Indian Country. It is because of this timing that Native critics drew attention to problematic depictions of Indians in these contemporary texts.[62] In a process that began in the 1970s and continues to gain momentum today, the American Indian population grew in both number and visibility, reversing trends that had been in place since the Indian Wars ended in the mid-1800s. Radicalized by the civil rights and Black Power movements, both detribalized and reservation-raised Indians began organizing politically. During the years spanning 1970 and 1995, the population of American Indians, Eskimos, and Aleuts grew from 827,000 to 2.2 million, and demographers expect the figure to nearly double again by 2050.[63] While some growth can be attributed to the improved collection of census data on reservations and in rural Alaska, the increase results primarily from individuals (and at times entire communities) choosing to identify as "American Indian/Alaskan Native" rather than as "White" or "Black," as they had done previously. Sociologist Joane Nagel has termed this phenomenon ethnic renewal, or "the process whereby new ethnic identities, communities, and cultures are built or rebuilt out of historical social and symbolic systems."[64] The combined factors of political consciousness-raising, tribal land suits, and improved conditions for ethnic and racial minorities in the United States challenged the notion of the vanishing Indian long embedded in mainstream America's consciousness. New children's novels about Indians continued to appear amid this transforming political climate. Those embraced by schools reacted to the changes in Indian Country in one of two ways: they denied political change and repeated the master narrative of vanishing (albeit minus the use of words such as "squaw," which had been acknowledged as offensive), or they celebrated Indians' renewed presence in American political life and actively promoted a counter-narrative that made the very idea of vanishing preposterous.

Indians, Land, and Modernity:
"The Return of the Indian"

Published in 1980, John Reynolds Gardiner's novella *Stone Fox* illustrates particularly well the aggressive reassertion of the vanishing Indian myth in the 1980s and beyond.[65] Set in Wyoming at the end of the nineteenth century, *Stone Fox* nonetheless responds to historical events of the late *twentieth* century. In telling the story, Gardiner draws on libertarian thought—particularly antistatist individualism and property rights by means of usage—that stands in stark contrast to the communal, nonpossessive values upheld by American Indians in both the nineteenth and twentieth century.[66] The central action of the story, a dogsled race, puts these social and economic principles head-to-head as a poor, white orphan living with his grandfather competes against a Shoshone man seeking to reclaim for his tribe land privatized by American law. The race's premise—land competition—is rooted in turn-of-the-century western history. The 1862 Homestead Act opened western lands for settlement, granting farmers who occupied and improved a 160-acre plot ownership of that land at minimal cost. In order to reach this territory newly opened for farming, however, settlers had to pass through Shoshone land. The tensions that emerged were addressed through a series of negotiations between the federal government and the tribe that lasted until 1904. First, a right-of-passage for land-seeking homesteaders traveling through Indian territory was established; next, boundary lines for a Shoshone reservation—land closed to homesteading—were determined; finally, those 1868 boundary lines were altered through land cessions that made additional land available for settlers.[67] Throughout the negotiation process, Shoshone people lost access to and possession of territory while non-Native individuals gained exclusive, private ownership of land once open to all.

The events of the late nineteenth century—Indian loss and settler gain—stand in direct contrast to the events of the late twentieth century—Indian gain and settler loss. Beginning in the 1970s, tribal nations on the east coast brought land suits to state and town governments, arguing that hundreds of thousands of acres of Indian land had been illegally seized in the previous centuries. Citing eighteenth-century law, tribes demanded compensation for their losses and, in many instances, won. On the west coast, Indian tribes used legal recourse to gain treaty-based hunting and fishing rights, much to the anger of many white residents in the Pacific and Rocky Mountain Northwest.[68] Stone Fox speaks to the frustration of white landowners like Gardiner who viewed twentieth-century Indian victories as a threat to private property and the privileging of occupancy and usage.

John Reynolds Gardiner's Stone Fox (1980)

Stone Fox tells the story of ten-year-old "little Willy," who lives with his grandfather on a Wyoming potato farm. The book opens with a crisis: Willy's grandfather is sick in bed and has not spoken in three weeks. Willy knows that something is seriously wrong, but the doctor finds nothing medically amiss when she examines him.[69] Unwilling to accept the physician's conclusion that Grandfather has simply decided to die,

Willy musters all his energy and harvests the potato crop alone, convinced that this will cure his parent figure. It doesn't. Not until a city
slicker appears threatening to take away the farm unless ten years of
back taxes are paid does Willy understand the cause of Grandfather's
malaise. Willy has never heard of taxes and doesn't understand their
point—the doctor's explanation that they care for people who cannot
care for themselves is unhelpful; Grandfather always said "we should
take care of ourselves . . . where there's a will, there's a way"—but Willy
nonetheless realizes that freeing the farm from debt is the key to saving
Grandfather's life.[70]

Willy has fifty of the five hundred dollars Grandfather owes in his
college bank account, and conveniently, the village's annual dogsled race
offers a first-place prize of five hundred dollars, with a fifty-dollar entry
fee. If he could just win the race, Willy tells himself, all problems would
evaporate. Willy hurriedly exchanges his college savings for an entry
ticket and exits City Hall feeling "ten feet tall" (50). That is, until he
meets his competitor. Also intent on winning is the Shoshone dogsledder
Stone Fox, who has never lost a race. Undaunted, little Willy and his dog
Searchlight practice the course repeatedly, noting in triumph that Stone
Fox takes just one trial run. The day before the competition, Willy hears
Stone Fox's team barking and reaches out to pet the magnificent animals.
The taciturn Shoshone punches the boy for interfering. The day of the actual race, however, Stone Fox's "stony" demeanor melts. After leading the
pack for the entire race, Willy is poised to win the coveted prize when,
ten feet from the finish line, Searchlight collapses in exhaustion. Instead
of pulling ahead to the finish, Stone Fox stops in his tracks, holds a gun
to the other competitors, and motions Willy to walk across the finish
line, Searchlight in his arms. The five-hundred-dollar prize secured and
back taxes paid, Willy's grandfather makes a full recovery.

The story of *Stone Fox* originated as a folktale, an oral genre defined
by its chameleonlike ability to change form as the contexts of its telling
shift. "The idea for this story came from a Rocky Mountain legend that
was told to me in 1974 by Bob Hudson over a cup of coffee at Hudson's
Café in Idaho Falls, Idaho," Gardiner states in his author's note (84).
Whatever the folktale's original form, by the time Gardiner heard and
retold the story, it revealed the concerns of rural white conservatives who
feared the power of newly politicized Indians (and perhaps other minority groups). Gardiner's version of the tale controls the threat of Native
power by using a historical setting to predict contemporary outcomes. In
Stone Fox, an Indian recognizes that it would be "unfair" to claim a prize
enabling him to buy back stolen Indian land when his white competitor

has worked so hard to save his small family farm. Thanks to carefully plotted reversals, Willy—ten years old, an orphan, one animal to pull his sled—figures as the underdog. The typical figure of sympathy, meanwhile, emerges as a silent, intimidating Goliath: "The boy's mouth hung open as he tilted his head way back to look up at the man. Little Willy had never seen a giant before" (52). On the day of the race, the Indian's magnanimous gesture of guarding the finish line transforms him into a noble savage, but it also renders him complicit in the disempowerment of his people. At a time when twentieth-century Indians were initiating court cases that ended in federal acknowledgment of their right to stolen property, *Stone Fox* asserts that even Indians can see that the "proper" owner of Indians' ancestral land is the white man who currently occupies it.

Like *Sign of the Beaver*, *Stone Fox* suggests that Indian removal is natural and inevitable, a logic that necessarily condemns Indians to the past. Gardiner tells readers that Stone Fox is "smart"; given American property laws and the nation's commitment to progress, however, he is also doomed. Only one dogsled team can win a race, and, according to American law, only one person or family unit can own a piece of land.[71] Little Willy—and white America—win both the race and the land. In book reviews and teacher lesson plans, much is made of the "tragedy" that occurs in *Stone Fox*'s narrative. "There is breathless excitement as we race with Willy and Searchlight to the finish line," reads the *New Yorker* review. "A word of warning: every victory has its price, and for the reader this one is a swift stab to the heart." The stab, of course, is the death of Willy's beloved pet. The tragedy of ancestral land lost and tribal sovereignty denied is so predictable that it doesn't even bear comment.[72] Textually reinforcing the loss of Indian land and culture as inevitable, however, doesn't make it so.

As indigenous communities across the United States experienced a numerical and cultural renaissance in the 1970s, an incubation process that would affect children's literature also began. The Native generation that came of age during and after the civil rights movement developed new ways of understanding its identity. A long, troubled history of American Indian boarding schools—historic centers of forced assimilation—finally came to a conclusive end in the West, while the offspring of detribalized Indians in the East discovered and reclaimed indigenous heritages that had been aggressively suppressed for generations.[73] The broad-based civil rights movement of the mid-twentieth century thus affected every corner of Indian Country. Whether born on western reservations, residing in western cities amid a population pocket of Indians, or living as white or black people in eastern cities or small towns, many members of this postwar generation came to see themselves as belonging not only to a specific tribal group but also to a community of Indians, a people that collectively shared attributes with other racial minorities.

Pan-Indianism and identification with civil rights aims—although never complete or uncontroversial in Indian Country—had important implications for children's literature. Traditionally, Native communities saw no compelling need for tribally or culturally specific children's novels. Their aim was to educate their own youth, and storytelling was the preferred means. By listening to elders, children learned tribally specific traditions not only through the stories told but also through their medium. Group interaction with a storyteller contrasted sharply with the solitary act of reading, particularly as performed in schools controlled by outsiders. Storytelling, moreover, was indigenous to Native communities, whereas the novel, a cultural production of the West, originated in a colonial milieu and emphasized individual rather than collective experience.[74] Yet in the wake of the civil rights movement, Christopher Columbus quincentennial, and multicultural initiative in schools, Native attitudes toward a Native children's literature began to change. Some Indians became interested in using novels as well as storytelling as a means of educating their own children. Others embraced the ideological goals of multiculturalism that activated mainstream K–12 reform and wanted authentic Native books to complement authentic African American, Hispanic American, and Asian American ones. Still others viewed multiculturalism as anathema to tribal sovereignty—which defined Natives as outside of and separate from the nation—but, recognizing the need for political allies, embraced school literature's capacity to educate mainstream youth about Native culture, history, and political rights.

The possibility of Native children's novels as mainstream school curriculum materialized at the turn of the twenty-first century in large part because Leslie Silko (Laguna/Pueblo), N. Scott Momaday (Kiowa), Louise Erdrich (Ojibwe), and others had claimed the novelistic form and written English as authentically Indian—that is, as "Native" as poetry and stories told in ancestral languages.[75] In the wake of favorable public attention to this adult fiction, educator activists initiated for Indians the pedagogical work other minority groups had begun: they drew attention to problematic representations in widely circulated children's books and called for culturally sensitive texts authored by Native people.[76] Contemporary realistic fiction such as *The Heart of a Chief* by Joseph

Bruchac (Abenaki) and *The Absolutely True Diary of a Part-Time Indian* by Sherman Alexie (Spokane) responded with Native protagonists who comment wryly on the world's distorted views of Indians.[77] Historical novels such as Louise Erdrich's *The Birchbark House* and its sequels—which parallel Laura Ingalls Wilder's Little House books—and Bruchac's middle-grade novels (for example, *The Winter People*, *Sacajawea*, and *Pocahontas*) responded by retelling familiar stories from a Native rather than Anglo-American perspective. Both genres challenge, narratively and extranarratively, older texts' assumptions about vanishing Indians, and both lay the groundwork for contemporary arguments about Indians' rights to land and sovereignty.

Joseph Bruchac's *The Winter People* (2002)

Set in the Quebec mission village of St. Francis during the French and Indian War, *Winter People* tells the familiar story of Rogers's Raid. In 1759, Major Robert Rogers commanded an elite group of Anglo-American scouts and Stockbridge Indian allies on a mission to destroy a French-Abenaki village that had become the launching pad for attacks on New England settlements—frontier outposts staked on Abenaki land. Rogers's letters and journals, now understood to be greatly exaggerated, reported that the mission of eradication was successful and that the St. Francis Abenaki were "chiefly destroyed."[78] Although French records and oral history suggest otherwise, Rogers's tale of triumph (and Indian vanishing) was widely circulated in the eighteenth and nineteenth centuries and popularized in the twentieth century by Kenneth Roberts's best-selling novel *Northwest Passage* (1936) and its Hollywood adaptation. Drawing on Abenaki sources and writing in response to Roberts and others, Bruchac's *Winter People* counters both the triumphal tone and Anglo perspective of mainstream accounts of the raid.[79]

Saxso, a fictional Abenaki adolescent, narrates Bruchac's tale, and he begins with the hushed warning, uttered in Abenaki but tinged with a Mahican accent, that he receives. "That whisper. It raises the hair on the back of my neck each time it creeps into my memory like a spider crossing your face as you sleep," Saxso confides, drawing on metaphors from the natural world to reverse traditional logic about Native-European conflict and suggest that it is *European* modes of attack that are sinister.[80] Having heard the furtive warning of ambush, Saxso carries it to his community and leads his mother and sisters to the woods and safety. Because he lost his father in an earlier European skirmish, Saxso feels responsible for protecting his womenfolk. At fourteen, however, he is only on the brink of adulthood and has difficulty judging where his responsibilities lie. In a moment he later deeply regrets, Saxso leaves the women to help another man rescue a child. As he and Great Simon retrieve the young girl, Rogers's men discover Saxso's family and take them captive. This, more than the Bostoniak (Anglo) bullet that penetrates his shoulder or the sight of his village in ruins, wounds Saxso; he has let his family down. Calmed by the skillful hands and words of the healer, however, Saxso regains strength and undertakes a journey to rescue his family.

Saxso's voyage up the St. Francis River in pursuit of Rogers's Rangers calls the Anglo-American heroism of Roberts's *Northwest Passage* into question. By describing a landscape "stripped of birds and animals," Roberts sheds superhuman light on the Rangers' military victory, accomplished as it was in a state of near-starvation.[81] Yet when Saxso moves across the same terrain days later, he reports, "I had only to drop in a hook and line to bring out a fat bass or trout. Our northern land may seem barren to those whose eyes are only used to the sight of villages, but there is food to be found everywhere" (107). And unlike the Rangers, who find the route arduous and their feet always wet, Saxso "knew the firm ground to follow" (117). Physical hardship, of course, was just one part of the journey's challenges. Both Saxso and the Rangers rehearse frightful stories to spur their travel. In *Northwest Passage*, Rogers urges his men forward by enumerating atrocities previously committed by St. Francis Indians. In *Winter People*, Saxso recalls the same incident differently; the Bostoniaks, having caught an Abenaki party by surprise, killed many men. When the survivors fled, the Bostoniaks began scalping the fallen. The fleeing Abenaki, upon witnessing what they considered a cowardly act, turned back and scalped the more than 140 Rangers who in their desecration of Abenaki dead had left themselves unguarded. Thus, as the Rangers buoy their spirits with thoughts of revenge, Saxso reassures himself with knowledge of his people's moral and military superiority.

Narrated in the first person and centered on the protagonist's solitary journey to rescue his family, *Winter People* is ostensibly Saxso's coming-of-age story. As a revisionist counternarrative, however, it rejects Anglo-American literary norms, including that of a heroic journey toward adulthood.[82] In shifting readers' perspective from English worldview to Abenaki way of knowing, Bruchac ensures that *Winter People* is only partially Saxso's tale. In recounting his story, Saxso incorporates numerous tales told to him by elders. Readers hear stories of the family's move from ancestral homes to St. Francis in the voice of Saxso's great-grandfather, stories of legendary battles in the voice of Saxso's uncle, and traditional tales—those of "the winter people," the rivers, the raccoon, and the tamarack tree—in the voice of Saxso's mother. Each of the stories contains a lesson, and in repeating them, Saxso both soothes himself and reviews elders' instructions. At a textual level, Saxso's rehearsing of Abenaki tales also transforms *Winter People* from a story about Saxso to a story about the entire Abenaki community, past and present.

Readers are immersed in Abenaki thought through Bruchac's choice of words, metaphor, and symbolism. Facing multiple life-and-death situations, Saxso struggles to render the unfamiliar familiar by tapping into his knowledge of the animal kingdom and the spiritual traditions of his people. When a Bostoniak bullet pierces Great Simon's skin and Saxso watches the lifeblood drain, his thoughts turn to the hunt. Great Simon's "body became limp as a deer when an arrow has cut its breath," Saxso notes, willing himself to comprehend the unthinkable: Great Simon has died (47–48). Seconds later, he himself is struck, and he notes through his haze that his enemy has "a face as hairy as that of a bear" (48).[83] Comparisons to the natural world and to the spiritual elements with which it is endowed enable Saxso to cope with a frightening environment and retain faith in his mission's ultimate success. As he rows upriver, Saxso appeals to the "little ones" who dwell underwater: "As I sang, I felt the river listening to me. I began to move more swiftly" (99). Reading symbolism into the movement of water and flight of animals fortifies him against despair. A large bird flies toward Saxso and the Worrier, his spiritual mentor, before his journey begins. The Worrier thanks this "brother loon" for "reminding us we may rise to fly again" (51). Throughout the narrative, the collective pronouns "we" and "us" dominate. As the Worrier emphasizes, Saxso is never really alone: he travels with his history and is guided by his animal siblings and guardian spirits, who operate in the present.

It is a community, not an individual, who plays the hero's part in *Winter People*, a fact made dramatically clear in the final moments of Saxso's mission. At the point when Saxso should have made his triumphal escape, retrieved captives in tow, a guard detects him and shoots. As he lies wounded, believing all chance of escape lost, Saxso hears his mother's voice behind him and sees her point his gun at the enemy. The family escapes, in part because the Stockbridge guard, admiring their collective courage, lets them go. Weak and injured, Saxso is carried most of the way home. He unquestionably displays bravery in conducting the mission, but Saxso's success is part of the larger glory of his family, his community, and his people. As he narrates in the novel's final chapter, "So it was that I brought my family home. I saved them and they saved me. Nothing that I did was done alone. I was helped by so many along the way. . . . I was helped by this land that loves us because we keep the summer in our hearts" (157).

Land is personified in *Winter People*, and it clearly prefers the Abenaki, who view it as kin, to the English, who view it as a commodity. The rightful owner of land, Bruchac argues, is the people whom the land loves—the Native inhabitants who imbue it with their peoplehood. This argument, like Gardiner's in *Stone Fox*, emerged from a specific historical context. The descendants of the St. Francis Abenaki who remained on mission land continue to live there today; Canada recognizes these Abenaki as a First Nation and has set aside the Odanak Reserve as its homeland. Descendants of eighteenth-century Abenaki who remained on ancestral land in New England, however, lost their public, collective identity during the nineteenth century. When American Indian policy made Native identities undesirable or dangerous, many of these New England Abenaki—Joseph Bruchac's maternal grandfather included— intermarried with other Native, European, or African peoples. Since the 1970s, however, Bruchac and other New England Abenaki have embraced their Native roots and struggled to secure federal recognition as a tribal nation. The St. Francis/Sokoki Band of the Western Abenaki gained state recognition from Vermont in 2006, but the law stipulates that it "shall not be construed to recognize, create, extend, or form the basis of any right or claim to land."[84] The various bands of New England Abenaki, therefore, continue to press for both federal recognition and the return of ancestral lands. *Winter People* participates in that process, declaring in its authorship the survival of a people and arguing in its narrative that these people, the Abenaki, are entitled to their stolen land.

Unlike *Stone Fox* and other novels discussed above, *Winter People* is not widely taught. Bruchac's books for young children, particularly those that fall in the folklore, myth, and picture-book categories, have entered classrooms at a much greater rate than his historical novels.[85] The reason behind Bruchac's scarcity in middle schools is multifaceted, but one factor is the lack of any standout text. Bruchac has published more than one hundred books that cross age levels and span genres including fiction, poetry, biography, autobiography, and traditional tales. Given the rapid pace of publication, it is not surprising that some works disappoint. Among the significant number praised for careful craftsmanship, however, none has received a major literary prize such as the Newbery, the Printz, or the National Book Award. By contrast, authors like Scott O'Dell, who published more than twenty-five novels for children, are generally known for one or two texts taught far more frequently than their other works. Pressed for time and directed by professional journals and associations to do so, teachers rely heavily on award-winning books in their curricula.

A more complex issue that may contribute to the way Bruchac has entered curricula involves the author's identity. As an Abenaki, Bruchac represents the newly reclaimed Indian of the eastern seaboard. Some indigenous peoples raised for generations on western reservations are reluctant to see Bruchac and those like him as Indian.[86] Ongoing debate, both within Native circles and between Native communities and the federal government, about who is "really Indian" only adds to sometimes bitter disagreement among Native people about what constitutes "real" Native American literature. Some Native literary critics insist that authorial "authenticity" is a precursor to the creation of Native literature— "Native American literature, it must be said finally (and we would have thought it was obvious), is literature of, from, by Native Americans"— while others argue that Native American literature must be defined first and foremost by *form*, not by authorship—"ultimately, the study of Native American fiction should be the study of style."[87] Depending on where one is positioned in the debate about who is Indian and what constitutes Native literature, Bruchac's books may or may not qualify as belonging to the genre.

Definitional debates have unfolded far from K–12 classrooms, and the majority of classroom teachers are unaware of the tensions involved; nonetheless, the disagreements affect what children read. Historically, curricular change around issues of representation has taken place when a unified group of activists has brought attention to an issue and offered a solution, often by facilitating the production and distribution of alternative narratives. The lack of consensus across Indian Country, as well as some ambivalence around the importance of new narratives reaching non-Native students, persists. Yet, powerful grassroots movements have coalesced on the Internet, suggesting that change is on its way. Two prominent websites focus on raising awareness about problematic representations of Indians in children's literature and promoting children's books authored by American Indians: Oyate, run by a 501(c)(3) by the same name, and American Indians in Children's Literature, a weblog maintained by Debbie Reese (Nambe Pueblo), formerly assistant professor of American Indian Studies at the University of Illinois at Urbana-Champaign. Both Reese and the Oyate board of directors have made clear the high value they place on Native-authored texts. In 2010, Oyate underwent a change in leadership and seems to be moving toward more flexibility in defining categories. Prior to that point, the organization openly discouraged non-Native authors from writing about Indians in any capacity, echoing the language and arguments employed by the Council on Interracial Books for Children in the early 1970s ("after reflecting on the potential damage your book could cause, we ask that you think again about publishing it").[88] From the inception of her blog, Reese has been more open to the possibility of a non-Native author respectfully, and with permission, writing about Natives.

Importantly, both Reese and Oyate have embraced as "authentic" detribalized Indians who identify as Native. Both praise Joseph Bruchac's work nearly universally, and without regard to whether a particular book focuses on his own or other Native peoples. Reese has stated that she chooses to review books on the Internet rather than in professional journals because on the web she can evaluate books for *what* they say as well as *how* they say it.[89] Equally important, online reviews published by Reese and Oyate are free and readily available to the public. In recent years, they have received considerable attention from both publishers and authors seeking to avoid stereotypes and classroom teachers aiming to introduce "bias-free" texts to their students. Given the sustained commitment to multicultural education in schools, it seems likely that the market for a now-flourishing world of Native literature will continue to grow. The particular development of that literature, however, remains to be seen. Will "authentic" authorship, literary form, or some combination of the two come to dominate educators' categorization of the genre? Will culturally specific literature written to foster tribal sovereignty be embraced by educators who have traditionally valued novels that foster national citizenship and cross ideological lines? The dizzying diversity of American Indians—manifest in tribal identity, relations to mainstream culture, and political engagement—undoubtedly has ramifications for both children's literature and multicultural education.

■ The widely taught novels discussed in this chapter, books written by Elizabeth George Speare, Conrad Richter, Scott O'Dell, and John Gardiner, describe mythic rather than historical Indians, a fact that makes putting these books to "multicultural" uses highly problematic. As adopted in today's K–12 schools, multiculturalism entails the celebration of diverse cultures. In theory, multiculturalism replaces the assimilation of the early twentieth-century "melting pot" ideal; nonetheless, in celebrating a "diverse America," it denies the possibility of affirming distinctive cultures as *alternatives to* Western values and mainstream narratives of the American past.[90] Native history and Native literature, in other words, do not sit well within the multicultural framework. As some

Native authors, critics, and activists have recognized, however, the multi-cultural agenda can be used to usher in Native texts that help non-Native children recognize Native rights to land and resources, a recognition that can serve as a precursor to embracing the idea of Native sovereignty.

Native-authored texts, however, cannot stand alone any more than texts privileging Anglo-American perspectives and featuring mythic Indians can. Students will come to understand the unique and troubled relations between the federal government and Indian nations, white settlers and Native inhabitants, mythic Indians and historical Indians, only if they are exposed to the history of representations of Indians in text. Most Native children grow up with an understanding of misrepresentations. Few non-Native children do. Stereotypes must be unlearned to be identified as literary trope. The pedagogical task for teachers is quite challenging: narratives such as *Island of the Blue Dolphins* and *Stone Fox* are essential to teaching American myth, but other books are critical to teaching Native history.

Chapter 3

War Novels

■ Ask Americans of any age to give a broad outline of U.S. history, and they will invariably start with Columbus, proceed to the Pilgrims, then mark the passage of time by a steady march of military engagements— the Revolution, the Civil War, and World Wars I and II—before adding the civil rights movement and returning to battles overseas.[1] This narrative framework is rehearsed in the nation's history textbooks and reinforced in popular media and museum exhibits. The progression facilitates a coherent, chronological narrative of the nation, but its confident shorthand also suggests inevitability and consensus, nation and citizenry as one. It is in part this conflation of people and country that makes war such an intriguing subject of study.

Children's authors have turned to military conflicts with frequency, sometimes to bolster the oft-repeated national themes of freedom, opportunity, and unity, but other times to raise questions about the character of the nation-state or the nature of war itself. Novelists' assumptions about what children would experience should war arrive at their doorsteps have changed substantially over the past seventy years—most significantly after the Vietnam War and 9/11—and these beliefs have shaped their portrayals of historical warfare. Novelistic depictions of the Revolution, the Civil War, and World War II have grown progressively harsher, less heroic, and more violent. The result is that three distinct generations of children's war fiction have emerged: that written between World War II and the Vietnam War (affected by the civil rights movement and rise of second-wave feminism), that written between the Vietnam War and 9/11, and that written after the start of the twenty-first century.[2]

All three generations of war novels view military conflict as constituting pivotal moments in the nation's history, moments that must be grappled with to understand one's identity as a citizen. By answering central questions differently, however, the novels offer distinct versions of the legacy forged by American warfare. The questions posed are complex and penetrate deep into personal and national self-understanding:

When a nation is at arms, where do citizens' responsibilities lie? Can patriotism and dissent coexist? How does the violence of war fit into the stories soldiers and politicians tell, at war's end, about the morality of peace? Ultimately, can wars bring about positive good, or is the violence they engender inherently destructive for the nation and its people?

Three Generations of Fighting for Independence: Johnny, Tim, and Octavian

The first generation of children's war novels still taught in today's schools were published during the 1940s and 1950s and fit into the larger category of bildungsroman narratives. Set against iconic backdrops, they rest on the assumption that war tested America but ultimately strengthened both the nation and its people. Whether the narratives unfold during the Revolution or Civil War, they share a number of features in common, the most important of which is a protagonist who symbolically figures as the nation as a whole.[3] In merging central character and country, first-generation war novels purport to tell not just a story about a particular war, but *the* story of the war—ultimately, a narrative of the nation, its people, and its destiny. The representative protagonist epitomizes the ideal of the self-made man; he is young, white, native born, English speaking, and northern. Hardworking and on the rise, he is either a farmer on his own land or an apprentice in a respectable trade.

Given first-generation war novels' regional bias, one might ask how they came to garner curricular popularity nationwide. Historian Joanne Pope Melish provides a partial explanation: in the years following the Civil War, southerners as well as northerners embraced the mythic idea that New England was the uncomplicated, historical center of a liberty-loving people who shunned slavery.[4] What facilitated the war novels' nationwide acceptance, therefore, was their inattention to slavery and silence on the issue of racial equality. In the case of Civil War narratives, authors' denial of slavery's importance to the war and, especially, their romanticization of the Old South's "contented slaves" led to books' removal from school curricula during the post–civil rights era. But first-generation war novels about the Revolution continued to benefit from their silence on slavery; by eliminating discussion of African Americans' uneven fate in the wake of war—as well as the rancorous sectional debate about black people's place within the republic after peace was achieved—novelists were able to render the War of Independence a more complete triumph.

Esther Forbes's *Johnny Tremain* (1943)

In American lore, "Johnny" is the boy who "has gone for a soldier." It is no surprise, then, that the most famous children's war hero bears that name. *Johnny Tremain* is known today as Esther Forbes's masterpiece, but Forbes was a prolific and profitable author for adults before she entered the children's market with her Revolutionary War novel.[5] Recognized for her historical romances—several were Book-of-the-Month Club picks—and popular history, Forbes turned to children's writing in part because of Pearl Harbor (she described the patriotic Johnny as "my great war effort") and in part because, after completing a Pulitzer Prize–winning biography of Paul Revere, she still had unanswered questions.[6] Like many authors who write both history and fiction, Forbes struggled to control her literary imagination while working in the historical mode. The *New England Quarterly* praised *Paul Revere and the World He Lived In* as "a novelist's biography," but despite its literariness, Forbes obeyed the rules of history writing in crafting it.[7] Her curiosity about what life was like for the apprentices who crossed Paul Revere's path, boys who, like other common folk of the eighteenth century, left scant records, was suppressed in *Paul Revere* and led to *Johnny Tremain*.

Paul Revere and *Johnny Tremain* share much in common despite their differences in genre and audience.[8] Both reflect deep historical research; feature protagonists who are "simple artisans" that rise to meet the extraordinary demands of war; and develop a historical argument that the Revolution's leaders fought to protect liberal values and American traditions of democracy, an interpretation that had fallen out of favor among professional historians who during the interwar period emphasized the economic rather than ideological roots of the rebellion.[9] As a local historian descended from a line of New England settlers and Revolutionary War soldiers, Forbes exemplified the interpretative tradition she disseminated in both books. She was born in Westboro, Massachusetts, in 1891 and grew up in a house filled with antiques and family stories about relatives captured by Indians. Her mother served as regent for the Worcester chapter of the Daughters of the American Revolution and engaged in serious research as an amateur historian. As Forbes phrased it, she was as "steeped in Colonial New Englandiana as a pickle is in brine."[10]

As an interpreter of the past, Forbes embraced antiquarian aims rather than the goals of "scientific" history. Antiquarians are concerned with heritage, and they connect to the past in deeply personal ways. As historians, they are less concerned with understanding change over time, the primary focus of scholarly inquiry, than with glorifying a particular historical moment and using that event to understand contemporary realities. In projecting forward from a fixed time in the past to the present day, antiquarians tend to gloss over intervening periods, assuming a kind of inevitability in the march of historical events. Like professional historians, however, they are firmly committed to accurately reporting details of the past. "At times maps of Boston or Salem would be spread out in the dining room and the whole family would work on deciding where old roads once ran. [Forbes] traveled about to do research and get the feel of places," a family member recalled.[11] Forbes conducted the majority of her research for both *Paul Revere* and *Johnny Tremain* at the American Antiquarian Society, and she bequeathed her "literary remains," the profit generated from her books, to this archive, whose very name captures its nineteenth-century founders' reverence for celebrating the American past.

Johnny Tremain tells the story of an orphaned silversmith apprentice. After suffering a debilitating injury in his master's Boston workshop, Johnny must acquire a new identity and sense of purpose, as well as a practical means of supporting himself. Because his injury coincides with the Sons of Liberty's final preparations for the Revolution, Johnny has the opportunity to remake himself as a Patriot, and he does so with gusto. In tracing Johnny's personal and political transformations from boy to man, elitist to egalitarian, Forbes's novel relates a familiar tale of the nation's birth, a narrative formulated by old New England families who in the nineteenth century created and preserved mythic tales of the nation's founding that placed Boston, Puritan values, and egalitarianism at the center of both the Revolution and the American project.

Employing a narrative device common to first-generation children's war novels, Forbes used an adolescent Johnny to symbolize the nascent American nation. The symbolism becomes most readily apparent in a textual contradiction. By writing a novel for children and making Johnny her unquestioned hero, Forbes invites young readers to participate in the struggle of founding the nation. Yet Forbes gives the adolescents in her book—Johnny and his friend Rab—only bit parts. In her rendering, Johnny is actually *asleep* when the war begins—not even "the shot heard 'round the world" disturbed his slumbers. And although Rab fights at Lexington, the young man is mortally wounded before firing a shot.[12] Johnny's passivity in battle makes sense given that he is a symbol (he stands for the nation being birthed by the war depicted) as well as a literary character. Moreover, peopled with heroes like John Hancock and Sam Adams, *Johnny Tremain* rests on the assumption that great men—not boy apprentices—make history.[13]

By merging Johnny and the nation, Forbes creates a subtle means of demonstrating American exceptionalism. Johnny, standing in for the nation, adheres to—and challenges—the literary trope of tragic hero. The "prize apprentice" of Hancock's Wharf, he is confident, ambitious, and presumptuous (100). Mirroring the American colonies, England's prize possession, Johnny flouts the rules of hierarchy and deference. Ignoring his master's admonishments that "pride cometh before a fall," he disobeys Mr. Lapham by pouring silver on the Lord's Day. His hand, a silversmith's most valuable tool, is burned beyond usefulness in the process. The novel's opening chapters read like a Greek tragedy: the best apprentice in Boston harbors a secret aristocratic identity (Johnny's mother died after arming him with proof of his high-status birth) and possesses a tragic flaw. Mr. Lapham interprets the burn as divine punishment for disregarding natural hierarchies and tells Johnny to find another master. Johnny's mistress predicts that the boy will end up on the gallows. Instead, Johnny becomes a Patriot. In Forbes's telling, an upstart can defy Old World destiny.

Before this bright future can dawn, however, Johnny Tremain must undergo a transformation that renders him an American. When first faced with the bleakness of his post-injury future, Johnny decides to capitalize on his high birth. He takes his mother's heirloom silver cup out of hiding and brings it to his rich maternal relations, Boston merchants "trying to ride two horses—Whig and Tory" (71). Mr. Lyte not only refuses to recognize Johnny as kin but goes so far as to frame him for theft. When the Observers (Forbes's name for the Sons of Liberty) intervene to secure his release, Johnny takes an important first step in embracing revolutionary values: he rejects the privilege of his birth.[14] While a prize apprentice, Johnny deemed all those less skilled than him as inferiors, and he showed little patience for those born less fortunate than himself.[15] By the time the war begins, however, he has learned to respect all people whose actions emanate from a desire to serve the common good. Johnny, representing the nation, has been swept up in the egalitarian language of the Revolution.

Johnny's transformation was imagined by Forbes during the 1940s, however, and it reflects the persistence of racial inequality at that time. Johnny's attitude toward the few African American characters appearing in the book remains static, despite his rejection of other natural hierarchies. As an apprentice, he enjoys ordering John Hancock's slave Little Jehu around the shop, and as a delivery boy for the Patriot *Observer*, he basks in the obsequious apology of Sam Adams's Sukey, who, after accidentally flinging dishwater on him, hurriedly stammers, "Oh, little master, I'se so sorry!" (13, 100). Far from being dismayed at the display of deference, Johnny takes pleasure in Sukey viewing him as an equal to Adams, a fellow white "master." The narrator tells us that Johnny is rewarded for accepting the apology: ever after, Adams invites Johnny into the house to talk to him "in that man-to-man fashion" (101).[16] The incident is presented as a lesson: Adams rewards Johnny for treating a social inferior with compassion. But Adams also views Johnny as a peer, a fellow Observer, because he "correctly" acts the part of a social superior to whom deference is due.

In writing *Johnny Tremain*, Forbes hoped to connect teenagers' responsibilities during the Revolution to her readers' duties during World War II. The novel's themes of moral military action and American egalitarianism parallel the rhetoric of the Second World War, best captured in Franklin D. Roosevelt's widely reproduced concept of fighting so the world could enjoy the Four Freedoms guaranteed to Americans. Within the context of *Johnny Tremain*, it is James Otis who formulates the rationale for war: "Why are we going to fight? Why, why? . . . For men and women and children all over the world. . . . Even as we shoot down the British soldiers we are fighting for rights such as they will be enjoying a hundred years from now. . . . There shall be no more tyranny. . . . Those natural rights God has given to every man, no matter how humble" (178–79). Forbes explicitly links the wars in her Newbery acceptance speech, noting that her readers "are not yet in the armed forces, but many of them soon will be. . . . [I] wanted to show that these earlier boys were conscious of what they were fighting for and that it was something which they believed was worth more than their own lives. And to show that many of the issues at stake in this war are the same as in the earlier one."[17] Johnny's practice of modeling himself after humble but gifted men, leaders who recognize the importance of ideals over self, becomes an example to Forbes's readers. Johnny is positioned to play a man's part at the novel's end, sacrificing life itself if called upon to do so. He is not perfect, but as a young Patriot, he's on the path to greatness.

When Forbes first submitted *Johnny Tremain* to Harcourt Brace, the publisher believed the novel's sophisticated prose and character development were inappropriate to a children's book. Suggestions for revision included shortening the manuscript, simplifying vocabulary, and altering characters so that they better conformed to straightforward notions of good and evil. Alarmed, Forbes wrote her agent:

> There are a number of things (like Johnny's getting locked up on
> Castle Island) that could be cut but what I object to is cutting almost

all of the paragraphs and scenes which show his changing relationship to many of the people with whom he is thrown. For if I had one predominating thought in mind while writing the book it was to show this flux and change—as is always done in good adult novels. I hoped by so doing to give a young reader a feeling of actuality—that these were real people such as he himself knew. . . . A little pathetically I'll admit I was trying to do a new sort of book for young people—not just a story but something of an actual "novel." I cannot say I have succeeded, but I am not ready too quickly to admit defeat.[18]

Forbes contended that Johnny could not be perfect or unwaveringly consistent because no real human is. But more important, Forbes needed Johnny to have flaws—and learn to overcome them—because this process of "flux and change" was central to her *historical* argument about the ideological roots of the Revolution. Johnny sheds English notions of class and privilege to embrace American values of opportunity, meritocracy, and egalitarianism. Instead of making the changes proposed, Forbes withdrew the manuscript and sent it to Houghton Mifflin, who published it with few changes. The result is that *Johnny Tremain* emerged as a *literary* novel, a book that has stood the test of time.

At various points since its appearance in 1943, critics have declared *Johnny Tremain* naive and out of touch. "In the more than fifty years since the publication of *Johnny Tremain*, much has happened to make young people more skeptical of government. . . . As a result, today's teenagers are less blindly patriotic than the World War II generation," Elizabeth Weiss Vollstadt wrote in her 2001 literary guide to the novel.[19] But as the collapse of the World Trade Center towers shortly thereafter demonstrated, the reality was more complex. Johnny's patriotism, self-assurance, and relentless self-making continue to speak to teachers and students. When readers identify with Johnny—and plenty of nonwhite, nonmale readers do—they can imagine themselves being present at the beginning, playing a vital if unsung role in the nation's founding. Such readers bask in the optimism the novel's argument about America's ideological roots, and hence its triumphal destiny, provides. Vollstadt was correct, however, in indicating that there have been moments when *Johnny Tremain*'s message seemed out of synch not only with professional historians' writings about the Revolution but also with the pulse of the American public. The early 1970s were such a time.

The second wave of widely taught war novels emerged as Americans questioned the link between U.S. military action and moral righteousness in light of the Vietnam War. In these second-generation texts, a young protagonist (male *or* female) infused with patriotism and excited about the activity war will bring becomes disillusioned by the so-called high ideals of the war's leaders and comes to recognize both the high cost of battle and the hypocrisy of those justifying power in the name of freedom. The novels deliver a message that war is tragic—and unnecessary. Whereas first-generation narratives emphasize the ideals for which soldiers fought, second-generation novels pay minimal attention to political ideology and eliminate discussion of justice and rights as a factor in waging war. By doing so, they make possible a pointed critique of war as a solution to mediating conflict. Johnny Tremain and other first-generation protagonists grow from childhood to adulthood in the course of a narrative, as wartime conditions demand; protagonists of second-generation novels, in contrast, remain largely rooted in adolescence, mirroring the state of their "misguided" nation, which has turned to violence as a means of solving problems.[20]

The pacifist arguments of second-generation war novels have no equivalent in the contemporaneous writings of professional historians, but they do reflect professional historiography of the 1960s and 1970s in other ways. Turning away from the consensus history of the post–World War II years, historians of the 1960s re-engaged progressive historians' arguments about the economic motivations undergirding much of American warfare, including the Revolution. Affected by the civil rights movement unfolding around them, young historians also began writing bottom-up social history that took seriously the lived experiences of previously ignored historical actors, including women, the working class, and African and Native Americans. The influence of both progressive historians and new social history can be seen throughout second-generation war novels, whose authors sought to complicate what they saw as oversimplified, bellicose war stories for children.[21]

Christopher Collier and James Lincoln Collier's *My Brother Sam Is Dead* (1974)

During the 1970s, Christopher Collier, then professor of history at the University of Bridgeport and future Connecticut state historian, collaborated with his novelist brother James Lincoln to craft a new kind of narrative of the American Revolution, one that spoke to their own times. Bolstered by the Vietnam War, which led some to view *Johnny Tremain's* heroism as misplaced, as well as by the bicentennial, which created a market for everything revolutionary, the novel filled a niche even before schools' movement to use authentic literature in the classroom.

The Collier brothers came of age almost half a century after Forbes, but like their literary predecessor, they trace their New England ancestry to the colonial period. On their paternal side, they are the tenth generation of American Colliers, the first of whom arrived in Plymouth County, Massachusetts, sometime before 1635. The Colliers' mother, Katherine Slater Brown, counted Samuel Sewell and Ann Bradstreet as ancestors and was a descendant of Samuel Slater, the industrialist whose mill in Pawtucket, Rhode Island, is credited with starting the American Industrial Revolution.[22] The brothers' favorite role model, however, was Uncle Bill, a member of the Lost Generation of expatriate American writers that included E. E. Cummings, John Dos Passos, Malcolm Cowley, and Edna St. Vincent Millay. William Slater Brown's leftist, bohemian, womanizing lifestyle—not to mention his imprisonment in a French jail after being "separated" from his ambulance corps during World War I—presented a stark contrast with previous generations' Puritan service and sacrifice.[23] James Lincoln (born 1928) and Christopher (born 1930) grew up hearing Uncle Bill's stories during the 1930s and 1940s; by the 1970s, they were writing stories of their own. The Vietnam-era novels the Collier brothers penned together grapple with some of the same themes—disillusionment, lost ideals, and the impossibility of heroism and sanctity—characterizing the work of the Lost Generation.

Of the brothers' many publications, both individual and collaborative, *My Brother Sam Is Dead* has been the most influential. When they set out to write *Brother Sam*, the Colliers had several aims: to create a narrative that would explicitly *teach*, to create a book dominated by progressive rather than Whig interpretations of the Revolution, and to create a story that prompted readers to consider pressing issues of their own day, particularly the Vietnam War. ("If the nation's most significant war brought so much suffering, shouldn't any war-like initiative cause deep concern?" an article written for teachers queried.)[24] Christopher Collier published two essays outlining the interpretative approach of *My Brother Sam Is Dead*, one in *Horn Book Magazine* (the preeminent publication for librarians) and one in the *ALAN Review* (a professional journal devoted exclusively to YA literature), as well as a book, *Brother Sam and All That*, dedicated to both teachers and librarians. Appearing over the course of three decades, each publication emphasized the brothers' second aim, to introduce children to progressive interpretations of the Revolutionary War. Whereas the Whig historians who influenced Forbes viewed the American Revolution as an expression of deep ideological commitments to political liberty, individual rights, and moral virtue, progressive historians emphasized the financial motives of revolutionary leaders. Progressive views necessarily challenged triumphal war narratives, a perspective Christopher Collier argued was greatly needed in children's literature: "Without denying its outstanding literary merit, Miss Forbes' presentation . . . present[s] history in simple, one-sided—almost moralistic—terms, [and to do so] is to teach nothing worth learning and to falsify the past in a way that provides worse than no help in understanding the present or in meeting the future."[25]

Christopher Collier contends that *Brother Sam*'s interpretation of the Revolution provides more nuance than *Johnny Tremain*'s; however, Collier's objective of creating a Revolutionary War novel that leads readers to better understand the contemporary concerns of the 1970s hints at the way *Brother Sam*, too, flattens out complexity in order to make a particular narrative argument. Exemplifying the approach of second-generation novels, *Brother Sam* downplays the importance of political ideology and eliminates discussion of rights and social justice, thereby enabling a pointed critique of war, generalized and in the abstract, as a solution to mediating political difference. A series of three narrative decisions facilitates this process. First, action is moved from iconic Boston to rural Connecticut, specifically to a town whose population had long been divided by religious allegiances; during the war, the historical split between Anglican and Presbyterian (or Congregational) churchgoers became political.[26] Second, instead of undergoing a process of political awakening that leads him to the Patriots, the protagonist, Tim Meeker, becomes increasingly disillusioned by the violence, hypocrisy, and greed of Patriot commanders. Third, the ideological rationale for the Revolution—and thus its liberating potential for all peoples—is discounted. This last technique in particular facilitates the novel's antiwar message. By narratively dismissing revolutionary ideology, the Colliers can argue that the Revolution lacked integrity and moral purpose.

The process of eroding the Revolution's liberating potential begins in the novel's opening chapter when Sam, Tim's older brother, bursts into the family tavern in a militia uniform and commences "[arguing] with the grownups."[27] Tim's description of the scene immediately suggests that although Sam is sixteen and nearly grown, his behavior remains childish. Sam reports military skirmishes as if they were sports matches, "shoves" food into his mouth, and whines, "You don't understand, Father, you just don't understand." Mr. Meeker, an apolitical pacifist, warns Sam of the harshness of war and reminds him of his obligation to obey authority, foremost his king. Sam remains defiant: "What right have the Lobsterbacks to be here anyway? . . . If they won't let us be free, we have to fight.

Why should they get rich off our taxes back in England? They're 3000 miles away, how can they make laws for us?" (3–8).

Echoing the words of Thomas Paine and countless political pamphleteers, Sam questions British imperialism, noting the wealth the colonies generated for England, the absence of colonial representation overseas, and the "tyrannical" presence of the king's troops in Boston. Sam's questions also echo the discourse in *Johnny Tremain* (chapter 8). But when Esther Forbes's Mr. Otis asks the Observers, "Why do we fight?" sixteen-year-old Rab Silsbee answers, "For the rights of Englishmen—everywhere" (178). Sixteen-year-old Sam's answer to the question of why he fights is startling in its contrast: "All my friends were going" (58).[28] The high ideals for which Sam claims to be fighting while in his father's presence are thoroughly undermined by his sophomoric bravado, something even his little brother detects. To make the point blatantly obvious, the Colliers have Sam Meeker serve under Benedict Arnold. Arguably the most well-known enemy of the American people, Arnold holds a place in U.S. history almost as mythic as that of George Washington, his historical foil. No metonym could better capture Sam's participation in an amoral, self-serving rebellion.

Just as Sam's behavior calls into question the reality behind revolutionary rhetoric, the manner in which both Sam and his father meet their death undermines the notion of heroic sacrifice in the name of country or king. The Colliers' extensive use of internal irony ends with the "meek" Meekers dying at the hands of armies they supported; the result, of course, is that Tim—and by extension, readers—becomes disillusioned with the Patriots and British alike. Convinced that war brings only misery and death, Mr. Meeker chooses to remain neutral. Ironically, the attempt to avoid conflict places him in the thick of it, and he, not his soldier son, becomes the family's first casualty. When the season for selling cattle arrives, Mr. Meeker insists on routine. "I've been selling my beef at Verplancks Point for ten years, and I haven't yet asked who was going to eat it," he tells the hostile "cow-boys" who warn him that the beef will end up in British soldiers' stomachs (94). Predictably, Meeker is ambushed on his return home. But because of "the confusion of war," he ends up imprisoned on a *British* prisoner ship, where he falls victim to neglect and disease. Meeker's Patriot son, meanwhile, dies at the hands of the American militia. When attempting to prevent cattle thieves from seizing his own family's livestock, Sam is framed for the burglars' crime. Since Sam's officers are as hungry to make an example of someone as the enlisted men are just plain hungry, they "didn't . . . care very much whether Sam was guilty or not" (185).[29]

The third major death to figure in the novel, that of a Patriot-owned slave, makes a subtle and complex argument about the futility of war by illustrating the emptiness of Patriot ideology. The Colliers' novel pays only slight attention to race because its central concern is with war as a political solution to problems, not with the issue of civil rights. But the Colliers do place an armed black man—an actual historical figure—in their story, and they align him, in belief and action, with the Patriots. Tim reports that it was "Samuel Smith's Negro" who announced that "the British were coming" (144). The decision to have Ned spread the alarm using the mythic language attributed to Paul Revere is telling: it conveys to readers Ned's belief in the Patriots' revolutionary promise of equality. In that, Ned was destined to be disappointed. He lived and died not so much a Patriot as "Smith's Negro." But for Ned, the British provided no better option. When the king's army arrives in Redding, Tim hears them call out, "There are some damned blacks in here, what shall we do with them?" In reply, an officer jabs a sword in and out of Ned's stomach before raising it to eye level. Tim watches in horror as "Ned's head jumped off his body and popped into the air" (144–45). *Brother Sam* depicts African Americans fighting for the Patriots but contends that the sacrifices made were worthless since the principles for which slaves believed they fought were empty at their core.[30] The consequence is profound; by eliminating ideology as the shaping force of the Revolution, the Colliers also erase the revolutionary potential of participating in the war. African American soldiers would have no special claims for a share in a republic shaped by liberty if the pillars of that republic were hollow. The interpretation is fundamentally less hopeful than that embedded in *Johnny Tremain* or contemporary U.S. history textbooks.[31]

In his essays for teachers and librarians, Christopher Collier describes the scholarship of progressive historians that informs the book's argument and distinguishes it from *Johnny Tremain*'s Whiggish argument. But the final question the Colliers pose in their authors' note in *Brother Sam* has nothing to do with whether one believes ideology or financial interest or some combination of the two motivated eighteenth-century colonists to wage a battle for independence. Instead, they ask a question whose answer depends on one's beliefs about human nature and the ethics of war as well as on one's understanding of history: "Could the United States have made its way without all that agony and killing?" (215). The question speaks to the novel's central purpose: to engage readers in thinking not only about the Revolution but also about the Vietnam War and, perhaps, warfare in general. Does a battle fought in the name of freedom always mean that those who fight make people free?

Can the young men who believe they are willing to die for a cause see beyond the rhetoric of officers, politicians, and media? Does war bring about lasting political change? In *Brother Sam*, the answer is repeatedly "no." Sam is lured by friends and Benedict Arnold to drop out of college and join the army. When his mother protests that he is needed at home, Sam reproaches her: "For God's sake, Mother, people are out there dying for you" (161). "Well they can stop dying," Mrs. Meeker responds; she doesn't need their so-called sacrifice. Tim similarly refuses to see Sam's soldiering as noble. "It seemed to me that we'd been free all along," he reflects (131).

Stripped of its revolutionary ideology, the War of Independence loses both its moral purpose and its position as glorious midwife to a nation. But by substituting one ethical argument for another, the Colliers made *Brother Sam* acceptable for classroom use. The very erasure of the *specific* ideology associated with the Revolution (life, liberty, and the pursuit of happiness) enables use of the Revolution in an argument that war—regardless of its stated aim—is inherently misguided. Peace and cross-cultural understanding is the ideal. In *Brother Sam*, the protagonist does not figure as the (fighting) nation; he stands distinct from and in opposition to his (misguided) country. By bravely defying communal expectations and following his own moral compass, he strengthens his community and nation. During the 1980s, many war novels emerged employing this same narrative technique. More recently, however, a third generation of children's authors has responded to the inherent weaknesses of the second generation's critique of first-generation war narratives. In substituting questions of universal morality for the narrower questions about national identity and purpose, second-generation war novels eliminate debate about the way rights and social justice, particularly for minority peoples, figure in war. To put it in the bluntest terms, second-generation war novels take the question of whether there are causes worth fighting for off the table.

Third-generation war novels combine aspects of both first- and second-generation narratives. These twenty-first-century texts return to iconic settings and entertain questions about just war while at the same time scrutinizing the "high ideals" of leaders willing to put soldier and civilian lives at risk in the name of national or "universal" principles. Rights and justice—issues eliminated in second-generation narratives—are reintroduced by applying the wartime ideology emphasized in first-generation novels to slaves, a group largely ignored by both first- and second-generation children's novelists.[32] In the case of fiction set during the American Revolution, slave protagonists, though initially inspired by revolutionary ideology, discover the emptiness of high-minded rhetoric for members of their race. As they attempt to unite their fate with the nation's, these protagonists are continually reminded of their status as property, not people. Third-generation war novels issue a radical critique of American war not because they point to the hollowness of treasured ideals, which African American characters embrace, but rather because they highlight the deviousness of the leaders promulgating them.

Third-generation war novels reflect both contemporaneous historiography and postmodern, postcolonial literature; as a result, they differ from their predecessors in both content and form. Like contemporary histories, third-generation novels recognize that Patriots politicized by rights rhetoric interpreted the broader application of that ideology in different ways. Some connected Patriot language describing America's enslavement by a tyrannical and virtueless Britain to the status of Africans enslaved by colonial Americans—a recognition that led to calls for emancipation—while others were horrified that the same spirit that awakened the elite to political action against Britain ignited the passions of "rabble" who refused to distinguish between political (i.e., national) and personal tyranny. This latter group was furious that the English, inflamed with desire to quell colonial rebellion, offered freedom to slaves who fought their masters, a practice that encouraged subordinates to embrace the very thoughts about autonomy and freedom that had led their white masters to rebel against Britain in the first place.[33] The critique of wartime rhetoric present in third-generation novels, particularly their attention to the hypocrisy implicit in ideals that apply unevenly across race, is more nuanced than that of second-generation texts, which, in their unqualified pacifism, flatten out the complexities and diversity of lived experience.

Like postmodern literature that recognizes late twentieth-century challenges to history as objective, scientific truth, third-generation war novels play with historical documentation: they frequently juxtapose actual primary sources with fabricated "historical" documents created by their twenty-first-century authors. Thus, even as the narratives question the ability to represent a "real" past (as opposed to an image of that past shaped by our modern-day ideas about a period fundamentally unknowable), they place value on "the real"—on artifacts of history. The primary sources necessary to tell the story of their slave protagonists do not exist, however, so the authors create them. In doing so, they seek to grant their characters equal status in the eyes of history and a voice through which to speak directly to Americans in the present.[34]

M. T. Anderson's *The Astonishing Life of Octavian Nothing,*
***Traitor to the Nation*, Vol. 1, *The Pox Party* (2006)**

Like Forbes and the Colliers before him, M. T. Anderson, author of two -
monumental YA war novels about the American Revolution, is a New
Englander. He came of age at a fundamentally different cultural moment
than the authors of the other central Revolutionary War children's novels,
however. Born in 1968, Anderson received his formal schooling after the
civil rights movement had morphed into multiculturalism in the K–12
arena and shaped debates about the Western canon in higher education.
A precocious Massachusetts teenager, Anderson entered Harvard as a
freshman but soon left the too-familiar environment for the other Cambridge, where he completed his bachelor's degree in literature in 1992.
The Astonishing Life of Octavian Nothing, Traitor to the Nation captures
a moment in which even a writer raised alongside a village green and
steeped in American history—family legend has it that his great-great-
grandfather was Mark Twain's cousin—could examine his nation's heritage with the distance of a tourist's eye. Written in the wake of a coalition
war against Iraq in which the rhetoric of liberty served as cover in the
hunt for nonexistent "weapons of mass destruction," *Octavian Nothing*
scrutinizes the ambiguous meaning of the American principle of liberty
at the very moment of its inception.[35]

   With *Octavian Nothing*, Anderson, describing himself as the editor
of Octavian's papers, created a Revolutionary War novel unthinkable a
generation previously. The story, purportedly "taken from accounts by
[Octavian's] own hand and other sundry sources," opens with the epony-
mous character detailing his childhood as an experimental subject at
Boston's Novanglian College of Lucidity, a fictional society of academicians imagined as "a provincial and incompetent" version of Benjamin
Franklin's American Philosophical Society.[36] Octavian arrives at the college's door in the womb of his thirteen-year-old mother, an Egba woman
from the Oyo region of West Africa. The details surrounding the college's
purchase and assimilation of Octavian's mother are murky, but by the
time Octavian is old enough to call her by name, she has become "Princess Cassiopeia" and he a prince dressed in silks and "brought up according to various philosophical principles, chief among [them] . . . tutelage
in the Classics" (33). Cassiopeia tells her son that she was "snatched"
from her father's kingdom in Oyo and later chose to resettle in New England. Perhaps because of his privileged position as a son, Octavian is
unable or unwilling to see the truth. In Greek mythology, Cassiopeia was

the queen of Ethiopia, a woman skilled in language but also arrogant and vain. When she bragged that she and her daughter were more beautiful than the children of the sea nymphs, she was forced to sacrifice her child as punishment.

From the moment of his birth, Octavian is simultaneously cherished and violated. Exalted as the key to quantifying the intellectual capacity of the African race, he was also subject to isolation from the world and made to weigh and record his daily intake and expulsion of food (33). Octavian writes at the beginning of his narrative, "I do not believe [the college fellows] ever meant unkindness" (13). But the academicians' behavior toward Octavian changes dramatically—and in ways unthinkable to readers of previous children's war novels—in the years preceding the Revolution. When British taxation leaves long-standing college benefactors short on cash, funds must be raised elsewhere. This requires that "the nature . . . of the experiment [on Octavian be] . . . changed." Tasked with menial labor, subject to corporal punishment, deprived of literary texts, and burdened by daily translation exercises of fragmented Greek and Latin passages "chosen for their convolution, recondite meaning, dryness, and insipidity," Octavian demands an explanation. The philosopher Mr. Gitney admits that the college now draws its funds from merchants and plantation owners with "some interest in proving the inequality of African capacities" (169). The final blow comes when Octavian's mother, ill from a smallpox inoculation administered by the college, dies and is dissected. Octavian erupts in rage when he forces the experimental chamber door and discovers his teachers destroying his mother's body to determine "whether the Negro suffer the affliction with the same degree of hardship as the European" (227). When told his outburst demonstrated innate African savagery, Octavian lapses into an enduring silence (231). For the next eighty pages, he speaks not a word; his story of flight, enlistment in the Patriot militia, and capture is narrated by others in a series of disorienting, one-sided letters marked by silence and omission.

In telling the story of the Revolution from the perspective of a slave disciplined to see the world with scientific objectivity, Anderson presents a startlingly new child's view of the war. Octavian Nothing takes as its subject not the armies on the ground but the intellectual giants in the chambers, the philosophers who architected the rebellion. By yoking the Founding Fathers' enlightenment thought with pseudoscientific nonsense, Anderson does more than illustrate the absurdity of the College of Lucidity's logic; he suggests that the Founding Fathers' propensity for slavery was fiendishly malevolent. Acting on behalf of patrons, the college generated scientific data that "proved" Africans' inferiority, thereby justifying economic extraction from Africa in perpetuity. When the Sons of Liberty seize Octavian from his Patriot regiment and return him to the college in shackles, the newly wise adolescent proclaims the argument of progressive historians—and contemporary American activists: "We smoke their sorrow contentedly; and we eat their sorrow; and we wear their sorrow; and wonder how it came so cheap" (326). Even as Octavian is given the iron bit, he refuses to be reduced to a mere body, a human form from which physical labor or "scientific" data are extracted. With help from the one tutor who resisted the changed nature of the experiment, Octavian flees the college, Boston, and the Patriots. Volume 2 of *Octavian Nothing* finds him in Virginia, fighting for Lord Dunmore's Ethiopian Regiment, a military unit composed entirely of the fugitive slaves of Patriot masters.[37] Surrounded by fellow African Americans, Octavian regains not only his narrative voice and physical body but also a connection to the continent of his ancestry, a homeland whose stories gradually come to nurture his soul alongside the classics of the Western canon. He regains, too, a reason to live and die: for liberty.

As a character, Octavian is difficult for modern children to connect with. His searing pain is thankfully beyond the ken of most American teenagers, especially those with the leisure and skill to read Anderson's erudite book. Novels set in slavery remain rare in children's literature, in part because it is difficult to show African American resistance—and thus the dignity of the enslaved—while simultaneously demonstrating the pervasiveness and tenacity of an utterly depraved system. Characters who have suffered the full brutality of chattel slavery do not emerge undamaged, and the injuries they bear are terrifying, incomprehensible, and often unspeakable. They are not, in short, for child eyes. Octavian's unusual education, and particularly his strict training in scientific disinterestedness, however, enables him to "be observant" and comment on slavery's horror without uttering that which must not be said. While this distancing makes Octavian's reportage tolerable, it holds the reader at arm's length. So too does Octavian's eighteenth-century prose and elevated vocabulary (for example, *houris, thanes, suppuration*), which places a barrier between Octavian and his readers just as much as it does between Octavian and his fictional peers. In this sense also, *Octavian Nothing* represents a radical departure from *Johnny Tremain* and *My Brother Sam Is Dead*; his story is too painful, too horrifying for modern American adolescents to imagine themselves living.

Unlike first- and second-generation war novels, third-generation narratives like *Octavian Nothing* have not yet entered school curricula for reasons both practical and philosophical. Their recent publication date means that affordable paperback editions for classroom use have not been available long. More important, however, *Octavian Nothing* fits squarely into the YA rather than middle-grade category. Written for high schoolers, YA literature competes with Shakespeare for curricula space and has been significantly less successful in penetrating school markets. Some YA novels migrate down into middle schools, but *Octavian Nothing*'s demanding vocabulary, postmodern form, and bleak message preclude that possibility. Laurie Halse Anderson's third-generation war novel *Chains*, which has been described as "a middle-grade companion to M. T. Anderson's ambitious 'Octavian Nothing' books," more readily fits the bill.[38] It echoes the themes of *Octavian Nothing* but is less dark, less radical, and much shorter. Despite the disappointments slave protagonist Isabel experiences as the Revolution begins, the feisty girl remains hopeful about her future in America. Like Johnny Tremain, who is politicized after suffering a career-ending burn and reading John Locke, Isabel is awakened by reading *Common Sense* and undergoing a painful public branding. Isabel discovers that neither the Patriots nor the Loyalists have her interests at heart, but when she must choose sides, she joins her fate with the rebels.[39] As she escapes British-occupied New York with an injured slave boy soldier in her cart, "the heavens [explode] into the red glare of rockets."[40] Her freedom and that of the nation, Anderson suggests, will be intertwined.

Reading a range of children's novels about the American Revolution side by side makes clear the generational influences on both literary style and historical argument. The extent to which temporal context affects how particular American military conflicts are used, however, becomes strikingly apparent when a series of children's war novels written during the same period—about any military conflict—are juxtaposed.

The View Post-Vietnam: War as American Tragedy

When the Collier brothers wrote *My Brother Sam Is Dead* on the eve of the American bicentennial, they said they hoped to start a "revolution" in children's literature. They were responding to the times, a moment in which Americans displayed newfound skepticism of U.S. military action as the war in Vietnam dragged on. In addition, the combined impact of the civil rights movement and second-wave feminism had begun eroding celebratory historical narratives of nation building and imperialism, preparing the way for *Brother Sam*'s acceptance. The Colliers' book was not the first widely embraced antiwar historical novel for children—Bette

Greene's *Summer of My German Soldier*, discussed below, claims that honor—but it was the most influential. Christopher Collier's credentials as a professional historian led credence to *Brother Sam*'s argument, and his efforts to publicize *Brother Sam*'s aims allowed for subsequent antiwar novels' warm reception by teachers and librarians. These pacifist books for children ask philosophical questions about war's relationship to morality, frequently skirting political questions about national duty and patriotic sacrifice in the process. Regardless of the novels' historical settings, the narratives expose political and military leaders' hypocrisy, question the machismo of battle, and blur the lines between good and bad, enemy and friend.

Two prolific children's authors followed the Colliers' publication of *Brother Sam* with pacifist Revolutionary War novels of their own. In 1980, the venerable master of children's historical fiction Scott O'Dell published *Sarah Bishop*. Based on an actual historical figure, *Sarah Bishop* replayed the argument of *Brother Sam* with a female protagonist. Like Tim Meeker, Sarah Bishop is caught between a Loyalist-leaning, pacifist father (killed by militiamen) and a Patriot brother (who dies on a British prison ship). Filled with "anger at the rebel and the King's men alike," Sarah retreats into the wilderness. She emerges to embrace the New Testament, convert to Quakerism, and, the narrator suggests, marry a pacifist.[41] Renowned children's author Avi joined the antiwar fray with *The Fighting Ground* (1984). In this book, Avi eliminated historical context as well as political ideology, creating a narrative that while set during the Revolution could really have taken place during any military conflict. The 152-page book contains only one sentence explaining why the Revolution was fought: over tyranny.[42] Avi spoke openly about his narrative goal to create a usable past, a history that readers could apply to political decisions in the present: "It is my desire to use the past to write about today. In short, there is a vital distinction to be made between the historian and the writer of historical fiction. They who write history get to alter the past. We who write historical fiction get to alter the future."[43]

Applying generalized antiwar arguments to specific historical contexts can have unintended consequences, however. By calling into question the political and ethical beliefs framing a particular war's meaning, antiwar narratives like *The Fighting Ground*, *Sarah Bishop*, and *Brother Sam* obviate the potential for understanding war as having brought about positive change. If one understands the Revolution as empty of principle, it can no longer be understood to have laid the groundwork for the abolitionist, women's suffrage, and civil rights movements. Historical African Americans and women of any race could no longer have pointed to the nation's founding documents—the principles for which the Revolution was fought—as justification for equal rights in their own day. The narrative cost of making antiwar arguments against the backdrop of wars widely understood to have been fought with ethical ends in mind is dramatic and troublesome. This becomes particularly apparent in examining second-generation novels set during the American Civil War and World War II.

Patricia Beatty's *Charley Skedaddle* (1987)

First-generation children's novels about the Civil War mirror their adult counterparts in presenting what cultural historian David Blight has described as a "reconciliationist" argument; they tell of a divided (white) American people reuniting after discovering that they are more alike than different. Reconciliationist narratives naturalize the postwar reunion of North and South while simultaneously erasing racial oppression as both cause and outcome of the war; African American liberation is sacrificed in the process.[44] The 1958 Newbery-winning novel, *Rifles for Watie*, is a classic example; the story ends with Union soldier Jefferson Davis Bussey declaring his intention to return south to collect his southern belle. Their marriage vows will symbolically reunite the nation.

As a second-generation war novel, Patricia Beatty's *Charley Skedaddle* is a pacifist rather than reconciliationist narrative. It views the Civil War as tragic not because of a lost cause but because of thousands of lives lost—unnecessarily. As Granny Bent, the Kentucky mountain woman who takes in Charley after he "skedaddles" from the Battle of the Wilderness, puts it, "Men like war. It makes 'em feel big. There's nothin' so bad it can't be talked out without fightin'. But some do dote on fightin'."[45] A white conductor on the Underground Railroad, Granny insists that slavery could have been destroyed without war; she does not acknowledge the nearly hundred-year period of failed diplomatic efforts to end the "peculiar institution."[46] In many ways, then, reconciliationist and antiwar Civil War narratives like *Charley Skedaddle* function similarly: they dismiss chattel slavery from being central to the origin and purpose of the struggle.

Charley Skedaddle opens with Charley Quinn, a rough-and-tumble Irish orphan, striving to emulate the older brother he lost at Gettysburg, first by joining the Bowery Boys street gang, then by attaching himself to the 140th New York Volunteers. Although Charley admires the "men in the Union blue . . . going off to fight for Abe Lincoln against slavery," he sneaks on board an army ship not because of his antipathy toward slavery, but rather because he wants to avenge his brother's death and escape being sent to a home for incorrigible boys, a fate he fears now that his sister is engaged (15). En route to Virginia, Charley discovers with disappointment that most volunteers enlisted for the bounty money, not to defeat "Johnny Reb" (21). Charley had envisioned the battle between the Blue and Gray as a street fight on a grand scale, a contest like those between the Bowery Boys and Dead Rabbits. Charley's naïveté may seem improbable, but it is essential to the novel's antiwar argument. He imagines that like the warring Irish street gangs who struggle over territory but hold beliefs and moral codes in common, the Union and Confederacy are more or less alike. The fight, in other words, is about following one's leader—determined by the Mason-Dixon Line rather than by neighborhood block—into battle. The issue over which the Civil War was fought is reduced to something "simple" that could have been eradicated without recourse to violence.

In order to deemphasize slavery and race as issues central to the Civil War, Beatty also ignores the historical tension between Irish and African Americans in Charley's natal New York. If Charley had been a real historical figure, he would have had more knowledge and stronger opinions about the way the war's outcome could change life for African Americans—and himself. In July 1863, a citywide draft riot erupted in New York. Because wealthy New Yorkers could avoid conscription by purchasing replacements to fight in their place, the draft, which affected all citizens, placed disproportionate burden on poor white men like the fictional adults in Charley's ethnic community. Enraged at the disparity and fearful of increased job competition from slaves freed by war, rioters attacked black institutions and individuals as well as wealthy men and offices associated with conscription.[47] *Charley Skedaddle* makes brief mention of the fact that "New York City was weary of the war . . . weary of the hated draft, of the violent riots protesting it," but the novel does not connect the protests with either their white, working-class perpetrators or their black victims (18). As a character, Charley expresses disgust with race-based slavery but conceptualizes it in narrow terms as a system equating people and property: "No person should ever be owned by any other person!" (40). His reductionist understanding of slavery's evils is narratively unconvincing given his sophisticated grasp of the importance of social as well as legal independence as a precursor to freedom in his own life as an Irish American. But Charley's ignorance helps enable Beatty's argument that the Civil War was *not* about fulfilling the promise of the Revolution and establishing black people's right to freedom in both legal and practical terms. Rather, slavery was a simple problem that could be solved without the radical upheaval of society.

We first see Charley's sensitivity to demeaning labor when the men onboard his Virginia-bound ship suggest that while he is too young to enlist, he could stay on as an officer's helper. Charley reacts with horror: "A *servant*? . . . Mother Mary, no—never a servant!" (24). Charley's attitude reflects what historian Sean Wilenz has termed "artisanal republicanism."[48] Traditionally, only property-holding men participated in the government of republics. Theorists reasoned that fully independent people could vote their conscience, whereas all other men had to consider the financial ramifications of voting differently from the people on whom their livelihoods depended. As the number of property-holding men in the United States shrank in the face of nineteenth-century urbanization and industrialization, however, definitions of "independence" expanded to include men who owned their time, labor, and tools, if not the land on which they lived. The propertyless Charley clings to this notion of independence, boasting that his sister makes a living trimming fancy hats (skilled labor) rather than working as a domestic servant. He is adamant that he will earn his keep in ways that ensure he remains "free." Luckily, the very ethnic stereotyping that puts him at risk of being associated with slavery and dependence saves him from that disgrace. Overhearing his Irish accent, the major signs Charley up as drummer boy: "Most Irish can sing," the major quips (31).[49] Charley accepts the assignment, but it is short-lived. After witnessing the death of a friend on the battlefield, Charley picks up a gun and shoots. The horror of having killed a man paralyzes him and—in a scenario reminiscent of Stephen Crane's *The Red Badge of Courage*, a novel similarly silent on the Civil War's cause—he "skedaddles" to the Blue Ridge Mountains.[50]

The wild landscape of Appalachia enables Charley to prove his mettle in a peaceful, noncombatant way. Drawing on literary tropes of the frontier, Beatty allows Charley to regain his self-pride and status as hero when he kills a panther, thereby protecting the community. He leaves the mountains soon after, when Confederate troops are poised to retreat through Appalachia's Blue Ridge. With Granny's urging and a heavy heart, Charley turns toward the Pacific coast. But he promises to return: "Charley Quinn drew himself up to his full height, looked Granny Bent full in the eyes, and said, 'I reckon when I get to be as tall as I'll ever be, I'll be back. This ain't so bad a place for a man to settle'" (180). His desire to return is only partly about Granny, who fills the place of the Irish grandmothers he never knew; it is also fueled by his wish to claim Sarie

Griffen, the young woman who gives him a lock of her "black, silken hair tied with . . . rose-colored ribbon" (177). Like a classic reconciliationist narrative, *Charley Skedaddle* ends with the promise of romance between North and South. The fate of slaves, who would ultimately be freed by the war Charley fled, is nowhere in the picture. In the mountains, Granny reports, there are "not none [black folk] up here—none at all" (119).

Charley Skedaddle ends with an author's note that includes discussion of the historical experience of African Americans during and after the Civil War. Given Beatty's omission of this focus within the narrative proper, the historical context is surprising.[51] It reveals that, consciously or not, Beatty realized that an exploration of slavery and the issues of emancipation and racial equity didn't sit well with the pacifist message she hoped to impart in a novel dedicated to her grandson—"in the hope that his generation will never have to go to war." To craft a pacifist argument against a Civil War backdrop, Beatty deemphasized the differences between warring soldiers and the ideologies under which they fought, limited Charley's contact with African Americans (no easy feat considering that New York boasted the largest antebellum population of African Americans in the North), and stripped her working-class Irish protagonist of any knowledge of tensions between the nation's Irish and free black residents.[52]

Bette Greene's *Summer of My German Soldier* (1973)

Charley Skedaddle's Civil War setting requires its antiwar message to sit side by side with the dehumanizing institution of chattel slavery; second-generation novels set during World War II must juxtapose their antiwar messages with the purposeful extermination of a racial other. The novels do so through the same means: eliminating discussion of the ideas for which the war in question was fought. First published in 1973, Bette Greene's *Summer of My German Soldier*, a World War II novel set in Arkansas and very loosely based on the author's own childhood in the South, sustained sixteen printings in its first decade, later inspiring both a sequel and a made-for-TV movie.[53] It has been widely taught since the year of its appearance. Surprisingly, it has received virtually no critical attention.[54]

Summer of My German Soldier opens with the arrival of German prisoners of war at the Jenkinsville, Arkansas, train station.[55] Like the rest of the town's 1,200 residents, twelve-year-old Patty Bergen rushes to witness the excitement. As the blond- and brown-haired POWs descend from the train and face the interracial crowd, Patty stands as the sole Jew.

Trapped in the segregated world of a pre–civil rights South, Patty faces a lonely summer: the town's "socially acceptable" residents are away at Baptist summer camp, and she is forbidden to play with either her African American peers or the children her neighbors deem "white trash." To make matters worse, Patty lives with unhappily married parents who harp on her appearance, dole out corporal punishment, and favor her picture-perfect younger sister. While decidedly unpleasant, the Bergen adults are not intolerable. In defiance of community pressure, they refuse to fire their "uppity" black housekeeper or inflate the prices of their department store goods for black customers.[56] The Bergens' precarious position as Jewish merchants dependent on gentile business, however, leads them to more or less conform to the town's racist social norms. Patty becomes entangled in the hypocrisies that result.

When POWs seeking field hats to protect themselves from the Arkansas sun request permission to enter the Bergens' store, Patty's parents don't refuse. Their decision has tremendous, unforeseen consequence, bringing Patty into contact with the enemy and smoothing the way for one of Hitler's soldiers to escape. When Patty sees the English-speaking POW with green-speckled eyes and "dark masculine eyebrows" waiting for help, she steps behind her parents' counter. It doesn't take long for her to decide that the handsome soldier is a good man, "not one of those—those black-booted Nazis" (35). When he compliments her sense of style, she is moved to prayer: "Oh, God, would it be at all possible for Frederick Anton Reiker to become my friend? I understand that it's not an easy request" (37). But in Greene's fictional world, the favor is granted because the historically improbable friendship facilitates the novel's antiwar argument. In the pages that follow, Greene inverts almost every convention of the widely produced Holocaust novel: Nazis, rather than Jews, are imprisoned in camps; a Jewish girl risks everything to hide a German soldier; Americans, rather than Germans, are racist and intolerant; and at story's end, readers mourn the death of a fugitive Nazi, rather than the loss of a Jewish girl's dreams to anti-Semitic hatred.

Shortly after meeting Anton at her parents' store, Patty spots the POW fleeing town by railroad track; instead of reporting his escape, she flags him down and hides him in her tree house.[57] The black housekeeper, Ruth, gasps when she learns what Patty has done, but she cooks up a proper breakfast and serves Anton on a table laid with china.[58] The unlikely interaction between Ruth and Anton is critical to Greene's repositioning of Americans (but not Nazis) as racist. Unlike the other white people Patty knows, Anton—somehow immune to Nazi indoctrination— expects Ruth to address him as a social equal. The black housekeeper feels his unstated, unqualified acceptance and tells a story that reveals the deep, enduring hurt racism has played in her life, a topic that Patty has never before heard her broach. Ruth's tale of white theft and deception highlights the hypocrisy of an America fighting for the Four Freedoms abroad while denying African Americans basic civil rights at home.

Patty adores Anton because he showers her with kindness and respect, qualities he also displays toward Ruth, the other outcast in the Bergen household. Patty remains uneasy with his enemy status, however, and she asks him a number of questions, including why he risked his life to escape the POW camp. Anton replies simply, "From now on I must be free" (80). Narrative details provide more information. Before he leaves the POW camp, Anton "borrows" a collection of Ralph Waldo Emerson's essays from the prison library, a measure he takes to ensure that his brain doesn't "starve" while in hiding (118). Unlike Henry David Thoreau, who prized *action*—living deliberately at Walden Pond or writing a "Plea for [radical abolitionist] John Brown"—Emerson believed that the journey toward freedom took place in the mind. A good person, in his view, embraced the divine within; there was no obligation to change the world through social action. Patty understands Anton's subtle message of stealing Emerson's essays no better than Greene's adolescent readers would, and she finds Anton's vague answer to her pointed question about escape unsatisfactory: "Can't you get hurt . . . and wouldn't you have been free sooner or later anyway? Wars don't last forever" (80). Patty may want proof that Anton rejects Hitler's worldview. Indeed, she has convinced herself of this fact, but it doesn't explain his flight.

Anton skillfully distracts Patty from her questions, but they are important. His actions highlight his extreme selfishness, which Patty—who directs the reader's vision—cannot see. As Anton explains, his family of academics disagreed with the Nazi regime—particularly its limits on free speech—but resisted only to the point at which they could ensure personal safety. "Some people [stood up to Hitler]," Anton explains, "but not many. My father chose acquiescence and life rather than resistance and death. Not a very admirable choice, but a very human one" (79). It is a course that Anton pursues as well, but by the end of the novel, he nonetheless emerges as a hero. Mr. Bergen catches Patty playing with "white trash" and, in a rage, punishes her with a leather belt. Seeing the beating, Anton rushes out of hiding to intervene, apparently unaware of his actions: "I came running out of hiding to—My God, I did, didn't I? . . . After almost two years of being as inconspicuous a coward as possible I had no idea that I would voluntarily risk my life for anyone . . . but I'm glad I could. I'm glad I still could" (119). Anton's reflex-driven act of protection falls far short of Patty's self-conscious risk to protect *him*, a decision that ends with reform school and being labeled a traitor to both the American and Jewish people. More important, Anton's sacrifice pales in comparison to that made by Christian families throughout Europe who knowingly and willingly risked their lives to hide Jews. When Anton next sees Patty, however, he compares Mr. Bergen to Hitler: "Cruelty is after all cruelty, and the difference between the two men may have more to do with their degrees of power than their degrees of cruelty" (117). Patty thanks him for the lesson, never considering the ways her father attempted to defy community mores; he failed by forbidding her to associate with impoverished white children, but he succeeded by treating Jenkensville's African Americans as equal citizens.

Incredibly, both critics and educators have missed the troubling implications of erasing the meaning of Hitler's war. Most contemporary reviewers described *Summer of My German Soldier* as "moving" and "sensitive." The Council on Interracial Books for Children criticized Greene's portrayal of Ruth (who quotes Scripture and speaks in dialect) but was silent on the juxtaposition of abusive Jewish parents and sweet Nazi soldiers.[59] By inverting the traditional Holocaust novel and removing Nazi ideology from the narrative, Greene developed a viable antiwar argument. The novel's message that "love is better than hate" and "there is more nobility in building a chicken coop than in destroying a cathedral" seems simple and unobjectionable (125). The implication is clear: if there could be a "good" Nazi soldier, one who was neither racist nor anti-Semitic, certainly there could be a "good" Viet Cong, and if military action was questionable in Hitler's Europe, it was even more so in Cold War Asia. *Summer of My German Soldier*'s brazen juxtaposition of pacifism in the face of systematic genocide and a catastrophic policy of appeasement brings into sharp relief the characteristics of second-generation war novels: in making arguments about the immorality of war, they obscure the humanitarian causes for which wars of the past have, at least at times, been waged.

■ In the almost seventy years since *Johnny Tremain* first made its appearance on school desks, stories of teenagers confronting the peril of battle and facing the task of defining their place in the nation-state have diversified, encompassing the experiences of girls, white ethnics, and African Americans as well as Anglo-American males. The Revolution remains the site of heartiest revision, perhaps because so much is at stake in its history.[60] Revolutionary War novels seek to answer a question fundamental to assessment of the United States: was the nation born of a misguided, duplicitous bloodbath, or did the rhetoric of leaders seeking liberty from imperial power set the course for a government and people committed to emancipation and individual rights in practice as well as in theory? The Revolution does not stand alone in raising such important issues, however. All military conflicts invite questions relative to ideology and morality, questions that can be answered only in relation to historical contexts. Why did the nation select military action as a means to resolve discord? Given information available at the time of declaring war, were other means of resolving conflict, methods with a smaller cost of human suffering, feasible? In retrospect, was the war waged in just and moral ways? As second-generation war novels demonstrate, a different mode of questioning is possible when war is considered in the abstract, as a concept severed from historical context and defined as violence directed at professional soldiers but affecting innocent civilians: can war *ever* be moral? This question is important, but it is also philosophical rather than historical. It requires removal from the specificity of time and place.

In the past, critics have labeled some first-generation war novels "dated" and some second-generation war novels "unpatriotic." Undoubtedly, third-generation war novels will come under fire for both their violence and "particularity" of vision. But as the longevity of books like *Johnny Tremain* and the Civil War novel *Across Five Aprils* (1965) demonstrates, well-written children's novels, once canonized, endure. If each generation—like each school of historiography—has weaknesses, these flaws are ultimately overshadowed by the novels' strengths. Taken together, the three generations of war novels tell a powerful story of particular historical moments as well as a nation's ongoing process of self-understanding.

Historian Michael Kammen explains that "wars have played a fundamental role in stimulating, defining, justifying, periodizing, and eventually filtering American memories and traditions."[61] For many children, wars are made vivid through the setting and plot of historical novels. When students read a range of historical fiction and experience the full interpretative spectrum of "defining" and "justifying" American wars, they are equipped to participate in, rather than be passive recipients of, that process Kammen terms "filtering." Instead of blindly accepting that the United States has *always* fought for freedom and democracy or that war is *always* avoidable and wrong, adolescents can turn to their sophisticated readings of American history to introduce nuance and balance. Armed with such knowledge, they are much better positioned to make decisions about the military's role in national and international diplomacy past, present, and future.

Chapter 4

Black and White

■ In 1950, four years before the landmark *Brown* case outlawed school segregation, the American Library Association (ALA) awarded its coveted Newbery Medal to Elizabeth Yates's fictional biography of Amos Fortune, an African who rose from chattel slavery to freedom and self-sufficiency in colonial New England. Yates's novel, *Amos Fortune, Free Man*, opens with the violent raid of a West African village in 1725. The fifteen-year-old protagonist is separated from his family, marched to the coast, and placed aboard a Boston-bound slaver. Nothing is known about the childhood of the historical Amos Fortune, but Yates imagined him as a tribal prince whose royal blood enabled him to withstand the dehumanizing Middle Passage with dignity.[1]

The boy's singular presence upon arrival in Boston intrigues Caleb Copeland, a Quaker. Seeing the proud youth positioned for the selling block, Caleb purchases him outright, sparing him the indignity of becoming haggled-over property. In an act projecting the boy's Christian future, Caleb renames the youth "Amos" and begins preparing him for freedom—eventually. As he explains to his wife, the boy cannot be freed immediately as he "is part animal now. What would he do but run wild?"[2] Caleb's speech demonstrates *Amos Fortune*'s politics: the novel condemns the slave trade but stops short of denouncing slavery; it champions African potential but praises Western institutions' civilizing influence. By adopting the form of a Christian conversion narrative, the text also implicates Amos in his servitude. Believing political freedom to be meaningless without the promise of eternal salvation, Amos refuses freedom papers once he is grown, insisting that he wants to remain a part of the Copelands' godly household. Predictably, Caleb dies insolvent and Amos is sold to pay the debts; he must once again earn his freedom.[3]

Amos Fortune's selection for the 1950 Newbery makes sense on many levels. At a time when the nation was thinking deeply about race, Yates's novel places an African American at the center of the narrative; praises the black protagonist's loyalty, character, and work ethic; and curbs the threat of black masculinity through the feminizing language of Christianity and the literary form of the conversion narrative. Yates's depiction of Amos as eternally childlike, moreover, matches contemporaneous representations of slavery. During the long years between Reconstruction and the civil rights movement, the prevailing interpretation of slavery was that it served as a "school for civilization" that prepared Africans for citizenship.[4] Initially, Yates worried that child readers wouldn't be able to relate to her adult protagonist. As she wrote, however, she decided that Amos's race compensated for the discrepancy of age; even as a grown man, "he gave of himself without caution or restraint, and in so doing forged a link forever with the childhood of the world."[5] Like the white apologist understanding of slavery that informed the book, Yates's conclusion that Amos's race made him childlike is unsurprising given the era of its origin. What is startling, however, is that *Amos Fortune* circulates in twenty-first-century schools. California's list of recommended titles for grades 6–8 praises *Amos Fortune* as a "classic story . . . useful in the study of America's slave history and the importance of human freedom."[6] The novel's continued classroom life testifies to the relentlessness of educators' efforts to project racial harmony and positive progress toward multicultural ideals backward into the colonial American settings captured in twentieth-century children's books.

Black protagonists were rare in children's literature when *Amos Fortune* first appeared in print in 1950. As more children's books featuring African Americans emerged in response to the civil rights movement, however, activists began scrutinizing the presence, absence, and character of black figures peopling children's books, and they pressed publishers for more stories depicting authentic black life. Their advocacy bore fruit: during the 1970s, four of the ten Newbery Medal winners featured prominent black characters, and two were authored by African Americans.[7] Problems persisted even as black characters became more common in children's literature, however. Antiracist critics called attention to the fact that many black characters continued to reflect stereotypes and that children's stories in general continued to assume a white rather than racially diverse readership.

By the 1980s, objections regarding individual children's novels' messages about race and assumptions about readership largely vanished from public memory, even as the number of new books featuring black protagonists diminished. Historical amnesia combined with mainstream publishers' retreat from racial themes in the conservative 1980s led to almost any novel about race being embraced by schools, which were now deeply committed to multiculturalism. Today's students have inherited the classroom canon forged in the 1980s, and they thus encounter a broad range of historical and historiographical interpretations in the novels they read. The individual arguments composing the cacophony about race, however, are each used to serve a larger multicultural message that equality, tolerance, and respect are the pillars of contemporary American society.

Teaching Tolerance

Fifteen years after *Amos Fortune* won the Newbery Medal, Nancy Larrick published what was to become a highly influential article in the *Saturday Review of Books*. The result of a three-year study, "The All-White World of Children's Literature" found that only 6.7 percent of children's trade books published between 1962 and 1964 included "one or more Negroes," and that most black characters were placed either in historical settings or foreign lands. Such statistics were devastating to "the Negro child's personality," Larrick argued, but "the impact of all-white books upon . . . white children is probably even worse." Her conclusion, which helps explain the embrace of *Amos Fortune*, reflected educational consensus in the 1960s: literary representations of diverse peoples were essential to "developing the humility so urgently needed for world cooperation."[8] The children's-book world agreed that interracial friendship must be characterized as American and its opposite as both uncivil and bigoted. The ALA's 1959 Newbery Medal selection, Elizabeth George Speare's *The Witch of Blackbird Pond*, captures the beginnings of the trend.

Like *Amos Fortune*, *Witch of Blackbird Pond* was written by a white woman born in the first decade of the twentieth century. Both novels are set in colonial New England. Whereas *Amos Fortune* features an enslaved African and justifies slavery as Christian, pedagogical, and humane, *Witch of Blackbird Pond* features a white Barbadian who learns to excoriate slavery, a practice she is told Connecticut Puritans eschew. How could these two books, one which looks favorably on New England slavery and one that both condemns and denies it, receive the same prize? Much had changed in the nine years separating Yates's award from Speare's. Notably, the Supreme Court argued several landmark civil rights cases, and new interpretations of slavery and race issued forth from the academy. By the early 1960s, the white apologist narratives that informed Yates's *Amos Fortune* had disappeared from college syllabi, replaced by scholarship seeking to understand the origin of racism and race-based slavery in North America. In a groundbreaking article, Oscar and Mary Handlin argued that in the United States, racism emerged subsequent to race-based slavery. This interpretation was hopeful as it suggested that laws had created racism (by means of chattel slavery), thus laws could eliminate it.[9] As political liberals in and out of the academy placed faith in law, children's book people invested hope in literature; the right books, they argued, could eradicate racism in the young.

Elizabeth George Speare's *The Witch of Blackbird Pond* (1958)

Witch of Blackbird Pond opens in 1687 with protagonist Kit Tyler en route to Puritan New England after her guardian, a plantation-owning grandfather, dies in debt. Raised from birth in a permissive Barbadian environment of privilege and slaves, Kit finds the transition to somber Connecticut difficult. In the process of striving to please the family that takes her in, she experiences a political and moral conversion that renders her "American" in the terms of 1950s convention. The first step is denouncing slavery. Although the historical region where Kit settles contained numerous slaves in the late seventeenth century, Speare eliminates their presence, reimagining the shameful institution as existing "mostly down Virginia way."[10] As scholars have argued, the erasure of slavery from historical narratives of New England heightened racism during the postbellum period by suggesting that contemporary African American poverty stemmed from innate racial qualities rather than past degradation.[11] In *Witch of Blackbird Pond*, however, the absence of human chattel that often facilitates racist thinking allows Speare to argue that tolerance of slavery and intolerance of difference is fundamentally un-American. When she first arrives in Connecticut, Kit cringes at domestic tasks that sting her eyes and callous her hands, work "a high-class slave in Barbados would rebel at" (78). But as months of toiling to put food on the table pass, Kit ceases to see physical labor as degrading. In the book's final chapters, Kit passes the test set for her by declining marriage to Wethersfield's wealthiest bachelor, a man who would staff his home with servants, and accepting instead the offer of a poor but hardworking sailor.

Kit's Americanization through the embrace of a Protestant work ethic and rejection of privilege dominates the narrative, but another Americanization process unfolds simultaneously. While Kit overcomes the racist assumptions she carried with her from Barbados, the townspeople rise above their provincial prejudice of foreigners, religious dissenters, and learned women. At the same time that political anxieties triggered by King James's retraction of Connecticut's colonial charter grow, sickness spreads over Wethersfield. Weakened by fear, the community rallies behind Goodwife Cruff's assertion that Kit and Quaker Hannah Tupper are responsible. Echoing Arthur Miller's *The Crucible*, published five years earlier, *Witch of Blackbird Pond* uses seventeenth-century witch trials to comment on McCarthy-era witch hunts. Kit's fate differs from that of the accused in both the 1690s and 1950s, however, as her "misbehavior" is ultimately recognized as a positive good. Encouraging the Cruffs' daughter to meet her at Hannah Tupper's for reading lessons, Kit teaches Prudence to read her Bible. Upon discovering his daughter's newfound learning, Adam Cruff makes a "declaration of independence," saying, "It's a new country over here, and who says it may not be just as needful for a woman to read as a man?" (222). His ahistorical words urge Speare's readers to abandon naturalized notions of differences. Kit and the people of Wethersfield must acknowledge as equal people of different race, religion, and gender; only then can the colonies move toward the founding of a republic. *Witch of Blackbird Pond* forcefully argues that tolerance and equality are American values, and that they were present at the beginning. Importantly, however, it does so with an all-white cast. In the next decade, the most influential historical novels would respond to Nancy Larrick's 1965 call for diversity. In placing black and white characters in conversation with each other, these books sought to transport (white) readers backward in time to reassess their assumptions about racial difference.

Theodore Taylor's *The Cay* (1969)

A decade after *Witch of Blackbird Pond*'s appearance, Theodore Taylor dedicated his novel *The Cay* "to Dr. King's dream, which can only come true if the very young know and understand." Taylor credits the experience of witnessing Ku Klux Klan violence at age four with profoundly affecting his life. His parents, a literary mother and Wobbly father, rejected racism, leaving Taylor baffled and greatly disturbed by the violence he saw directed toward black people. Taylor's adult politics, however, defy easy classification. He presented himself as apolitical, anti-intellectual, and "un-PC" in a memoir that establishes clear distance between himself and his "communist sympathizer" father, whom he disparages as selfish, lazy, and most of all, absent. Having left home at seventeen, Taylor's faith in hard work and relentless self-making were strong.[12] His fifty-plus action-packed books developed this all-American theme again and again, attracting a loyal fan base. No book, however, came close to achieving the popular and critical success of *The Cay*. More than a simple adventure tale, this book about interracial friendship struck a chord with a nation deep in the throes of the civil rights movement. Translated into fourteen languages, *The Cay* ranks fifty-seventh among all-time best-selling children's paperbacks; as Taylor proudly noted in 2000, "some teachers have taught it for a quarter-century."[13]

The Cay opens in Curaçao, where eleven-year-old Phillip Enright has lived since his father was called from their Virginia home to wage war against Hitler. When German submarines reach the Dutch island, Phillip's mother insists on returning to the relative safety of the United States, and she and her son promptly board a ship bound for Miami. Two days later a torpedo strikes, and Phillip, who sustains a blow to the head, lands alone on a raft with a West Indian man, Timothy. As the two drift to a deserted island, Phillip becomes blind as an aftershock of the head wound; he soon finds himself utterly dependent on the illiterate, dialect-speaking man. The young boy expresses his fear and frustration in racially loaded remarks: "You ugly black man! I won't do it! You're stupid, you can't even spell." Timothy ignores the insults but not Phillip's refusal to fight for his life. When the boy fails at the tasks set him, then blames the old man for asking him to try, Timothy issues a cuff that pulls the boy out of his self-wallowing pity and prejudice, enabling him "to change."[14] The intervention proves critical as Timothy dies in a vicious hurricane shortly thereafter, leaving the blinded Phillip to shift for himself until a rescue plane arrives.

The Cay is a survival story that places the key to a white child's safety not in his ability to secure food or shelter, but rather in his capacity to overcome racism. To flourish on the island, Phillip must listen to and learn from a black man who knows the ocean and its ways. Whereas Kit's transformation in *Witch of Blackbird Pond* takes place at a distance from actual African peoples, Phillip's conversion unfolds before Timothy's eyes, a task Taylor deemed more challenging. The West Indian's "color"—the first characteristic Phillip confronts—poses a barrier to the racist child. Immediately after the boat is struck, when Phillip realizes that he and Timothy share a raft, the boy's fear and disgust is palpable: "He crawled over toward me. His face couldn't have been blacker, or his teeth whiter. . . . He had a big welt, like a scar, on his left cheek. I knew he was West Indian. I had seen many of them in Willemstad, but he was the biggest one I'd ever seen" (31). Soon after, Phillip loses his sight. Immediately, his ability to see Timothy's humanity expands. After Timothy brings him ashore, builds shelter, provides food and water, and compassionately offers company, Phillip wonders whether Timothy had become white: "I had now been with him every moment of the day and night for two months, but I had not seen him. I remembered that ugly welted face. But now, in my memory, it did not seem ugly at all. It seemed only kind and strong. I asked, 'Timothy, are you still black?' His laughter filled the hut" (100).

In presenting colorblindness as a solution to racial tension, Taylor drew on discourses of race popular during the middle phase of the civil rights movement. Historian Kenneth M. Stampp's influential book *The Peculiar Institution: Slavery in the Ante-Bellum South* (1956) begins with the statement that "slaves were merely ordinary human beings, that innately Negroes *are*, after all, only white men with black skins, nothing more, nothing less."[15] Timothy echoes Stampp's words when Phillip asks him about the purpose behind racial difference: "Why b'feesh different color, or flower b'different color? I true don' know, Phill-eep, but I true tink beneath d'skin is all d'same" (75). Timothy's answer, unlike Stampp's explanation, does not construe the "sameness" as white. His actions, however, reveal Taylor's continued privileging of white skin. The climax of the novel occurs when a ferocious hurricane hits the cay, putting Phillip and Timothy's fragile existence in peril. Hugging a tree and instructing Phillip to do the same, Timothy places himself between the boy and the storm's biting winds and flying debris. When the fury subsides, the West Indian's body appears exactly like that of a slave: stripped of clothing, his "flayed" back and legs are bloody and "cut to ribbons by the wind" (111). The next morning he is dead.

The experience of being stranded on an island with a man of another race utterly transforms Phillip. Importantly, however, it leaves Timothy's character untouched. Before Timothy's death, Phillip Enright fulfills the promise of his name, "ending right" by learning to see the West Indian as equal. Blindness facilitates the transformation, of course, but so too does temporary "blackness." Phillip early on wonders whether Timothy has become white; after Timothy's death, however, he realizes that it was not Timothy that had changed, but himself. Hearing an airplane near the island, Phillip begins waving frantically only to have the plane pass him by. The boy concludes that the pilot must have mistaken him for "just another native fisherman waving at an aircraft. I knew that the color of my skin was very dark now" (131). Historian John Stauffer has described white radical abolitionists' efforts to "become black" as part of a process that would usher in a world free of hierarchy.[16] Likewise, Phillip not only ceases to see Timothy's skin color but also moves toward embracing blackness, rather than whiteness, as the norm and ideal. In the case of *The Cay*, however, this transformation does not lead to the eradication of hierarchy. While Phillip ultimately rejects the presumed superiority of whiteness, Timothy does not. In fact, he dies in the act of serving as whipping boy for his "young bahss."

Paula Fox's *The Slave Dancer* (1974)

In 1974, the closing year of the "long 1960s," another novel centered on a young white protagonist's changed attitudes toward race garnered praise from the children's book world.[17] Paula Fox's *The Slave Dancer* differed from its predecessors in that its protagonist—and by extension, its readers—witnesses the structural racism obscured in *Witch of Blackbird Pond* and *The Cay*. Jessie Bollier's experience of white privilege, even as he is kidnapped and forced to labor on a slave ship, helps him understand the role American law plays in keeping black and white humanity apart—and unequal. In its darkness, violence, and distrust of interracial understanding, *The Slave Dancer* anticipated much later children's books, even as it maintained that white children's attitudes were the key to transforming racial tension in the United States. *The Slave Dancer* also differed from earlier works in that it met with mixed reviews, despite the fact that it captured the 1974 Newbery. As *School Library Journal* quipped, "Fox's books are easier to admire than they are to love."[18]

Paula Fox was born just two years after Theodore Taylor and shared his childhood experience of poverty and reckless parenting. The daughter of a nineteen-year-old Cuban mother and peripatetic Anglo-American father, she was given up for adoption at birth. Her maternal grandmother rescued her from the orphanage, and after six years in foster care, Fox was unhappily returned to her parents. The childhood chronicled in her memoir is a story of astounding neglect by intellectuals who drank, had affairs, and generally ignored their daughter. Fox spent a brief (and pleasant) period of her girlhood in Cuba, where she learned that her once wealthy grandparents had owned considerable land but no African slaves. The family's political commitments rubbed off. As a young woman attempting to support herself in Los Angeles, Fox was drawn to leftist circles, particularly those of communists, because they promoted "equality for black people, an astonishing thought in those days." Her first publications appeared in *Negro Digest* in the 1940s, and the themes of race and class continued to dominate her novels, which began appearing in the 1960s. While her adult fiction soon went out of print, not to be rediscovered until the 1990s, her children's books prospered.[19] In 1978, the International Board of Books for Young People (IBBY) recognized her children's literature with the prestigious Hans Christian Andersen Award.[20]

The Slave Dancer opens in 1840 when greedy slavers kidnap a fife-playing boy from a New Orleans dock and throw him onboard their Africa-bound ship. Torn from home and family, Jessie Bollier experiences an approximation of short-term slavery as he is forced to play his instrument at the crew's command. Abducted to accompany the "dancing" of slaves—what traders called the only movement chained people could make during exercise sessions above deck—Jessie involuntarily participates in the transformation of African people into chattel. As difficult as it is to confront the human misery onboard ship, Jessie finds the transformation taking place within himself harder still:

> I found a terrible thing in my mind. I hated the slaves! I hated their
> shuffling, their howling, their very suffering! I hated the way they spat
> out their food upon the deck, the overflowing buckets, the emptying
> of which tried all my strength. I hated the foul stench that came from
> the holds no matter which way the wind blew, as though the ship itself
> were soaked with human excrement. I would have snatched the rope
> from Spark's hand and beaten them myself! Oh, God! I wished them
> all dead! Not to hear them! Not to smell them! Not to know of their
> existence![21]

Jessie's horror at his own lack of sympathy leads him to defy orders to dance the slaves. He suffers the lash for insubordination, but it is subversive obedience, not docile fear, that the crew beats into him. After receiving his strokes, Jessie identifies with the Africans below deck instead of the white sailors above it.

By placing Jessie on a slave ship, Fox makes the white boy complicit in the degradation of Africans even as he expresses horror at slavery and even when he himself suffers at the slavers' hands. Jessie's growth—at least in terms of understanding the way race and power intersect in his world—is thus much deeper than either Kit's or Phillip's. Kit learns to live without slaves in *Witch of Blackbird Pond* but never recognizes the way all North America benefits from the slave trade; Phillip learns to view black men as equal in *The Cay* but cannot see how structural racism ensures Timothy's continued deference toward him. Jessie, however, perceives that capitalist greed drives men to use whatever power they possess to dominate others for profit. The potential gains of the slave trade thus corrupt even those sailors who began their careers as victims of impressment. Jessie refuses to let this happen to him. When the crew spies an American flag near Cuba and begins to destroy evidence of its illegal business, throwing shackles, restraints, and slaves overboard indiscriminately, Jessie acts on his determination to align with the oppressed rather than the oppressors. Grabbing an African boy near his own age, he proceeds to a hiding place until it is safe to dive undetected. The adolescents emerge from the water (somewhat inexplicably) on the shores of Mississippi.

When Daniel, a fugitive slave, tends to their needs, Jessie learns the limits of his ability to identify with Africans. Race and power are bound up in ways he can neither disentangle nor control. After a blissful week of healing and friendship, Daniel provides the African boy with an escort to the North and freedom. Turning to Jessie, he demands secrecy, then provides a "chart of words that would lead [him] home to New Orleans" (121). At parting, Daniel's affection is reserved for the black child. "I wanted [Daniel] to touch my head as he had Ras's," Jessie narrates. "But his arms remained unmoving at his sides. I looked into his face. He didn't smile. The distance between us lengthened even as I stood there, listening to his breathing, aware of a powerful emotion, gratitude mixed with disappointment. . . . 'Go on now,' he said. I stepped out of the hut. Daniel had saved my life. I couldn't expect more than that" (121).

The interracial friendship described in *The Slave Dancer* is far more complex than that depicted in *The Cay* because it recognizes the need to confront a history of inequality and distrust before egalitarian relationships can be forged. Fox spent a year at the library reading what she described as the "tremendous area of books on slavery" before writing *The Slave Dancer*.[22] Such scholarship proliferated during the 1960s and early 1970s, and Fox's knowledge of the historiographical shift that took place between the King-dominated moment that informed *The Cay* and the Black Power moment in which she wrote assisted her in creating a protagonist who recognizes difference, as well as similarity, between black and white. Jessie and Ras may have been imprisoned on the same slave ship by the same evil white men, but after his interaction with the fugitive slave Daniel, Jessie comes to understand that their race ensures fundamentally different experiences—on the slaver and in their new lives of freedom.

The Slave Dancer explores the horrors of the Middle Passage through the perspective and narrative voice of a white boy. At the time of its publication, however, calls for black authors to write books featuring fully developed, three-dimensional African American characters were growing in number and volume. Even as the ALA nominated *The Slave Dancer* for the Newbery Medal, antiracist critics censured the book for presenting anonymous black slaves below deck. In the weeks before the ALA banquet, Fox learned that protests were planned. She invited Augusta Baker, prominent African American librarian and author of *Books about Negro Life for Children*, to give the traditional "About the Author" Newbery address. Baker carefully outlined Fox's identity as an American of Spanish and English-Irish descent who had spent considerable years of her childhood in Cuba.[23] Nonetheless, Fox said later, "I was a total wreck when I found out what was going on. . . . On the evening of the Newbery Award . . . I literally thought I would die. There I was in my evening gown, shaking like a leaf. But I gave my speech, and afterwards one or two of the previously hostile critics approached me, to let me know I was 'forgiven.'"[24]

Not all antiracist critics were willing to forgive the ALA, however. For some, the changes taking place in American children's literature—captured in miniature by the books and authors honored by the literary establishment—paled in comparison to the continuity. "While interracial children's fiction has increased from about ten books a year in the early fifties to over fifty in the late sixties, it has usually been written with the white reader primarily in mind," a 1970 *Childhood Education* article lamented. "In over two-thirds of the books, the major character is white and the character development possible for black roles consequently is limited."[25]

In 1965, a group of concerned librarians, teachers, parents, and political activists came together to form the Council on Interracial Books for Children (CIBC); their aim was to address the needs of African American children (and later, youth of other minority groups), who lacked books reflective of their culture and life experiences. Their efforts to raise awareness within the fields of publishing, education, and library science were far reaching, with three strategies proving particularly successful. First, the CIBC published *Interracial Books for Children*, a bulletin aimed at uncovering the bias present in those nonwhite characters who did figure in children's books. The bulletin included critical commentaries on children's classics that contained racist caricatures—for example, *Charlie and the Chocolate Factory*, *Mary Poppins*, and *Pippi Longstocking*—as well as recently released books like *The Slave Dancer*, whose CIBC review asked, "Should a white author use the Black Experience as mere background for a white-oriented adventure story?"[26]

Next, the CIBC called attention to the way prizing children's books for "literary quality" translated into awards being conferred on texts that contained racist, sexist, or otherwise offensive elements. Because the Newbery Medal reigned supreme in American children's literature, guaranteeing longevity, increased sales, and often a place in school curricula for its winning books, it became a primary target. Since its 1922 founding, all but one Newbery-winning author, a South Asian, had been white.[27] To address this issue head-on, the CIBC established its third winning strategy: it created a series of contests for unpublished children's authors of color. Successful contenders received CIBC assistance in placing their manuscript with mainstream publishing houses. Issued at the fringe of the literary establishment, these racially specific awards served as corrective to and critique of the ALA's Newbery. By the final decades of the twentieth century, the ALA adopted the practice itself, granting the Coretta Scott King (for African Americans) and Pura Belpré (for Latinos and Latinas) awards in addition to its annual Newbery Medal.

Despite the CIBC's victories, the organization was fraught with conflict. Not everyone involved—including the writers and illustrators who entered its manuscript contests—agreed with the organization's method of determining qualified entrants, a process that essentialized race. Nor was there consensus among CIBC supporters about whether white authors could create black characters without inserting, consciously or unconsciously, "white racist bias." The artists selected to judge the manuscript contests discovered, to their great disappointment, that many authors of color were liable to the same stereotypes as white authors.[28] Ultimately, a number of the CIBC's bulletin readers asserted that it was what a text *did* rather than who wrote the text that mattered most.[29] Ideological and pragmatic disagreements dogged the organization to its end in the late 1980s; however, there was also wide consensus among those involved that the CIBC's unique and sometimes provocative perspective was healthy for the children's book world.

The Limits of Tolerance: Controversy Erupts

Of all the books that came under attack in the CIBC's bulletin as racist, none is more illustrative of the interpretative complexity common to widely taught historical novels than William Armstrong's *Sounder*. Winner of the 1970 Newbery, Armstrong's story of a black sharecropping family and its beloved coon dog was widely acclaimed by the literary establishment and quickly adopted for classroom use. Unlike its award-winning predecessors, *Sounder* told a story of race from the voice of a black child, a strategy that hadn't been employed in a high-profile historical novel since *Amos Fortune* (1950). By the late 1960s, however, this narrative strategy had become more of a liability than a boon. *Sounder* and its white author found themselves enmeshed in racial politics in much the same way that William Styron garnered praise, then condemnation, for imagining the thoughts, feelings, and desires of a nineteenth-century slave in *The Confessions of Nat Turner* (1967), a Pulitzer Prize–winning book that sparked publication of *William Styron's "Nat Turner": Ten Black Writers Respond* (1968). The CIBC recognized the parallel. "You will be interested to learn that we are taking the position that the 1970 Newbery Medal to 'Sounder' is, to the children's book field, what Styron's 'Nat Turner' is to adult literature," CIBC director Brad Chambers wrote to the editor of *Moneysworth* magazine. "That the book received the book industry's top accolades is a manifestation of white supremacy pervading the field. 'Sounder' is a very, very racist book."[30]

The disparity between *Nat Turner* and *Sounder*'s fate speaks to the fundamental difference prize winning makes in the worlds of children's and adult fiction. Bookstores, libraries, and teachers pay no particular attention to Pulitzer-winning literature decades after the award has been granted, but each holds up Newbery-winning books as the best (and most enduring) in the children's literature field. Thus, while *Nat Turner* and the controversy associated with it have been filed away as history, the relic of a particular moment in U.S. race relations, *Sounder*—that is, the novel, not the controversy—remains a living presence in children's lives.[31] The storm surrounding the book entirely forgotten, *Sounder* ranks ninety-fourth on the list of all-time best-selling children's paperbacks, having sold 2,394,340 copies as of 2000 (and almost 500,000 between 1996 and 2000 alone).[32]

William Armstrong's *Sounder* (1970)

In telling a story about a black sharecropping family's struggle for survival—and in setting that story in an unspecified time and place in the past—William Armstrong's *Sounder*, discussed in Chapter 1, delivers a message about life and dignity that strives to be both universal and particular to the African American experience. Critics who praised *Sounder* at the time of its publication marveled at the novel's ability to transcend time. "Written with quiet strength and taut with tragedy. . . . Grim and honest, the book has a moving, elegiac quality that is reminiscent of the stark inevitability of Greek tragedy," one reported. "The writing is simple, timeless, and extraordinarily moving," another seconded.[33] Approaching *Sounder* as a literary text, the critics described what they understood to be the universal human truths captured in the narrative. But when *Sounder* is approached as historical fiction—as a text whose vision of the past is shaped by the present—its truths appear less transcendent.

A shift takes place in the novel after the protagonist's father is hunted down for having stolen a pig to feed the family. In the process of the father's arrest, the boy witnesses the degree to which white men deliberately conflate black men and dogs. The boy assumes that the police's command to "chain him up" is directed at Sounder, who is trying to protect his master, "but then he saw that one of the men had snapped a long chain on the handcuffs on his father's wrists."[34] As the deputies pull away, they shoot the dog, who, unlike his master, can still fight back. Before the father disappears into the white man's jail and the injured Sounder retreats into the brush, the family participates in meaningful, culture-making activities. Mother sings and tells Bible stories, and father teaches the boy coon-hunting lore. After man and dog leave, however, the bleak cabin becomes desolate. Culture making has been stamped out by the grim struggle for survival.

Armstrong's interpretation of the way black sharecroppers coped with a social, political, and economic system that entrapped them in poverty and second-class citizenship parallels the interpretations of contemporaneous historiography that understood nineteenth-century American slavery as a "closed system." In his influential work *Slavery: A Problem in American Institutional and Intellectual Life* (1959), historian Stanley Elkins argued that in the face of overwhelming, authoritative control over mind and body, the vast majority of enslaved Africans couldn't imagine themselves breaking free; in order to cope, they resigned themselves to bondage.[35] Armstrong applies the same logic to his protagonist's parents, who, despite their free status, lead lives little different from their enslaved predecessors.

Unlike his parents, the boy protagonist has been shielded from servile dependence on white landowners. Cocooned in the family's cabin, he holds fast to a dream of literacy and draws hope from the biblical Joseph, whose divinely inspired dreams always come true. The boy's faith is rewarded when, spurred to search for his father, who was sentenced to hard labor, he finds instead a learned black man who invites him into his school and home. Upon hearing the news, his mother exclaims, "The Lord has come to you, child." She recognizes that her son has found a way out of poverty and hopelessness (103, 105).

According to the argument laid forth in Elkins's *Slavery*, the boy and his parents' differing fates and outlooks stem from their differing opportunities. Elkins claimed that when placed in a closed system with no means of escape or access to the outside world, adults regressed to childlike behavior, maintaining a kind of split personality in which one part of the self remained intact and the other played out a perpetual role for those in power. A select few with specialized skills (plantation artisans, for example) could escape the closed system and its concomitant regression. The boy in Armstrong's novel is thus privileged. While the mother and father lack vitality and a fighting spirit, the boy glitters with the promise of a better future. In the early 1970s, *Sounder* captured the hopefulness of an era of federally mandated school desegregation: provided with appropriate mentorship, superior education, and reason to hope, the boy can escape degradation.

But there was another way to read the novel. Assistant professor of language arts at Richmond College in Staten Island and a prolific reviewer for the CIBC bulletin, Albert V. Schwartz read *Sounder* as reproducing the white privilege that kept African Americans oppressed. As the headline of his review—"*Sounder*: A Black or a White Tale? Flaws in Newbery Award Winner Obscured by Innate White Bias"—suggests, Schwartz characterized Armstrong's novel as a tale written by and for white people, at African Americans' expense.[36] When Schwartz's critique is remembered at all today, it is simplified: Armstrong was white, and he gave his canine character a name while denying his black, human characters individual identities. For those schooled in literary analysis, such a critique is easy to dismiss—authorial erasure of names is a common means of communicating universal experience. Schwartz's real criticism, however, was more profound, and it centered on Armstrong's assumptions about the way structural racism of the pre–civil rights South affected African American adults. Why, Schwartz asks, did Armstrong omit the rich African American culture and community that, even in the midst of poverty, sustained a family like the one depicted in *Sounder*? Where in the book is evidence of resistance and rebellion? By the mid-1970s, professional historians, filmmakers, and children's authors were beginning to create historical narratives that answered these questions, making *Sounder* seem out of date.

As Schwartz suggested but did not fully articulate, there remains a discrepancy between the structural racism *Sounder* exposes and the solution its narrative offers. The boy protagonist escapes the cycle of poverty through a combination of individual effort (pulling newspapers from trash barrels) and chance (finding, in the rural South, a learned black teacher with a classical library).[37] Such tales of self-making have been reproduced in Anglo-American, immigrant, and African American literary traditions for centuries, and they often read as apolitical to an American public. During the early 1970s, however, heated civil rights debates made the implications of this Horatio Alger myth more visible than usual. In

1965, assistant secretary of labor Daniel Patrick Moynihan published *The Negro Family: The Case for National Action*, a controversial report that sought to explain the contemporary "problem" with black families, particularly of the female-headed variety. Moynihan argued that the way for a black individual to break the cycle of poverty and rise to success was by dissociating himself from home and heritage.[38] In the context of the Moynihan report, Armstrong's novel read not as an iteration of the American tale of self-making but as part of a larger societal failure to understand the strengths of African American culture.

Born in Lexington, Virginia, in 1911, Armstrong understood rural poverty and appreciated the realities of southern black life. Like the protagonist he created in *Sounder*, however, he left home as a young man and began a new life. He graduated college, "married up," and settled in New England, where he taught at an elite boarding school. It was during his time at Kent School that Armstrong wrote the manuscript that would become *Sounder*. In its original version, the story of the black family and its dog was linked to another story of three white children and their dog; when the manuscript was divided for publication, however, the story of the white family was relegated to a quickly forgotten sequel (*Sour Land*), while the story of the black boy and his dog became a best seller.[39]

The final version of *Sounder* included an author's note explaining that the narrative that followed "is the black man's story, not mine. It was not from Aesop, the Old Testament, or Homer. It was history—*his* history" (viii; emphasis in original). For those CIBC members for whom authorial "authenticity" was becoming increasingly important, this statement captured all that was wrong with Armstrong's novel. It both revealed and concealed the origin of *Sounder*. Who was "the black man"? Was it *really* his story? If so, why didn't he write the book himself? Furthermore, they argued that as long as novels such as *Sounder* were written, they crowded out space for authors of color.[40]

This was not the only response to Armstrong's novel, however, or the most popular. In featuring a black protagonist and making a historical argument about the destructive nature of racism, *Sounder* filled an important gap in children's literature. Recognizing this, three of the most prominent black artists of the early 1970s—director Lonnie Elder III and actors Cicely Tyson and Paul Winfield—collaborated on a big-screen movie adaptation of *Sounder* (1972, dir. Martin Ritt) that was nominated for three Academy Awards. As artists, they rejected the notion that only black people could create black characters, a fundamentalist belief that had kept African American actors from access to "white" parts for years.[41] Yet in embracing Armstrong's text, the artists also transformed it in ways that responded to the CIBC critique. In the screenplay, characters have names; the family attends church, plays baseball, and sings spontaneously; and the mother attempts to prevent her husband's arrest. Most important, the boy is not an individual hero who breaks from his "damaging" cultural heritage but a child uplifted by his family. His mother shoulders extra burdens so that he can leave home to acquire an education.[42] The CIBC praised the film but worried about the "substantive ethical questions" it raised. In an unfinished memo, CIBC director Brad Chambers asked,

1. Who benefits financially? How ethical is it for any white writer to profit from the Black Experience? Should a white man get the royalties from a work that has been restructured by Black writers?
2. Should the movie rightfully bear the same title as the book, remembering that a nonracist movie is going to result directly in the sale of a racist book?[43]

As was the case for other CIBC critiques of contemporary award-winning books, Chambers's questions were largely dismissed. Attracted to *Sounder*'s strong black hero and American tale of self-making, librarians and teachers continued to recommend and assign it.

Even after the CIBC folded in the 1980s and William Armstrong died in 1999, *Sounder* lived on. In 2003, a new movie version of the book appeared, this time on television. Kevin Hooks, the actor who played the adolescent lead in the 1972 film, now held the reins as director. His made-for-TV movie adhered more closely to the novel. "It's ironic to me that we were making a much more hard-hitting film for the Wonderful World of Disney in 2003 than the feature was able to deal with in 1972. . . . Audiences have matured," Hooks said of the new version, which universalizes the black family by erasing personal names, depicts the boy's lonely path to acquiring an education, features evil white men, and has the father return home to die onscreen.[44] But subtle differences between the movie and novel—as well as quiet nods to Schwartz's critique—remain. Most notably, the movie closes with the boy protagonist, now literate, writing the story of Sounder—his story, his history—for himself. The explanation of *Sounder*'s authorship has moved from overlooked addendum in the novel to dramatic climax in the movie.

■ Undeterred by its limited success in turning public opinion against *Sounder*, the CIBC redoubled its efforts in 1974 when it learned about plans for a made-for-TV movie based on *The Cay*. While bypassed for the Newbery, Taylor's novel had received considerable attention, including the Jane Addams Brotherhood Award for promoting peace, social justice, and world community.[45] The CIBC knew that *The Cay*'s projected telecast, featuring the popular James Earl Jones as Timothy, would greatly increase the novel's circulation. With hopes of convincing NBC to cancel production, the CIBC communicated its reading of the novel's dialect-speaking black character and colorblind message to the studio: "Rather than praise for literary achievement on behalf of 'brotherhood,' *The Cay* . . . should be castigated as an adventure story for white colonialists to add to their racist mythology."[46] The campaign to call off production failed, but the CIBC nonetheless achieved considerable success in promulgating its message. Partnering with the National Education Association, the CIBC developed and distributed lesson plans centered on the book and its adaptation prior to the film's release.[47] What most educators had failed to see in 1969 many could recognize in 1974: *The Cay* detailed the antiracist growth of a white boy but remained silent on the impact racism had on a black man.

The CIBC's biggest victory in connection with *The Cay* came unexpectedly. As part of its effort to dissuade NBC from airing the film, the council contacted the current chair of the Jane Addams book award committee. Bertha Jenkinson quickly joined her voice to the CIBC's, stating that her organization's honoring of *The Cay* five years earlier had been "a mistake." She went on to qualify her remarks, noting that given the level of political awareness at the time, "*The Cay* probably deserves the awards which it received in 1969." But the CIBC seized on her regret and published a bold article in its bulletin headlined, "Revoking 'The Cay' Award." Deeply offended, Taylor removed the Jane Addams plaque from his wall and returned it to Jenkinson, collect.[48] Yet in a trajectory that mirrors that of *Sounder*, the story doesn't end there. Taylor heard the loud criticism leveled against his novel and responded by publishing a co-narrated "prequel-sequel," *Timothy of the Cay* (1993). This book provides a reason for the black man's self-sacrifice (guilt over having inadvertently caused the death of a white child years earlier) and access into the West Indian's thoughts and feelings. The first printing sold out immediately, and despite its unsuccessful narrative, reader demand remains steady. Dust surrounding the 1974 film settled quickly, and *The Cay* emerged with reputation intact.[49] In 2010, California, Indiana, New York, North Carolina, and Massachusetts included the novel on their respective lists of recommended middle-grade titles.

As the case of *Sounder* and *The Cay* illustrates, the CIBC was only moderately successful in changing the destiny of contemporary novels already prized by the literary establishment. Newbery-winning books in particular not only entered the school curriculum but stayed there, regardless of criticism about black characters, white authors, or their imagined readers' racial identities. Interested in fostering student empathy for the downtrodden, satisfying multicultural aims, and integrating literature into the social studies, teachers have continued to use a range of novels about race and slavery in their classrooms. The books chosen differ in message but share in common an ability to satisfy both the political left and right: in addition to including "positive" black characters, they advocate tolerance and self-making, praise education, and encourage self-discovery. Collectively, they speak to mainstream Middle America. The CIBC, by contrast, was a radical organization whose bulletin never penetrated the conservative institution of the public school. Yet the council had tremendous impact in other ways. It not only called attention to "the all-white world of children's literature" but also *changed* that world by launching the careers of several highly successful authors of color, people who in turn paved the way for future generations of children's authors, including Asians and Latinos/Latinas as well as African Americans. The work of these authors stands side by side with children's novels published during earlier phases of the civil rights movement in today's schools.

Recentering the Narrative: Black as the Norm

When the CIBC began its manuscript contests for novice children's writers, the judges read many wooden, amateurish entries. Included among the submissions, however, were several glittering gems, stories so good that they awakened mainstream children's editors to the value of what was then called "minority fiction."[50] Mildred D. Taylor's submission to the 1974 "middle grade—Black" contest was one such treasure. The manuscript, *Song of the Trees*, turned into the first book in a series of novels and novellas set in the American South and rooted in family stories of resistance and survival. Children's literature scholar Barbara Bader has compared the series—in theme, impact, and influence—to that of Laura Ingalls Wilder: "It takes no deep thought to name *Little House in the Big Woods* as the most important American children's book of the first half of the twentieth century . . . and [Taylor's *Roll of Thunder, Hear My Cry*] is arguably the most important of the century's second half."[51] By connecting Taylor to mainstream publishers, the CIBC contest launched an author whose first full-length novel, *Roll of Thunder, Hear My Cry* (1976), won the Newbery and whose prequels and sequels collectively won six Coretta Scott King Awards.[52] There could be no better testimony to the ALA's transformation; the mainstream organization now recognized and prized books with minority themes written by minority authors. And those books, whose paperback covers glistened with golden ALA award stamps, entered the school curriculum in force.

Mildred D. Taylor's *Roll of Thunder, Hear My Cry* (1976) and *Let the Circle Be Unbroken* (1981)

Mildred Taylor was born in Jackson, Mississippi, in 1943. The family patriarch, Taylor's great-grandfather, was the product of an Alabama slave and her white master; he grew up to see freedom, purchase land, and establish an economic and psychological legacy that would sustain his family during three generations of Jim Crow. Taylor, a member of the fourth generation, would capture this legacy for a fifth, post-*Brown* generation. Like many of her future readers, she spent her childhood in the North and attended at least nominally integrated schools (her father's involvement in a racial incident had propelled the family north to Toledo, Ohio). Regular trips to Mississippi, however, enabled Taylor to experience firsthand both the fear and confusion associated with restricted access to public facilities as well as the warmth and security tied to arriving on family land. Adult experiences also shaped the budding author's self-understanding. After graduating from college in 1965, Taylor joined the Peace Corps, traveled to Ethiopia, and was welcomed "home" by a village who recognized her as a long-lost descendant. Upon her return to the United States two years later, Taylor's racial pride, strengthened and clarified by her experience, meshed with a generation of students who embraced Africa, viewed "Black as Beautiful," and sought curricular changes that reflected their new worldviews.[53]

When Taylor began transforming her father's stories of life in Depression-era Mississippi into historical fiction, she filtered his oral history through her own experiences as a child of the mid-twentieth-century civil rights movement. Her Logan series thus captures several generations of views on black history and black political priorities, combining the sensibilities about race and race relations of her parents' and grandparents' generation with her own 1970s readings of blackness in America. Her Newbery acceptance speech for *Roll of Thunder* responded to the 1965 Moynihan report and to contemporary media images of "broken" black families. As Taylor said, she wanted to capture "a Black family united in love and pride, of which the reader would like to be a part." She explained, "I had a driving compulsion to paint a truer picture of Black people. I wanted to show the endurance of the Black world, with strong fathers and concerned mothers; I wanted to show happy, loved children about whom other children, both Black and white, could say: 'Hey, I really like them! I feel what they feel.'"[54]

In stark contrast to *Sounder*, which draws inspiration from 1950s historiography understanding slavery as a closed system, *Roll of Thunder* is in dialogue with 1970s historiography that focuses on the world slaves made; despite its oppression, scholars of the 1970s argued, plantation slavery and its Jim Crow legacy left "living space" for cultural creation.[55] Accordingly, Taylor's stories are filled with joyous, heartfelt living. The Logan children grow up not only with their mother and father but also with a grandparent, an uncle, cousins, and nonfamily members who become like family; everyone tells stories, makes music, and socializes at church. The four kids, moreover, form a social group all their own, playing games, telling jokes, and plotting revenge on enemies large and small. Stacey, Cassie, Christopher-John, and Little Man invite reader identification regardless of race. Taylor knew that the concept of a warm, safe family circle was attractive to all; she correctly surmised that in the 1970s, white readers, as well as black ones, would embrace her narrative. But her greatest innovation in children's literature has operated below most readers' recognition: she recast a "timeless"—but arguably *not* universal—school classic, retelling it through a Black Power lens.

Taylor has never named a literary model for her Logan books, describing them instead as autobiographical, but *Roll of Thunder* and its first sequel, *Let the Circle Be Unbroken*, unmistakably echo Harper Lee's *To Kill a Mockingbird* (1960), one of the best-selling and most frequently taught American novels of all time.[56] Lee's story takes place in a small town in Alabama between 1933 and 1935; Taylor's stories unfold in rural Mississippi during the same years. All three books are narrated by a school-age girl who expresses annoyance at her pubescent older brother's withdrawal. Both the Finch and Logan children learn to recognize their parents' education and access to resources, factors that set them apart from their peers. And most notably, both *Mockingbird* and the Logan stories climax in the trial of an innocent black man by a bigoted white jury. In linking her narrative to Lee's in setting, plot, character, and theme, Taylor draws attention to the way race shapes characters' experiences and authorial agency determines readers' perspective. The result can be seen most clearly when comparing the books' concern for education and preoccupation with transgression and its punishment.

Mockingbird opens with Scout Finch's much-anticipated foray into public school. Her first day is quickly ruined when Miss Caroline discovers that Scout not only knows the alphabet but can also read and write; the teacher demands that Scout's father stop teaching her. The experience worsens when Scout earns a whipping for attempting to explain why a country boy won't take a loan to buy a "forgotten" lunch: "You're shamin' him, Miss Caroline. Walter hasn't got a quarter at home to bring you."[57] *Roll of Thunder* repeats the scene almost exactly. While Little Man's first-grade classmates express delight at receiving textbooks, the Logan six-year-old spies the word "nigra" juxtaposed with "'very poor' condition" on his book's student registration page and angrily brushes the offending text to the floor. Cassie explains that Little Man can read, information that only further provokes the teacher, who orders both children to the "'whipping' chair."[58]

Book learning is valued by both the Logans and Finches, but the more important lessons are ones of survival. Both sets of parents require their children to bear witness to adults who have suffered as a result of poor choices. Atticus counsels Scout and Jem to keep a level head when criticized for their father's legal defense of a black man. When Jem fails to heed the advice and decapitates a woman's flowers after being verbally abused, his father backs the demand for repayment: Jem must tend her garden and read aloud to the woman, who suffers from drug withdrawal. Similarly, when the Logan children disobey strict orders to stay out of the Wallaces' general store, Mama awakens them at dawn to introduce them to a man whose "face [now] had no nose, and the head no hair; the skin was scarred, burned, and the lips were wizened black, like charcoal" (97). The man, accused of flirting with a white woman, had been set on fire by the Wallaces.[59]

In light of these similar child-rearing strategies, the differences Atticus and the Logan parents display become striking; each set of parents prepares their children for the starkly different realities they will face as adults of a particular race. As a lawyer, Atticus appreciates rules and their enforcement but dislikes coercion. Thus, he displays a patient leniency when Scout adopts an unladylike swearing streak. Uncle Jack, who steps in to clean up his niece's mouth, is astounded when his spanking meets with indignation. As Scout protests, he "lit into her" before she was given the opportunity to defend herself. Atticus explains to his brother, "So far I've been able to get by with threats. Jack, she minds me as well as she can. Doesn't come up to scratch half the time, but she tries" (92). The Logans, by contrast, know that for their black children trying won't cut it, as there will be no opportunities to tell one's side. Convincing therefore takes the form of coercion, and misdeeds are punished regardless of circumstance. When Mrs. Logan catches Stacey with a crib sheet, she whips him, even though she knows with certainty that her son would never cheat (81). The fact that Stacey's sometimes-friend T.J. had slipped the notes under Stacey's papers is superfluous. The humiliation of squirming under his mother's hand in front of classmates serves a dual purpose: in addition to teaching Stacey's peers that cheating will not be tolerated, Mrs. Logan teaches Stacey that associating with people who make poor choices implicates *him* in the dangerous situations they create. Unlike Scout, Stacey accepts the whipping—and the warning— without a murmur.

In both novels, parental lessons prepare children for a horrifying narrative climax, a tragedy neither family can prevent. The sexual overtones of Tom Robinson's alleged crime in *Mockingbird* are substituted for accidental homicide in *Roll of Thunder*, but the premise is the same: a black man is accused of wrongdoing by the white person responsible for the act. Trial by an all-white jury seals the accused's fate, even when a sympathetic white lawyer has proved the black man's innocence beyond a shadow of doubt. In *Roll of Thunder*, T.J., the conniving neighbor with whom the Logan children have grown up, is the accused. By luring Stacey to the Wallace store, T.J. triggers a chain of events that lead Mrs. Logan to organize a community-wide boycott of the establishment. Yet even as the black community takes great risks to carry out the politically dangerous boycott (echoes of 1960s activism can't be missed), T.J. ingratiates himself with the censured family, tagging behind the Wallaces' swaggering teenage sons. Having learned through his schoolroom humiliation the lesson of guilt by association, Stacey breaks contact with T.J. Nonetheless, it is to the Logans that T.J. turns when the Wallaces frame him for murder. The family prevents a lynching, but legal trial brings the same result: certain death.[60]

Like *Mockingbird*'s Finch children, the Logans learn the meaning of "justice" in the Jim Crow South; moreover, they do so by watching a member of their own black community be sentenced to hang. A white lawyer plays the hero in *Mockingbird*, placing both himself and his children in physical danger by taking on a black defendant. In *Roll of Thunder*, however, it is the Logans who assume the greatest risks and achieve the best results. A white lawyer defends T.J. in court, but it is Mama's boycott that demonstrates that vigilante justice will not be tolerated and Papa's decision to set his own family's cotton on fire that prevents T.J.'s lynching. Thus, despite *Roll of Thunder*'s and *Mockingbird*'s similar story lines, the lessons each imparts are distinct. Atticus uses the trial to reinforce to his children, the community, and *Mockingbird* readers the danger of stereotypes: "You never really understand a person until you consider things from his point of view . . . until you climb into his skin and walk around in it" (34). As literary scholar Janice Radway has argued, the novel aims "for nothing less than the re-conceptualization of women and 'Negroes' as collections of individually different human beings rather than as categories of people rendered identifiable by certain common properties." That message resonated with white, middle-class readers during the 1960s, when television cameras captured through close-ups both white violence and peaceful black resistance.[61] Tom Robinson's jurors might not be able to look past deeply engrained beliefs about "Negroes," but Harper Lee optimistically concluded that Jem and Scout's generation would.

Mildred Taylor's books are less optimistic. Writing a decade and a half after Lee, Taylor warned that friendship between blacks and whites must be approached warily, and with no illusion of equality. If *Mockingbird* emphasized the accessibility of individuals different from oneself, Taylor's books emphasized their mystery. In *Let the Circle Be Unbroken*, young Jeremy Simms risks social suicide to befriend the Logan children, with whom he walks daily to his separate, white school. The adults strongly disapprove of the friendship, and Uncle Hammer explodes in rage when he discovers that Jeremy has given a photograph of himself to Cassie: "Stacey, you soon gonna be fourteen. Now that ain't so very old, but it's old enough to know how things stand, and if you don't know it already, you better start learning right fast how white men think 'bout black women."[62] Again and again, the Logan children are shown the dangerous consequences of trusting white people who offer "friendship." In *Roll of Thunder*, T.J. pays for his naïveté with his life. In *Let the Circle Be Unbroken*, Cousin Suzella, a biracial beauty who passes as white in the North, pays with her pride. When the white boys who flirted with her discover she is a Logan, they punish Suzella by stripping her father in her sight, proving that he (and she) is black: "We'll see jus' how light the nigger is. . . . All right, nigger, go 'head, get them clothes off" (344). Taylor's pessimistic message about interracial possibilities is softened by hope for a better future. "Maybe in fifty or a hundred years, folks won't have to even think 'bout it . . . whether you're black or white," Papa tells Cassie in *Let the Circle Be Unbroken*. "Way it seem now, it ain't likely, but maybe" (180). And in the final Logan book, *The Road to Memphis*, Jeremy Simms defies expectations by sacrificing his birthright of white privilege to protect the Logan children. But the real optimism of the Logan stories lies not in the rare benevolent white character, but rather in the moral strength and purposeful action of the African American community.

In 2002, more than a quarter century after *Roll of Thunder*'s release, the novel ranked as the ninth most-frequently challenged book in the nation, with readers objecting to its "insensitivity, racism and offensive language."[63] Some critics of the novel detect its Black Power message, finding the book "angry," but the vast majority of objections to *Roll of Thunder*'s place in schools echo a segment of 1970s antiracist criticism. These detractions come from people—often parents of black schoolchildren—who seek literary representations of African Americans that place them on par with white characters. In their eyes, neither Taylor's race nor the feistiness with which her characters fight racism compensates for the fact that Cassie, Stacey, and siblings are pushed off sidewalks, splattered with mud, and attacked with racial epithets, all because they are black. "There are those who do not want to remember the past or who do not want their children to know the past and who would whitewash history, and these sentiments are not only from whites," Taylor explained in a speech for yet another literary award. "My stories might not be 'politically correct,' so there will be those who will be offended, but as we all know, racism is offensive. It is not polite, and it is full of pain."[64]

Taylor's enthusiasts far outnumber her detractors, and *Roll of Thunder* figures as one of the most assigned novels of the entire middle-grade canon.[65] Its popularity stems from a number of factors. First, of course, the novel is engaging and beautifully written. Even more important, however, is the fact that most people read into the book a *moderate* political stance: ugly white characters are joined by Jeremy Simms and the compassionate lawyer Mr. Jamison, messages of racial exclusion dovetail with the family's strong American values, and the Logan children's warm African American English is balanced with Mama's schoolmarm vocabulary and grammar.[66] A final factor, however, has less to do with Taylor's craft and audiences' desires than with publishing trends and educators' needs. Taylor's literary career coincided with the rise of multiculturalism as a high priority in K–12 schools. As federal funds for school book purchases dried up in the 1980s, however, publishing houses' commitment to discovering and promoting the work of minority authors diminished. As a result, Taylor's stories were among the few books available in the 1980s and early 1990s that fulfilled a set of categories then in high demand: they explicitly dealt with racial issues, were appropriate for middle-grade readers, were authored by an African American, and could be used in interdisciplinary ways. Recognizing Taylor's books as a gold mine, California had, by 2002, placed six of her nine titles on its list of recommended literature and at least one in each of its age-level categories for elementary, middle, and high school.

Christopher Paul Curtis's *The Watsons Go to Birmingham—1963* (1995)

It was not until a full two decades after *Roll of Thunder*'s publication that another African American author captured a Newbery Medal. Christopher Paul Curtis's entry into the children's literature world mirrored Taylor's in remarkable ways. Not only did he win award after award in mainstream and race-specific categories—his second novel, *Bud, Not Buddy* (1999), is the first book ever to secure both the Newbery and Coretta Scott King awards—but like Taylor, his timing was perfect. Passage of the No Child Left Behind Act (2001) provided K–12 schools with federal money for book purchases and placed significant emphasis on literacy, a policy that in practice sent elementary and middle school teachers scuttling for ways they could combine history instruction with reading practice. It would be hard to identify a more opportune moment for a talented black author of children's historical fiction to appear on the scene; his books were all but guaranteed a place in school lessons.

Both Taylor and Curtis were raised in midwestern Rust Belt cities, and just a decade apart. Yet it is the difference between their respective cultural and psychic orientations—and the effect this has on their books—that is intriguing. Taylor's sense of home is rooted in land, both that of her family in the South—cotton fields wrested from plantation owners during Reconstruction—and that of her ancestors in Africa. Trees, fields, and the rich earth are recurring motifs in her books, and it is land that differentiates the Logans from their sharecropping neighbors, giving them financial security, leadership within the black community, and a sense of purpose and belonging. Curtis, by contrast, is shaped by the urban experience. Born in 1954 to an auto worker father and stay-at-home mother, both college educated, Curtis grew up in a self-contained African American neighborhood; his family's comfort and security stemmed not from ownership of farmland but from a well-paid union job and the material goods it could buy.[67] For Curtis, the Midwest, not the South, was home, and it had been for generations. His grandfathers, models for two characters in *Bud, Not Buddy*, were northerners: Earl "Lefty" Lewis was a redcap, union organizer, and Negro League pitcher, and Herman E. Curtis was a classically trained violinist who played in orchestras by night and did odd jobs by day.[68]

Taylor's books participate in an African American literary tradition that romanticizes the rural folk as authentic and life-giving, especially in comparison to the corrupting and fracturing influence of the city; Curtis's books, by contrast, poke fun at that tradition.[69] Whenever Momma of *The Watsons Go to Birmingham* waxes eloquent about the South, Dad assumes a blistering hillbilly accent and tells "Southern style stuff"—that is, the hard truth of racism, masked for the children's sake in absurd comedic form.[70] Sprinkled with references to brands (an Ultra-Glide record player, Jell-O, Old Spice, Buick, Maytag) and technological innovations (washing machines, telegrams, railroads), Curtis's historical novels celebrate the (relative) freedom and prosperity of African American life in northern cities.[71]

In describing his own, unorthodox journey to becoming a children's author, Curtis explains that as a teenager in Flint, Michigan, he was lured by the power of easy money. A steady job could buy him a new car and his own apartment—attractions too tempting for the urban youth to resist. Much to his parents' chagrin, he joined the assembly line after high school, hanging car doors ten hours a day and taking college classes at night. Not until age forty did Curtis leave the plant, taking a year off to write *The Watsons Go to Birmingham—1963*. The product of a year's labor in the children's section of the public library—Curtis's preferred writing spot—*The Watsons* was an overwhelming success. The book won honor citations in both the Newbery and Coretta Scott King contests, sold more than 300,000 copies by 2002, and attracted Whoopi Goldberg to the movie rights.[72] Curtis never went back to Fisher Body Plant No. 1.

The Watsons tells the story of a close-knit family of five whose oldest son, Byron, is a struggling student, schoolyard bully, and pyromaniac. Keenly aware of the racial terror exploding in the South, the Watsons worry that their thirteen-year-old's childish misbehavior will blossom into teenage delinquency and land him in serious trouble. The way to straighten him out, they conclude, is by sending him to Grandma Sands. For reasons unexplained, the "Weird Watsons" haven't been to Birmingham since younger son Kenny was born a decade earlier. In the interim, Momma has romanticized the slow pace and rustic housing (no indoor plumbing or air conditioning) while "forgetting" the ever-present possibility of violence and humiliation. Even as Momma suppresses the fact that once south of Ohio, "y'all colored folks cain't be jes' pullin' up tuh any ol' way-uh," her knowledge of Jim Crow realities drives her desire to send Byron south (132). As Dad explains, "We think it's time Byron got an idea of the kind of place the world can be" (123). The parents get more than they bargained for. The historical bombing of the Sixteenth Avenue Baptist Church coincides with the family's first Sunday in Birmingham, and six-year-old Joetta is at Sunday school. Although she escapes physically unharmed, the Watsons head north immediately thereafter, the need to "straighten Byron out" having evaporated as the teenager proves himself thoroughly transformed (123).

Like *Roll of Thunder*, *The Watsons* is a work of African American literature as well as a historical novel about the black experience. Characters switch between northern and southern American dialects, as well as between middle- and working-class forms of African American English; use humor as a means of negotiating racism; and make hearty use of exaggeration, telling "truthful lies" that draw on the tradition of black folklore.[73] The innocence of Curtis's naive narrator, Kenny, enables him to both comprehend and misinterpret.[74] Much to the ten-year-old's amusement, Momma has planned every mile of the fifteen-hour drive to Birmingham before the journey begins: "Where we'd eat, when we'd eat, who got baloney sandwiches on Day One, who got tuna fish on Day Two . . . how long we could hold ourselves between going to the bathroom . . . everything" (133). When Dad discovers that the car's movement lulls its passengers to sleep, however, he determines to drive straight through. In addition to throwing off Momma's meticulous plans, the executive decision lands the Watsons in some tight spots, precisely what Momma's road guide was designed to avoid. "Instead of being in a motel you've driven us straight into Hell!" an exasperated Momma exclaims as the family pulls into a rest stop late at night. Shaken by Momma's "cuss" word, Kenny comments, "Hell? I thought you said this was Tennessee!" (146).

The most striking aspect of *The Watsons* may well be what happens when naive child reader meets naive child narrator. Older kids laugh at Kenny's confusion, knowing that Tennessee *is* hell for black men and women at an isolated truck stop late at night. But Kenny, who lives in an entirely segregated world, rarely thinks about race; even Byron's explanation of why the family is in danger sails over his head. The result is that white children reading *The Watsons* often express surprise upon "discovering," late in the novel, that its characters are black.[75] For African American children and experienced readers, race is everywhere apparent: Momma speaks "Southern style" when agitated, Kenny recites Langston Hughes, and Joey's hair smells of pomade. Contemporary white children living in worlds as socially segregated as Kenny's, however, sometimes miss the cues. Scholars have argued that an unintended consequence of the naive narration is that *The Watsons* fosters nonblack readers' "colorblind" identification with Kenny. By inserting themselves within the protagonist's family before racial violence erupts, (white) readers, through narrative identification, experience the actions of white racists as committed against themselves.[76]

Editors urged Curtis to add a white character to *The Watsons*—someone like Mildred Taylor's Jeremy Simms—in order to appeal to a more diverse readership, advice that he rejected: "As a writer, I don't think of the audience in those terms: I don't consciously say, *I'm targeting this book at this particular group*. I think what is most important . . . is that you tell your story."[77] Curtis's decision proved astute; *The Watsons* has appealed to white children and white teachers as well as to African American ones. That *The Watsons* achieved, casually and unintentionally, the colorblind identification Theodore Taylor belabored in *The Cay* speaks to the contradictions of today's multicultural moment: cultural heritages are celebrated by all, but the social liabilities inherent in a minority status remain oddly invisible to children whose worlds, in practical terms, continue to be largely segregated.

By focusing reader attention on the violence and bigotry of the Jim Crow South, *The Watsons* comments only passively on the pedestrian but equally pervasive structural racism that affected Americans throughout the postwar nation. In the early 1960s, Flint was on the verge of becoming a depressed inner city. As part of the Second Great Migration, African Americans had flocked to the Midwest to fill lucrative war-related jobs during the 1940s. In response, Flint's leaders built George Washington Carver Elementary, the school the fictional Watson children attend, in 1945. Carver was not only an attempt to ease school crowding but also a strategy to segregate the city's schools, which now swelled with black children. At the war's end, a combination of government and corporate policies increased segregation. The Federal Housing Administration and Veterans Administration's mortgage program facilitated the building of white suburbs, while General Motors built new industrial complexes outside the city, draining Flint of both well-paying jobs and tax revenues. Squeezed into substandard housing and poorly funded schools, Flint's black residents fought back. Just four years after the setting of *The Watsons*, race riots erupted in nearby Detroit, and the reverberations in Flint led Michigan's governor to declare a state of emergency. Hundreds of people took to the streets protesting police brutality, unfair housing, and other race-related issues.[78]

Such tensions are entirely absent from *The Watsons*. While signs of economic distress figure in the narrative—Momma tells Byron that the family has at times relied on "welfare food," and the ever-observant Kenny realizes that both the schoolyard bully and his victim lack money for winter clothing—they are minimized. The novel's focus on the warmth and stability of the Watsons' home legitimizes the urban black culture most African American children know today. But its child's-eye view of the 1960s also romanticizes and exaggerates the safety and security of the urban North. In Curtis's telling, racial violence is something that happened in Birmingham, not Flint. It begs comparison with Elizabeth George Speare's *Witch of Blackbird Pond*, which places seventeenth-century slavery in Virginia, but not Connecticut. *The Watsons* does not address the racist policies that created poor, segregated, urban neighborhoods precisely at the time of the novel's setting. Yet the legacy of those postwar policies is painfully evident today. At the beginning of the twenty-first century, Flint ranked among America's most dangerous cities, while Birmingham stood as a shining example of the *new* New South, a place *Black Enterprise* voted as one of the best cities for African Americans to live and work in 2004.[79] It is in part the novel's silence on federal failures in regard to racial equality that facilitated its entry into the classroom canon. *The Watsons* differs from earlier middle-grade novels about African Americans in that it celebrates the urban North rather than the rural South and is authored by a black man who takes brown rather than white skin as the norm. But the book's rehearsal of all-American values—the strength of a nuclear family, the benefits of self-discipline, and the joys of consumer goods—makes it the consummate text of a multicultural, capitalist moment.

■ The Civil War has long been the starting place for understanding the nineteenth century, and from the vantage point of the early 2000s, it appears that the civil rights movement, the long-delayed fulfillment of the Civil War's promise, will become the starting point for interpreting the twentieth. K–12 students are already immersed in study of the civil rights movement's iconic heroes. During Black History Month in particular, they celebrate change: once there was slavery, now there is freedom; once there was racial violence, now there is racial harmony. Once black and white children attended separate schools, now people of diverse backgrounds study and learn together. Picture books and middle-grade novels, history textbooks and PBS documentaries, family stories and students' own experiences convince them that change has occurred. Rarely, however, do students learn how it happened and why it took so long. Nor, in most classrooms, do students grapple with the extent to which the narrative of progress we tell disguises continued inequalities and ongoing resentment and distrust.

What students don't know about the continuing struggle for civil rights and social justice can be bridged in part by examining the way progress toward these issues has been conceptualized over time. Children's historical fiction captures the stages of an ongoing project. At midcentury, white novelists created texts designed to cultivate empathy among young white readers who were assumed to view the racial other with fear, disgust, or worse. In the last quarter of the twentieth century, black authors created novels designed to delight black children and attract white readers, who were assumed to be open-minded enough to enjoy the company of black characters who seemed much like themselves. Rather than seeking white readers' empathy, these novels strived for readers' *identification with* their black characters.

Collectively, the books' arguments about race are complex and contradictory. Yet when read in classrooms, the novels are interpreted in much the same way: as reinforcing a narrative of progress in which Americans have moved toward recognizing all peoples as equal and the United States has evolved into a nation embracing multiculturalism as a core strength. This explanation is employed even when a novel's narrative thwarts such a reading. Many children, for example, read the ending of *Roll of Thunder, Hear My Cry* as predictive of future racial harmony because the final chapter features black and white farmers working together to extinguish a fire. This reading ignores the fact that the men join forces only because Mr. Logan ensures that they do.[80] By surreptitiously setting fire to his family's cotton fields, Papa endangers the white men's crop. Faced with financial ruin, the white farmers are handily distracted from their planned lynching of T.J. The scene communicates anything *but* harmonious cooperation and racial equality in the making. Instead, the book ends with the threat of raw, racially inflicted violence.

Students who read multiple novels about race written by different authors over a span of time will be less apt to apply a universal interpretation of progress to every text encountered. As they read conflicting accounts side by side, they will discover that it is not just relations between the races that have changed over time but also the way people talk about the history of those interactions. In every post–Civil War generation, narratives about slavery's legacy reveal the author's aspirations for contemporary society as well as his or her reflections on the contemporary moment. Given the gap between a historical novel's setting and composition, this in itself complicates the narrative of progress and, particularly, the conclusion that "that was then, this is now." The journey to justice is ongoing, and historical interpretations of past inequalities can stimulate action toward addressing civil rights issues today instead of reinforcing the status quo as a promise already fulfilled.

Chapter 5

Historical Fiction
in the Classroom

■ The novels whose analysis composes this book appear regularly in today's elementary and middle schools, and generally speaking, their presence in the lives of generations of American children is a good thing. As teachers attest and research supports, the books appeal to young adolescents, generating interest and excitement about a school subject, history, that usually elicits little enthusiasm. Nonetheless, the novels' mythic portrayal of Indians, promotion of a colorblind ideal, and rehearsal of a celebratory nation-state narrative are problematic. If the books are not taught critically—that is, with attention to their role in an ongoing and at times contentious debate about the American past and its meaning in the present—they can alienate nonwhite readers and cultivate among all a heritage-based collective memory of the United States. This strips history, as both a school subject and an approach to knowledge, of its significant and creative power.

How did the historical fiction that forged a middle-grade canon come to be taught in ways that largely ignore the novels' participation in contested debates about the meaning of the American past? The nationwide cohesion of curriculum—not just what books are taught, but also *how* they are taught—is not coincidental; rather, it results from a confluence of educational research, policy, and practice unfolding at all levels of government (federal, state, and local) and schooling (K–12, undergraduate, and graduate). Educational research on literacy, state processes of teacher training and certification, and in recent decades, the federally initiated standards and accountability movement have all affected the way teachers and students engage with historical novels in school. For historical fiction to figure in curricula in new ways, as aids to developing historical thinking, new priorities must guide academic research, federally mandated curricular standards, and the training and professional development of teachers. Only then can historical novels help students understand that history's very elasticity of form grants it the ability to support diverse political agendas; only then can students become critical readers of history and cultural references to the national past.

Historical Fiction in Social Studies Classrooms: Novels as Heritage Primers and "Banks of Fact"

The "expanding horizons" model for social studies curriculum currently employed in many states calls for U.S. history instruction twice in middle school (at grades 5 and 8) and state history once (at grade 4).[1] For upper elementary and middle school teachers whose professional education has emphasized the benefits of using authentic literature and interdisciplinary approaches to teaching, the thought of using a U.S. history textbook year after year is unattractive, even in the tension-filled environment of state standards and accountability. By drawing on approaches recommended in education methods courses, citing literacy research that highlights the "inconsiderateness" of textbook prose, and pointing to history pedagogy research that documents textbooks' ineffectiveness in teaching historical thinking, teachers can justify the partial or total abandonment of textbooks in favor of other instructional tools, including historical novels.[2] The historical fiction that makes up the middle-grade canon figures prominently in textbooks' replacement primarily because their settings—colonial New England, American wars, the Great Depression, the civil rights movement—correspond so well to the content of state learning standards, which favors a progress-oriented narrative of the nation-state.

Substituting fiction for a textbook, however, does not automatically transform the way history is conceived, taught, or learned. Remarkably, when historical novels are used in place of textbooks, the *conception* of history—and at times the conception of the text read—differs insignificantly. The class studies "accurate" historical novels to gain information about real historical figures (George Washington, Abraham Lincoln, Amos Fortune) and the real tasks of daily life in the past (making soap, traveling on horseback, suffering inequality). The instructional delivery system changes from textbook to trade book, but powerful factors affecting curriculum endure. Most important, teacher understanding of history as a school subject to be learned rather than as an epistemic stance to be acquired remains unaltered.

For many teachers, neither undergraduate coursework in education nor subsequent professional development or master's level education presents opportunities to scrutinize the nature of historical knowledge.

Teachers with K–6, K–8, or middle-grade certifications frequently hold undergraduate majors in education. Over a four- or five-year undergraduate program, they may have taken as few as one (for elementary education majors) or three (for middle-level education majors with a concentration in social studies) college history courses.[3] In many universities, moreover, the history courses required of education students are fulfilled by means of large introductory lectures taught through textbooks and multiple-choice tests. The instruction in these classes differs insubstantially from that most teacher candidates received in high school. The result is predictable: if prospective teachers enter an undergraduate history course with an understanding of the past as static, knowable, and absolute, the class alone will be insufficient to shift their conception of the field. Only if a history course explicitly grapples with historical thinking as a way of knowing, introducing students to interpretative puzzles, evidentiary gaps, and discrepant interpretations, will students' orientations to history shift.[4]

If introductory history courses fail to transform prospective teachers' understanding of history, so, too, do educational methods courses. Methods courses for prospective elementary and middle school teachers invariably focus on materials and instructional strategies for teaching *all* the social studies—sociology, anthropology, geography, psychology, economics, history, and political science.[5] By design, they are rooted in professional practice—that is, effective delivery of instruction—rather than in disciplinary scholarship and the nature of historical (or other disciplinary) knowledge.[6] It is within the context of these multidisciplinary, pragmatically focused courses that pre-service teachers are empowered to break from the tyranny of the textbook and explore innovative ways to meet state social studies standards. Historical novels, therefore, emerge as pedagogical tools in an environment unmoored from questions about the nature of history and historical narrative.

As products of such education programs, many elementary and middle school teachers understand history as both irrefutable fact and heritage, a celebration of the past that, while attempting to be "accurate," privileges the creation of memory that fosters identity, patriotism, and personal pride.[7] School instruction built around the concept of heritage—which highlights those aspects of the past that a community treasures and wholeheartedly embraces—looks profoundly different from school lessons rooted in the concept of disciplinary history.[8] A heritage-based approach to the past assumes a static, knowable, *objective* history, one that can and should be embraced by all participating in a common culture or tradition. The hallmark of a historical approach to the past, by contrast, is *questioning*: asking not only what happened but also why it happened (and why we know it happened), how people understood what was happening, and who was affected—and in what ways—by the event. The process, which is acknowledged as imperfect, involves searching for evidence, scrutinizing conflicting sources, building an argument, subjecting the analysis to review, and revising conclusions after taking into consideration new questions, new perspectives, and new evidence. Throughout, there is an understanding that the past is knowable only through the lens of the present, a refracted vision always subject to change.

The historical novels composing the classroom canon are often used to facilitate history-as-heritage—a static, patriotism-infused relationship to the past. They frequently serve this end even when teachers use them as springboards for student research on the historical actors and events figuring in the novels, tasks that *appear* to match the work of professional historians.[9] Central to this process is an understanding of historical fiction as being like the history textbooks it replaces; the novels, like the textbooks, are understood to capture "truth." An individual historical novel typically enters the middle-grade canon in part because book reviewers praise it as both exceptionally crafted and historically "accurate." The reviewers' very language reveals underlying assumptions that history is objective, neutral, and uncontested—that it is, in short, heritage. There is considerable interpretative diversity among the historical novels judged accurate by book reviews, but historical novels can foster history-as-heritage regardless of whether they present a top-down or bottom-up interpretation of historical change. Student identification with the iconic figures and events peopling war novels (for example, Paul Revere, the Delaware Crossing, the Gettysburg Address) can foster patriotism, but so too can identification with the collective and unnamed citizens remembered solely for their deeds (taming the wilderness, weathering the Great Depression, marching for civil rights).

The similarity between classroom projects developed around novels with iconic characters and top-down understandings of historical change and those developed around novels with average historical characters and bottom-up understandings of historical change sheds light on the process. Students participate in a "Pioneer Day" or reenact the hiding of a fugitive slave (alternatively, a fugitive slave is hidden *during* Pioneer Day). They build model log cabins or host a local Native American who talks about enduring (that is, timeless) cultural traditions.[10] They reenact the Second Continental Congress or stage a Revolutionary War campsite. They research Civil War generals or write reports on grassroots civil rights heroes. Each of these activities celebrates heroic deeds and lives purposefully led. Each strives to unite students around a common set of historical figures, behaviors, and values associated with a healthy nation-state. History in this scenario is knowable (we can reenact it, re-create it, look it up), consensual (traveling to unknown places, fighting for what one believes in, and preserving one's heritage requires bravery and dedication), and positive. Such relationships to the national past differ substantially from that of professional historians. For discipline-based scholars, the past is frustratingly unknowable and at times bafflingly complex. Far from harmonizing, historical narratives are understood as powerful social and political tools that reflect authorial perspective and divide as frequently as they unite. The "facts" of history and the *uses* of those facts cannot be disentangled.

Not all teachers who elect to use historical fiction in their social studies classes do so with the intention of forging a common cultural heritage. In fact, some teachers attuned to the importance professional historians place on evaluating authorial perspective in historical documents (primary sources) and historical narratives (secondary sources) embrace historical fiction precisely because they recognize its potential to teach students about point of view. Unlike their colleagues who use novel extension projects to further heritage-based history instruction, these instructors design projects with the express intention of cultivating disciplinary-based skills in history. They encourage students to think about the perspective of the novels' protagonists, who normally represent the dominant viewpoint (for example, Union soldiers, Anglo-American settlers, nonviolent civil rights demonstrators), and contrast it with that of minor characters, who frequently voice alternative or conflicting views. These teachers are cognizant of the fact that the range of vantage points present in fiction generally exceeds that present in textbooks, facilitating student discussion about perspective.

Nonetheless, there are severe limits to exploring perspective through literary characters alone. Unless students interrogate the positioning of the text itself—not just the characters *in* the text—they fail to read as professional historians do, with attention to context and subtext.[11] It is precisely at this juncture that many middle-grade students and their teachers get stuck. This is understandable; the educational resources teachers rely on to select historical novels for study emphasize over and over again the books' historical accuracy instead of the books' historical argument. Understanding a historical novel as presenting "fact" rather than "interpretation," teachers create curricular projects mired in heritage even when they have sought out historical novels for the purpose

of cultivating the disciplinary-based skills of identifying and contextualizing perspective.

A teacher-created "webquest" designed as the culminating project
for Elizabeth George Speare's *The Witch of Blackbird Pond* provides a
window into this phenomenon.[12] Created by award-winning gifted education teacher Ruth Sunda, "Consider the Source: Evaluating Source Reliability through the Study of *The Witch of Blackbird Pond*" is among
the most sophisticated webquests available on any historical novel; it
appeals to students' imagination, poses challenging historical questions,
and scaffolds the process of historical investigation. The webquest's historical lessons build on the literary theme of character bias and motivation introduced in *Witch of Blackbird Pond*'s climax, the moment when
Kit stands accused of witchcraft in part because she is a foreigner and
Anglican. The webquest asks students who have thought about the fictional character's dilemma to consider the prejudice latent in the actions
of historical peoples (real-life, seventeenth-century witch accusers) and
the narratives of twenty-first-century websites describing life in colonial
New England. In setting these tasks, the webquest complicates the notion
of history as "fact"—a simple, objective account of what happened.

The instructions and student resources provided, however, reveal an
intriguing gap in application. The issue of bias and reliability as a general
concept and as a *particular* concern of historical research is conflated and
the disciplinary goal of recognizing source bias compromised by heritage
and presentism—that is, viewing the past through the eyes of the present.
The webquest reads,

> The journey across the Atlantic was a challenge, and life in early New
> England was difficult. We'll look at the reasons for these pilgrimages,
> and the harsh realities of what these brave families found waiting.
> Freedoms were hard-earned. In Elizabeth George Speare's novel,
> *The Witch of Blackbird Pond*, the heroine, Kit, discovers that life in
> Connecticut Colony has many hardships. She also endured false
> accusations of being a witch. But who were these accusers? Were they
> credible witnesses? How can you know what information is reliable?
> Along our voyage through this WebQuest, we'll learn how to ask
> questions before making a decision, and how to "consider the source"
> or evaluate the reliability of an information source.

The webquest divides students into four groups, each with a specific
task. The Reliability Consultant is charged with becoming "an expert on

determining source reliability"; the Star Witness with preparing a defense for the accused witch, Quaker Hannah Tupper; the Puritan Speech Writer with composing an address to encourage Englishmen to emigrate to Connecticut Colony; and the Loyalist Pamphlet Distributor with writing a broadside to convince Englishmen to remain in England. The group names reveal pedagogical goals designed to cultivate disciplinary-based skills in historical analysis: evaluating sources (Reliability Consultant), considering how perspective shapes narrative (Puritan Speech Writer/ Loyalist Pamphlet Distributor), and scrutinizing point of view (Star Witness). In practice, however, the tasks encourage the kind of ahistorical and uncritical thinking characterizing history-as-heritage.

Students in the Puritan and "Loyalist" (note the ahistorical term) writing groups are directed to engage in research, acquiring the historical details and linguistic voice necessary to approximate seventeenth-century documents. Links to museum, public television, and heritage organization websites are provided. Additionally, students are directed to three primary source documents: a letter from a (miserable) indentured servant to his parents in England (1623), an indentured servant's reflection on his passage from Holland to the New World (1750), and a transcript of proceedings from the Salem witch trials (1692). Notably, the primary sources cover vastly different time periods and geographic areas (Dutch *and* English colonies, Massachusetts *and* Pennsylvania). While a tip sheet on how to evaluate sources is provided, the information needed to properly assess primary sources—who is the author? when and why was the document written? how and why was the document preserved?—is not.[13] In fact, the two indentured servant sources include only the author's name, a date, and a web address. An involved search, discouraged by the webpage formatting, would be needed to even assure that the documents are authentic.[14] The targeted pedagogical goal of determining reliability, then, is understood not as the historical skill of evaluating sources for perspective, bias, and authenticity, but rather as an issue of student behavior. Students are expected to produce a pamphlet that is "reliable" because it draws from teacher-approved sources of historical information, information that is equated with "fact." In this framework, history remains heritage: uncritical, un-debatable, and associated with patriotism.

If the creative writing tasks above illustrate the continued vision of history as knowable and objective, the Star Witness task highlights the dominance of presentist thinking. To prepare testimony on behalf of accused witch Hannah Tupper, students are provided with transcripts of the Salem witch trials. Reliability is again the theme. Given that the circumstances, religion of the accused, and geographical setting of *Witch of Blackbird Pond* differ from that of 1692 Salem, one might expect students to consider how the Salem record could be useful in preparing a defense of Hannah. Instead, the webquest prompts students to read the Salem transcript ahistorically: "For several years in the late 17th Century . . . people were accused of being in league with the devil for absurd reasons like: '*When his shadow fell on me, I cut my finger with my knife.*' . . . Think about the actual witnesses in terms of how UN-reliable they were. . . . What characteristics or circumstances of the Puritans may have made them unreliable sources?" (italics in original). As this line of questioning makes clear, trial evidence is to be judged unreliable if it fails to conform to twenty-first-century ideas of rational thought. Yet the ministers who presided at Salem carefully weighed evidence, judging some data permissible and others not.[15] The webquest dismisses out of hand the standards the Puritans themselves used. Absent the attempt to understand the worldview of seventeenth-century colonists, however, historical actors can't be deemed "reliable" or "unreliable" witnesses by twenty-first-century researchers; the rules of historical discourse disallow it. Given the framing of the webquest's question, students can only conclude that those who believed in witches (that is, learned and uneducated seventeenth-century Anglo-Americans alike) were stupid.

A central strength of historical fiction as curriculum is that it allows adolescents to scrutinize historical narrative as a construction. A novel like *Witch of Blackbird Pond* can be a reliable source of information on seventeenth-century domestic life but an unreliable source of information on seventeenth-century political ideology. It can be a reliable source of information about the way critiques of McCarthyism appeared in children's literature in the 1950s but an unreliable source of information about the proceedings of seventeenth-century witch trials. The task of determining reliability, then, is more complicated than it initially appears. To effectively wrestle with the issue, students must be involved in inquiry-based research that encompasses *both* the historical setting of the novel *and* the historical (or contemporary) setting of its publication. Such investigative work enables students to "do history" while *also* realizing the moral and political power inherent in shaping narratives about the past. But teachers can guide students in such intellectual work only if they themselves understand the way historians frame questions, read texts, and conduct research. The current system of educating elementary and middle school teachers leaves most classroom instructors far short of these skills.

Historical Fiction in Language Arts Classrooms: Novels as Tools for Tapping Student Ideas and Teaching Empathy

Historical fiction frequently appears in elementary and middle schools to supplement or replace social studies textbooks. Because historical novels have captured a disproportionate number of literary awards and are frequently recommended by curriculum experts, however, English language arts teachers have turned to them as exemplary texts as well. In part, this trend stems from the fact that regardless of whether or not they are certified to teach social studies, most K–8 teachers understand the subject as being central to character education. They want students to respond emotionally to stories of people in the past, identifying with renowned leaders and empathizing with mistreated victims. The professional identity of K–8 educators, which is tied to the teaching of students rather than to the teaching of academic subjects, encourages teachers to incorporate social studies, a subject area associated with civic virtue, when appropriate.[16]

Educational researcher and scholar Linda Levstik exemplifies this phenomenon in both her intellectual lineage and her current position as the foremost advocate for both literature-based social studies instruction and historical fiction's utility in engaging children with ethics and "the possibilities of human behavior."[17] Now a professor of curriculum and instruction at the University of Kentucky, Levstik completed a PhD in education at Ohio State, where she was mentored by social historian Robert Bremmer and leading children's literature scholar Charlotte Huck. Levstik's doctoral thesis analyzed historical children's literature, considering the books as markers of social history and useful tools for social studies instruction. Her intellectual grounding in elementary education and faculty appointment in a department of curriculum and instruction, however, prompted Levstik to shift her focus slightly in subsequent research, exchanging textual analysis of literature for qualitative research that sought to capture and analyze students' ideas as they interacted with historical narratives. Her initial classroom-based research, Levstik explained, was stimulated by questions about "the breadth, depth, [and] accuracy of the history that readers encountered [and] recalled in the process" of reading biographies, historical literature, and historical fiction. This work was informed by literacy and cognitive research as much as, if not more than, by theories of history and historical thinking.[18] In its primary focus on student ideas rather than text, Levstik's research is less attuned to the way children's books restrict what is possible for students to think while reading, particularly given their limited knowledge of history and exposure to historical thinking. In this regard, Levstik's scholarship—like much classroom-based research—mirrors (and helps reproduce) the classroom practices in which it is generated.

This phenomenon is evident in Levstik's writing about moral issues, which she has found to form "students' understanding of the object of studying history." Because children associate moral decision making with the personal and particular, Levstik has argued that students better understand a fictional character's decision to join the Patriot cause or assist a fugitive slave than they do the political, military, or economic explanations for the related behaviors of writing the Declaration of Independence or issuing the Emancipation Proclamation, topics frequently presented in history textbooks.[19] This research both supports and confirms language arts teachers' own beliefs about why historical novels make good instructional tools. Yet there is a critical weakness to this claim: children may be emotionally engaged by the actions of a fictional character in ways they are not by a textbook, but they need just as much assistance understanding the *import* of a fictional character's behavior as they do understanding textbook explanations of historical significance. In endowing their fictional characters' behavior with moral and political significance, historical novelists make characters' thoughts and actions constitute historical argument.

In Mildred Taylor's novel *Roll of Thunder, Hear My Cry*, Cassie Logan believes that she, her family, and her black community will ultimately transform the Jim Crow South, bringing social and political equality to Mississippi. In Harper Lee's *To Kill a Mockingbird*, Scout Finch trusts that her father and other liberal-minded southern lawyers (all white) will bring justice to Alabama, eradicating generations of bigotry. Both novels are set in the Deep South during the Great Depression, and the fictional characters' differing beliefs about how change will occur are rooted in their author-creators' time, place, and personal convictions. The characters' actions—for example, Scout's ability, by means of childhood innocence alone, to disperse an angry white mob gathering against what it disparages as her "nigger-loving" father—are guided by these beliefs and help build the author's historical, as well as moral, argument.[20] Levstik's research suggests that adolescents would be strongly attracted to both *Roll of Thunder* and *To Kill a Mockingbird*, as each pivots on questions of ethical and moral behavior. The two books make quite distinct arguments about how the civil rights movement generated change, however. Adolescent readers need assistance not only in extracting this argument from the narrative but also in identifying it as such.[21] In taking seriously the ideas students derive from historical narratives, researchers and teachers alike must consider how the constraints of a particular narrative shape the range of views possible.

In many language arts classrooms, teachers' instructional practice makes clear the high value placed on student ideas derived from fiction reading. When the authentic literature movement reshaped conceptions of the purpose and form of students' interface with books, K–8 language arts was profoundly influenced by Louise Rosenblatt's reader-response theory, which understands meaning as adhering not in a text itself, but rather in the interactions between text and reader.[22] In grade school classrooms, this thinking informed the creation of literature circles, peer discussion groups designed to foster students' ability to discuss a literary work and its connection to their lives in meaningful ways, with minimal teacher prompting. The image of a teacher standing to elucidate the meaning of a novel was to be replaced by that of students huddled around a text, discovering meanings together.[23] Many teachers who sought to transform their classrooms in this way found the ideal difficult to achieve in practice. Students new to literature circles—and perhaps new to the concept of reading for pleasure—struggled to spontaneously connect what they read to their own lives or other texts. Responding to this challenge, educators Susan Zimmermann and Ellin Oliver Keene identified specific strategies for teaching students to activate prior knowledge and trigger emotional responses to texts. In language later widely adopted in elementary and middle-grade curricula, they described student connections as taking one of three forms: text-to-self, text-to-text, and text-to-world.[24]

Historical fiction's elevated place in language arts classrooms has ensured that it figures prominently in literature circles. The historical novel's identity as both literature and interpretative history, however, poses analytical challenges for students because the genre lays claim to two ways of knowing. As fiction writers, historical novelists assume the right of artists to create characters and convey through their imagined personalities truths about both a particular landscape and the human condition more generally. Historians, however, contend that human behavior, feelings, and worldviews, far from being universal, are in fact shaped by the particularities of time, place, and culture.[25] Historical novelists understand this. Despite their best efforts to minutely document and describe the world in which their characters live, work, and love, they acknowledge the past that their characters inhabit as inherently foreign. As a genre, then, historical fiction straddles the history-fiction divide. This makes the standard reader-response approach employed in classrooms especially difficult. Students' efforts to connect a work of historical fiction to themselves, their (contemporary) world, and realistic fiction almost inevitably result in ahistorical, presentist thinking.

When teachers ask students to respond to historical fiction (and occasionally nonfiction) by making text-to-self comparisons, both teacher and student conceptualize the narratives as primarily literature, not history. Students seize on the similarities between themselves and the historical actors depicted. When they find gaps between their lives and those of the historical actors, they fall back on familiar narratives of progress (e.g., we're smarter now than people were in the nineteenth century) and nationalism (e.g., such practices would never take place here, in the United States) to explain them away. The educational philosophy behind text-to-self connections is that students need encouragement to see themselves in a text, to empathize with characters. As works of historical interpretation, however, historical novels caution against this very identification. Sam Wineburg, a researcher interested in the intersection of cognition, pedagogy, and historical study, explains: "'Presentism'—the act of viewing the past through the lens of the present—is not some bad habit we've fallen into. It is, instead, our psychological condition at rest, a way of thinking that requires little effort and comes quite naturally."[26] This perspective—widely shared by historians—challenges the logic articulated in educational literature. It suggests that students don't need help finding themselves in historical novels or nonfictional histories; rather, they need help understanding just how foreign the world depicted therein is.

In a participant-observer study of a sixth-grade classroom using a literature-based approach to the social studies, Levstik recorded a conversation in which a student who read Anne Frank's *The Diary of a Young Girl* confidently asserted, "I would have run away! Why didn't they run away?" The book, which was the student's first encounter with Nazi-occupied Europe, triggered empathy for Anne and European Jews more generally. The student's exclusive focus on the individual, however, led her to "blame the victim" rather than identify how social and political institutions radically different from her own curtailed the Franks' options. By contrast, a student reading a nonfiction trade book about the Holocaust journaled, "I don't understand how this could happen! It's like prejudice against Black people." This student made a sophisticated text-to-world connection, recognizing the parallel race-based prejudice in America and Nazi Germany. Drawing on knowledge of history across time and space, the student displayed movement toward a historical question: what combination of ideology,

racialized law, and institutionalized practice enabled the dehumaniza-
tion of a people at different points of history in different social and political contexts? The middle schoolers' different responses did not derive
from different modes of writing (diary versus nonfictional history). Another student responding to the same nonfiction book about the Holocaust wrote, "The book made me glad I live here, and not back then.
I'm lucky."[27] The comment, of course, reveals the student's conflation of
historical time and geographical (or national) space, and thus an ahistorical approach.

What made one student successful in interacting with a text historically while others failed was awareness of additional historical contexts.
Adolescents generally lack what Denis Shemilt has called "a conspectus
of the whole of human history," a long view of the past that spans centuries and regions, enabling detection of patterns and themes.[28] Without
this knowledge base, text-to-world comparisons follow the same pattern as text-to-self comparisons: they descend into ahistoricism. Students
cannot use the reader-text-world triad successfully when their points
of reference are limited to their own experiences. The reader-response
model as first articulated by Rosenblatt rests on the idea that aesthetic
and efferent responses to literature build on one another, meaning that
personal connections to text spur a reader into deeper, critical exploration.[29] As the theory has migrated into K–12 practice, however, the
movement between various aesthetic and efferent responses has often
been compromised. In emphasizing independent and peer-generated
meaning making, the reader-text-world triad has discouraged teachers
from intervening to address the important questions and *mis*readings
that students derive from their encounter with texts. This is particularly
vexing given what Wineburg has dubbed the "unnaturalness" of historical thinking.[30] Young adolescents cannot propel themselves to higher-
level analysis without access to knowledge of times and places beyond
themselves. With guidance, however, the reader-text-world triad can
provide a powerful platform for taking adolescents' ideas seriously *and*
helping them recognize the importance of genre in conducting literary
analysis.

An instruction booklet on *Witch of Blackbird Pond* illustrates the
problems that can arise when the past is viewed as transparent, but also
the possibilities that emerge when personal connections to a text serve
as a catalyst for, not the stopping point of, analysis. The guide states, "Kit
is having a difficult time finding people with whom she feels comfort-
able, and she feels disturbed by others' reactions to her. Have you ever
found yourself in a similar 'outcast' situation? Have you ever felt the

same way?"[31] The questions center on the ethical issues adolescents find appealing in historical study. By tapping into adolescent anxieties about social exclusion, they also help readers find themselves in the story of seventeenth-century Kit Tyler. This is a good start. But how deeply can a twenty-first-century person "know" what an orphaned English Barbadian transported to Puritan America felt? Kit's "differentness" from her Wethersfield, Connecticut, peers is decidedly *not* that of a twenty-first-century fifth grader who feels rejected by her classmates.[32] Kit's Anglican faith and trust in the king's decisions clash with the social norms and legal authorities of her new world; they put her very life in danger. Will students urged to make text-to-self connections realize how starkly different their lives—and problems—are from Kit's?

A sophisticated line of questioning can help bring students toward this realization. After asking adolescent readers if they have ever felt as Kit did (a text-to-self query), teachers can prompt students to consider how—and why—their situations differed from Kit's because of their profoundly different historical milieus. In other words, teachers can provide specific guidance on the kind of text-to-world connection that fosters critical reading. Examining the historical context in which Speare wrote *Witch of Blackbird Pond* would prove useful, particularly because she selected a historical setting for her story of ostracization that facilitates an argument about parallels between 1950s and 1680s America. After providing appropriate supportive materials, teachers could ask, "Who might feel ostracized in postwar New England, the period in which there was a so-called Cold War consensus?" In both the late seventeenth century and mid-twentieth century, American citizens holding a potent mixture of political, religious, and cultural beliefs out of step with the powerful majority were not merely viewed as outcasts—they were criminalized as dangerous to the body politic. With teacher guidance, this text-to-world comparison can lead students to unpack the historical—and moral—argument embedded in Speare's decision to make her protagonist not only a foreigner, religious minority, and political dissident but *also* the hero of the novel, the most "American" character of all. *Witch of Blackbird Pond* reflects Speare's belief that future witch hunts can be prevented only if thoughtful, informed citizens recognize dangerous historical reasoning reiterated in the present.

Published in 1958, *Witch of Blackbird Pond* is a product of its time. We may be tempted to read its passionate call for tolerance of all peoples as universal and timeless, but it bears the markings of its historical context: the novel denies New England complicity in both chattel slavery and violence between English settlers and Native peoples. Carefully selected text-to-text comparisons can help students recognize this. A number of twenty-first-century historical novelists have responded to Speare's subtext by writing children's books that highlight New England slavery and the English taking of Indian captives. Comparison of these narratives can lead students to comprehend the complexity associated with claims about "truthful" or "accurate" historical accounts. Cognizant of the flaws of a building-block notion of history that assumes an inching forward to truth, students should be wary of seeing new historical novels as faultless correctives to Speare's, however. These books, too, contain subtexts and cross-purposes, ones we (and their authors) might not be aware of for another half century. Ultimately, this reinforces a basic principle about reading historical fiction: it is *how*, not *what*, we read that generates historical insight.

Students' belief that the object of studying history is to explore moral issues and teachers' understanding of the social studies as key to character education point to historical novels' utility in literature-based instruction. However, given the complexity of historical fiction—which by definition is both literature and historical interpretation—students need considerable support to develop their initial readings of historical novels into critical analysis of text. Applications of reader-response theory can be useful, but only if paired with strong teacher scaffolding, which depends on teachers' understanding of historical as well as literary texts.

Novels as Tools to Teach Reading and Writing: No Child Left Behind, the Standards Movement, and Content Area Literacy

Like reader-response theory, the No Child Left Behind Act (NCLB; 2001) has significantly affected the way historical novels figure in today's classrooms. In fact, its "back to basics" thrust has in some cases swayed classroom practice away from the student-centered learning associated with reader-response theory and toward more teacher-directed instructional methods and sustained "reading practice." NCLB mandated that every student in grades 3–8 be tested in reading and mathematics every year (less frequent testing in science began in 2006); the timing of tests in other academic subjects was left to states. Consequently, NCLB demoted social studies as an academic discipline of high priority. No state tests elementary or middle-grade students in history annually, and half do not test students in social studies *at all* during the elementary and middle school years.[33] Given that performance of schools and states is measured by test scores, it is unsurprising that history has been squeezed out of the curriculum in favor of double instruction in reading and mathematics, especially in struggling or failing schools.[34] But social studies has not disappeared from classrooms. At the same time high-stakes testing devalued social studies, it elevated reading comprehension and basic literacy. Many teachers preserved history instruction by means of language arts classes and independent reading programs.

Using historical fiction to meet English language arts standards positions the novels in ways quite distinct from literature circles' emphasis on student ideas; nonetheless, the approaches yield similar results when it comes to historical understanding. In both cases, decontextualized, presentist thinking dominates. An Internet-published lesson plan on Irene Hunt's Civil War novel *Across Five Aprils* (1964) illustrates the point. Students are instructed to rewrite a letter (printed in the novel) sent by a fictional Union soldier to his family in southern Illinois; the student's rewritten version is to correct the spelling, punctuation, and grammar of the original.[35] Many state language arts standards include writing grammatically correct "friendly letters," and this assignment was undoubtedly crafted with just such a benchmark in mind. When *Across Five Aprils* doubles as a history text, however, the exercise is problematic.

The letter's colloquial language, haphazard spelling, and dialect markers situate the novel's characters in a particular time, place, and culture. These social identities are crucial to understanding the characters' beliefs and actions, including the decision of Jethro's favorite older brother, Bill, to muster with the Confederacy: "I won't fight fer arrogance and big money against the southern farmer. I won't do it. . . . I've studied this thing, Jeth, and I've hurt over it. My heart ain't in this war. . . . But if I hev to fight, I reckon it will be fer the South."[36] As a struggling but independent white farmer, Bill sees himself aligned with the agricultural South, not the urbanizing North. Slavery is conspicuously absent from his reasoning. For Bill and his historical counterparts, regional identity was of vital importance. After the Civil War, however, this identity weakened as the reconciliation between North and South gradually produced a national culture that attempted to put differences in the past. The characters in *Across Five Aprils* exemplify this process; at the book's end, young Jeth goes to college, a move that will mute the linguistic and cultural markers of region and class he carried throughout the novel. Yet even as Jeth fulfills the hopes and dreams of his rural family, education and its concomitant upward mobility will remain largely out of reach for the South's freed slaves. Their ambitions were sacrificed as a national culture was forged by means of regional reconciliation.

What does it mean for a twenty-first-century child to erase the social markers of a southern white farmer in a fictional Civil War letter? Perhaps a better question is what *could* it mean? In addition to honing skills in "correct" grammar and Standard English, this exercise could stimulate historical thinking around a range of important issues. Students might consider what Jethro would learn as a student at McKendree College, the oldest institution of higher learning in Illinois. What areas of knowledge would be valued, and what kind of teachers and students would he encounter? The fact that Jethro attends a Methodist institution, not one of the new land-grant colleges that emerged after the war, tells us that this youngest son was being educated to leave the family farm. How does this decision figure in the South's modernization, and in the ending of a predominantly agricultural economy? In addition to deepening students' skills in asking and answering historical questions, this line of inquiry complicates the assumptions implicit in notions of "correct" grammar and spelling. Without engaging in lost-cause sentimentalism, students might consider what was destroyed when a national culture (notably, one that excluded African Americans) emerged.

Just as historical novels are put to service in meeting English language arts standards, they are used as tools for reading practice aimed at raising student test scores. Under both Republican and Democratic administrations in the first decade of the twenty-first century, education policies have emphasized "reading first."[37] George W. Bush's NCLB, like the Johnson-era Elementary and Secondary Education Act before it, provided substantial funds for schools to purchase trade books. It also provided federal dollars for schoolwide literacy initiatives. All money channeled through federal coffers, however, had to be spent on programs backed by "scientifically based research," a term defined by the federal government. As a result, many schools, districts, and states turned to commercial literacy program providers who had the means, know-how, and capacity to meet federal standards.[38] Renaissance Learning is one such company; its website includes links to dozens of scientifically based studies, produced by its staff, demonstrating its adherence to federal research standards and its "proven results." Currently used in more than seventy-five thousand schools across North America, Renaissance Learning's Accelerated Reader program engages students in reading one of the more than 100,000 trade books to which it has assigned a readability score.

Each trade book included in the Accelerated Reader program has a multiple-choice "reading practice" quiz tied to it.[39] The fact-based quizzes assess literal understanding, as the program's purpose is to reinforce practice and provide feedback on comprehension. Many historical novels, including those that have been dropped from school curricula because of their representations of minority figures and dated historiography, are included in the Accelerated Reader program.[40] This is cause for concern, as the objective, fact-based nature of the Accelerated Reader practice quizzes neither encourages nor rewards students for recognizing the unstated assumptions—the subtext—embedded in books. The structure of Accelerated Reader as an independent reading program, moreover, precludes opportunities for students to discuss these discoveries with more skilled readers. Backed by research and eligible for federal funds, Accelerated Reader demonstrates how narrowly constructed conceptions of literacy shape the way students read historical novels in school.

The Discovering Literature Series novel guide for Scott O'Dell's *Island of the Blue Dolphins* brings these shortcomings into relief. Unlike Accelerated Reader, the publisher producing the Discovering Literature Series is too small to afford the high cost of establishing that its products are scientifically based on reading research.[41] Nonetheless, its guidebooks make clear its reliance on current federally approved reading research: "While many skills reinforce a student's ability to comprehend what he or she reads . . . two skills are vital. They are: discerning *main ideas* and *summarizing* text. Students who can master these two essential skills develop into sophisticated readers."[42] In the seventy-plus pages of questions and exercises that follow, students gain considerable practice in both skills. The problem, however, lies in the fact that basic reading skills are insufficient for reading literature in sophisticated ways. Nowhere in the novel guide is *Island* described as a work of historical fiction. As a result, students are never prompted to consider how O'Dell's tale is an imaginative interpretation of an actual historical figure's experiences, one that is both different from and similar to earlier and contemporary accounts written by anthropologists, journalists, and historians. Without assistance, students are unlikely to see Karana as a victim of both historical colonialism (her tribe was removed to missions in California because of the Spanish policy of *reducción*) and literary colonialism (O'Dell imagines Karana as a "girl Robinson Crusoe" despite the fact that she is a victim of imperialism rather than its benefactor). Clearly, students cannot become sophisticated readers of historical novels without considering the way they function as interpretative history with a stake in how the past is conceived in the present.

As the nation's energy and research dollars have been directed at uncovering the most scientific means to teach literacy, a group of researchers has pointed to the way reading skills are related to the context in which reading occurs. The subfield of "content area literacy" attempts to address the gap between the basic reading skills needed to decode text and the more advanced task of reading for knowledge in a particular domain such as history. Unlike research that focuses on basic literacy, content area literacy understands reading as a social act; evaluation of students' interaction with a text must take into consideration genre and a student's purpose for consulting the text. When applied to reading history in schools, however, content area literacy research has been as narrowly construed as basic literacy research; it has focused almost exclusively on the challenges textbooks present for student comprehension.[43] Textbooks remain an important delivery system for K–12 history instruction, but as the prevalence of historical fiction in middle-grade classrooms demonstrates, they are only one means by which students are introduced to study of the past. Moreover, they are little valued by professional historians. Therefore, even as literacy experts pay more attention to the different reading skills required by discrete academic subjects and their associated texts, a breach between school and academy remains. Students who become "skilled" readers of history textbooks have not become skilled readers of history.[44]

Sam Wineburg's analysis of the way Advanced Placement U.S. history students and out-of-field professional historians evaluated accounts of the Revolutionary War's Battle of Lexington makes this abundantly clear. The two research groups were presented with a collection of documents including primary sources, a textbook excerpt, and a novelistic account of the battle; they were then asked to talk out loud as they read them. Wineburg reports at length on the vocalizations of one high school student: "As I listened to and later analyzed Derek's reading of these documents, I was struck by how well he embodies many of the features of the good reader described in the education literature. He carefully monitors his comprehension and uses reading strategies such as backtracking when meaning breaks down; he pauses and formulates summaries after each paragraph; and he tries to connect the content of what he reads to what he already knows."[45] Nonetheless, Derek (like his high school

peers) ranked as "most reliable" the document the professional historians ranked as *least* reliable: the U.S. history textbook. How can we make
sense of this? Clearly, the reading skills the high school students had
mastered stopped short—substantially short—of the reading competencies essential to reading and thinking historically. When the high school
students in the study read the unmarked sources placed before them,
they didn't look for or detect the polemic of the text and they didn't infer
authorial intent. In fact, they failed to see the text itself—and not just the
content *in* the text—as requiring a critical stance.

The discrepancy between students' and historians' approach to reading points to the problem with state curriculum standards that assign
the task of critical reading exclusively to English language arts.[46] There
is nothing inherent in English as a discipline that renders it more condu-
cive than history to fostering sophisticated reading skills. In fact, in the
United Kingdom, where school history instruction is organized around
history as a discipline instead of history as a factual narrative, historical
reading skills are cultivated beginning in elementary school.[47] There *is* a
difference, however, between the literary texts assumed to form the core
of an English curriculum and the history textbooks assumed to be the
primary mode of delivering history instruction in the United States. State
standards reflect this; they match targeted student learning with the type
of text associated with the school subject, not with the practices of the
school subject's corresponding academic discipline.

The experience of reading a novel differs dramatically from that of
reading a textbook. Textbooks seek to transmit stable, predetermined
meaning to the reader; in Roland Barthes's terms, they are "readerly."
Novels, by contrast, are frequently "writerly": they allow and often require
the reader to converse with the text to draw out potential meanings.[48]
School instruction tied to the different types of text differs accordingly.
When novels are assigned, teachers ask questions about what a text says
but also about how authorial choices (regarding diction, imagery, narration, genre, and so on) shape the narrative's meaning. Teachers employing textbooks rarely pose such questions because the form of the
text—which seems to present a definitive meaning—discourages it.[49]
Textbooks hide authors' interpretative processes, eschewing hedging language, footnotes, and bibliographic essays. They also come packaged with
end-of-chapter questions, objective unit tests, and teacher editions with
"correct" answers provided. Each encourages what Bruce VanSledright
has dubbed "encyclopedia epistemology." If students are told that "the
answer is on page 15" enough times, it becomes nearly impossible for

them to imagine that textbooks contain anything but unmediated truth. The unfortunate outcome is that students learn that the critical reading skills they practice in English language arts classes do not apply to historical texts or historical questions. This might explain why historical novels tend to be read uncritically; characters' motives are scrutinized, but authors' intent is not. Nothing better captures the way history as a school subject has been stripped of its power to cultivate critical readers and thinkers, students who recognize the stakes involved in constructing narratives about the nation's past.

Bringing Change to the Classroom

The use of historical novels in today's schools represents a tremendous missed opportunity; whether they figure in social studies curricula, English language arts instruction, or as stand-alone texts in independent reading programs, they fall far short of their pedagogical potential. The current pattern of historical novels' use in classrooms stems from an array of policy decisions, research recommendations, and inherited practice at federal, state, and local levels. It is no surprise, therefore, that the path to reform must also be multifaceted. The sections below identify problem areas and potential solutions. Taken collectively, change in each domain could transform the way students and teachers engage with historical fiction, and thus with the power of historical narrative in the classroom.

Standards and Accountability

In the past decade, many educational researchers have questioned the utility of curricular standards and accountability as a means of raising children's academic achievement. Given that both Republican and Democratic presidential administrations have supported standards and accountability and that a bipartisan coalition of state governors and school chiefs initiated a movement toward Common Core State Standards, however, it seems unlikely that either will soon disappear. The question then becomes, how can historical novels be taught in ways that assist in the powerful transformation of K–12 history in an era of high-stakes testing? Pedagogy experts have wrestled with the challenge implicit in the question for years.[50] The unavoidable reality is that teaching historical thinking and history-as-inquiry is time consuming and politically contentious, and its learning outcomes are less frequently measured by standardized tests than the outcomes of teaching history as a factual narrative to be memorized.[51] Moreover, there are limits to standardized tests' ability to document the kind of historical thinking and research a student should be prompted to engage in when encountering a historical novel (or for that matter, any historical document). For real change to occur, state and federal governments must find ways to assess the performance of students, teachers, administrators, and schools that push beyond the narrow data collected through high-stakes tests.

Despite this bleak reality, the Common Core State Standards Initiative provides a fresh opportunity to think about what skills and intellectual projects should be central to a K–12 education. Thus far, the Common Core has been innovative primarily in its effort to establish nationwide unity in learning expectations. Like NCLB before it, the initiative has privileged English language arts and mathematics above all other subjects, creating draft standards for only these disciplines in its initial phase. And like preexisting state standards, it has made English language arts the primary home for defining and delivering literacy. In a promising move, however, the English language arts standards for grades 6–12 include sections on literacy in science and history/social studies. Unfortunately, and unsurprisingly, the middle school history/social studies benchmarks make the same assumptions as current content area literacy research: they presume that students learn history primarily from textbooks. Passing attention is given to primary source documents, but historical novels receive no mention, despite their widespread presence in middle-grade classrooms.

The history/social studies literacy competencies for all grade levels, moreover, fall far short of what a historical approach to any given text demands. Not until grades 9–10 do the history/social studies standards include reading for context ("cite specific textual evidence to support analysis of primary and secondary sources, attending to such features as the date and origin of the information"), and not until grades 11–12 does a (weak) hint of reading for subtext appear ("evaluate an author's premises, claims, and evidence by corroborating or challenging them with other information").[52] Yet there is strong evidence that when properly guided, children can learn as early as fifth grade to read with attention to context and subtext.[53] Acknowledging that disciplines require different reading skills is a good start, but as long as the standards continue to define literacy in narrow terms, teachers will have little incentive to devote the time and energy required to teach students to think historically. The

Common Core's position as a game changer will be significantly compromised as a result.

Teacher Training

The 2001 passage of NCLB established the expectation that every K–12 teacher would be "highly qualified," a status achieved in part through evidence of an instructor's intellectual grounding in the disciplines taught. Despite this assertion, K–12 teachers overall and elementary and middle school teachers in particular remain woefully ill prepared to teach history. At all grade levels, teachers deemed highly qualified in social studies may have their primary training in any one of the disciplines included in the social studies, even if the majority of their teaching consists of history courses. At the middle-grade level, this issue is compounded by the fact that a highly qualified teacher must gain endorsement in two subjects taught in middle schools, a requirement that in practice translates into fewer university and professional development courses in each discipline. Highly qualified teachers at the elementary level, of course, are defined as generalists; they receive minimal college training or professional development in history.

Effective history instruction and meaningful classroom engagement with historical fiction—regardless of its place in the curriculum—require rethinking the way federal law defines "highly qualified" and U.S. states educate and support K–12 teachers. Educators responsible for social studies curriculum at all levels need sufficient disciplinary training in history to read historical fiction and nonfiction critically. At most universities—the source for the vast majority of the nation's teachers—teacher training is a joint task of the college of education and the college of arts and sciences. University professors across campus thus have a shared responsibility to ensure that students majoring and minoring in education acquire the disciplinary-based skills to do their jobs well. Wherever teacher candidates encounter historical narratives—whether in children's literature courses, history department surveys, general education requirements, or methods seminars—they must be given opportunities to see historical questioning modeled and to ask, and answer, historical questions of their own. Explicit discussion of historiography as a component of a disciplinary approach to history is critical; teachers need to understand how and why historical narratives change when different questions are posed and different evidence is brought to the table. Too often, pre-service elementary and middle school teachers fulfill their history course requirements in large lecture halls where they study from textbooks and where their idea of history as an uncomplicated, fact-based narrative goes unchallenged. This is a major stumbling block to schoolchildren's early exposure to history as a meaningful, intellectually challenging, and politically charged field of study.

Educational Research

Policy makers at every level of K–12 education are increasingly turning to academic research to guide decision making. The breadth and depth of history pedagogy research published in the past decade is remarkable, but unlike research in literacy, it has barely penetrated the institutional entry points where classroom instruction is in large part determined: curriculum standards, pre-service teachers' course of study, and the collection of texts read by students. Sam Wineburg's elegant exploration of historical thinking discusses in detail the practice of reading historically, while Bruce VanSledright's groundbreaking study of fifth graders documents how ten-year-olds can learn to read and reason in the way Wineburg describes.[54] But for all the emphasis educators have placed on reading and writing across the curriculum, the assumption that reading (and writing) is a skill devoid of disciplinary context flourishes in the K–12 arena. The challenges of reading in history, science, and math continue to be described as challenges of vocabulary and genre—nonfiction versus fiction, textbook versus authentic literature—rather than of understanding the disciplines' different uses of evidence, construction of argument, and hierarchy of questions. The nationwide emphasis on "reading first" provides a platform for challenging this conception. In order to be heard in the current educational environment, however, historians must speak the language of literacy and join the conversation about what good reading looks like at every age.

Current curricular frameworks listing historical fiction among their recommended trade books understand the novels as literary texts or tools for reading practice. Titles are matched to suggested grades based on their age-appropriateness and readability as determined by the length and complexity of sentences and words. Critics of readability measures have long noted the formulas' limitations: they don't take into consideration a reader's prior knowledge and cannot measure the sophistication of ideas conveyed. Importantly, both elements are essential to determining a text's level of difficulty for *historical* reading. John Reynolds Gardiner's novella *Stone Fox*, for example, has an Accelerated Reader readability score of four and is commonly taught in third or fourth grade.

Its large print and short length marks it as a transitional text for students just beginning to move from picture to chapter books. In terms of vocabulary, sentence structure, and length, this illustrated novella is among the easiest books in the middle-grade canon. The book's relatively simple prose, however, stands in stark contrast to its complexity as a work of historical interpretation. *Stone Fox* never explains the historical issues— nineteenth-century federal land and Indian policy—behind the novel's narrative conflict. To recognize the narrative inversion of a young white protagonist figuring as an underdog trying to hold on to family land, readers must detect and analyze subtext, drawing on an understanding of social institutions in the process.

Studies of children's historical understanding suggest that many third-grade students would struggle mightily to read *Stone Fox* in this way. In a yearlong qualitative investigation of a fourth- and fifth-grade classroom, Keith Barton found that the students understood change as stemming from the extraordinary effort and achievement of individual people working alone.[55] The logic of *Stone Fox*'s narrative reinforces this belief: little Willy wins the dogsled race and the right to his family's land because he works hard, displays admirable bravery, and holds the moral high ground (all in contrast to his strong, adult, Indian foe, Stone Fox). In order to read the story as a historian would, elementary school students would need to not only read against the grain of the text but also recognize the way the narrative simplifies and distorts the causes of historical change in precisely the same way that they themselves typically do.

At what age could students read *Stone Fox* and other novels historically? Only empirical research can answer that question. A number of studies suggest that with careful scaffolding, elementary and middle school students can learn to read for subtext. At this point, however, it is unclear whether developmental barriers prevent upper elementary school students from understanding the role of social institutions in history, or whether that lack of understanding is instead a product of their limited exposure to the concept and their abundant familiarity, through textbooks, biographies, historical fiction, and mass media, with the importance of "great men and women." Most classroom-based research on students' historical understanding and on the effect of teacher instruction on students' ideas has focused on classrooms using nonfiction. Neither these studies nor those focusing on student ideas in literature-based history programs have scrutinized the historical arguments present in the texts students read. Significantly more research is needed to elucidate the ways the narratives to which students are exposed shape not only their current historical understanding but also the *possibilities* of their historical understanding at any given age or grade level. The analysis of widely taught historical novels in this book may provide a starting point for researchers interested in uniting analysis of the arguments in particular texts with the student ideas generated from reading them.

The Novelists' Craft and Professional Historians

The artistic labor of authors who write children's historical novels is far removed from the realm of educational research and policy, but as the creators of widely used curricular material—whether intentionally or not—novelists have the opportunity to positively influence classroom instruction. Many novelists have shown a marked interest in helping teachers introduce new historical perspectives to their students. In the three decades since the Collier brothers published *My Brother Sam Is Dead*, "author's notes" have become increasingly common features of children's historical novels. In these afterwords, authors often distinguish the characters, plot details, and settings that are historical from those that are partially or purely the fabrication of their imaginations. They also explain what purpose the imagined elements play in their story—how they fill in gaps in the historical record, for example, or allow the author to probe an unanswered question of historical interpretation. Invariably, the authors convey in their afterwords their own fascination with the puzzles of history, and they urge children to read more about the era depicted in the novel.

As a professional historian who also wrote fiction, Christopher Collier arguably felt a more pressing need to justify his interpretative decisions than the majority of his novelist colleagues, who generally let their books speak for themselves. Not only did Collier write an author's note for each of his coauthored historical novels for children, he also published two professional articles and a two-hundred-page collection of essays detailing his methodology.[56] Collier's efforts are exceptional, but his transparency can serve as a model for those interested in transforming K–12 education through artistic endeavors. Children's novelists frequently mention in interviews and speeches the primary sources and secondary scholarship that most influenced their stories. By making these sources widely known to readers, either by discussing them in published author's notes or by providing bibliographies on their author websites, novelists can facilitate classroom conversations about "doing history" and entering historiographical debates.

Professional historians can assist in the process as well. Classroom teachers rarely have the time or access to resources that enables them to read decades' worth of key scholarly texts on a given historical topic. Historiographical knowledge, however, is immensely useful when analyzing historical fiction because it gives readers a tool to detect the kind of arguments authors are making through their characters, action, and dialogue. If historical novelists' share with readers the secondary literature that most influenced their thinking, classroom teachers need to be able to place that literature within a larger conversation about the historical period discussed. Clear, accessible essays that trace the development of historical arguments around central questions and events in American history would equip teachers and their students with these important analytical tools. In much the same way that the Internet has made primary source material widely available to K–12 classrooms nationwide, online publishing has the capacity to render cutting-edge, synthetic scholarship accessible to teachers everywhere. As Gary Nash and others have argued forcefully, professional historians have a responsibility to bridge the gap between K–12 schools and the academy, thereby ending the "long walk" away from secondary classrooms that commenced after World War I.[57] Production and distribution of historiographical essays written for the nonspecialist are one such way they can do this.

■ During the 1980s and 1990s, while debate raged about national heroes and neglected heroines, multiculturalism and traditional values, the national press focused its attention on textbooks and the short-lived national history standards.[58] Historical novels, meanwhile, flourished quietly as teachers continued to employ them in cultivating civic identity, encouraging multicultural thinking, bolstering self-esteem, building confident readers, and developing literary taste. No one "important" paid attention to the books, which engaged students and generally avoided controversy. The same trend is apparent today. The public and scholarly neglect that has enabled children's historical fiction to prosper, however, has also limited the books' effectiveness as pedagogical tools for the twenty-first century. In the current climate of educational reform, the time might be right to bring historical fiction into the center of conversations about good reading, critical thinking, and inquiry-based research. The afterword that follows presents a vision for using historical novels effectively in today's classrooms.

Afterword

Pedagogical Possibilities

■ In the summer between my seventh- and eighth-grade years, all students in my midwestern school were required to read and write an essay about Bette Greene's *Summer of My German Soldier*. I don't remember much about the summer of 1989, but I do remember reading that book. I *hated* it. Perhaps because I knew that the essay I wrote would be the first piece of writing my new English teacher saw—and because he would be grading it—I muted my anger in the book report I submitted. Nonetheless, I can see it now as I reread the essay, saved in a basement filing cabinet along with other middle school mementos. The fury and frustration I directed at *Summer of My German Soldier* was no doubt exacerbated by the fact that I was one of only two Jewish eighth graders in my school, and this was the first book I had read about Jews in the three years I had been a student there. The novel featured abusive Jewish parents and their twelve-year-old daughter, who hid an escaped Nazi soldier. Worse yet, the book preached tolerance—of *Nazis*.

The directions for the summer reading assignment asked students to state the date of the novel's publication, but it did not ask for commentary on this fact. The central task was to write an essay analyzing the novel. My analysis of the book's protagonist read,

> As a result of being left alone most of the time, no one really
> explains the war to Patty. She gets the impression that Nazis are
> all cruel people when in fact many are nice if they have nothing
> against you. It's their cause that is so terrible. Patty becomes
> acquainted with Anton, a friendly P.O.W. who speaks English
> fluently. She can't understand how he can be nice and polite. She
> gets the impression that everyone is deceiving her when they talk
> about how awful the Nazis are.

In reading my thirteen-year-old self's words now, I think I grasped Greene's argument, although I certainly didn't know *why* she was making it. I didn't realize that the 1973 publication date offered a clue, linking Greene's argument about World War II to the Vietnam peace movement that inspired it. I only knew that the book made me uncomfortable, and that I had to express this to my new teacher in a politic way. I wrote,

> I think *Summer of My German Soldier* is a good book because
> it gives a different outlook on World War II. I have read other
> books on the subject but they all take place in Europe and most
> are about Jews in hiding. Although I think this book is interesting,
> I didn't like it very well. I didn't like any of the characters (their
> personalities not the way they were developed). It seemed like
> there was something unforgivable about all of them except maybe
> the policeman or Freddy. It's not the type of book I personally like
> to read.

My teacher barely responded to my disguised disgust: "Still, it seems that you got a lot out of it!" I'm not sure that I did. Fifteen years later, when I discovered that *Summer of My German Soldier* was still widely taught and that I therefore must consider it in my research, I was filled with dread. I still didn't want to touch the book. Had I been provided with the opportunity to critically analyze it as an eighth grader, however, I don't think I would have been haunted by the novel. When students are empowered to understand historical fiction—like all history—as narrative construction, they can engage in debate about how the past has been represented.

Toward a New Vision

The teaching strategies outlined in the tables that follow build on historical fiction's long-recognized curricular strengths. They begin with a teacher's selection of a novel of high literary quality, a book that develops students' appreciation for language, characterization, and complexity of plot. Such literature invites reader identification, thereby cultivating students' empathy for the historical actors featured and stimulating students' "need to know" about the past.[1] Historical fiction is recognized as literature in this teaching strategy, but it is read with attention to its role as interpreter of the past. History is foreign and unknowable; we moderns can only access it through the imperfect lens of the present. By supporting an approach to reading novels that attends to historical argument and historiographical influence, teachers will help students develop into readers capable of recognizing referential illusion and approaching narratives of all kinds with attention to the moral and political arguments they support. These lessons indisputably preserve school history's role in citizenship education; no skills could be more potent in a democracy.

At the same time that the recommended teaching strategies emphasize disciplinary-based skills and empower students to participate in national debates about knowledge, truth, and perspective, they reinforce familiarity with the celebratory narrative of the nation-state, thereby ensuring that it continues—at least in some form—to be part of a shared American culture. A brief examination of Revolutionary War novels demonstrates the point. Esther Forbes's Johnny Tremain rubs shoulders with the "great men" of colonial Boston: Sam Adams, John Hancock, James Otis, and Paul Revere, among others. In the small town of Redding, Connecticut, the Colliers' "Brother Sam" also knows the great figures of history; in fact, he enlists under turncoat Benedict Arnold. The protagonist of Laurie Halse Anderson's *Chains*, a New York slave girl (and sometimes spy), hears tell of Nathan Hale's "pretty speech" in which "he was sorry that he could die only one time for his country."[2] The great men take different roles in each book, but they are essential to all three. To understand the critiques of *Johnny Tremain* present in *My Brother Sam Is Dead* and *Chains*, young readers must recognize Benedict Arnold as a traitor and Nathan Hale as a hero (albeit, one whose heroism the protagonist questions). War novels are not alone in this trend; historical fiction that has gained the greatest recognition by teachers and librarians takes as its subject significant events and figures in national history. They engage the celebratory narrative of the nation-state even if they call its assumptions into question.

In the following tables, I summarize the approach to reading historical fiction adopted in Chapters 2–4 of the book. Teachers may find the step-by-step approach in these tables useful as they write lesson plans that capitalize on novels' form, structure, and argument. Note that the process outlined in the tables is iterative. In proceeding, one will undoubtedly find oneself looping back to earlier steps; this is to be expected.

Preparing to teach

Step 1: Select historical novel for potential curricular use

Rationale and procedure: Among the factors to consider: novel's setting (does it fit grade-level curriculum?), reading level, literary quality, price of classroom set. Novels with contentious reception histories or a detailed author's note providing references to primary source documents may be especially promising for classroom study.

Step 2: Gather information about the novel and its author

Rationale and procedure: Before beginning to read, make a note of the book's publication date and, if necessary, refresh memory about major social, political, and cultural trends during that period.

Locate biographical information about the author. The book jacket, websites, and reference books such as Anita Silvey's various editions of *Children's Books and Their Creators* provide useful information about authors both deceased and living. Newbery and other award acceptance speeches (available through *Horn Book Magazine*) can provide insights as well. Helpful information: where can the author be placed culturally, geographically, generationally, and politically?

Step 3: Read and annotate the novel

Rationale and procedure: While evaluating the story as a work of literature, strive to isolate and articulate the novel's historical argument. The book's subject (e.g., a particular American war, frontier settlement, racial violence) will suggest a range of interpretative possibilities. Because the historical argument of a novel is implicit rather than explicit, however, extracting it requires both focus and skill. It is helpful to be especially alert to the following:

- Appearance of historical figures—what is the protagonist's opinion of these iconic individuals?
- Appearance of canonical texts (everything from Shakespeare's plays to political pamphlets and African American classics)—do they reveal or influence the protagonist's politics?
- Historical or mythic events of national or local importance (e.g., the disappearance of Connecticut's 1662 charter, the Boston Tea Party, the Emancipation Proclamation, the Sixteenth Street Baptist Church bombing)—what significance do these events hold in the protagonist's eyes?
- Presence of racial others—how does the protagonist behave toward people different from him- or herself? Is there a gap between words or beliefs and actions?
- Historical inaccuracies, erasures, or omissions—are African slaves, indigenous peoples, or immigrants absent where historically they should be present?
- Literary tropes (e.g., the last Indian of the tribe, happy slaves, marriage between a Union soldier and Confederate belle)—does incorporation of these stock literary devices reveal the author's interest in preserving a celebratory history of the nation-state? Or is the author using familiar literary devices in ironic ways?
- Presentism—do characters hold beliefs that mirror those of today, especially with regard to race, gender, social class, and "natural" hierarchies?

Step 4a: Conduct exploratory historical research: consult primary sources and contemporary scholarship

Rationale and procedure: The critical reading process undoubtedly generated questions about historical facts, questions that historical research can answer definitively: Were there slaves in eighteenth-century Connecticut? Did college students in the revolutionary era leave their studies to join militias fighting the British? Did well-to-do girls sail from England to the Americas unescorted in the 1830s? It is not necessary to check on each historical detail, but pursuing areas of doubt can be a helpful way to begin thinking through a novel's narrative argument and historical interpretation. Often, historical omissions or the use of historically possible but improbable occurrences provide clues as to the perspective of the novel as a whole.

Remember: the goal is not to prove a novel historically "accurate" or "inaccurate." Rather, it is to determine how the combination of historical facts, authorial interpretations, and fictional inventions together produce the novel's historical argument.

Step 4b: Consider historiographical debates

Rationale and procedure: The novel's subject and theme (e.g., women on the frontier, freedmen in the rural South, apprentices during the Revolutionary War) place the book in conversation with a larger body of historical scholarship. From the moment a historical event takes place, people begin interpreting it. Over a period of decades, interpretations of that historical moment shift and points of disagreement emerge: Did frontier women experience greater or lesser hardship than their sisters back east? To what degree did freedmen have the ability to resist and transcend oppression? What role did mass protest play in generating support for the American Revolution? Familiarity with the central areas of disagreement can help place a novel within a school of historiographical thought.

If an author provides information about the primary sources consulted during the writing process, it is very helpful to read these documents and consider how the author has interpreted them. For example, Elizabeth George Speare read *A Narrative of the Captivity of Mrs. Johnson, containing an account of her sufferings, during four years, with the Indians and French* (1796) quite literally, taking what the narrative reports Mrs. Johnson seeing and experiencing at face value. Mrs. Johnson's narrative, however, is rooted in an Anglo-American perspective; Speare unselfconsciously incorporated this bias, along with the narrative's details, into her historical novel *Calico Captive* (1957).

Historiographical essays, or articles that review scholarship on a particular topic over a period of several decades, appear regularly in professional history journals (searchable through online databases). Some college-level history textbooks (e.g., Alan Brinkley's *American History: A Survey* [2009]) also contain historiographical essays on key topics. These can be excellent places to start reading. Those interested in learning more can supplement these overviews by examining the key texts mentioned. When reading historical monographs, pay particular attention to introductions and conclusions, which often spell out the author's argument and explain how and why it differs from that of earlier historiography.

Step 5: Determine student learning goals and develop final project

Rationale and procedure: After considering the particulars of each novel as well as relevant curricular goals, choose an appropriate instructional approach from the examples that follow.

Walking Students through the Project

Every historical novel has the capacity to figure within a curriculum in a range of ways that support students' growth in historical understanding. A teacher need not exhaust every angle of a particular book in the classroom. Instead, one approach can be selected for one novel, another for a different novel, and so on, each tied to a different unit of historical study. Over time, students will gain familiarity with various techniques and, ideally, draw on each as they read independently. The approaches described below share in common an appreciation of literature's unique capacity to transport readers into the disorienting world of the past. They differ in emphasis, however, highlighting three discrete (if related) tasks of historical study: "doing history" through investigative research, reading historically, and thinking historiographically.

Approach 1: "Doing History"
The Novel as Springboard for Investigative Research

This pedagogical approach can be applied to almost any historical novel, although it will be most satisfying when a book contains a mixture of actual and fictional historical figures, events, and documents, or when authors have specifically named primary sources that inspired their stories. This approach aids students in understanding that although a historical narrative's confident voice may make it *seem* definitive—the last word on what happened in the past and why it matters—it is in reality the result of research and analysis that leave considerable doubts. Students who engage with this approach will begin to understand that historical narrative does not replicate what "really" happened in the past. History by definition is interpretative. It is always open to revision.

Approach 1: Example using Scott O'Dell's *Island of the Blue Dolphins* (1960)

Step 1: Assemble classroom archive

Rationale and procedure: An archive (online or in print) makes the process of historical research more manageable and significantly less frustrating for beginning researchers. Archives can include historical maps; census reports; contemporaneous newspaper articles and advertisements; books, speeches, or laws mentioned in the text; and copies of any sources the novelist cites as inspiration for the story. Museums and historical societies have assembled packets organized around some widely taught novels. See Appendix B.

> **Example:** Archival sources could include nonfictional nineteenth-century accounts of the lone woman's life on the island, contemporary anthropological scholarship, interviews in which O'Dell discusses his research methods, and press coverage detailing new interpretations of the lone woman's life. For a list of suggested documents, see Appendix B.

Step 2: Introduce historical fiction as a genre of literature and type of historical narrative

Rationale and procedure: Explain that historical novelists, like professional historians, conduct research before writing. They strive to create settings, characters, and dialogue that could have existed in the past. Unlike historians, however, novelists have a literary license to invent people, personalities, and events that better enable them to tell their story. They may also compress time and simplify complex events for the sake of storytelling.

> **Example:** Teachers might discuss how *Island* also fits into the genre of the "survival tale." This form is a product of Western literary traditions, which raises interesting questions about its appropriateness as a model for understanding the lone woman's experience of solitude. For more on how to discuss literary tropes with students, see Approach 2.

Step 3: Support students' reading of the novel

Rationale and procedure: After assessing prior knowledge, work with students to situate the novel within a larger historical and geographical context so they can enter the world of the text: What did other parts of the United States look like at the time? What features dominated the landscape described in the book before and after the novel's action? If one population group is featured in the novel, how might other populations have experienced the same setting? Next, guide literary analysis and reader response as necessary. The aim at this stage should be students' enjoyment and understanding of the story *as literature*.

> **Example:** *Island* is set in the larger context of European colonialism and Indian removal. Karana's tribe had already felt the impact of European arrival through depleted populations and disrupted ecological systems. During the years spanning the novel's setting (1835–1853), California was contested territory, moving from Mexican to U.S. hands. Russians continued to hunt on coastal islands. In the eastern United States, the Cherokee were forced from their homelands during the infamous Trail of Tears that took place three years after Karana's isolation began.

Step 4: Present the novel as a work of historical analysis

Rationale and procedure: Upon completion of the novel, revisit the narrative with an eye toward history. A good way to begin is by having students list, in small groups or as a class, the qualities that make the book a work of *historical* fiction. Where does history appear? Ask students to consider ideas and beliefs as well as events, objects, and people. Teachers might scaffold this process by providing students with a list of historical items for one chapter and asking students to create a similar list for the rest of the book. The teacher-created webquest "Fact or Fiction: An Analysis of Historical Fiction Literature by Elizabeth George Speare" provides a good example of this technique.[a]

> **Example:** Topics that might emerge for *Island* include the following:
>
> - Spanish/Mexican missions and the policy of *reducción* (Native resettlement)
> - Russian trade in the New World and Native-European trade partners
> - Effects of European contact on ecosystems, populations, and traditional ways of life (including gender roles)
> - The power of names, name changes, and secret names
> - Karana's diet and attitudes toward animals and plants as food
> - Karana's inability to communicate with people, European and Native, with whom she comes into contact

Step 5: Model research questions

Rationale and procedure: Help students identify questions for historical investigation. For example: What (and who) in the story is real, realistic, and invented? Is the protagonist ordinary or extraordinary for his or her time? Are the protagonist's experiences ordinary or extraordinary? What questions about the past does the story leave unanswered? The class might decide which questions are most interesting or pressing and establish investigative teams to pursue them.

> **Sample questions:** Were Karana and her family members real? If so, is the account of the lone woman's years alone realistically rendered? Did the lone woman become a vegetarian? Did the attitudes toward food Karana displays in the novel exist within her culture?

Step 6: Facilitate historical research

Rationale and procedure: Direct students to use the primary and secondary sources in the classroom archive, as well as on the Internet and in local libraries, to attempt to answer the questions they have posed. Of course, students will discover that not all questions can be answered definitively—the available evidence might be insufficient or open to multiple interpretations, just as it is in real archives. The absence of pertinent information or presence of healthy disagreement about a particular incident, historical personality, or group of people may have been what led the novelist to craft a fictional story in the first place. Bruce VanSledright's "Questions Historical Detectives Ask to Solve the Mysteries of the Past" is a helpful resource for classrooms beginning to engage in research and historical thinking about the evidence found.[b]

---

[a]Kirk, "Fact or Fiction." The list appears in the "hints" section of the "process" page.
[b]VanSledright, *In Search of America's Past*, 40.

Example: Students will undoubtedly point to the discrepancy in reports about Karana's brother/son—did he even exist? They may debate the degree to which this matters. They will notice that historical evidence for Karana's actions, and especially for her thoughts, is lacking.

Step 7: Lead reflection and discussion

Rationale and procedure: After students have exhausted their resources and made the best conclusions they can, convene the class to discuss the findings, as well as the experience of "doing history." Did the process of research and interpretation lead everyone to the same place, or did readings of the available evidence vary? Which primary sources posed interpretative difficulties? This debriefing step will generate opportunities to discuss both the challenges of research and the challenges of interpretation. Ultimately, students should come to some conclusion about the degree to which the historical novel read reflects the historical record. They should also wrestle with the question of whether it matters that the narrative deviates from the evidence or invents scenarios or explanations. Why or why not? What's at stake?

Example: In the historical record, much of what we "know" about the lone woman is the result of sailors' and mission priests' interpretation of her "signs" and anthropologists' analysis of Native and European informants' description of her years after the fact. After studying the sources in the classroom archive, students might conclude that they are less confident about their ability to imagine Karana's thoughts—particularly given her distance from them culturally and temporally—than O'Dell was.

Given that the myth of the vanishing Indian has, historically, facilitated settler-colonialism, students may question O'Dell's decision to represent Karana as "the last of her tribe."

Step 8: Assign final project

Rationale and procedure: Teachers might conclude the unit by presenting students with a collection of book reviews published over a range of years. How do reviewers speak of the novel's historical accuracy? Students might write their own reviews that modify or elaborate on the criticism published.

Alternatively, teachers might ask students to write a diary entry or letter in the voice of a character, a conversation between two characters, or a sequel chapter to the book. After completing the creative piece, students should write an essay explaining the narrative decisions made: Is the writing typical or atypical of a historical actor of the character's time, place, race, class, religion, and gender? What historical models were used by the student? The essay should be accompanied by a list of primary and secondary sources consulted.

Sample assignment: The lone woman was buried under the baptismal name Juana María. A plaque erected at the Santa Barbara Mission by the Daughters of the American Revolution commemorates her life. If you could erect another plaque to stand beside the one currently in place, how might it differ from that in existence? Design the plaque and write a paper explaining your decisions. In your essay, (1) be sure to cite material from the classroom archive where appropriate, and (2) address the question, is the currently standing plaque *wrong*?

Approach 2: Looking for Argument and Subtext
The Novel as Tool for Historical Reading

This approach works best with novels tightly organized around a literary trope: for example, *Sounder*'s tale of self-making, *The Sign of the Beaver*'s "vanishing Indians," *Be Ever Hopeful, Hannalee*'s postwar marriage between North and South, and *Johnny Tremain*'s understanding of the American Revolution as a national (as well as personal) rite of passage. Students who engage with this approach will gain understanding of how narrative structures shape the way we talk about the past; in prioritizing certain themes over others, we make a story cohere. But we also downplay or ignore evidence that may complicate the analysis. Awareness of what has been omitted can make students think critically about offhand references to history as justification for ideologically motivated actions in the present.

Approach 2: Example using Theodore Taylor's *The Cay* (1969)

Step 1: Introduce historical fiction as a genre of literature and type of historical narrative

Rationale and procedure: Explain that historical novelists, like professional historians, conduct research before writing. They strive to create historical settings, characters, and dialogue that could have existed in the past. Unlike historians, however, novelists have a literary license to invent people, personalities, and events that better enable them to tell their story. They may also compress time and simplify complex events for the sake of storytelling.

> **Example:** Teachers might point out that a novel does not need to have any "real" historical figures to be classified as historical fiction. *The Cay*'s setting (World War II) is historical, and its fictional characters behave in ways appropriate to the historical time and place imagined; this makes the book historical fiction.

Step 2: Support students' reading of the novel

Rationale and procedure: After assessing prior knowledge, work with students to situate the novel within a larger historical and geographical context so they can enter the world of the text: What did other parts of the United States look like at the time? What features dominated the landscape described in the book before and after the novel's action? If one population group is featured in the novel, how might other populations have experienced the same setting? Next, guide literary analysis and reader response as necessary. The aim at this stage should be students' enjoyment and understanding of the story *as literature*.

Example: *The Cay* opens in 1942, the year after the United States entered World War II. At the beginning of the novel, Phillip and his family are temporarily living in Curaçao, a Dutch Caribbean island that served as a major depot for African slaves in the seventeenth century. The majority of Curaçao's population is of African descent. In 1942, however, Curaçao remained a colony of the Netherlands.

Phillip's permanent home is in Virginia. Like the rest of the U.S. South during the 1940s, Virginia was a Jim Crow state where racial segregation was the norm. Segregation was *also* the norm in the U.S. armed forces, even as the Allies fought a war denouncing Hitler's vision of Aryan superiority.

Step 3: Introduce the concept of literary tropes

Rationale and procedure: The stories we tell—about fictional people in books and movies and about ourselves—often adhere to formulas that help us make sense of life. The figurative language we use is familiar, comforting, and comprehensible. Using picture books, television episodes, and movie clips, present common literary tropes and help students to recognize and identify them. Tropes might include the following:

- A happily-ever-after marriage that unites warring parties
- Friendly vs. hostile Indians
- The benevolent rich patron and grateful servant (or slave)
- A poor boy who through "luck and pluck" rises to riches and respectability
- The United States as a nation that from its earliest conception spread freedom and democracy to the world

> **Example:** Teachers should draw from resources readily available in their classroom or school collections. It is not necessary to have the theme match that of the novel being studied. Rather, the central goal is to have students learn to recognize literary tropes as such.

Step 4: Scaffold identification of tropes in the novel

Rationale and procedure: Ask students to summarize (orally or in writing) the plot of the novel. Encourage them to pay particular attention to the ways the protagonist changes over the course of the narrative: What leads to his or her growth? If growth is impossible, why? Does the region (e.g., the frontier, the South) or nation-state change or remain static?

After students have arrived at the novel's argument—that is, they have detailed change over time and identified cause and effect—ask them if it matches a literary trope.

> **Example:** When *The Cay* opens, Phillip shares the racist assumptions of his parents and peers. Although the majority of Curaçao's population is black, Phillip has little contact with island natives. In no way does he see black people as equals. After he sustains an injury to the head, however, Phillip loses the ability to see at the same time he is stranded on a deserted island with a black man. As Phillip grows to trust, depend on, and ultimately love this West Indian, he stops thinking of him as "black." Race, in Phillip's view, no longer matters. Phillip has become colorblind.
>
> Colorblindness—that is, ceasing to see race—is presented as a solution to racism. It is extolled as a societal ideal.

Step 5: Reflect and discuss

Rationale and procedure: Teachers might explain that the use of literary tropes helps us make sense of the past. But it also *confines* our understanding of the past. If we told the story from another character's perspective—for example, from the point of view of the antagonist instead of the protagonist—how might the novel's argument change? What if we told the story from the perspective of a character who doesn't exist in the novel but who did exist in the historical setting the novel depicts?

Teachers might ask: Is it possible that the entire *premise* of the literary trope is just a metaphor rather than historical reality? If so, what is at stake in omitting historical evidence that contradicts the story?

> **Example:** While Phillip undergoes substantial change during the course of the novel, Timothy, the West Indian man, does not. When he first meets Phillip, he calls him "young bahss." He continues to show deference to the white boy throughout the novel, ultimately sacrificing his own life during a hurricane to ensure that Phillip survives. Phillip may come to see Timothy as a friend, but Timothy does not reciprocate; he knows that the racial hierarchy that exists—in the Caribbean and in the United States—precludes a relationship of equals. Phillip can afford to go blind, but Timothy cannot.
>
> The story of Timothy and Phillip is purely fictional. Since the 1940s, however, there has been change in the way people of African and European ancestry interact in both the United States and the Caribbean. Students might discuss the following: Was colorblindness the key to this transformation? If so, in what ways? What does colorblindness suggest about the role black people played in the civil rights movement, in bringing about change? Thinking for a moment about the present rather than the past, is colorblindness an ideal in today's society?

Step 6: Explore context of the novel's publication

Rationale and procedure: Historical fiction provides information about *two* historical time periods, the time and place in which the story is set (say, colonial Virginia) and the time and place in which the story was written (say, 1970s Texas). The latter can affect interpretation of the former. Does the historical context or the background of the author help explain the choice of literary trope? What contemporaneous national events, if any, are relevant to the history the author told in the novel? Teachers might ask their classes to investigate the intellectual history of the author: Who is he or she? How does he or she think about history? What life events may have influenced the author's perspective on the past, or on the present in which he or she wrote? Author interviews, websites, and, if time and interest permit, other books written by or about the author can be useful resources.

> **Example:** Taylor dedicated *The Cay* (1969) "to Dr. King's dream," a reference to the civil rights leader's famous "I Have a Dream" speech, which was delivered in Washington, DC, in 1963. Throughout the 1960s, American thinking about slavery was greatly influenced by historian Kenneth Stampp's book *The Peculiar Institution: Slavery in the Ante-Bellum South* (1956). Its preface includes the memorable line, "Slaves were merely ordinary human beings. . . . Innately Negroes *are*, after all, only white men with black skins, nothing more, nothing less" (vii).

The Cay, which won the Jane Addams Brotherhood Award for promoting peace, social justice, and world community, was very much a product of its time. By the late 1960s and early 1970s, however, many civil rights groups had grown frustrated with the slow pace of progress and some turned from nonviolence and interracial cooperation to violent protest and Black Power. A spokesperson for the Jane Addams award committee stated that *The Cay*'s 1969 award was "regrettable."

Step 7: Assign final project

Rationale and procedure: Pair the novel with a text that offers a competing historical interpretation of the same time and place. See Approach 4.

Example: Students could read Paula Fox's *The Slave Dancer* (1973), a novel in which the white protagonist recognizes the impossibility of friendship between blacks and whites in the midst of a slave society. Alternatively, they could read Taylor's prequel-sequel, *Timothy of Cay* (1993), a novel that attempts to address the critiques that emerged against *The Cay* in the 1970s.

Approach 3: Considering Context
The Novel as Tool for Historical Reading

This approach works best for older novels that have enjoyed a long and storied reception history, perhaps including adaptations into film and theater: for example, *The Cay, Sounder, To Kill a Mockingbird*, and *The Sign of the Beaver*. This approach builds on and extends Approach 2 by bringing even more attention to historical context and shifting historiography.

Approach 3: Example using William Armstrong's *Sounder* (1969)

Step 1: Guide students' reading for argument and subtext

Rationale and procedure: Follow steps 1–6 of Approach 2.

Example: Set in the Jim Crow South sometime between Reconstruction and the civil rights movement, *Sounder* depicts a world in which rural African Americans are largely trapped in a cycle of poverty and dependence on the white people whose land they sharecrop. Public schooling is segregated and grossly inadequate. *Sounder* employs a literary trope prevalent in American literature: a journey of self-making that culminates in literacy and respectability.

Published in 1969, *Sounder* shares a historical context with *The Cay* (see Approach 2). See Chapters 1 and 4 for analysis of the novel, its author, and the historical context of its publication.

Step 2: Support student investigation of the novel's initial positive reviews

Rationale and procedure: Ask students to read book reviews, summarizing the praise. The class might also examine and discuss the criteria award-granting organizations used to select prize-winning children's novels at the time of the book's publication.

Book Review Index Online (Gale Cengage Learning) has a searchable database of books reviewed in major journals and newspapers.

> **Example:** As a Newbery-winning novel, *Sounder* was reviewed by every major children's book editor. See, for example, 1969 reviews by *Horn Book Magazine*, *Children's Book Bulletin*, *Commonweal*, *Library Journal*, and the *New York Times Book Review*. Critics noted the heroism of the characters, commenting on their quiet stoicism in the face of cruelty.

Step 3: Support student investigation of subsequent unfavorable reviews

Rationale and procedure: Ask students to summarize the critique that emerged in the wake of the novel's awards. Consider the following: What do the detractors interpret differently from the supporters? What objections do they raise?

Critical responses may be found among alternative presses or media outlets such as the CIBC's bulletin, *Interracial Books for Children*, and Debbie Reese's blog, *American Indians in Children's Literature*.

> **Example:** Albert V. Schwartz's "*Sounder*: A Black or a White Tale? Flaws in Newbery Award Winner Obscured by Innate White Bias," published in the CIBC's bulletin, will provide much fodder for discussion. Schwartz objected to the characters' lack of resistance against racial oppression, the absence of black community in the novel, the withholding of characters' proper names, and the fact that the novel's author was white. More broadly, Schwartz disagreed with *Sounder*'s assumptions about the way Jim Crow and the legacy of slavery affected African American adults.

Step 4: Lead reflection and discussion

Rationale and procedure: What distinguishes the supporters from the detractors? Ask students to examine the time period of each review and the background of each reviewer (e.g., professional allegiances, political views, racial or ethnic identities). The differences discovered will provide *partial* answers to the question of why there are divergent views of the book. Teachers might also ask students to consider whether the two groups hold fundamentally different assumptions about the role of (children's) literature in society.

> **Example:** Members of the Newbery Medal committee and reviewers for mainstream publications viewed *Sounder* as a work of high literary quality. In describing the novel's strengths, they compared it to epic literature and Greek tragedy; it was "timeless." Many reviewers acknowledged the book's particular relevance in light of the civil rights struggle, but their reviews lingered on language, form, and character.

Schwartz's critique focused on the implications of *Sounder*'s argument in 1969, a moment when black children's writers had difficulty getting published, black youth craved intellectual role models within an African or African American tradition, and social scientists argued that black poverty stemmed largely from the failures of African American culture rather than the continuance of structural racism.

Step 5: Introduce artistic responses

Rationale and procedure: Many popular children's books are turned into films. Others spawn sequels. Still others inspire writers to create a novel of their own in response. Share one or more of these artistic responses with students. Discuss where this work fits into the larger conversation about the book and its critics.

Example: *Sounder* was adapted into a movie twice, once in 1972 and once in 2003. Both adaptations respond to the CIBC's criticism of the original novel, but they do so in different ways. Whereas the 1972 film inserts black culture and community, gives characters proper names, adds a sympathetic white character, and shows the family actively resisting racial violence, the 2003 film remains much closer to the novel. Its central point of revision comes at the end of the film: the protagonist is seen writing the novel *Sounder*, thereby transferring the book's authorship from white to black hands.

Step 6: Assign final project

Rationale and procedure: Teachers might ask students to summarize previous generations' reaction to the story, then write their own review, justifying their critical appraisal for contemporary audiences.

Alternatively, teachers might invite students to create their own artistic response to the novel, filming a key scene, writing an additional chapter, composing a graphic novel, or crafting an entirely new story set in a similar time and place. An accompanying essay would explain the interpretative choices made.

Example: *Sounder*'s film adaptations drew media attention of their own. Students may wish to read film critics' assessments of the movies in the *New York Times* or other major publications. After evaluating critics' responses to the films, students may choose to stage a scene of *Sounder*. Next, they should write a short essay explaining the artistic choices made in their staging: how does their version interpret Armstrong's novel differently from the professionally produced movies? How does their version respond to critical reviews of each of *Sounder*'s adaptations, and to reviews of the novel itself?

Approach 4: Reading Historically, Thinking Historiographically
Novel Pairings

This approach has wide utility. Pairings work best when both novels provide compelling narratives. Novels with similar settings but different historical arguments (and typically, different publication dates) or novels with different historical settings but similar subjects and historical arguments (and typically, similar publication dates) work equally well. An example of the former would be *Johnny Tremain* (1943) and *The Astonishing Life of Octavian Nothing, Traitor to the Nation*, vol. 1 (2006), both novels about the American Revolution that make radically different arguments. An example of the latter would be *My Brother Sam Is Dead* (1974) and *Summer of My German Soldier* (1973), novels about different American wars that make similar antiwar arguments. Students exposed to this pedagogical approach will gain increased understanding of historiography and the impact contemporary politics and sensibilities can have on interpretations of the past.

Approach 4: Example using Esther Forbes's *Johnny Tremain* (1943) and M. T. Anderson's *Octavian Nothing, Traitor to the Nation*, vol. 1 (2006)

Step 1: Guide students' reading for argument and subtext

Rationale and procedure: Select first novel of pair—in the case of contrasting historical arguments, the "model" narrative with the earlier publication date. Follow steps 1–5 of Approach 2.

> **Example:** *Johnny Tremain* opens in Boston on the eve of the American Revolution. The prize apprentice of Hancock's Wharf, Johnny is ambitious and presumptuous, like the American colonies themselves. Clearly, he is destined for a bright, *independent* future. Before becoming a Patriot, however, he must embrace the egalitarian values of the Revolution. Importantly, his newly acquired understanding of equality does not extend to the African slaves peopling the narrative. Given that *Johnny Tremain* appeared at a time when U.S. soldiers fought in segregated units, this is perhaps unsurprising.
>
> Published in 1943, *Johnny Tremain* draws parallels between the Revolution and World War II, interpreting both as being fought against tyranny and for the natural rights of all people.

Step 2: Repeat with second novel

Rationale and procedure: Although the task in reading the second novel is the same, students will inevitably begin comparing the books, especially if the novels share the same historical setting. Depending on the novel pairing, however, students may detect similarities more readily than differences, and they may describe both in terms of character and plot rather than in terms of *argument*. At this stage of reading, this is appropriate.

Example: *Octavian Nothing* opens in Boston on the eve of the American Revolution. Octavian lives in the Novanglian College of Lucidity with his mother, an African princess. He studies classics, natural philosophy, and music. As the Revolution approaches, the college's patron dies, leaving its scholars to secure funding from Virginia planters. Unbeknownst to him, Octavian has from the beginning been the subject of an experiment to determine the intellectual capacities of Africans. With new funders, the experiment is biased toward proving his *in*equality to Europeans. Octavian learns firsthand the hypocrisy of Patriots who speak of liberty and equality at the same time they hold slaves in bondage.

Published in 2006, *Octavian Nothing* emerged in the context of the War on Terror and scrutinizes the American rhetoric of liberty.

Step 3: Bring the novels together

Rationale and procedure: Once students have had the opportunity to read and process both novels, teachers should direct students to think deeply about the authors' arguments, articulating both their overarching shape (considering literary tropes, for example) and their means of *making* the argument. Students will need to gather textual evidence to demonstrate how a novel's historical argument is constructed. In *My Brother Sam Is Dead*, for example, Sam enlists in the militia under future traitor Benedict Arnold. In *Summer of My German Soldier*, a Nazi POW is the only white adult to treat the African American housekeeper as a social equal.

In the case of novels with contrasting historical arguments, students should detect the way similarities in character and plot actually point to *differences* in the authors' historical arguments.

Example: Both *Johnny Tremain* and *Octavian Nothing* are novels of revolutionary Boston. Like Johnny, Octavian has an inflated sense of self-importance and (so he believes) status as "apprentice"—he studies under the Novanglian College of Lucidity's natural philosophers and hopes to one day join their ranks. While Johnny's position changes with a burned hand that leads him to the Patriots, Octavian's changes with a brutal whipping that leads him to acknowledge his identity as a slave. Johnny doubles as a symbol for America, a nation shaped by egalitarian values and stirred by freedom; Octavian, who is excluded from the body politic and hence the war's promise, does not. When *Johnny Tremain* closes, the protagonist is positioned to muster for the Patriots. As *Octavian Nothing* concludes, the protagonist has "left the Patriots behind" (351); the sequel finds him fighting for the British.

Step 4: Explore context of the novels' publication

Rationale and procedure: Once the arguments of both novels have been outlined, teachers can help students begin to understand their origins. Divergent historical interpretations emerge when researchers ask different questions, use different evidence, or read primary sources differently. Often, a historian's own background, convictions, or milieu lead him or her to approach a topic in ways distinct from earlier scholars. In this step, students will think historiographically, seeking to understand the questions and sources underlying a particular novel's interpretation.

Teachers should make biographical information on the authors available. Accounts of any significant historical events or trends unfolding during the author's lifetime—wars, the civil rights movement, the McCarthy period, second-wave feminism—will also prove critical.

> **Example:** Forbes's interpretation of the Revolution aligns with Whig historiography; she understands the Founding Fathers to be motivated primarily by ideals—a deep commitment to political liberty, individual rights, and moral virtue. Through the character of Johnny Tremain, she explores the process of political transformation, notably the embrace of natural rights instead of natural hierarchies. Forbes is unconcerned about race; she considers the meaning of revolutionary rhetoric for a young white apprentice but not for a black slave. Forbes addresses the issue of class in *Johnny Tremain*, but in fairly narrow ways. Johnny sheds his class privilege when he learns that American Loyalists, but *not* American Patriots, are interested in their pocketbooks. Unlike the progressive historians that were her contemporaries, Forbes ignores the wealth of the Founding Fathers and the post-Independence policies intent on reestablishing natural hierarchies in the new nation.

> Anderson's interpretation of the Revolution participates in historians' ongoing debate around the question, how revolutionary was the American Revolution? The book's philosophers embrace enlightenment ideals, and yet they easily sacrifice both Octavian and the integrity of their scientific experiment in order to preserve their institution. When Octavian asks Mr. Sharpe how he can call himself a Son of Liberty, he is told that "the world . . . the real world of objects . . . is engaged entirely in commerce" (340). Money as well as ideals motivate Anderson's Patriots, and they affect Octavian as well: he "steals" himself and fights for liberty under the British.

Step 5: Lead reflection and discussion

> **Rationale and procedure:** What is gained by reading the novels together? In the case of differing historical interpretations, what "truths" does each novel capture? Are different narratives necessary to tell each story? If so, why? How does each add to an overall understanding of the historical period described, and of history as an academic discipline?

> In the case of similar historical arguments developed in different historical settings, teachers might ask students to consider the following: Does the argument work better in one setting than it does in another? Why or why not? What does the repetition of the same argument in different settings say about the power of the argument for its intended audience, and about the way history as narrative works?

> **Example:** *Johnny Tremain* provides a clear distillation of a Whig interpretation of the Revolution; through Johnny's transformation, readers gain an understanding of the principles undergirding American republicanism. Johnny grows from an arrogant, disagreeable child to a thoughtful, selfless young man. Comprehension of the principles undergirding *Johnny Tremain* enables readers to understand Octavian's disillusionment and disgust with the Sons of Liberty, his rage at the hypocrisy he sees in the "enlightened" men surrounding him. Both novels capture a "truth" about the Revolution: the power of the era's political ideology, on the one hand, and the yawning gap

between the meanings it suggested and the realities that transpired, on the other. Reading the books together reinforces the challenges historians and historical novelists face when attempting not only to capture what happened in the past but also to explain the significance of what did and did not occur.

Step 6: Assign final project

Rationale and procedure: Historical arguments about the nation and its people are adapted for changing circumstances and repeated across generations. After reviewing the historical argument made in either novel, ask the class to locate a forum in which it has been used in the recent past (e.g., by political leaders, news reporters, or artists). Teachers might ask, how do you feel about its use now that you recognize the argument as a literary trope? The discussion could conclude with students writing individual essays analyzing the way the argument figures in the contemporary source identified.

Example: Students may wish to consider the way the ideals embedded in the United States' founding documents have been used to justify military action in the twentieth and twenty-first centuries. In contemporary discourse, can they identify speakers like Johnny and Octavian?

Appendix A

Nationwide Trends in Middle-Grade Historical Fiction

■ A long history of local control over curricular decisions in the United States makes it impossible to obtain an exact measure of any one book's penetration into primary and secondary school classrooms. Even as the nation inches toward standardization in educational aims and achievement goals, decisions about how curriculum is delivered—that is, which books are taught and how—continue to be made by individual districts, school faculties, and even single teachers. We can't create a definitive list of the most widely taught novels in the middle-grade curriculum, but we can track nationwide trends.

More than 10 percent of U.S. states—Alaska, California, Indiana, New York, North Carolina, and Massachusetts—publish on their Department of Education website lists of fiction titles or, in the case of Massachusetts, authors that the state endorses or that classroom teachers within the state use and publicly recommend. Many states, both those with and without recommended reading lists, also specifically encourage teachers to select trade books that have won major children's literature awards. The Common Core State Standards in English Language Arts, which a majority of U.S. states adopted in 2010, provides a short list of illustrative texts for each grade level.

Publication of children's book titles in multiple formats offers an additional gauge of circulation. The creation of a motion picture based on a children's book documents a title's popularity—the book helps sell the big-screen or made-for-TV film—as does a book's recording as an audio book or translation into Spanish (both suggest use in school settings as these formats support the learning of special-needs populations). The Internet also provides a tangible if inexact measure of a book's classroom use, leaving a trail of student and teacher projects on particular novels as well as their queries for academic help or professional assistance. Websites like SparkNotes.com and PinkMonkey.com have responded to student demands for comprehension aids by providing in-depth summaries and analyses of particular middle-grade novels, a service that attests to a book's assignment in classrooms. Finally, museums' development of successful school-group programs centered on a particular children's book suggests wide readership of the novel in the geographic region of the museum.

Sales numbers provide additional insight into a book's use in schools. *Publishers Weekly*'s list of the all-time best-selling children's books documents the significance of particular titles over the period of their print life. This system of measuring popularity favors older titles; however, *Publishers Weekly*'s longitudinal data can be compared to up-to-the-minute (literally) sales rankings on Amazon.com, the largest North

Book	State list				
Across Five Aprils		CA	IN	MA NC	
Amos Fortune, Free Man	AK	CA			NY
And Then What Happened, Paul Revere?[a]		CA		MA	
The Astonishing Life of Octavian Nothing, Traitor to the Nation, vol. 1[b]					
Ben and Me: An Astonishing Life of Benjamin Franklin by His Good Mouse Amos[a]	AK	CA	IN	MA	NY
The Birchbark House[a]		CA		MA	CC[c]
Bud, Not Buddy		CA		MA	CC
Caddie Woodlawn[a]	AK			MA	NY
The Cay		CA	IN	MA NC	NY
Chains[b]					
Charley Skedaddle	AK				
A Day No Pigs Would Die[a]				NC	
Dragonwings[a]		CA		MA	NY CC
Esperanza Rising[a]		CA			
Fighting Ground		CA		MA	
A Gathering of Days[a]		CA		MA	
The Island of the Blue Dolphins			IN	MA	NY
Sequel, *Zia*	AK	CA			

American book retailer. Amazon sales records demonstrate that a book like *Island of the Blue Dolphins*, which ranks sixth on *Publishers Weekly*'s list, does so not only on the strength of long-ago sales; during the summer of 2010, the novel consistently ranked around 1,500 on Amazon's current list of best-selling books (adult or child).

Books that do not appear in the following table might merit checkmarks in a number of the criteria boxes. They might also enjoy great popularity in a particular school district, region, or state. However, they have not consistently surfaced in ongoing searches of children's literature spaces, online and on the ground, in the past ten years.

Best-selling children's paperback ranking	Newbery	Other major award	SparkNotes	Other student-centered reading guide or presence on paper-mill website	Movie adaptation	Museum program	Accelerated Reader	Audio book	Sequel	Spanish translation
		X	X	X	X		X	X		
	X			X		X	X	X		
							X	X	X	
		X					X	X	X	
					X		X	X		
				X			X	X	X	
	X	X		X			X	X		X
	X			X	X		X	X	X	
57		X		X	X		X	X	X	X
		X					X	X	X	
		X		X			X	X		
			X	X			X	X	X	
		X		X			X	X	X	
				X			X	X		X
		X		X			X	X		
	X			X			X	X		
6	X		X	X	X	X	X	X	X	X

Continued on next page

Book	State list					
Johnny Tremain	AK	CA	IN	MA NC	NY	
Journey to Topaz[a]		CA		MA		
The Light in the Forest	AK			NC		
Little House on the Prairie[a]		CA	IN	MA	NY	
Lyddie[a]		CA	IN		NY	
My Brother Sam Is Dead	AK	CA		MA	NY	
Rifles for Watie[b]						
The River between Us		CA		MA		
Roll of Thunder, Hear My Cry		CA	IN	MA	NY	CC
Sarah, Plain and Tall[a]		CA	IN	MA	NY	CC
Sarah Bishop[a]	AK			MA		
The Sign of the Beaver	AK		IN	MA	NY	
Sing Down the Moon[a]	AK			MA		
The Slave Dancer	AK		IN	MA		
Sounder	AK		IN		NY	
Stone Fox		CA	IN	MA	NY	
Summer of My German Soldier	AK	CA	IN	MA	NY	
To Kill a Mockingbird	AK	CA	IN	MA	NY	CC
Turn Homeward, Hannalee						
The Watsons Go to Birmingham—1963		CA	IN	MA		
The Winter People[b]				MA		
The Witch of Blackbird Pond		CA	IN	MA		

a. Indicates books that have been widely adopted but which, for reasons of thematic organization, are not discussed in depth in *Child-Sized History*. In a number of cases, these books have received critical attention from other scholars.

b. Indicates books that at the time of this printing had not penetrated school curricula nationwide. These titles are included in this study because they illustrate new directions in children's and YA historical fiction that may soon enter and influence the classroom canon or, alternatively (in the case of *Rifles for Watie*), approaches that have been eliminated or muted in the canon as currently composed.

c. The Common Core State Standards (CC) for English language arts provides a short list of illustrative texts, only ten or so titles for each grade category (K–1, 2–3, 4–5, 6–8, 9–10, 11–12). The list is also aspirational, including a number of titles that are not currently widely taught.

Best-selling children's paperback ranking	Newbery	Other major award	SparkNotes	Other student-centered reading guide or presence on paper-mill website	Movie adaptation	Museum program	Accelerated Reader	Audio book	Sequel	Spanish translation
16	X		X	X	X	X	X	X		
				X			X		X	
NA	NA		X	X	X		X	X		
12				X	X	X	X	X	X	X
				X	X	X	X	X	X	X
		X	X	X		X	X	X	X	
	X						X	X		
		X		X			X	X		X
80	X		X	X	X		X	X	X	X
45	X			X	X		X	X	X	X
							X	X		
101	X			X	X	X	X	X		X
	X			X			X	X		
	X			X			X	X		X
94	X		X	X	X		X	X	X	
72				X	X		X	X		X
		X		X	X		X		X	
NA	NA	X	X	X	X		X	X		X
				X		X	X		X	
	X	X		X			X	X		
							X	X		
22	X			X		X	X	X		X

Notes: States that as of 2010 made lists of trade books publicly available on their Department of Education websites include Alaska, California, Indiana, Massachusetts, New York, and North Carolina. Alaska, New York, and North Carolina preface their lists with the caveat that the books are not meant to be "recommended" or "required" but rather are compilations of titles that have been deemed effective by teachers within the state. Indiana notes that the list is "designed as a companion piece" to the state's English Language Arts Standards, but that it is not meant to be all-inclusive. Massachusetts, which lists authors rather than individual titles, recommends books actively: "Knowledge of these authors, illustrators, and works in their original, adapted, or revised editions will contribute significantly to a student's ability to understand literary allusions and participate effectively in our common civic culture" (Massachusetts Department of Education, *English Language Arts Curriculum Framework*, 100). California uses similar language, emphasizing that district book selection policies should be used in connection with the state's list of "recommended literature." The North Carolina list is for English I, ninth grade, exclusively.

"Other major award" includes the Newbery Honor, Printz Award for Young Adult Literature, National Book Award for Young People's Literature, Scott O'Dell Award for Historical Fiction, and, for adult literature, Pulitzer Prize.

Publishers Weekly data for all-time best-selling children's paperbacks is as of 2000. *Publishers Weekly* does not distinguish between picture books, middle-grade novels, and crossover titles (which attract child and adult readers alike) in its ranking. Thus, the historical novels above are measured against toddler classics like *Goodnight, Moon* and *Where the Wild Things Are* as well as the books in the Harry Potter series.

Ten- to fourteen-year-olds use the Internet for school assignments at a significantly higher rate than five- to nine-year-olds according to the most recent U.S. Department of Education statistics. This may explain the absence of SparkNotes and other online study guides for books like *Stone Fox, Ben and Me, And Then What Happened, Paul Revere?, Little House on the Prairie, The Birchbark House,* and *Sarah, Plain and Tall,* which are commonly assigned at the third-grade level (National Center of Educational Statistics, "Digest of Educational Statistics" [2007], table 414, *nces. ed.gov/programs/digest/d07/tables/dt07_414.asp*).

The Accelerated Reader program was used by nineteen thousand U.S. schools and 6.2 million students in 2010. Many of the titles listed in the chart above were among the most popular books read during the 2009–2010 school year. *Stone Fox* was the ninth most frequently read book among fourth graders, and *Sign of the Beaver* the tenth most frequently read book among fifth graders. *Island of the Blue Dolphins* was widely read among students in grades 4–6; it was the thirty-first most frequently read book among fourth graders, the sixteenth among fifth graders, and the thirty-fifth among sixth graders. (By contrast, the highest ranking received by *The Birchbark House* was 5,028 among fifth graders, and by *The Winter People,* 7,424 among sixth graders.) Three generations of books about race and racism show strong popularity among fifth through eighth graders using Accelerated Reader. *The Cay* ranked 83rd for fifth grade, 16th for sixth grade, 27th for seventh grade, and 80th for eighth grade; *Roll of Thunder, Hear My Cry* ranked 293rd for fifth grade, 57th for sixth grade, 24th for seventh grade, and 29th for eighth grade; *The Watsons Go to Birmingham* ranked 51st for fifth grade, 21st for sixth grade, 19th for seventh grade, and 40th for eighth grade. War novels were also widely read through the Accelerated Reader program, with *My Brother Sam Is Dead* ranking as the 25th most frequently read book among eighth graders; *Johnny Tremain* ranked 93rd and *The Astonishing Life of Octavian Nothing* 7,745th among eighth-grade students. (Statistics prepared for author by Eric Stickney, director of educational research for Renaissance Learning, 8 Sept. 2010. In author's possession.)

Thanks to Konrad Mugglestone, who assisted with initial data collection.

Appendix B

Historical Sources Discussed in Pedagogy Charts

Museum Sites and School Tours

Boston By Foot offers a 1.5-hour guided tour of downtown Boston, or "Johnny Tremain's Boston": *www.bostonbyfoot.org/tours/arrange/youth*.

Local historian Brent Colley offers classroom tours of Redding, Connecticut, and teacher workshops on incorporating *My Brother Sam Is Dead* into school curriculum: *www.historyofredding.com/HRmbsd.htm*.

The Wethersfield (Connecticut) Historical Society offers a *Witch of Blackbird Pond* program for students: *www.wethhist.org/wethersfield-education-tours.htm*.

Storyteller and historical interpreter Cathy Kaemmerlen offers a school drama program based on *Turn Homeward, Hannalee*: *tattlingtales.com*.

Classroom Archival Material for Historical Novels

The Amos Fortune Forum prints a booklet to accompany the teaching of *Amos Fortune, Free Man*. It can be obtained by contacting the Jaffrey, New Hampshire, public library: *town.jaffrey.nh.us/PublicLibrary/Public%20Library.htm*.

The Santa Barbara Museum of Natural History provides online resources in connection with *Island of the Blue Dolphins*: *www.sbnature.org/research/anthro/chumash*.

The History of Redding website provides online archival material and contemporary photographs in connection with *My Brother Sam Is Dead*: *www.historyofredding.com/HRmbsd.htm*.

The Hudson Museum of the University of Maine provides an online classroom archive to accompany reading of *The Sign of the Beaver*: *www.umaine.edu/hudsonmuseum/Beaver.html*.

The Wethersfield (Connecticut) Historical Society provides a "Teacher's Resource Kit" for *The Witch of Blackbird Pond*: *www.wethhist.org*.

Sample Contents for a Teacher-Created *Island of the Blue Dolphins* Archive

The following resources, if not available in a teacher's local library, can often be obtained through interlibrary loan:

John E. Bennett, "Our Seaboard Islands on the Pacific," *Harper's Monthly Magazine* 97, 582 (1898): 852–62.

Marla Daily, "The Lone Woman of San Nicolas Island: A New Hypothesis on Her Origins," *California History* 68, 112 (1989): 36–65.

Travis Hudson, "Recently Discovered Accounts Concerning the 'Lone Woman' of San Nicolas Island," *Journal of California and Great Basin Anthropology* 3, 2 (1981): 187–99.

Interview with Scott O'Dell in Justin Wintle and Emma Fisher, eds., *The Pied Pipers: Interviews with the Influential Creators of Children's Literature* (New York: Paddington Press, 1975), 171–81.

Joe Robinson, "Marooned: 18 Years of Solitude" and "Adrift in a Sea of Fiction," *Los Angeles Times*, 15 June 2004.

Notes

Introduction

1. Hancock, "Children's Books," 225–44; Huck, "Literature-Based Reading Programs"; Cullinan and Person, *Continuum Encyclopedia*, 645.
2. The middle school movement originated in the 1960s but gained nationwide prominence in the 1970s and 1980s. The term "middle school" remains imprecise, however, as it encompasses institutions serving a variety of grades with a range of educational practices. Middle schools nonetheless share points of convergence; during the early 1990s, 76 percent of middle schools included—but weren't necessarily limited to—either grades 5–8 or 6–8. More recently, the trend has turned toward a grades 6–8 configuration. As of the mid-1990s, about half the nation's middle schools organized teachers into interdisciplinary teams in addition to or instead of disciplinary departments. Thompson and Homestead, "Middle School Organization."
3. Marcus, *Minders of Make-Believe*, 298–303; Anderson et al., *Becoming a Nation of Readers*.
4. The American Library Association has bestowed the Newbery Medal on "the most distinguished contribution to American literature for children" annually since 1922. Receipt of the Newbery substantially increases book sales and often ensures the winning title an indefinitely long shelf life. Cosgriff, "The Newbery Awards." Since its inception, the Newbery Medal has been awarded to historical novels with great frequency. Kidd, "Prizing Children's Literature."
5. Fellman, *Little House, Long Shadow*, 177–78.
6. On high school students' dislike of history, see Loewen, *Lies My Teacher Told Me*, 1, and Rosenzweig and Thelen, *Presence of the Past*, 109–14. On educators' support of literature integration in the social studies, see Cianciolo, "Yesterday Comes Alive"; Gallo and Barksdale, "Using Fiction in American History"; McGowan, "Children's Fiction as a Source"; Hickman, "Put the Story into History"; Fuhler, "Add Spark and Sizzle"; and Savage and Savage, "Children's Literature."
7. Speare, "On Writing *The Sign of the Beaver*"; Dresang, "Interview of Joseph Bruchac."
8. See VanSledright, *In Search of America's Past*.
9. The term is Howard Zinn's. His book *A People's History of the United States, 1942–Present*, first published in 1980, has become a best seller.
10. The "expanding horizons" social studies model calls for U.S. history to be taught in fifth and eighth grade and state history to be taught in fourth grade; see Chapter 5 for a more extensive discussion of this curriculum model.

11. The Common Core State Standards Initiative, a movement originated by U.S. governors and state superintendents, seeks to replace disparate state learning standards with a set of academic standards by subject and grade shared by every U.S. state and territory. The Core Standards movement gained considerable momentum in 2010 with more than three-fifths of U.S. states adopting them. See the Common Core State Standards website, *corestandards.org*. See Chapter 1 for a discussion of state textbook adoption.

12. See Appendix A for individual titles' ranking on the 2001 *Publishers Weekly* list.

13. Children's books first published exclusively in hardback take several years to penetrate the curriculum; books enter classroom instruction only when inexpensive paperbacks are available for school purchase.

14. Appendix A presents data used to gauge popularity for each text examined in this study.

Chapter 1

1. Armstrong, *Sounder*. Lessons are drawn from two teacher-created websites: *www.aea267.k12.ia.us/curriculum/webquest02/porisch/sounder.htm* and *www.nashville.k12.tn.us/CyberGuides/sounder/teachertemplate.html* (accessed 17 Aug. 2005; no longer available). Typographical errors have been corrected for clarity.

2. On heritage, see Lowenthal, *Possessed by the Past*, and Kammen, *Mystic Chords of Memory*, esp. chapter 9. On the pervasiveness of "progress" and "freedom" as a framework for understanding the narrative of U.S. history in K–12 schools, see Barton and Levstik, *Teaching History*, chapter 10.

3. See Wineburg, *Historical Thinking*. The skills associated with reading narratives like *Sounder* as a historian would—engaging in the practices of sourcing, contextualizing, close reading, and corroborating—are discussed in greater depth in Chapter 5.

4. *Horn Book Magazine* was founded in 1924 and quickly became one of the most important sources of children's book reviews. While today's parents may consult the *New York Times Book Review* or online sources, *Horn Book* remains a central source for librarians who manage purchasing at public and school libraries.

5. Epstein, "Publishing Children's Books." Individual consumer purchases of children's books—only available in hardback—tended to cluster around the holiday season. Mass market titles such as the Little Golden Books and Stratemeyer Syndicate series books (Nancy Drew, Hardy Boys, etc.) were initially eschewed by libraries.

6. Kidd, "Prizing Children's Literature." The origin of U.S. children's literature as a distinct entity is commonly traced to the 1920s, the decade that also saw the creation of the Newbery Medal. As early as 1929, the *Historical Outlook*, a journal for history teachers, printed "The Historical Novel as an Aid to the Teaching of Social Studies"; similar articles advocating the use of historical fiction in history classrooms appeared during the next decades, well before the rise of the authentic literature movement, in *Wilson Bulletin for Librarians*, *Social Education*, *Elementary English*, *High Points*, and *Education*.

7. Kidd, "Prizing Children's Literature." On the relationship between children's librarians and children's editors, see Marcus, *Minders of Make-Believe*, and Mickenberg, *Learning from the Left*.

8. The term is Dee Garrison's, from *Apostles of Culture: The Public Librarian and American Society, 1876–1920.*

9. On the novel's short print record, see Mickenberg, "Communist in a Coonskin Hat?"

10. *Amos Fortune, Free Man* and *Sign of the Beaver* are discussed in Chapters 4 and 2, respectively. The left-leaning African American author Ann Lane Petry provides another instructive example. Her novel *Tituba of Salem Village* (1964) is still in print and occasionally appears in classrooms, but its curricular presence pales in comparison to Elizabeth George Speare's *The Witch of Blackbird Pond* (1958), a novel that shares a colonial Connecticut setting and plot device of using a witch trial to comment on McCarthy-era political persecution. Speare, who was white, did not engage in leftist political activity and in fact presented herself publicly as a model 1950s housewife. Her *Witch of Blackbird Pond*, which does surpass Petry's literarily, ranks as the twenty-second best-selling children's book of all times; Petry, meanwhile, is featured in *Recovered Writers/Recovered Texts: Race, Class, and Gender in Black Women's Literature*, edited by Dolan Hubbard. *Witch of Blackbird Pond* is discussed in Chapter 4.

11. Rollins authored the first of multiple editions of *We Build Together: A Reader's Guide to Negro Life and Literature for Elementary and High School Use* in 1941, and Baker published and updated a pamphlet, *Books about Negro Life for Children*, beginning in 1946. See Marcus, *Minders of Make-Believe*, 224–25. Pura Belpré is memorialized today by the ALA Belpré Award for a children's book authored or illustrated by a Latino or Latina. The award was established in 1996, thirty years after the similar Coretta Scott King Award for African American authored and illustrated literature, and it was not granted annually until 2009. Unlike the Newbery Medal, the Belpré Award's criteria do not specify that winning books must be written in English, an important stipulation given that Belpré initiated bilingual story hours in Harlem. Hernández-Delgado, "Pura Teresa Belpré." A significant presence of Latino characters (let alone Latino authors) in widely taught middle-grade historical fiction has yet to appear, although it seems forthcoming.

12. Ten years later, teachers and librarians would be more attuned to such linguistic markers, but most remained blind to the more subtle colonial or racist assumptions embedded in the novels they reviewed. Willett, "*Rifles for Watie*." On Keith's openness to change, see Harold Keith to editor Elizabeth M. Riley at the Thomas Y. Crowell publishing company, 6 Aug. 1956, Harold Keith Papers, Kerlan Collection, University of Minnesota, box MF 503. On Hollins, see Marcus, *Minders of Make-Believe*, 224, and Mickenberg, *Learning from the Left*, 101–2. On reconciliationist Civil War narratives, see Blight, *Race and Reunion*, chapter 7.

13. Despite significant attention to diversity, librarianship remains largely white, female, and middle class today; see Office of Research and Statistics and Office of Diversity, "Diversity Counts." The publishing industry also remains overwhelmingly white at its upper echelons, despite efforts to diversify. Since the 1960s, however, the market for children's books and types of critical reviews available in both scholarly and public forums has changed considerably.

14. C.B.G., "A Big Business"; Marcus, *Minders of Make-Believe*, 238.

15. At the time of the novel's publication, editors were concerned about length.

Crowell's Elizabeth M. Riley wrote to Keith, "We have given the matter of the book's length considerable thought. We have consulted with librarians, with parents, and with young people to see if we could not find justification for publishing the book in its present length. Unfortunately we have been told over and over that we will limit the audience if we publish a 400 page book in small type. When I was discussing the book with Mr. Crowell, I rashly said that it ought to be cut to about 90,000 words in order to make the book a length and price your young audience will accept. I am only now finding out how exceedingly rash my statement was!" Ninety thousand words would have meant cutting the original manuscript by 46 percent. A compromise of 20 percent was reached. Riley to Keith, 23 July 1956, Harold Keith Papers, Kerlan Collection, University of Minnesota, box MF 503. For an article recommending *Rifles for Watie* as a read-aloud, see Fuhler, "Add Spark and Sizzle."

16. Since the turn of the twenty-first century, critics have once again accused the Newbery selection committee of being out of touch, in part because the stylistically and thematically innovative texts chosen as award winners have proved difficult for and unpopular among child readers. Silvey, "Has the Newbery Lost Its Way?"

17. Federal money as a percentage of K–12 funding increased from 4.4 percent in 1964 to 8.8 percent in 1968 to 9.8 percent in 1980, distributed proportionately according to the number of students per district living below the poverty line. Graham, *Schooling America*, 132–39.

18. U.S. Congress, *Books for Schools*.

19. Moreau, *Schoolbook Nation*; DelFattore, *What Johnny Shouldn't Read*.

20. FitzGerald, *America Revised*.

21. Ravitch, "Thin Gruel."

22. Exceptional minority figures were also used as historical examples of a particular phenomenon—for example, scientific innovation that fueled the Industrial Revolution. This could be quite confusing because within the context of the story told, such success seemed to appear out of nowhere: the education of African Americans had never been discussed. Moreau, *Schoolbook Nation*, 264–330.

23. Ravitch, "Thin Gruel." See also CIBC, "10 Quick Ways to Analyze Children's Books for Racism and Sexism," *Director's Files*, reprinted in *Guidelines for Selecting Bias-Free Textbooks and Storybooks*.

24. Association of American Publishers, "Interactive Textbook Adoption/Open Territory Map." For a useful overview of the rationale behind and influence of state adoption policies, see Apple, "Regulating the Text"; Leahey, *Whitewashing War*; Keith, "Choosing Textbooks"; and Squire, "Textbooks to the Forefront."

25. DelFattore, *What Johnny Shouldn't Read*, 123.

26. Moreau, *Schoolbook Nation*, 310–11.

27. Poorly funded districts generally replaced textbooks every seven years. A five- or three-year cycle of textbook replacement was standard in districts with more money. Congressional representatives were surprised when they learned that most school administrators spent federal funds not on new textbooks, but rather on trade books. U.S. Congress, *Books for Schools*; Moreau, *Schoolbook Nation*, 306.

28. On the larger failures of the War on Poverty, see Matusow, *The Unraveling of America*, chapter 8.

29. Graham, *Schooling America*, 106–9; Hartman, *Education and the Cold War*, 175–86. On the ESEA's effect on the children's book industry, see Brown, "Into the Minds of Babes," 69–75, and Durell, "If There Is No Happy Ending."

30. U.S. census data did not include information about Americans of Hispanic origin until 1970; the drive for diversifying characters in children's literature was centered primarily on African Americans during the 1960s and 1970s.

31. Gibson, "The Black Image in Children's Fiction," xxiv. See also Taxel, "The Black Experience in Children's Fiction."

32. Larrick, "All-White World." Larrick was a passionate advocate of multicultural literature and outspoken critic of reading textbooks containing artificial, formulaic stories of the Dick and Jane variety; her life work captures the way calls for authentic literature and for more diverse characters, literary forms, and children's authors coalesced during the final decades of the twentieth century. Bayot, "Nancy Larrick"; "Nancy Larrick Succumbs to Pneumonia."

33. It remained difficult for new minority voices to make inroads with mainstream publishers; those who had forged relationships with publishers during the brief window of opportunity created by the CIBC and Great Society continued to be published throughout the 1980s. A new cohort of minority authors wouldn't appear in mainstream presses until the 1990s.

34. "Pooh and Pals in Paper." See also Brown, "Into the Minds of Babes," 69.

35. Scholastic paved the way for publishers' entry into the children's paperback market, but others soon followed. Dempsey, "A Second Chance—in Paperback"; Hancock, "Children's Books," 225–45; Marcus, *Minders of Make-Believe*, 242–44. The school paperback market continues to be a crucial factor in the production of children's and young-adult books with multicultural themes. See Morgan, "A Bridge to Whose Future?"

36. It is estimated that in 1950, 80 percent of first graders were encountering Dick and Jane in the classroom. Toppo, "See 'Dick and Jane'—Again"; Moran, "Dick and Jane Readers."

37. In practice, neither approach is used in such strict isolation from the other. See Chall, "The New Reading Debates," esp. 316. Reading-acquisition theorist and Dick and Jane author William S. Gray in fact suggested that beginning readers should be prompted to use a *variety* of strategies, including phonics, when confronted with a new word (i.e., using context cues; noting configuration of letter shapes; relying on structural clues such as roots, prefixes, and suffixes; using phonic clues; and finally, consulting a dictionary). Today, this is called a "blended approach," and it is widely used. Gray, *On Their Own in Reading*.

38. Flesch, *Why Johnny Can't Read*.

39. In his *Atlantic Monthly* article on the politics of elementary school reading, Nicholas Lemann described whole language instruction as spreading "like wildfire" during the 1980s; Lemann, "The Reading Wars."

40. Early critiques of Dick and Jane focused on race, but later criticism extended to the issue of stereotypical representations of gender; see Women on Words and Images, *Dick and Jane as Victims*.

41. David, *Moving Forward from the Past*.

42. Shannon, *Broken Promises*. See also Baumann, "Commentary: Basal Reading Programs and the Deskilling of Teachers," and Shannon, "Commentary: Critique

of False Generosity." On Shannon's influence, see Monaghan, "Phonics and Whole Word/Whole Language Controversies."

43. Shannon, *Broken Promises*, 78.

44. An additional eighteen states offer middle-level "endorsement," meaning that a teacher can add to an elementary or high school licensure certification to teach one or more subjects at the middle level (defined variously but including grades within the 4–9 range). National Middle School Association (NMSA), "Position Statement on the Professional Preparation of Middle Level Teachers"; NMSA, "Middle Level Teacher Certification/Licensure by State." Data is from 2007, the last time a comprehensive study of middle-level credentialing was conducted.

45. For the state superintendent's articulation of the program's goals, see Honig, "The California Reading Initiative." Interestingly, California does not offer a middle-grade licensure or endorsement; teachers are certified in either a single academic subject (enabling them to teach in a high school) or multiple subjects (enabling them to teach in an elementary or middle school).

46. Comparing the first edition of this recommended reading list to subsequent editions highlights California's attention to multicultural aims. A number of books written by Euro-American authors that were initially praised for their "multicultural" perspective and later criticized for inaccurately portraying the experience of minorities appear in early editions of *Recommended Readings* but not in later ones (e.g., Paula Fox's *The Slave Dancer*, Scott O'Dell's *Island of the Blue Dolphins*, and Elizabeth George Speare's *The Sign of the Beaver*). Classic books critiqued by antiracist critics (e.g., Carol Ryrie Brink's *Caddie Woodlawn*, Astrid Lindgren's *Pippi Longstocking*) also disappear from the list over time. California Department of Education, *Recommended Readings*.

47. Ravitch, "Thin Gruel," 19.

48. Egoff, "The Problem Novel," 356–69; Zipes, "Taking Political Stock."

49. Honig, "The California Reading Initiative," 240.

50. Home education has long been practiced as an alternative to public schooling, but it did not become legal nationwide until 1993, largely as the result of the grassroots efforts of evangelical Christians. The number of children homeschooled has increased steadily, growing from 850,000 (1.7 percent of school-age children) in 1999 to 1.1 million (2.2 percent of school-age children) in 2003 to 1.5 million students (2.9 percent of school-age children) in 2007. Religion is a factor in many families' decision to homeschool; in a 2007 survey of homeschooling parents, 83 percent cited the desire to provide religious or moral instruction as a reason for providing home education. Bielick, "Issue Brief."

51. Armstrong, *Sounder*, 59; hereafter cited in text.

52. In the boy's wanderings in search of his father's chain gang, he walks through a small town containing a "large brick schoolhouse with big windows"; he successfully avoids jeers by crossing the street and "walking close up against the hedge on the other side" (92). Later, the painted houses give way to cabins, and the boy relaxes. Here, he hugs the book he is carrying close to his body because he thinks people might "laugh," not "jeer," at him. The boy spies another school. Unlike the town children who play on swings, these schoolchildren stand outside pumping water. Race is not mentioned, but it is obvious that the country children are black, as is their elderly teacher with the white hair.

53. Armstrong, "Author Interview #69." See also Bryon, "William Armstrong's Old

Masters," which quotes Armstrong as saying, "I was writing about people's hearts and feelings. There's no color to feeling. There's no color to heart." The tide against colorblindness was turning fast, however. The Student Non-Violent Coordinating Committee (SNCC) began ejecting its white members and turning to Black Power in 1966.

54. Armstrong, "Author Interview #69."

55. This is expressed particularly clearly in Armstrong, "Author Interview #69": "The mother has learned to lose, you know, but she loses gracefully, and with nobility, simply. A lot of people can lose with a great explosion of fury. But it takes nobility to lose quietly."

56. Less generously, of course, the message could also be that black sharecroppers had the capacity to escape the cycle of poverty and degradation if they only tried hard enough, like *Sounder's* boy.

57. Brophy and VanSledright, *Teaching and Learning History*, 74.

58. Exactly what developing citizenship means can differ among social studies educators. For an articulation of the concept of teaching history for democratic citizenship, see Barton and Levstik, *Teaching History*, esp. chapter 2.

59. Sonlight Curriculum, "How Literature-Rich Homeschooling"; emphasis in original.

60. Tomlinson, Tunnell, and Richgels, "The Content and Writing of History," 53. A more technical article on the same topic appears in the *Journal of Educational Research*: Richgels, Tomlinson, and Tunnell, "Comparison."

61. Beck et al., "Learning from Social Studies Texts" and "Revising Social Studies Text"; McKeown et al., "Contribution of Prior Knowledge."

62. Cianciolo, "Yesterday Comes Alive"; Smith and Johnson, "Dreaming of America."

63. Diane Ravitch has argued that multiculturalism has two definitions, one pluralistic and the other particularistic, and that only the latter makes the concept controversial. Ravitch, "Multiculturalism" and *Left Back*. For an examination of the way "diversity" came to be embraced by political conservatives, see Hall, "The Long Civil Rights Movement."

64. The practice of modifying history textbooks to include the "heroes" of minority peoples in fact dates back at least to the 1920s, when various European ethnic groups—Italians, Irish, Jews—advocated for inclusion. Prior to the civil rights movement, however, publishers did not feel such pressure to include African Americans among the nations' heroes. See Zimmerman, *Whose America?*

65. Miller, *U.S. History through Children's Literature*; Howard, *America as Story*. In doing so, they echo book reviews published in education and library journals. The children's librarians and teachers who review historical fiction emphasize again and again the "accuracy" of the history contained in the books. I drew this conclusion after reading reviews of all novels included in this study from the time of publication until today. Periodicals and education and library journals examined include *Booklist, Catholic Library World, Chicago Tribune, Center for Children's Books Bulletin, Childhood Education, Commonweal, English Journal, Grade Teacher, Horn Book Magazine, Instructor, Journal of Adolescent and Adult Literacy, Journal of Reading, Language Arts, Library Journal, New York Times Book Review, New Yorker, Publishers Weekly, Reading Teacher, School Library Journal, Social Education, Social Studies, Teacher, Times Education Supplement,* and *VOYA*.

66. Lowenthal, *Possessed by the Past.*
67. Anderson, "Using Children's Literature," 88.
68. Barton and Levstik, *Teaching History*, chapter 11. Anderson's article specifically recommends four middle-grade novels as pedagogical tools: *The Slave Dancer, Amos Fortune, Free Man, Sounder* and *Roll of Thunder, Hear My Cry.* Each of these books, as well as critics' objections to their representation of black life, is discussed in Chapter 4.
69. Disagreement about the purpose of K–12 history instruction exists, of course, but it has been limited to debates among scholars and researchers of education. At regular intervals, it is reported in alarmist language by the media. Importantly, however, this conflict has remained largely isolated from actual K–12 curriculum, as the longevity of the middle-grade canon demonstrates. The tension surrounding national history standards in the 1990s is illustrative. The short-lived nature of the controversy only reinforces the degree to which there was more consensus than dissension about how history as a school subject should be conceived. Despite their public outcries, the harshest critics of the standards ultimately approved them after only slight revisions were made. See Nash, Crabtree, and Dunn, *History on Trial*, chapter 7, and Symcox, *Whose History?*
70. Wineburg, "On the Reading of Historical Texts"; VanSledright, *In Search of America's Past.*
71. The phrasing "access to accountability" is borrowed from Patricia Albjerg Graham, *Schooling America.*

Chapter 2

1. Byler, *American Indian Authors*, "Introduction."
2. Paris, *Children's Nature*; Deloria, *Playing Indian*. Elizabeth George Speare cited her 1920s participation in Camp Fire Girls as a formative experience in her acceptance speech for the Laura Ingalls Wilder Award.
3. "All-Time Bestselling Children's Books" (2001).
4. As M. Daphne Kutzer has argued, doing so enabled Omri to reclaim the glory of the British Empire at a time when the United Kingdom was experiencing a decline in economic and political power. Kutzer, "Thatchers and Thatcherites."
5. Banks, *The Indian in the Cupboard*, 69; hereafter cited in text.
6. Moore and MacCann, "The Ignoble Savage"; Slapin and Seale, *Through Indian Eyes*; LaBonty, "A Demand for Excellence"; Giese, "Native American Books."
7. May, *Homeward Bound*; Spigel, *Make Room for TV.*
8. Richter, *Writing to Survive*, 3, 113–14.
9. Johnson, *A Writer's Life*; LaHood, *Conrad Richter's America*, quotation p. 11.
10. Richter, *Light in the Forest*, viii; hereafter cited in text.
11. Conrad Richter to John F. Kennedy, 9 Oct. 1961, quoted in Johnson, *A Writer's Life*, 327.
12. Jaenen, "Thoughts on Early Canadian Contact," 58. Native peoples similarly questioned the costs of progress during the 1950s, the "era of termination." Federal policy aimed to remove Native people from reservations and relocate them, assimilated, into urban communities, a practice that spawned nostalgia for the past. Deloria and Lytle, *The Nations Within*; Nagel, *American Indian Ethnic Renewal*; Philp, *Termination Revisited.*
13. Dowd, *A Spirited Resistance*, 23–46.

14. On Native people's effect on the ecosystem—and the myth of "virgin land"—see Cronon, *Changes in the Land*, and Kretch, *The Ecological Indian*.
15. Berkhofer, *The White Man's Indian*, 71–111.
16. In fact, children were usually taken prisoner and would have only very rarely been scalped. Axtell, *The European and the Indian*, 207–44.
17. Slotkin, *Regeneration through Violence*, 496–506.
18. Brickell, "Narrative of John Brickell's Captivity," 54. This source is discussed in Schmaier, "Conrad Richter's *The Light in the Forest*."
19. Axtell, *The European and the Indian*, 168–207; Demos, *The Unredeemed Captive*. In the Ohio Valley, white captives strengthened newly syncretic Indian communities that contested American expansion well past the War of 1812.
20. Richter was not the first author to write about a captive who preferred to remain among Indians. Lois Lenski's Newbery Honor–winning *Indian Captive: The Story of Mary Jemison* (1941), for example, featured a protagonist who chose to remain among the Seneca. The girl does so, however, only after she learns that her biological parents and siblings had been killed during the raid on Deerfield. What was striking about True Son was his refusal to recognize where his "true" loyalty lay.
21. Richter uses approximately 180 Algonquian words in the novel. LaHood, *Conrad Richter's America*, 101.
22. Edmunds, "Native Americans, New Voices."
23. Morison to Alfred A. Knopf, 27 Apr. 1953, Conrad Richter Papers, Princeton University Library, box 15, folder 1. These same sentiments were expressed by ethnohistorians, scholars using the interdisciplinary tools of history and anthropology to reconstruct the Indian past. An article about *Light in the Forest* in ethnohistory's flagship journal argued, "Richter's novel . . . confronts the reader with the hard-to-believe but entirely genuine fact that most adopted White captives were not happy to return to White civilization. . . . Richter does more than any conventional scholar has done to bring mid-18th century Delaware-White relations into clear, three-dimensional focus." Schmaier, "Conrad Richter's *The Light in the Forest*," 372–73.
24. Alfred A. Knopf to Conrad Richter, 15 Dec. 1966, box 13, folder 1; Herbert Barr to Conrad Richter, 4 May 1953, box 15, folder 3. Both are in Conrad Richter Papers, Princeton University Library.
25. In addition to its ahistorical, racially deterministic thinking, the novel features an African American slave who is a redeemed captive; he equates True Son's "confinement" in Paxton with his own enslavement. In contrast to the freedoms he and True Son enjoy in Indian Country, he argues, everything in white society is equally enslavement. The claim is problematic. After the American Revolution, Pennsylvania's Act for the Gradual Abolition of Slavery (1780) called for slaves to be freed by their twenty-eighth birthday. That the elderly basket maker may not have lived to see freedom only reinforces the likelihood that he would understand his confinement as utterly different from True Son's: he was chattel, whereas the boy was in control of his own destiny.
26. Speare wrote her last children's book for her grandsons. Unlike its 1950s predecessors, *Sign of the Beaver* features a male protagonist. The two female characters, sisters of protagonists Matt and Attean, however, are described as "spunky" (134).
27. "All-Time Bestselling Children's Books" (2001).

28. *A Visit with Scott O'Dell* (Boston: Houghton Mifflin, 1983). On *Harper's* as a source see Tarr, "An Unintentional System of Gaps," 70. For a bibliography of articles on the lone woman, see Woodward, "Juana María." Magazine accounts differ, but the "fact" that she jumped overboard to rescue a child left on the island does not appear before the 1880s. Robinson, "Marooned: 18 Years of Solitude"; Heizer and Elsasser, "Original Accounts of the Lone Woman."

29. Archeologists now believe that the lone woman spoke a language belonging to the Takic linguistic family (Uto-Aztecan stock), whereas Natives gathered at the Santa Barbara Mission spoke languages from the Chumash family (Hokan stock). Lightfoot, *Indians, Missionaries, and Merchants*, 30–48; Santa Barbara Museum of Natural History, "The Lone Woman of San Nicolas Island."

30. Nidever, "Life and Adventures of a Pioneer," 21; Woodward, "Juana María." The famed ethnologist and linguist John Peabody Harrington interviewed Chumash peoples who were alive when the lone woman arrived in Santa Barbara; the 1970s processing of Harrington's extensive notes unearthed details unavailable when *Island* was published. See Travis Hudson's articles in the *Masterkey*.

31. Quoted in Robinson, "Adrift in a Sea of Fiction." Sources published since the 1980s reveal few new details about the lone woman's life. For research conducted post-1960, see Morgan, "Account of the Discovery of a Whale-Bone House"; Hudson, "Recently Discovered Accounts"; and McCawley, *The First Angelinos*. An exception is Daily, "Lone Woman of San Nicolas Island"; Daily suggests that the lone woman was not indigenous to the island, but rather relocated from the north (Kodiak or Aleutian Islands) as part of the sea otter trade.

32. O'Dell, *Island of the Blue Dolphins*, 182; hereafter cited in text. Many of the eighteenth-, nineteenth-, and early twentieth-century stories available to O'Dell also describe the lone woman as a Crusoe figure.

33. O'Dell wanted Karana to be an agent of change, transforming a world "where everything lived only to be exploited, into a humane and meaningful world." O'Dell, "Adventure with Memory and Words."

34. At least at some level, O'Dell recognizes that Karana's relationship to the island should differ from Crusoe's given that it is her natal home. When Karana's brother Ramo acts in Crusoe-like ways, declaring, "I am now Chief of Ghalas-at. All my wishes must be obeyed" (44), he is fatally attacked by wild dogs, a punishment exacted, perhaps, for acting the part of conqueror rather than conquered.

35. Maher, "Encountering Others," quotations p. 216.

36. O'Dell describes Karana's death in the sequel, *Zia*, published many years later, in 1976.

37. Historical records suggest that the lone woman's community arrived safely in California; however, when the lone woman was brought to the mission eighteen years later, none could be located. In *Island*, the implication that they perished is strongly suggested by the ambiguous detail Karana reports; when she asks (through signs) what happened to the ship that had taken her people away, Father Gonzales tells her that "this ship had sunk in a great storm soon after it reached his country," which explained why no one came back for her (180). Did the ship sink before or after the people disembarked? If after, why didn't survivors insist on Karana's rescue? The ambiguity leaves many, Maher included, to assume that all of Karana's people perished. Maher, "Encountering Others."

Island's sequel, *Zia*, alters this assumption, but the ambiguity remains. Karana's niece states that her brother and aunt (Karana) are "the last of my kin" (20). Zia's deceased mother had married a man outside the Ghalas-at community.

38. Wintle and Fisher, *The Pied Pipers*, 179.

39. See McGirr, *Suburban Warriors*, for a discussion of the political context in which O'Dell wrote.

40. Wintle and Fisher, *The Pied Pipers*, 171–81.

41. In discussing the Newbery Honor book *Sing Down the Moon* (1970), which features a Navajo protagonist, O'Dell quipped, "I'm not interested in the Navajos particularly—they're not my favorite tribe even. They were marauders." O'Dell's grammar and tone suggest that the Navajo were extinct; yet, at the time of the 1974 interview, the Navajo were the second-largest Indian group in the United States; they had decidedly not vanished, which might explain why they struck O'Dell as distasteful. Wintle and Fisher, *The Pied Pipers*, 174–75.

42. Wintle and Fisher, *The Pied Pipers*, 174–75.

43. European contact with the indigenous population of the Channel Islands dates to at least 1542, with Russian hunters, accompanied by Alaskan Natives, arriving on San Nicolas sometime between 1811 and 1825. By the nineteenth century, San Nicolas's indigenous population had declined from several hundred to twenty or fewer. McCawley, *The First Angelinos*, 3–9, 202–20; Heizer and El-sasser, "Original Accounts of the Lone Woman," 3; Lightfoot, *Indians, Missionaries, and Merchants*.

44. Tarr, "An Unintentional System of Gaps," 62, 70. Others have made similar claims, suggesting that adherence to some Western perspectives and stereotypes works in *Island* but not in other novels. Schon, "Master Storyteller and His Distortions"; Stott, "Native American Narratives," 46.

45. *Island* had sold 400,000 copies in thirty-two hardback editions at the time of O'Dell's death in 1989. The thirty-third hardback edition appeared one year later, in celebration of *Island*'s thirtieth anniversary. "Scott O'Dell, Children's Author, Dies"; McDowell, "Scott O'Dell."

46. Speare, *Sign of the Beaver*, 1; hereafter cited in text.

47. Speare, "The Survival Story."

48. Smith, *A History of Maine*, 263–64. Speare changed the boy's name and lowered his age to make him more accessible to readers. Her decision to move the story back in time (from 1802 to 1769) most likely stems from a desire to place the action before the Revolution, thereby creating an American New England free from indigenous peoples. Speare, "On Writing *The Sign of the Beaver*" and "The Survival Story."

49. On the sixteenth century, see Kupperman, *Indians and English*, 117–20; on the seventeenth and eighteenth centuries, see Lepore, *In the Name of War*. In *Sign of the Beaver*, Matt and Attean's comparison of flood stories (prompted by Matt's reading of Noah) reflects observations of colonial figures such as Roger Williams, Alexander Whitaker, and Andrew White, who argued that Indians had "distant recollections" of the Judeo-Christian past.

50. Speare, "The Survival Story."

51. The Native characters' stereotypically cinematic speech has been a source of critique. Maine's Indians had traded with Europeans since the mid-seventeenth century. While the Penobscot formed kinship ties with the French, they were

increasingly dependent on trade relations with the English following the end of the French and Indian War. Seale, "The Sign of the Beaver"; MacDougall, *The Penobscot Dance of Resistance*.

52. Slotkin, *Gunfighter Nation*, 10–16.

53. Matt is invited to play games, a boyhood equivalent of war, and acquires a black eye, deliberately delivered: "It was no accident, [Matt] knew. . . . These boys were putting him to the test" (102). The description of the village life, including the sign of the beaver as a territorial marker, derive from anthropologist Frank Gouldsmith Speck, *Penobscot Man*, esp. 47, 175–76, 206. Speare discusses this source in "The Survival Story."

54. In his musings, Matt admits that he now understands the decisions of white people who, captured by Indians and adopted into families, decided to stay rather than return to the society of their birth. But he insists that "it wouldn't be the same to make that choice deliberately" (114).

55. West, *The History of Milo*. According to local histories, Theophilus Sargent was given the honor of naming the town.

56. Kertész, "Skeletons in the American Attic"; O'Brien, *Dispossession by Degrees*.

57. Thoreau, *The Maine Woods*, 8, 179.

58. Brooks, *The Common Pot*, 247–52.

59. Thoreau, *The Maine Woods*, 140. Joe Polis, Thoreau's guide during his final trip in Maine, also shares characteristics with Speare's fictional Attean, particularly in his role as nature and survival instructor. In a 1993 interview, Speare cited an "ancient tombstone" on a reservation in Oldtown, Maine, as the source of her character's name Attean. Speare, "On Writing *The Sign of the Beaver*."

60. Speare, "The Survival Story," 168. Speare herself was part of the process of Anglo-Americans "becoming Native"; her ancestry dates to the colonial period on both the maternal (New England) and paternal (South) sides, and her husband's family traces its ancestry to the Massachusetts Bay Colony. See Schwebel, "Rewriting the Captivity Narrative." When Speare accepted the Laura Ingalls Wilder Award for "a substantial and lasting contribution to literature for children" in 1989, she said that children often asked her if she had any Indian friends: "I wish I could answer that I do, but the state of Connecticut where I live long ago did a very thorough job of obliterating Native Americans." Today, it is obvious that Native culture may have been hidden, but was far from obliterated. The Mashantucket Pequot and Mohegan tribes are highly visible in Connecticut, thanks in part to thriving casinos. Speare, "Laura Ingalls Wilder Award Acceptance Speech." Yet by the time Speare wrote *Sign of the Beaver*, she was primed for potential criticism. In an unpublished interview given in 1989, Speare said she made Attean a member of the Penobscot Beaver clan because a professor in Maine had told her that clan was extinct: "I thought I'd get in less trouble that way." Elizabeth George Speare, interview by Marilyn Fain Apseloff, Easton, Connecticut, 18 July 1989 (recorded CD in author's possession).

61. Hudson Museum of Maine, "Curriculum Connection." The word "squaw," now viewed as a racial slur, likely originated as an English derivation of several Algonquian words referring to women and females. Its negative connotation emerged in a colonial context in which women, especially nonwhite women, assumed a lower social status relative to white men. MacDougall, *The Penobscot Dance of Resistance*, 33.

62. Seale and Slapin, *A Broken Flute*; Oyate, "Books to Avoid: *Sign of the Beaver*"; Reese, *American Indians in Children's Literature*. See also Bradford, *Unsettling Narratives*, 125–27.

63. Paisano, "Population Profile of the United States."

64. Nagel, *American Indian Ethnic Renewal*, 9–10.

65. Lynne Reid Banks titled the sequel to *The Indian in the Cupboard*, in which Little Bear returns to Omri's cupboard to be brought back to life, *The Return of the Indian*. The name of this section derives from that title. The Indians who return in children's literature of the 1980s and 1990s do so in forms both mythic and historic.

66. Gardiner, an engineer who wrote children's books as an avocation, pays tribute to Andrew J. Galambos, a libertarian who lectured widely in the Los Angeles area during the 1960s and 1970s, "for the many ideas and concepts of his, based on his theory of primary property and the science of volition, that appear in this book." *Stone Fox*'s message parallels that of the popular Little House series, whose uncredited coauthor, Rose Wilder, was also a libertarian. In her book *Little House, Long Shadow*, Anita Clair Fellman tracks the waning presence of the Little House books in elementary school curriculum because of their portrayal of Indians; it is ironic that *Stone Fox* rose to take their place.

67. Copies of all relevant treaties are available on the Eastern Shoshone tribal website, *www.easternshoshone.net*.

68. Prucha, *The Great Father*, 1172–79; Volmann, "Survey of Eastern Indian Land Claims"; Campisi, *The Mashpee Indians*; *Drumming Up Resentment*; Wilkinson, *Messages from Frank's Landing*.

69. The town doctor's gender is a nod to Gardiner's contemporary readers.

70. Gardiner, *Stone Fox*, 38–39; hereafter cited in text.

71. Beginning in 1906, implementation of the 1877 Dawes Act established individual ownership of land even on reservations, part of the U.S. government's attempt to detribalize Indians. Stamm, *People of the Wind*, xiii, 241–42.

72. McNulty, "Children's Books for Christmas."

73. Scholarship on the Indian boarding schools is vast. Dates of school closings, as well as the degree to which schools assailed Native heritage, differed by tribe. The boarding school legacy, particularly as manifest in parenting and in language and culture loss, persisted for generations after closure, however. Womack, Justice, and Teuton, *Reasoning Together*, 11–12.

74. Stott, "Native American Narratives," 46. That is not to say that Natives didn't write novels prior to the end of the twentieth century; they did. But throughout the 1970s and 1980s, Native authors such as Michael Dorris (Modoc) wrote that "there is no such thing as 'Native American literature,' though it may yet, someday, come into being." Dorris, "Native American Literature," 147. Consensus had shifted by the beginning of the twenty-first century, with most critics asserting that a distinctly Native literary tradition, a tradition that included novels, existed.

75. Simon J. Ortiz articulated the authenticity of the Native novel in his landmark article, "Towards a National Indian Literature: Cultural Authenticity in Nationalism."

76. For a historical overview of these efforts, see Tjoumas, "Native American Literature for Young People." The lack of children's books by Native people is reflected

in early compilations of recommended books: Stensland, *Literature by and about the American Indian*, and Lass-Woodfin, *Books on American Indians and Eskimos*. Byler, *American Indian Authors*, which recommends only works written by Native authors, is a rare exception.

77. Bruchac's Penacook protagonist tells his English teacher, who assigns Speare's *Sign of the Beaver*, that the author was wrong in concluding that Indians "vanished" from New England. Bruchac, *Heart of a Chief*, 19–21.

78. Rogers, *Journals of Major Robert Rogers*, 129. This discussion of *The Winter People* draws on the more extensive textual analysis presented in Schwebel, "Rewriting the Captivity Narrative."

79. In particular, Bruchac is in conversation with *A Narrative of the Captivity of Mrs. Johnson, containing an account of her sufferings, during four years, with the Indians and French* (1796), Kenneth Roberts's, *Northwest Passage* (1936), and Elizabeth George Speare's *Calico Captive* (1957).

80. Bruchac, *The Winter People*, 6–7; hereafter cited in text. The Indian who gives warning was part of Rogers's party, but he had once lived at St. Francis and was an unwilling accomplice to its destruction. He ends up shot in the back, four times, for his treason.

81. Roberts, *Northwest Passage*, 238–39.

82. Just as Joseph Conrad was Scott O'Dell's literary model, Chinua Achebe, the Nigerian author best known for *Things Fall Apart* (1959), was Bruchac's. In fact, Achebe advised Bruchac's dissertation, "Border Crossings." Innovative in language and form, *Things Fall Apart* tells the story of African colonization from the Nigerian perspective just as Bruchac's *Winter People* tells the story of American colonization from the Abenaki perspective. See Achebe, "An Image of Africa."

83. The practice of conceptualizing enemies as animals is a common trope in colonial literature and not unique to Indians. Saxso's use of animal imagery, however, comforts and strengthens him more than it serves to demonize racial others.

84. General Assembly of the State of Vermont, Bill S.117, section 853(c), 3 May 2006; "State of Vermont's Response to Petition for Federal Acknowledgment of the St. Francis/Sokoki Band of the Abenaki Nation of Vermont," Dec. 2003.

85. Massachusetts recommends Bruchac as an author for their Pre-K–2 and 3–4 categories but not for their 5–8 category (Laura Ingalls Wilder and Carol Ryrie Brink, however, are listed for 5–8); Massachusetts Department of Education, *English Language Arts Curriculum Framework*. California recommends four Bruchac titles, three for grades 3–5 and one for grades 6–8; California Department of Education, *Recommended Readings* (2009). New York recommends one Bruchac book under its "folklore" category in both 3–5 and middle school; New York State Department of Education, *English Language Arts Resource Guide*, 10, 27. Indiana recommends one Bruchac picture book for grades 3–5 and Bruchac's poetry (but not historical fiction) for grades 6–8; Indiana Department of Education, *Indiana Reading List*.

86. Nagel, *American Indian Ethnic Renewal*, 237–45.

87. Weaver, Womack, and Warrior, *American Indian Literary Nationalism*, 16; Treuer, *Native American Fiction*, 4.

88. Oyate, "Frequently Asked Questions" ("Would you please review my manuscript because I don't want to make any mistakes?"), *www.oyate.org/faqs.html* (accessed

11 Oct. 2009; no longer available). Beverly Slapin, cofounder of Oyate and formerly its executive director, wrote a highly critical review of Sharon Creech's *Walk Two Moons* that was published on Oyate's website; it stands in stark contrast with the review published in *MELUS*: Stewart, "Judging Authors by the Color of Their Skin?"

89. Reese, "Reviewing Children's Books for Major Journals," posted 23 Jan. 2008 on *American Indians in Children's Literature*; Kauanui, "For the Seventh Generation," interview with Debbie Reese.

90. In other words, the "pluralistic" rather than "particularistic" vision of multiculturalism, to borrow Diane Ravitch's terms, has dominated. See Chapter 1, note 63.

Chapter 3

1. Researchers have documented some deviance from this standard narrative among members of racial and ethnic minorities, particularly when interviews have been conducted outside schools or other institutional settings. What is remarkable, however, is the degree to which Americans at large have adopted this framework of the narrative, what Peter Novick characterizes as "the defense of freedom," and Keith Barton and Linda Levstik as "the story of national freedom and progress." Novick, *That Noble Dream*, 333; Barton and Levstik, *Teaching History*, chapter 9. On the impact of racial and ethnic diversity on the story of U.S. history told, see Epstein, "Deconstructing Differences," and Rosenzweig and Thelen, *Presence of the Past*.

2. Demarcations of generation are never exact; books published during a later time period may adhere to an earlier generation's ethos for a variety of reasons, including an author's coming-of-age during an earlier period. With less frequency, a book written during an earlier generation may anticipate later developments. See note 32 below for an example of the latter.

3. First-generation children's war novels use literary devices well established in adult fiction. Kammen, *A Season of Youth*; Blight, *Race and Reunion*.

4. Melish, *Disowning Slavery*.

5. Read by generations of schoolchildren, *Johnny Tremain* inspired a Disney movie in 1957, mention on the TV show *The Simpsons* in 1993 ("Whacking Day," season 4, episode 20), and staging in children's theaters nationwide beginning in 2001. During the 2008 presidential election, Republican hopeful Michael Bloomberg cited *Johnny Tremain's* influence ("I must have read it 50 times") in the *Newsweek* cover story about his campaign (Meacham, "The Revolutionary"). The stage adaptation of *Johnny Tremain* was written by John Olive (before 9/11) and first produced in the Seattle Children's Theater in 2001. The production's ability to capture the patriotic mood sweeping the nation in the wake of the World Trade Center collapse led to stagings across the country.

6. Esther L. Forbes to Dale Warren (Houghton Mifflin), May 1942, quoted in York, "Son of Liberty," 426.

7. Forbes, *Paul Revere*; French, "*Paul Revere*"; Forbes, "Acceptance Paper," 249.

8. A number of details can be found in both books: Johnny's craftsman mark, for example, mirrors Paul Revere's, and Johnny's master Mr. Lapham shares much in common with Revere's father's master, Mr. Coney.

9. Forbes's writing emphasizes what Peter Novick has called "the defense of free-dom as the thread which wove American history together." Novick, *That Noble Dream*, 333. On progressive historians, see Beard, *An Economic Interpreta-tion*. SparkNotes identifies "class" as a central motif in *Johnny Tremain*, thereby reinforcing Forbes's argument that American leaders of the rebellion were *not* influenced by economic interests.

10. Quoted in Bales, *Esther Forbes*, 1.

11. Erskine, *Esther Forbes*, 21–22.

12. Forbes, *Johnny Tremain*, 218, 250; hereafter cited in text.

13. In the same way that Johnny represents America, Isannah Lapham, the youn-gest daughter of Johnny's master, symbolizes England. Weak and sickly, she is adopted by Lavinia Lyte and turned into a plaything whose behavior associates her with the mother country's decadence and loss of virtue. At the novel's end, Isannah departs for London with Lavinia (who is engaged to a lord), where she will be trained as an actress, a profession associated with promiscuity (230–32).

14. "I want nothing of them. Neither their blood nor their silver. . . . Mr. Lyte can have the old cup" (164). For a fascinating discussion of silver as a recurring mo-tif in the novel, see Rubin, "Silver Linings."

15. Johnny's literacy is critical to his transformation. His first post-injury job is with the *Observer*, and he reads pamphlets and John Locke at the printing office when he is not delivering the papers (96). On the importance of pamphlets in estab-lishing the ideological justification for war, see Bailyn, *Ideological Origins*.

16. Similarly, Johnny's egalitarianism does not extend to Native people. Like his real-life historical counterparts, Johnny "plays Indian," to borrow Philip Deloria's term (*Playing Indian*), as he participates in the Boston Tea Party.

17. Forbes, "Acceptance Paper."

18. Esther Forbes to Ruth Boyd, n.d., reprinted in Erskine, *Esther Forbes*, 27–30.

19. Vollstadt, *Understanding Johnny Tremain*, 9.

20. Roberta Seelinger Trites argues that such novels of adolescence are a post-modern phenomenon. Coming-of-age bildungsroman narratives, standard in the nineteenth century, have been largely replaced by novels of development in which adolescents gradually recognize the limits of their power in a repressive environment seeking to shape and control them. Second- and third-generation war novels largely fit this pattern. Trites, *Disturbing the Universe*.

21. Novick, *That Noble Dream*, 71–86, 234–39, 354–60; Newman, "Writing the History"; Turley, "By Way of DuBois." On the aggression of first-generation chil-dren's war novels, see MacCann, "Militarism in Juvenile Fiction."

22. Wade Collier, *The Colliers of Massachusetts* (2004, 2009); James Lincoln Collier to Wade Collier, 6 Apr. 2000, reprinted in Wade Collier, "Notes Prepared for Sara Schwebel," 3 June 2009 (in author's possession).

23. Collier, "B [William Slater Brown]." William Slater Brown is identified as the friend and companion "B" in E. E. Cummings's book *The Enormous Room* (1922). On the Lost Generation, see Cowley, *Exile's Return*.

24. Collier, "Fact, Fiction and History," quotation p. 6; "Johnny and Sam"; and *Brother Sam and All That*. Collier envisioned students' reading of the novels being supplemented by teachers' guidance: "Let me say that the books will not teach themselves. Students will . . . need considerable guidance if they are to

fully comprehend the themes that constitute the core of the books" ("Fact, Fiction, and History," 6).

25. Collier, "Johnny and Sam," 138.

26. Christopher Collier chose Redding as the novel's setting because its historical divisions provided a means of emphasizing the brother-against-brother aspect of the Revolution as civil war. Collier, "Fact, Fiction and History," 6. Collier knew his local history exceedingly well; research notes exchanged between the brothers detail everything from parish boundaries to family names. James L. Collier Papers, Kerlan Collection, University of Minnesota.

27. James Lincoln Collier and Christopher Collier, *My Brother Sam Is Dead*, 8; hereafter cited in text.

28. Sam's radicalization at Yale is more a commentary on the 1970s than on the 1770s. Only a tiny minority of men attended college in the eighteenth century, and most Yale students continued their studies rather than enlist when war broke out. Johnston, *Yale and Her Honor-Roll*, 8–9.

29. The Colliers explain in their authors' note that a Revolutionary War soldier was "executed by [General Israel] Putnam very much as we have described the death of Sam Meeker" (215). Military executions were extremely rare during the Revolution, however, as the vast majority of condemned men received pardons. The irony that the Colliers develop, then, rests on meticulously researched but statistically rare evidence. Estimates of disciplinary executions during the war range from forty to seventy-five, mostly for mutiny, treason, or plundering. Royster, *A Revolutionary People at War*.

30. The Colliers' treatment of Indians, interestingly, does not follow this strategy of placing minority groups on the "right" side. Although described mythically as "the last Indian we had in Redding" (11), Tom Warrups—a real historical figure—fits contemporary historians' understanding of indigenous people acting out of local and individual interest in choosing (and changing) sides. In *Brother Sam*, Tim states that he "couldn't figure out which side [Warrups] was on" (67). See Calloway, *The American Revolution in Indian Country*.

31. It also differs profoundly from the narratives African Americans have historically told about the Revolution, which emphasize the war's ideological roots and cast black soldiers' participation in the struggle as the key to demanding African Americans' full inclusion in the rights of citizenship.

32. The Collier brothers' Arabus trilogy (*Jump Ship to Freedom, War Comes to Willy Freeman, Who Is Carrie?*) is an exception among second-generation war novels. Published between 1981 and 1984, the novels are ahead of their time in narrating a story of the Revolution from the perspective of a northern African American. Unlike third-generation novels, however, the central black characters align themselves with the Patriots and earn freedom from slavery. The trilogy is significantly less violent and more hopeful than the twenty-first-century narratives that follow. Literarily, the books are also somewhat weak; they never achieved the status of the Colliers' earlier *Brother Sam*.

33. On British military policy regarding fugitive slaves fleeing rebel owners, see Holton, *Forced Founders*. On the effect of revolutionary rhetoric on the antislavery movement, see Melish, *Disowning Slavery*.

34. In many ways, third-generation war novels are neo-slave narratives, stories of slavery imagined and written in contemporary times as a means of reshaping the

memory of bondage in and for the present. On neo-slave narratives, see Rushdy, *Neo-Slave Narratives*.

35. Horning, "Patriot Games," 41.
36. Anderson, *Astonishing Life of Octavian Nothing*, vol. 1, *The Pox Party*, author's note; hereafter cited in text.
37. Anderson, *Astonishing Life of Octavian Nothing*, vol. 2, *Kingdom on the Waves*. On Lord Dunmore and the Ethiopian Regiment, see Holton, *Forced Founders*.
38. Just, "Bookshelf: *Chains*." Laurie Halse Anderson, who envisions *Chains* as the first book in a trilogy, has said she is waiting to complete her own narrative journey before reading M. T. Anderson's *Octavian* books. Corbett, "A Talk with Five NBA Finalists." Although slightly older than M. T. Anderson, Laurie Halse Anderson (no relation) belongs to the same generation. She was born in Potsdam, New York, in 1961.
39. *Forge*, the sequel to *Chains*, traces the journey of Curzon, the enslaved Patriot soldier Isabel smuggles out of the British prison. Hiding his history of bondage, Curzon enlists in the Sixteenth Massachusetts Regiment and is accepted as an equal by the white farmer-soldiers who are his peers. Even after being reenslaved by his former master, a congressman quartered at Valley Forge, Curzon insists that the Americans, not the British, have his interest at heart. The book ends with Curzon and Isabel once again on the run; flanked by the protection of thousands of American foot soldiers, Curzon is back in the army fighting for his, and his nation's, freedom.
40. Anderson, *Chains*, 298.
41. O'Dell, *Sarah Bishop*, quotation p. 81. The novel's suggestion of marriage differs from both the historical record and the typical second-generation war novel ending, which features continued adolescence.
42. "He had heard his father and his father's friends talk many times about the tyrannical British; their cruel mercenary allies, the German-speaking Hessians; and the hated Tories, those American traitors who had sided with the brutal English king." Avi, *The Fighting Ground*, 4.
43. Avi, "On Historical Fiction." Avi (Edward Wortis) was born in New York City in 1937 and raised in a politically active family of artists and writers attracted to radical causes. He attended Antioch College and the University of Wisconsin–Madison in the 1950s before earning a master's degree in library science from Columbia. Tait, *Avi*; "Avi Wortis"; Avi, "Autobiographical Sketch."
44. Blight, *Race and Reunion*. Reconciliationist narratives reached their height in adult literature between the 1860s and the Gilded Age but remained prominent in children's literature long after that point. Harold Keith's Newbery-winning *Rifles for Watie*, discussed in Chapter 1, is a prime example.
45. Beatty, *Charley Skedaddle*, 127; hereafter cited in text.
46. The majority of Underground Railroad conductors were black; narratives of white involvement in aiding escaping slaves is a common trope in reconciliationist literature. Blight, *Race and Reunion*, 231–33. *Charley Skedaddle*'s Granny, who is described as being one-quarter Creek, plays into the vanishing Indian trope discussed in Chapter 2. The view that violence—however terrible—was necessary to eradicate American slavery was even held by ardent pacifists. Although the official doctrine of the Society of Friends forbade war-related activity, many

Quakers viewed the Civil War as a special case that required arms. Nelson, *Indiana Quakers*.

47. Bernstein, *New York City Draft Riots*, 17–42.

48. Wilenz, *Chants Democratic*.

49. During the mid-1800s, Irish immigrants fresh from the potato famine were the lowest-paid, most despised, and most foreign workers in the North. Far from "independent" in the traditional republican sense, they shared much in common with their underpaid black counterparts. Ultimately, Irishmen's *racial* differentiation from black Americans—the only people lower on the social scale than themselves—secured their status as citizens. See Roediger, *The Wages of Whiteness*.

50. On *The Red Badge of Courage*, see Blight, *Race and Reunion*, 240–41.

51. Like James Lincoln Collier, the novelist who relied on his brother's historical expertise in drafting *My Brother Sam Is Dead* and other historical novels, Patricia Beatty relied on her husband, a professional historian, for research expertise. Her first novels were written collaboratively with John Beatty; the pair checked every word uttered by their characters against Shakespeare, the Bible, and the OED to ensure temporal accuracy. McElmeel, *100 Most Popular Young Adult Authors*, 27.

52. When Granny asks Charley whether there are black folk in New York, he replies, "Not many at all" (119). The only significant black character in the novel is flat and stereotyped.

53. On the novel's popularity, see Bachelder et al., "Looking Backward," and Flaherty, "Books." The made-for-TV movie aired on NBC in 1978 and was nominated for three Emmy Awards. A musical of the novel was staged by Encore Theater Company in 2001.

54. Bette Greene experienced a lonely childhood as the daughter of merchant parents in small, southern, and overwhelmingly Christian Parkin, Arkansas. Like her protagonist, she developed a close friendship with her family's black housekeeper. Both of Greene's parents were born to Eastern European Jews who opened mercantile stores in the American South. LeMaster, *Corner of the Tapestry*, 262–63; Lamm, "Betty Evensky Greene."

55. More than 430,000 POWs arrived in the United States during World War II; most spent the duration in rural towns like the fictional Jenkinsville. Robin, *The Barbed-Wire College*; Krammer, *Nazi Prisoners of War*, 44–45.

56. Greene, *Summer of My German Soldier*, 62; hereafter cited in text. The Bergens' fair treatment of customers is suggested in *Summer of My German Soldier* but directly acknowledged in the book's sequel, *Morning Is a Long Time Coming*, 93.

57. Records indicate that only 0.28 percent of German POWs held in the United States escaped, and fewer than twenty of those received help from American citizens; all abettors were adults. Krammer, *Nazi Prisoners of War*, 130.

58. Hypocrisy figures in small details. Ruth fries bacon for breakfast, despite the fact that Mrs. Bergen complains about the high cost of kosher salami, and the dishes on which the family eats are made in (Axis) Japan (109, 120).

59. Jane Abramson's book review for the *Library Journal* is a rare exception, stating that Greene "never deals with her religion—what it's like to be Jewish in Jenkinsville, Arkansas, or how being Jewish conflicts with her feelings about Anton."

On the CIBC, see MacCann, "Militarism in Juvenile Fiction," 19. *Summer of My German Soldier* appears as the eighty-eighth most challenged book of the 1990s and the fifth most challenged book of 2001; its reasons for being banned include "offensive language, racism, sexually explicit." American Library Association, "Banned and Challenged Books."

60. The Civil War, French and Indian War, and World War II have also inspired revisions. I discuss French and Indian War stories in the context of representations of indigenous Americans (Chapter 2), but they can also be examined through the lens of war-novel generations. Children's books about the Vietnam War are slowly beginning to appear in school curricula.

61. Kammen, *Mystic Chords of Memory*, 13.

Chapter 4

1. On African royalty in the American literary imagination, see Foster, *Witnessing Slavery*. Yates was the daughter of a wealthy Buffalo businessman who made his fortune in coal. Yates, *My Diary—My World* and *My Widening World*.

2. Yates, *Amos Fortune*, 35.

3. Eighteenth-century slave narratives frequently took the form of conversion stories, as in Phillis Wheatley's well-known poem, "On Being Brought from Africa" (1773). Constanzo, *Surprising Narrative*; Foster, *Witnessing Slavery*. Yates's decision to have Amos refuse freedom from Caleb solved a puzzle encountered in the historical record: the existence of unsigned, and thus unbinding, manumission papers. Lambert, *Amos Fortune*, 5–6.

4. The most influential study was Ulrich Bonnell Phillips, *American Negro Slavery: A Survey of the Supply, Employment and Control of Negro Labor as Determined by the Plantation Regime* (1918). Challenges to the idea of slavery as a benevolent institution existed, but were subordinated by Phillips's popularity. Williams-Myers, "Slavery, Rebellion, and Revolution." Local histories praised Amos Fortune as an exemplary product of slavery: see, for example, Annett and Lehtinen, *History of Jaffrey*, 748–56.

5. Yates, "Acceptance Paper," 370–71.

6. California Department of Education, *Recommended Readings* (2009). The novel is also on the list of recommended titles for the states of New York and Alaska.

7. Stories written and illustrated for black children predated the civil rights movement but did not circulate in the mainstream book world; not until the 1980s did books written by African Americans become widely adopted in schools. On histories of earlier African American children's literature, see Johnson, *Telling Tales*; Kutenplon and Olmstead, *Young Adult Fiction by African American Writers*; and Martin, *Brown Gold*.

8. Larrick, "All-White World."

9. Handlin and Handlin, "Origins of the Southern Labor System."

10. Speare, *Witch of Blackbird Pond*, 26; hereafter cited in text. Connecticut slaves appear only once in the 249-page book, when Kit "glimpsed the familiar black faces that must be slaves" at the back of the meeting house (53). In the 1690s, about one in ten estate inventories in Connecticut included slaves. Main, *Society and Economy in Colonial Connecticut*, 177. This discussion of *Witch of Blackbird Pond* draws on the more lengthy analysis of the novel presented in Schwebel,

"Historical Fiction and the Classroom." (Reprinted with kind permission from Springer Science+Business Media.)

11. Melish, *Disowning Slavery*.
12. Taylor, *Making Love to Typewriters* and "Exploding the Literary Canon."
13. "All-Time Bestselling Children's Books" (2001); Theodore Taylor to Steve Waterman, 22 Aug. 2000, Theodore Taylor Papers, Kerlan Collection, University of Minnesota, box MF 2829, folder 2.
14. Taylor, *The Cay*, 71–72; hereafter cited in text.
15. Stampp, *Peculiar Institution*, vii.
16. Stauffer, *Black Hearts of Men*.
17. The "long 1960s" refers to the period stretching until 1974, the year of Nixon's resignation. Isserman and Kazin, *America Divided*.
18. Silver, "From Baldwin to Singer," 29. Prominent black children's author Julius Lester wrote in the *New York Times Book Review*, "Jessie is our window on the slave trade and it is here that the novel fails. As a character, Jessie simply is not interesting and thus his observations are not interesting. He becomes a mere device for the transmission of information about life on a slave ship and the slave trade in Africa and the Americas. The information, however, never takes on a living reality, because we do not care about Jessie." Lester, "*The Slave Dancer*." The editors of *Childhood Education* noted the book's wide praise but admitted they found the tale "curiously wooden. . . . The characters lack vitality; the plot frays out." "*The Slave Dancer*."
19. Fox, *Borrowed Finery*, quotation p. 194; Tillman, "Artist's Voice since 1981"; Rehak, "Life and Death of Paula Fox."
20. The Hans Christian Andersen Award is the highest international recognition in the world of children's literature; it is granted by IBBY to a living author or illustrator "whose complete works have made a lasting contribution to children's literature." *www.ibby.org*.
21. Fox, *The Slave Dancer*, 69; hereafter cited in text.
22. Kovacs, *Meet the Authors*, 34–35.
23. Baker, "Paula Fox." Although Fox's Cuban relatives were members of the aristocratic elite who fled when Batista came to power, Fox used her fluent Spanish to identify with the oppressed, becoming an advocate for Mexican Americans in San Francisco and teaching English in New York. Fox, *Borrowed Finery*.
24. *Contemporary Authors*, 215.
25. Glancy, "Beautiful People," 365. The article went on to praise *Sounder*, discussed later in this chapter, as an exception to the norm.
26. Schwartz, "Black Experience as Backdrop."
27. Cosgriff, "The Newbery Awards." The 1928 Newbery Medal went to Dhan Gopal Mukerji, who was born in a village outside Calcutta. Publishing house consolidation, the rise of big-box stores, and the proliferation of new children's and YA prizes are slowly eroding the monopoly children's librarians and their awards have enjoyed in the book industry. Marcus, *Minders of Make-Believe*; Kidd, "Prizing Children's Literature."
28. Many authors checked multiple boxes in indicating their racial or ethnic category; some created their racial category and marked it on the form. CIBC, *Director's Files*, box 12; Brad Chambers to Donnarae MacCann, 13 June 1978, in CIBC, *Director's Files*, box 17.

29. No comprehensive study of the CIBC has been conducted, and the organization's papers, housed in the Schomburg Center for Research in Black Culture (New York Public Library), are incomplete and largely unprocessed. Available correspondence, however, makes clear the range of views held within the organization. Bulletin reviews discussed multiple aspects of text. Critiques of *The Cay* and *The Slave Dancer*, for example, noted not only the "whiteness" of the texts' authors but also the fact that the texts aligned reader vision with the racist attitudes of their protagonists. Schwartz, "'The Cay': Racism Still Rewarded" and "Black Experience as Backdrop."

30. Bradford Chambers to Mr. Warren Boroson, 5 Nov. 1970, in CIBC, *Director's Files*, box 6. Not all members of the CIBC leadership agreed; June Meyer Jordan, an African American author who had served as a judge for the CIBC manuscript contest in the "Black" category and who helped push for passage of the ALA's Racism and Sexism Awareness resolution, wrote a positive review of *Sounder* for the *New York Times*, although she did suggest that "perhaps parents should loiter nearby, ready to enforce their child's revulsion from violence so truly and so well described. Perhaps parents should prepare to clarify the questions never raised, explicitly." Jordan, "*Sounder*."

31. The amnesia in relation to controversy over race is illustrated by the fact that *Sounder* frequently appears on librarian and teacher lists of "dog stories." In 2007, Harper Perennial published *Three Dog Tales*, a YA paperback that includes the story of *Sounder*, *Old Yeller*, and *Old Yeller*'s sequel, *Savage Sam*.

32. "All-Time Bestselling Children's Books" (1996, 2001).

33. *Center for Children's Books Bulletin* 23, 4 (1969): 54; *Commonweal* 91, 8 (1969): 257.

34. Armstrong, *Sounder*, 26; hereafter cited in text.

35. Elkins, *Slavery*.

36. Schwartz, "*Sounder*: A Black or a White Tale?" From internal evidence in several documents contained in the CIBC director's files, it is clear that Schwartz is white. Unfortunately, no papers specific to Schwartz remain in the CIBC collection; the folder labeled with his name is empty.

37. The boy also extracts a collection of Montaigne's essays from the trash. This narrative detail is important as it shows that the boy and his teacher draw inspiration from canonical (and imperialist) Western texts. The teacher tells him, "This is a wonderful book. . . . People should read [Montaigne's] writings . . . but few do. He is all but forgotten" (98).

38. Moynihan, *The Negro Family*; Feldstein, *Motherhood*, 139–52. The adolescent boy in *Sounder*, of course, fled a female-headed home.

39. The original manuscript was divided in four, producing companion novels (*The MacLeod Place* and *The Mills of God*) as well as a sequel to *Sounder* (*Sour Land*). William Armstrong Papers, Kerlan Collection, University of Minnesota, box MF 37; author interview with Christopher (Kip) Armstrong.

40. The man described but not named in the author's note, Charlie Jones, is of course a real man who Armstrong discussed at some length in interviews. Armstrong's son has explained that the story of *Sounder*, however, originated in Armstrong's imagination, not in Jones's storytelling: "He wrote the author's note to make it seem as if Charlie Jones had told him the story." In other words, the

prefatory comments were an authenticating device. E-mail from Christopher Armstrong to author, 9 July 2008.

41. Suzzanne Douglas, who played the mother in the 2003 Disney remake of *Sounder*, said during a 2005 interview that she wasn't aware of the 1970s-era CIBC criticism. Her response at the time was, "Oh, not that again. I've run up against that my whole life, that I wasn't black enough. I have to speak a certain way, act a certain way. That's not how I define myself. I think I'm bigger than black; that's just one attribute I have. In an effort to be progressive, [those critics] have taken the humanity out of things—anyone can feel injustice. God doesn't know culture. I applaud that Armstrong chose to [write about an African American family] at a time when there wasn't much of that nature written, even by our own folks." Telephone interview by author, 2 Nov. 2005.

42. Earlier drafts of Armstrong's *Sounder* manuscript had included reference to a meeting house picnic and other cultural activities ultimately displayed in the movie. William Armstrong Papers, Kerlan Collection, University of Minnesota, box MF 37. For comparison of the novel and 1972 film, see Rutherford, "New Dog with an Old Trick"; Deutsch, "Named and the Unnamed"; and Farmer, "Black Experience."

43. Unedited memo (typos corrected for clarity), n.d., in CIBC, *Director's Files*, box 16.

44. Telephone interview of Kevin Hooks by author, 4 Nov. 2005.

45. The award has been granted annually since 1953 by the Women's International League for Peace and Freedom and the Jane Addams Peace Association.

46. Schwartz, "'The Cay': Racism Still Rewarded." The CIBC eventually used *The Cay* as a model of a genre of books to avoid: CIBC, *Guidelines for Selecting Bias-Free Textbooks and Storybooks*, 11.

47. "NEA Alerts Teachers/Parents to Controversy Over 'The Cay,'" n.d., in CIBC, *Director's Files*, box 16; "Statement by Samuel B. Ethridge" (director of Civil and Human Rights Program for the NEA), n.d., Theodore Taylor Papers, Kerlan Collection, University of Minnesota, box MF 777, folder 9; Banfield, "Commitment to Change."

48. Theodore Taylor to Bertha Jenkinson, 27 Jan. 1975, Theodore Taylor Papers, Kerlan Collection, University of Minnesota, box MF 777, folder 4; Taylor, letter to the editor, and "Exploding the Literary Canon"; Schwartz, "Revoking 'The Cay' Award" and "'The Cay': An Award Regretted, Not Revoked."

49. Taylor, *Timothy of the Cay*; McLellan, "'Cay' Author Wins Ruling on Sequel." Unhappy with the film adaptation's script, and certainly with the film's reception, Taylor refused to allow Universal to produce videos of the film. Despite tremendous teacher demand for any adaptation of widely taught novels, it is therefore impossible to find a copy of the made-for-TV movie. Taylor, *Making Love to Typewriters*, 127.

50. Lillian McClintock, senior editor of children's books, Rand McNally, to Bradford Chambers, 19 June 1968: "What is the Council's method of choosing publishers for the manuscripts? It seems to me that since the Council obviously needs and wants the cooperation of all publishers, that all publishers should be given an opportunity to consider the manuscripts that are received in the competition. . . . I do know that we were not asked whether we were interested in any

of them." CIBC, *Director's Files*, box 6. See also Brad Chambers to Donnarae MacCann, 13 June 1978, in CIBC, *Director's Files*, box 17, and Horning, "An Interview with Rudine Sims Bishop."

51. Bader, "How the Little House Gave Ground."

52. Taylor was the second African American author to win the Newbery. The first, Virginia Hamilton, had also entered the field through the CIBC. Virginia Hamilton's Newbery winner, *M. C. Higgins, The Great*, was less specifically historical, less recognizably "black" (the protagonists' rural identities come across much more forcefully than their racial ones), and less plot-driven than *Roll of Thunder*; it never gained strong footing in the school curriculum.

53. Drew, *100 Most Popular Young Adult Authors*, 406; McElmeel, *100 Most Popular Young Adult Authors*, 425–27; Crowe, *Presenting Mildred D. Taylor*.

54. Taylor, "Newbery Medal Acceptance," 26.

55. The terms are from Eugene D. Genovese's *Roll, Jordan, Roll: The World the Slaves Made*.

56. I have located only one critical article that addresses the ways *Roll of Thunder* and *Let the Circle Be Unbroken* echo *To Kill a Mockingbird*; it focuses on the trial scenes. Whitehead, "The Mockingbird Encircled." Barbara Bader wrote that Taylor originally thought of *Roll of Thunder* not as a book for children, "but rather as an adult novel along the lines of *To Kill a Mockingbird*." Editor Phyllis Fogelman convinced her otherwise. Bader, "How the Little House Gave Ground." No documentation is provided.

57. Lee, *To Kill a Mockingbird*, 26; hereafter cited in text.

58. Taylor, *Roll of Thunder*, 25; hereafter cited in text.

59. Papa had warned, "If I ever find out y'all been up there, for any reason, I'm gonna wear y'all out. Y'all hear me?" The narrator continues, "Papa always meant what he said—and he swung a mean switch" (41). Mama's lesson is supplemented by Papa's whipping, which is administered some hundred pages after his initial warning.

60. Hamida Bosmajian has written about the trial at some length: "Mildred Taylor's Story of Cassie Logan: A Search for Law and Justice in a Racist Society."

61. Radway, *A Feeling for Books*, 337.

62. Taylor, *Let the Circle Be Unbroken*, 174; hereafter cited in text.

63. American Library Association, "Harry Potter Series." It is likely that the ALA's data capture far fewer challenges than actually occur; see Kidd, "Not Censorship but Selection."

64. Taylor, "Acceptance Speech."

65. *Roll of Thunder* is one of six books selected as a representative text for grades 6–8 in the *Common Core State Standards: English Language Arts*. The year 2002 was the only one in which it appeared on the ALA's top ten list of banned books.

66. During the 1960s and 1970s, the period when Taylor wrote her first children's books, linguists used the term "Black English" to describe African American language that differed from Standard English in systematic ways. The term was also embraced by black educators and artists who not only acknowledged the speech pattern as a "real language" but also celebrated its richness of expression. Of course, the speech of actual African Americans often overlapped with that of their white neighbors (as it does in *Roll of Thunder*), and it did not always fit neatly into the patterns of linguistic features researchers now identify as African

American English or African American Vernacular English. Yet it is clear that language—the medium of the Logan family's storytelling—is a part of *Roll of Thunder*'s project of celebrating black life and culture. For insight into the issues surrounding the use of African American English by children's authors in the 1970s, see Tremper, "Black English in Children's Literature."

67. Morgan, "History for Our Children."

68. Curtis, "Afterword," *Bud, Not Buddy*. As an adult, Curtis makes his home in Windsor, Ontario.

69. Carby, "The Ideologies of Black Folk," 125–43.

70. Curtis, *The Watsons Go to Birmingham*, 132; hereafter cited in text.

71. Curtis's third historical novel, *Elijah of Buxton*, is an exception. It is set in a small nineteenth-century community of freed people who escaped slavery by crossing into Canada.

72. Morgan, "History for Our Children." A movie has not yet been made.

73. McNair, "I May Be Crackin'"; Barker, "Naive Narrators." Curtis also draws inspiration from (adult) African American literature. His image of death in *The Watsons* borrows from Zora Neale Hurston in *Their Eyes Were Watching God*, and his depiction of slavery "from the periphery" in *Elijah of Buxton* stemmed from his thinking about Toni Morrison's *Beloved*. Morgan, "History for Our Children," 204; Schneider, "Talking with Christopher Paul Curtis."

74. Walter Dean Myers's *Riot* (2009), a novel set in New York City during the 1863 draft riots, parallels *The Watsons* in portraying a northern girl's naïveté about the meaning of race. Fifteen-year-old Claire is the daughter of an Irish mother and black father who together operate a tavern. Before violence erupts against the city's black people and institutions, however, Claire—unbelievably—seems to never have given her racial or legal identity a thought. Given the fact that she does not live in a racially segregated world, her naïveté is significantly less plausible than Curtis's narrator's. Myers, a prolific and critically acclaimed African American writer for children and teens, is better known for his contemporary realistic fiction, including the Printz-winning *Monster* (1999).

75. TeachingBooks.net, Interview with Christopher Paul Curtis. Some children similarly experience Bud (of *Bud, Not Buddy*) as white.

76. Wyile, "Expanding the View of First-Person Narration"; Barker, "Naive Narrators." White children's misreading of the Watsons' race may also stem from the extent to which African American cultural products (music, language, humor, fashion) dominate today's youth culture.

77. Quoted in Morgan, "History for Our Children," 212; emphasis in original.

78. Highsmith, "Demolition Means Progress," 342–51, 423; Sugrue, *Origins of the Urban Crisis*; Jackson, *Crabgrass Frontier*, esp. chapters 11–16. A historical marker now stands on the site of the school, which closed in 1982, to memorialize Michigan's "separate but equal" policies. "Carver Elementary School."

79. "Report Finds St. Louis Most Dangerous U.S. City"; Brown, "10 Best Cities for African Americans."

80. The SparkNotes reading of the novel reinforces this misconception: "At first, the reader thinks that a miraculous fire brought together the community. Then, the reader learns that it was Papa who started the fire. At first, it may seem that it was slightly criminal of Papa to fool the men by starting a fire. But, on the other hand, he burned his own land. . . . It may seem contrived to some readers that

the novel has such a happy ending. . . . There is no lynching; no one dies. In fact, the whole community is forced to work together. What is Mildred Taylor trying to say? Obviously, she is saying that black and white people can and should work together. But she is also saying that they are most likely to work together in a state of emergency, when their material resources are endangered." SparkNotes, reading guide for *Roll of Thunder, Hear My Cry*.

Chapter 5

1. The expanding horizons model, first adopted around 1955, remains the dominant K–8 design despite the National Council for the Social Studies' position that it is "insufficient for today's young learners" ("Powerful and Purposeful"). Now entrenched as a matter of habit rather than theory, the principle of "expanding outward" from self and home to nation and world was originally rooted in the child development work of Jean Piaget and Bärbel Inhelder. Theories of domain-specific learning have discredited the easy translation of Piagetian research (which was rooted in natural science) to the social sciences and humanities. Sunal and Haas, *Social Studies*, 13–15; Superka, Hawke, and Morrissett, "Current and Future Status," 362–69; Hallam, "Piaget and the Teaching of History"; Booth, "Ages and Concepts," 22–38; Wineburg, *Historical Thinking*, chapter 2.
2. For examples of literacy research, see Beck et al., "Learning from Social Studies Texts" and "Revising Social Studies Text"; McKeown et al., "Contribution of Prior Knowledge"; and Richgels, Tomlinson, and Tunnell, "Comparison." For the application of such research by a classroom teacher, see Villano, "Should Social Studies Textbooks Become History?" On history pedagogy research, see VanSledright, *In Search of America's Past*; Paxton, "Someone with Like a Life"; and Wineburg, "On the Reading of Historical Texts."
3. Jerald, "No Action"; Ingersoll, "Problem of Underqualified Teachers"; Ravitch, "Educational Backgrounds"; Martel, "Can 'Social Studies' Standards Prepare History Teachers?"
4. McDiarmid and Vinten-Johansen, "Catwalk across the Great Divide," 156–77. When given the opportunity to experience historical methodology and study historical pedagogy, even those educators who have been teaching K–12 history for years can be empowered to reconceptualize the knowledge undergirding the school subject and alter their practice. Bain, "Into the Breach," 331–52; Kelly and VanSledright, "Journey toward Wiser Practice," 183–202.
5. On the place of history within the field of social studies, see Sunal and Haas, *Social Studies*, 13–15, and Superka, Hawke, and Morrissett, "Current and Future Status." On the disciplinary background of teacher educators, see Ravitch, "Educational Backgrounds," 141–55, and McDiarmid and Vinten-Johansen, "Catwalk across the Great Divide," 156–77.
6. Lee Shulman has argued that to be effective, history teachers need not only strong teaching methods and deep knowledge of their discipline but also what he terms "pedagogical content knowledge"—the ability to integrate good teaching methods with the particular nature of a discipline. In the teaching curriculum described in the text, prospective teachers' failure to gain disciplinary knowledge also renders it impossible for them to acquire pedagogical content knowledge. Shulman, "Knowledge and Teaching."

7. Others have argued that the same is true for high school history teachers, particularly given the high percentage who are teaching "out of field." Since passage of the No Child Left Behind Act, which stipulates that states must work toward having "highly qualified" teachers at all grade levels in all subjects, state departments of education have begun requiring students seeking certification in secondary education to major in the academic discipline they intend to teach. Not all prospective high school social studies teachers major in history, however. Those who major in a different social science may never enroll in upper-level history courses that shift their epistemic stance. This is almost universally true of elementary and middle-level teachers. McDiarmid and Vinten-Johansen, "Catwalk across the Great Divide," 156–77.

8. Lowenthal, *The Past Is a Foreign Country* and *Possessed by the Past*; Kammen, *Mystic Chords of Memory*. Kammen explains that at times, heritage "involves an explicit element of anti-intellectualism—the presumption, for example, that history experienced through sites and material culture must be more memorable than history presented on the printed page" (625).

9. In their introduction to scholarly essays on the teaching of history in the K–12 setting, Peter N. Stearns, Peter Seixas, and Sam Wineburg comment on schools as a site for forging collective memory and a heritage-based understanding of the past, and they wonder at the lack of scholarly attention directed at the process: "Perhaps the problem is that historians fail to see what happens in elementary and high school history as a memory project, as heritage. Perhaps they prefer to understand the subject of school history less as practice of public memory than as the first steps toward a critical, disciplinary practice of history" (*Knowing, Teaching, and Learning History*, 2).

10. For an example of curricular guides that advocate these kinds of activities, see Miller, *U.S. History through Children's Literature* (1997) and, for comparison, Ellermeyer and Chick, *Multicultural American History* (2003). Despite the shift in content, similarities are evident. School and teacher websites also provide one (albeit imperfect) means of gauging curricular activity nationwide. Because many of these extension projects are the culmination of units of study, pictures of student projects often appear online for school communities to view. A Google search for "pioneer day" and "elementary school" yields more than forty thousand hits while a search for "colonial day" and "school" yields more than seventy thousand; clearly, the practice is widespread.

11. See Wineburg, *Historical Thinking*.

12. The term "webquest" was coined by Bernie Dodge and Tom March and is defined as an online "inquiry-oriented activity" with six steps: introduction, task, process, resources, evaluation, and conclusion. March, "WebQuests 101." I analyze only the published webquest, not the oral teacher instructions or student-teacher discussion that undoubtedly accompanies its use each year. There are limits to such analysis, but they differ from the limits characterizing participant-observer studies conducted by researchers such as Keith Barton and Linda Levstik and teacher-research studies like that conducted by Bruce VanSledright. One disadvantage of participant-observer studies is that researchers who have developed relationships with teachers they have observed can become reluctant to critically (and publicly) evaluate the shortcomings of their work. By analyzing

published lesson plans, I evaluate static text, but I do so unclouded by a relation-ship with its author.

13. Students are provided with a link that brings them to what appears to be a teacher-created form for checking source reliability. The tips are by any account ill designed to help students evaluate the primary source material on the website. Questions include "Date—is the information current, or does it need to be cur-rent?" and "Equipment—what kind of equipment was used to record informa-tion?" A final pointer basically acknowledges the tips' questionable usefulness: "Answer as many of the questions as you can, and determine if the answer would indicate a reliable source, an unreliable source, or an uncertainty for each."

14. Such a search would ultimately reveal that the documents were selected and ed-ited for the online course companion to a college textbook: Garraty and Carnes, *American Nation*.

15. There is an extensive literature on witchcraft in colonial America. For the con-nection of the accused with issues of gender and status, see Karlsen, *Devil in the Shape of a Woman*; for discussion of witchcraft in relation to local politics, see Boyer and Nissenbaum, *Salem Possessed*; and for an examination of the motiva-tions and psychology of the accusers, see Demos, *Entertaining Satan*.

16. The mission statement for the National Council for the Social Studies reads in part, "Social studies educators teach students the content knowledge, intellectual skills, and civic values necessary for fulfilling the duties of citizenship in a par-ticipatory democracy" ("About National Council for the Social Studies").

17. Levstik, "Relationship between Historical Response and Narrative," 27.

18. Levstik has captured her own intellectual biography in "Narrative as a Primary Act," 1–9, quotation p. 4.

19. Levstik, "I Wanted to Be There," 65–77, quotation p. 70. In an earlier yearlong case study of a fifth grader's reading and understanding of historical narratives (in both novel and textbook form), Levstik observed that the student, Jennifer, was *most* concerned about the moral issues raised. Because fictional protago-nists and antagonists frequently differ in their views about the central events of the narrative, Jennifer felt that the novels, but not her textbook, enabled her to see multiple perspectives. As Levstik notes, however, Jennifer never indicated an understanding of the way novelists shaped the views of both protagonists and antagonists, and hence the readers' access to interpretations of the past. None-theless, Levstik argues that the novels Jennifer read facilitated her understanding of the interpretative nature of history. Among the books on Jennifer's reading list were *The Witch of Blackbird Pond* and *My Brother Sam Is Dead*. Would Jen-nifer's experience of grappling with what Levstik terms "different kinds of right and wrong" look different had she read *Johnny Tremain* instead of *My Brother Sam Is Dead*? Levstik, "Historical Narrative and the Young Reader," quotation p. 117.

20. See Morris, "Birmingham Confrontation Reconsidered," for competing interpre-tations of the engines driving the civil rights movement (the work of politi-cal moderates who patiently but persistently persuaded others to modify their beliefs and practices, the success of marginalized peoples who attracted the at-tention of liberal third parties who intervened in local power structures, and the organizational efforts of the radicalized margins that created change themselves by disrupting, through coordinated effort, the power of oppressors). For a cogent

analysis of these issues in *To Kill a Mockingbird*, see Gladwell, "The Courthouse Ring."

21. *Mockingbird* has long been a staple of high school English curricula, and *Roll of Thunder* is virtually required reading in middle schools. In overwhelming numbers, then, children move "backward" in historiography, reading an interpretation of race relations embraced during the 1950s and early 1960s after having being exposed to an interpretation of race relations rooted in the late 1970s. If teachers juxtaposed the narratives, however, students would not only be exposed to two literary masterpieces but also have the opportunity to see the stakes involved in making historical arguments. Applebee, "Study of Book-Length Works."

22. Rosenblatt, *The Reader*; Rosenblatt's theory had been developed decades earlier, but it wasn't until authentic literature became a reality in the K–12 arena that it was translated into practice in classroom instruction. See Hancock, "Children's Books," 225–44.

23. Daniels, *Literature Circles*. As the term has entered the K–12 classroom vocabulary, it is sometimes misapplied to teacher-created student groups structured by reading level rather than by student interest in a particular text.

24. Zimmermann and Keene, *Mosaic of Thought*, quotation p. 55.

25. In the best historical novels, characters are embedded in a richly detailed, three-dimensional, temporal world, and they *think* like characters of that world. When they don't—as when a nineteenth-century girl rejects all gender constraints—readers can detect the influence of modern-day sensibilities and cry foul. Anne Scott MacLeod does just this in "Writing Backwards: Modern Models in Historical Fiction"; the widely taught Newbery winner *Sarah, Plain and Tall* (1985) by Patricia MacLachlan is singled out as an example.

26. Wineburg, *Historical Thinking*.

27. Levstik, "Relationship between Historical Response and Narrative," 10–29, quotations pp. 15–16.

28. Shemilt, "The Caliph's Coin," 99.

29. Rosenblatt, *The Reader*.

30. Wineburg, *Historical Thinking*.

31. The question is quoted from Rice, *A Guide for Using "The Witch of Blackbird Pond" in the Classroom*, 14. The guide suggests that teachers use reader-response journals with their students.

32. This is not to dismiss the seriousness of an adolescent's social isolation; in extreme cases, it, too, can lead to death in the form of suicide. I merely want to suggest that casual association of Kit's isolation and the average middle schooler's feelings of isolation is misguided.

33. Data are drawn from state Department of Education websites.

34. Pederson, "What Is Measured Is Treasured." For a discussion of the way high-stakes testing has affected teaching in a variety of states that regularly test in social studies or history, see Yeager and Davis, *Wise Social Studies*. In low-performing schools, an additional incentive to shift instructional time away from social studies texts and toward trade books arises from students' inability to comprehend grade-level textbooks; trade books offer many more discrete reading levels than do U.S. history textbooks, which are usually produced for fifth-, eighth-, or eleventh-grade readers.

35. The lesson plan appears on a number of teacher websites; the original appears to have been created by Donna Gogas.

36. Hunt, *Across Five Aprils*, 45–46.

37. The much-decried "No Child Left Behind" name disappeared with Barack Obama's election in 2008, but the implications of the Bush-era policy have endured. The Elementary and Secondary Education Act that preceded NCLB was renewed under Obama's administration, and in its new form, it emphasizes accountability as measured by "scientific" data.

38. The criterion for "scientifically based research" not only shaped language arts and reading programs for students and professional development for teachers but also shaped the design of research and inquiry as scholars applied to the federal government for grant support. Eisenhart and Towne, "Contestation and Change."

39. Renaissance Learning produces a number of different types of quizzes, some of which are designed to measure higher-order thinking. Reading practice quizzes are by far the most popular, however, and unlike the other quiz types, they are produced for every title with an Accelerated Reader score. As of 2010, Accelerated Reader had produced reading practice quizzes for more than 125,000 titles. The most popular are for books with a readability level score of 4–8, or fourth to eighth grade. Telephone interview with Eric Stickney, director of educational research, Renaissance Learning, 7 Sept. 2010. Census data chart the number of K–12 schools in the United States at about 115,000.

40. Novels that have accompanying Accelerated Reader quizzes but were removed (between 1986 and 2010) from California's *Recommended Readings in Literature: Kindergarten through Grade Eight* include *Caddie Woodlawn, Island of the Blue Dolphins, Sign of the Beaver,* and *The Slave Dancer*. Other titles that never appeared on California's list, such as the reconciliationist Civil War narrative *Rifles for Watie,* also have Accelerated Reader scores and quizzes associated with them.

41. E-mail communication between Garlic Press and author, 28 Dec. 2009.

42. Spicer, *Teaching Guide*, 5; emphasis in original.

43. Instructional interventions designed to improve content area literacy reflect this as they often entail little more than attempting to improve *basic* reading skills, albeit with expository text. See, for example, Bryant et al., "Reading Outcomes," and Texas Reading Initiative, *Research-Based Content Area Reading Instruction,* as well as the research studies it cites in its bibliography.

44. The phrase "breach between school and academy" is from Wineburg, *Historical Thinking.*

45. Wineburg, *Historical Thinking*, 68–69, and "On the Reading of Historical Texts."

46. English language arts standards in every state include benchmarks for distinguishing between fact and opinion, differentiating between literal and figurative language, and identifying perspective and point of view.

47. On reading skill development in the United Kingdom, see Lee and Ashby, "Progression in Historical Understanding."

48. Barthes, "The Reality Effect."

49. This referential illusion, to borrow Barthes's term, exists to some extent in all narrative history, but by forgoing footnotes, bibliographic essays, and clearly identifiable authors, K–12 textbooks bolster rather than break down the illusion. The textbook's form frustrates students' awareness of what Bruce VanSledright

terms "the inner interpretive machinery of doing history." Barthes, "The Reality Effect"; VanSledright, *In Search of America's Past*, quotation p. 50.

50. See Yeager and Davis, *Wise Social Studies*.
51. On the time-consuming nature of teaching historical thinking skills and reading for subtext, see VanSledright, *In Search of America's Past*, and Brophy and VanSledright, *Teaching and Learning History*.
52. *Common Core State Standards: English Language Arts.*
53. VanSledright, *In Search of America's Past.*
54. Wineburg, *Historical Thinking*; VanSledright, *In Search of America's Past*. Their work, of course, is part of a larger body of research in the field. For a sampling of the best work, see Stearns, Seixas, and Wineburg, *Knowing, Teaching, and Learning History.*
55. Barton, "Bossed around by the Queen."
56. Collier, "Johnny and Sam"; "Fact, Fiction, and History"; and *Brother Sam and All That.*
57. Nash, Crabtree, and Dunn, *History on Trial*, 36–39.
58. On the controversy over the national history standards, see Nash, Crabtree, and Dunn, *History on Trial*, chapter 7, and Symcox, *Whose History?*

Afterword

1. The phrase is from Levstik, "I Wanted to Be There," 65–77.
2. Anderson, *Chains*, 197.

Bibliography

Abramson, Jane. "*Summer of My German Soldier.*" Book review. *Library Journal* 98, 18 (1973): 3154.

Achebe, Chinua. "An Image of Africa: Racism in Conrad's *Heart of Darkness.*" In *Hopes and Impediments: Selected Essays, 1965–1987.* London: Heinemann, 1988.

Alaska Department of Education and Early Development. *Common Ground: Suggested Literature.* Juneau, AK: Department of Education and Early Development, 1991.

Alexie, Sherman. *The Absolutely True Diary of a Part-Time Indian.* New York: Little, Brown, 2007.

"All-Time Bestselling Children's Books." Edited by Diane Roback and Jason Britton and compiled by Debbie Hochman Turvey. *Publishers Weekly* 243, 6 (1996): 27–33; 248, 51 (2001): 24–32.

American Library Association. "Awards and Grants." 2010. *www.ala.org/ala/ awardsgrants/index.cfm.*

———. "Banned and Challenged Books." 1990–2009. *www.ala.org/ala/ issuesadvocacy/banned/frequentlychallenged/challengedbydecade/index.cfm.*

———. "Harry Potter Series Tops List of Most Challenged Books Four Years in a Row." Press release. 13 Jan. 2003.

Anderson, Laurie Halse. *Chains: Seeds of America.* New York: Simon and Schuster, 2008.

———. *Forge: Seeds of America.* New York: Atheneum, 2010.

Anderson, M. T. *The Astonishing Life of Octavian Nothing, Traitor to the Nation.* Vol. 1, *The Pox Party.* Cambridge, MA: Candlewick Press, 2006.

———. *The Astonishing Life of Octavian Nothing, Traitor to the Nation.* Vol. 2, *The Kingdom on the Waves.* Cambridge, MA: Candlewick Press, 2008.

Anderson, Nancy. "Using Children's Literature to Teach Black American History." *Social Studies* 78, 2 (1987): 88–89.

Anderson, Richard C., et al. *Becoming a Nation of Readers: The Report of the Commission on Reading.* Washington, DC: U.S. Department of Education, 1985.

Annett, Albert, and Alice E. E. Lehtinen. *History of Jaffrey.* Jaffrey, NH: Town of Jaffrey, 1937.

Apple, Michael W. "Regulating the Text: The Socio-Historical Roots of State Control." In *Textbooks in American Society: Politics, Policy, and Pedagogy,* edited by Phillip G. Altbach et al. Albany: State University of New York Press, 1991.

Applebee, Arthur N. *Literature in the Secondary School: Studies of Curriculum and*

Instruction in the United States. Urbana, IL: National Council of Teachers of English, 1993.

———. "A Study of Book-Length Works Taught in High School English Programs." Report 1.2. Albany, NY: Center for the Learning and Teaching of Literature, 1989.

Appleyard, J. A. *Becoming a Reader: The Experience of Fiction from Childhood to Adulthood*. New York: Cambridge University Press, 1990.

Armstrong, William H. "Author Interview #69." Audiotape. Morristown, NJ: Pathways to Children's Literature, 1974.

———. *The MacLeod Place*. New York: Coward, McCann and Geoghegan, 1972.

———. *The Mills of God*. Garden City, NY: Doubleday, 1973.

———. *Sounder*. Reprint, New York: Harper and Row, 1989. First published 1969 by Harper and Row.

———. *Sour Land*. New York: HarperCollins, 1971.

Aronson, Marc. "Slippery Slopes and Proliferating Prizes." *Horn Book Magazine* 77, 3 (2001): 271–78.

Association of American Publishers. "Interactive Textbook Adoption/Open Territory Map." *www.aapschool.org/map.html* (accessed 15 Jan. 2011).

Avi. "Autobiographical Sketch." In *Sixth Book of Junior Authors and Illustrators*, edited by Sally Holmes Holtze. New York: H. W. Wilson, 1989.

———. *The Fighting Ground*. Reprint, New York: Harper Trophy, 1987. First published 1984 by J. B. Lippincott.

———. "On Historical Fiction." *Children's Book Council Magazine*. *www.cbcbooks .org/cbcmagazine/meet/avi.html* (accessed 8 Apr. 2006; no longer available).

"Avi Wortis." *Major Authors and Illustrators for Children and Young Adults: A Selection of Sketches from "Something About the Author,"* 2nd ed., 8 vols. Detroit: Gale Group, 2002.

Axtell, James. *The European and the Indian: Essays in the Ethnohistory of Colonial America*. New York: Oxford University Press, 1982.

Bach, Alice. "Cracking open the Geode: The Fiction of Paula Fox." *Horn Book Magazine* 53, 5 (1977): 514–21.

Bachelder, Linda, et al. "Looking Backward: Trying to Find the Classic Young Adult Novel." *English Journal* 6, 9 (1980): 86–89.

Bader, Barbara. "How the Little House Gave Ground: The Beginning of Multiculturalism in a New Black Children's Literature." *Horn Book Magazine* 78, 6 (2002): 657–73.

Bagnall, Norma. "Theodore Taylor: His Models of Self-Reliance." *Language Arts* 57, 1 (1980): 86–91.

Bailyn, Bernard. *The Ideological Origins of the American Revolution*. Cambridge, MA: Harvard University Press, 1992.

Bain, Robert B. "Into the Breach: Using Research and Theory to Shape History Instruction." In *Knowing, Teaching, and Learning History: National and International Perspectives*, edited by Peter N. Stearns, Peter Seixas, and Sam Wineburg. New York: New York University Press, 2000.

Baker, Augusta. "Biographical Note on Paula Fox." *Horn Book Magazine* 50, 4 (1974): 351–53.

———. *Books about Negro Life for Children*. New York: Bureau for Intercultural Education, 1946.

Bales, Jack. *Esther Forbes: A Bio-Bibliography of the Author of Johnny Tremain.* Lanham, MD: Scarecrow Press, 1998.

Banfield, Beryle. "Commitment to Change: The Council on Interracial Books for Children and the World of Children's Books." *African American Review* 32, 1 (1998): 17–22.

Banks, Lynne Reid. *The Indian in the Cupboard.* Reprint, New York: Avon, 1982. First published 1980 by J. M. Dent, London.

———. *The Return of the Indian.* New York: Doubleday, 1986.

Barker, Janet L. "Naive Narrators and Innocent and Experienced Perspectives on Race in Three Historical Novels by Christopher Paul Curtis." Paper presented at the annual meeting of the Children's Literature Association, Charlotte, NC, June 2009.

Barthes, Roland. "The Reality Effect." In *The Rustle of Language,* translated by Richard Howard. New York: Hill and Wang, 1996.

Bartoletti, Susan Campbell. "The Power of Work and Wages: Working toward Historicity in Children's Fiction." *Children's Literature Association Quarterly* 24, 3 (1999): 112–18.

Barton, Keith C. "Bossed around by the Queen: Elementary Students' Understanding of Individuals and Institutions in History." In *Research History Education: Theory, Method, and Context,* edited by Linda S. Levstik and Keith C. Barton. New York: Routledge, 2008.

Barton, Keith C., and Linda S. Levstik. *Teaching History for the Common Good.* Mahwah, NJ: Lawrence Erlbaum, 2004.

Bates, Albert Carlos. *The Charter of Connecticut: A Study.* Hartford: Connecticut Historical Society, 1932.

Baumann, James F. "Commentary: Basal Reading Programs and the Deskilling of Teachers: A Critical Examination of the Argument." *Reading Research Quarterly,* 27, 4 (1992): 390–98.

Bayot, Jennifer. "Nancy Larrick, Author of a Guide to Children's Reading, Dies at 93." *New York Times,* 21 Nov. 2004.

Beard, Charles A. *An Economic Interpretation of the Constitution of the United States.* Reprint, New Brunswick, NJ: Transaction Publishers, 1998. First published 1913 by Macmillan.

Beatty, Patricia. *Be Ever Hopeful, Hannalee.* Reprint, Mahwah, NJ: Troll, 1991. First published 1988 by William Morrow.

———. *Charley Skedaddle.* Reprint, Mahwah, NJ: Troll, 1988. First published 1987 by William Morrow.

———. *Turn Homeward, Hannalee.* Reprint, New York: Beech Tree, 1999. First published 1984 by William Morrow.

Beck, Isabel L., et al., "Learning from Social Studies Texts." *Cognition and Instruction* 6 (1989): 99–158.

———. "Revising Social Studies Text from a Text-Processing Perspective: Evidence of Improved Comprehensibility." *Reading Research Quarterly* 26, 3 (1991): 251–76.

Bennett, John E. "Our Seaboard Islands on the Pacific." *Harper's Monthly Magazine* 97, 582 (1898): 852–62.

Berkhofer, Robert F., Jr. *The White Man's Indian: Images of the American Indian from Columbus to the Present.* New York: Vintage, 1978.

Berlin, Ira. *Many Thousand Gone: The First Two Centuries of Slavery in North America*. Cambridge, MA: Harvard University Press, 1998.

Bernstein, Iver. *The New York City Draft Riots: Their Significance for American Society and Politics in the Age of the Civil War*. New York: Oxford University Press, 1990.

Bielick, Stacey. "Issue Brief: 1.5 Million Homeschooled Students in the United States in 2007." Jessup, MD: National Center for Education Statistics, 2009.

Blackhawk, Ned. "Look How Far We've Come: How American Indian History Changed the Study of American History in the 1990s." *OAH Magazine of History* 9 (2005): 8–12.

Blight, David W. *Race and Reunion: The Civil War in American Memory*. Cambridge, MA: Harvard University Press, 2001.

Blos, Joan W. *A Gathering of Days: A New England Girl's Journal, 1830–32*. Reprint, New York: Aladdin, 1990. First published 1979 by Charles Scribner's Sons.

Booth, Martin. "Ages and Concepts: A Critique of the Piagetian Approach to History Teaching." In *History Curriculum for Teachers*, edited by Christopher Portal. New York: Falmer Press, 1987.

Bosmajian, Hamida. "Mildred Taylor's Story of Cassie Logan: A Search for Law and Justice in a Racist Society." *Children's Literature* 24 (1996): 141–60.

Bostrom, Karen Long. *Winning Authors: Profiles of the Newbery Medalists*. Westport, CT: Libraries Unlimited, 2003.

Boyer, Paul, and Stephen Nissenbaum. *Salem Possessed: The Social Origins of Witchcraft*. Cambridge, MA: Harvard University Press, 1974.

Bradford, Clare. *Unsettling Narratives: Postcolonial Readings of Children's Literature*. Waterloo, Ont.: Wilfrid Laurier University Press, 2007.

Brantingham, Barney. "Island Woman's Origins Still Hotly Debated." *Santa Barbara News Press*, 11 July 1993.

Brickell, John. "Narrative of John Brickell's Captivity among the Delaware Indians." *American Pioneer* 1, 2 (1842): 43–56.

Brink, Carol Ryrie. *Caddie Woodlawn*. Reprint, New York: Aladdin, 1990. First published 1935 by Macmillan.

Brinkley, Alan. *American History: A Survey*, 13th ed. New York: Glencoe/McGraw-Hill, 2009.

Brooks, Lisa. *The Common Pot: The Recovery of Native Space in the Northeast*. Minneapolis: University of Minnesota Press, 2008.

Brophy, Jere, and Bruce VanSledright. *Teaching and Learning History in Elementary Schools*. New York: Teachers College Press, 1997.

Brown, Carolyn M. "10 Best Cities for African Americans." *Black Enterprise*, 1 May 2007.

Brown, Joshua. "Into the Minds of Babes: Children's Books and the Past." In *Presenting the Past: Essays on History and the Public*, edited by Susan Porter Benson, Stephen Brier, and Roy Rosenzweig. Philadelphia: Temple University Press, 1986.

Bruchac, Joseph. *The Arrow over the Door*. New York: Dial, 1998.

———. "Border Crossings: Poems and Translations." PhD diss., Union Institute and University of Ohio, 1975.

———. *Bowman's Store: A Journey to Myself*. New York: Dial, 1997.

———. *The Heart of a Chief*. New York: Dial, 1998.

———. *Pocahontas*. New York: Harcourt, 2003.

———. *Sacajawea: The Story of Bird Woman and the Lewis and Clark Expedition.* New York: Harcourt, 2000.

———. *The Winter People.* New York: Dial, 2002.

Bryant, Dianne Pedrotty, et al. "Reading Outcomes for Students with and without Reading Disabilities in General Education Middle-School Content Area Classes." *Learning Disability Quarterly* 23, 4 (2000): 238–52.

Bryon, Jennifer. "William Armstrong's Old Masters." *Writer's Digest* (March 1978): 24–25.

Butterfield, Herbert. *The Whig Interpretation of History.* Reprint, New York: AMS Press, 1978. First published 1931 by G. Bell and Sons, London.

Byler, Mary Gloyne. *American Indian Authors for Young Readers: A Selected Bibliography.* New York: Association on American Indian Affairs, 1973.

C.B.G. "A Big Business, a Big Problem." *Publishers Weekly,* 21 Feb. 1966.

California Department of Education. *Recommended Readings in Literature: Kindergarten through Grade Eight.* Sacramento: California State Department of Education, 1986, 1989, 1990, 1996, 2002, 2009.

Calloway, Colin G. *The American Revolution in Indian Country: Crisis and Diversity in Native American Communities.* New York: Cambridge University Press, 1995.

Campisi, Jack. *The Mashpee Indians: Tribe on Trial.* Syracuse, NY: Syracuse University Press, 1991.

Carby, Hazel. "The Ideologies of Black Folk: The Historical Novel of Slavery." In *Slavery and the Literary Imagination: Selected Papers from the English Institute,* New Series, no. 198, edited by Deborah E. McDowell and Arnold Rampersad. Baltimore: Johns Hopkins University Press, 1989.

"Carver Elementary School." Michigan Historical Marker Website. *www.michmarkers.com* (accessed 15 Jan. 2011).

Chadwick-Joshua, Jocelyn. *The Jim Dilemma: Reading Race in "Huckleberry Finn."* Jackson: University of Mississippi, 1998.

Chall, Jeanne. "The New Reading Debates: Evidence from Science, Art, and Ideology." *Teachers College Record* 94, 2 (1992): 315–28.

———. *Stages of Reading Development.* New York: McGraw-Hill, 1983.

Cianciolo, Patricia. "Yesterday Comes Alive for Readers of Historical Fiction." *Language Arts* 58, 4 (1981): 452–61.

CIBC. *See* Council on Interracial Books for Children.

Civil War Diary. Based on *Across Five Aprils,* by Irene Hunt. Directed by Kevin Meyer. Santa Monica, CA: Rhino Home Video, 1991.

Cochran-Smith, Marilyn. *Walking the Road: Race, Diversity, and Social Justice in Teacher Education.* New York: Teachers College Press, 2004.

Collier, Christopher. *Brother Sam and All That: Historical Context and Literary Analysis of the Novels of James and Christopher Collier.* Orange, CT: Clearwater Press, 1999.

———. "Fact, Fiction, and History: The Role of Historian, Writer, Teacher, and Reader." *ALAN Review* 14, 2 (1987): 5–8.

———. "Johnny and Sam: Old and New Approaches to the American Revolution." *Horn Book Magazine* 52, 2 (1976): 132–38.

Collier, James Lincoln. "B (William Slater Brown)." *Spring: The Journal of the E. E. Cummings Society* 6 (1997): 128–51.

Collier, James Lincoln, and Christopher Collier. *Jump Ship to Freedom*. New York: Doubleday, 1981.

———. *My Brother Sam Is Dead*. Reprint, New York: Scholastic, 2005. First published 1974 by Four Winds Press.

———. *War Comes to Willy Freeman*. Reprint, New York: Dell Yearling, 1987. First published 1983 by Delacorte Press.

———. *Who Is Carrie?* Reprint, New York: Bantam Doubleday Dell, 1987. First published 1984 by Delacorte Press.

Collier, Wade. *The Colliers of Massachusetts: The Descendants of Thomas and Susannah Collier, Who Arrived in Hingham, Massachusetts in 1635*. Vol. 1, *The First Five Generations*. Lunenburg, MA: Privately published, 2004.

———. *The Colliers of Massachusetts: The Descendants of Thomas and Susannah Collier, Who Arrived in Hingham, Massachusetts in 1635*. Vol. 2, *Generation Six*. Lunenburg, MA: Privately published, 2009.

Common Core State Standards: English Language Arts. National Governors Association Center for Best Practices and Council of Chief State School Officers. 2010. *corestandards.org/the-standards/english-language-arts-standards*.

Constanzo, Angelo. *Surprising Narrative: Olaudah Equiano and the Beginnings of Black Autobiography*. New York: Greenwood Press, 1987.

Contemporary Authors: New Revision Series. Vol. 105. Detroit: Gale Group, 2002.

Corbett, Sue. "A Talk with Five NBA Finalists." *Publishers Weekly*, 30 Oct. 2008.

Cosgriff, Elizabeth. "The Newbery Awards." *Open Spaces* 2, 1 (2004): 49–53.

Council on Interracial Books for Children (CIBC). *Director's Files, 1954–84*. Sc MG 438, Manuscripts, Archives and Rare Books Division, Schomburg Center for Research in Black Culture, New York Public Library.

———. *Guidelines for Selecting Bias-Free Textbooks and Storybooks*. New York: Council on Interracial Books for Children, 1980.

Cowley, Malcolm. *Exile's Return: A Literary Odyssey of the 1920s*. Edited and introduced by Donald W. Faulkner. New York: Penguin, 1994.

Creech, Sharon. *Walk Two Moons*. New York: HarperCollins, 1994.

Cronon, William. *Changes in the Land: Indians, Colonists, and the Ecology of New England*. New York: Hill and Wang, 1983.

———. "A Place for Stories: Nature, History, and Narrative." *Journal of American History* 78, 4 (1992): 1347–76.

Cross, Helen Reeder. "Biographical Note on Elizabeth George Speare." In *Newbery and Caldecott Medal Books, 1956–1965*, edited by Lee Kingman. Boston: Horn Book, 1965.

Crowe, Chris. *Presenting Mildred D. Taylor*. New York: Twayne, 1999.

Cullinan, Bernice E., and Diane G. Person, eds. *The Continuum Encyclopedia of Children's Literature*. New York: Continuum, 2003.

Curtis, Christopher Paul. *Bud, Not Buddy*. Reprint, New York: Dell Yearling, 2002. First published 1999 by Delacorte Press.

———. *Elijah of Buxton*. New York: Scholastic, 2007.

———. *The Watsons Go to Birmingham—1963*. Reprint, New York: Bantam Doubleday Dell, 1997. First published 1995 by Delacorte Press.

Daily, Marla. "The Lone Woman of San Nicolas Island: A New Hypothesis on Her Origins." *California History* 68, 112 (1989): 36–65.

Daniels, Harvey. *Literature Circles: Voice and Choice in the Student-Centered Classroom.* Portland, ME: Stenhouse, 1994.

David, Robert, ed. *Moving Forward from the Past: Early Writings and Current Reflections of Middle School Founders.* Columbus, OH: National Middle School Association, 1998.

DelFattore, Joan. *What Johnny Shouldn't Read: Textbook Censorship in America.* New Haven, CT: Yale University Press, 1992.

Deloria, Philip J. *Playing Indian.* New Haven, CT: Yale University Press, 1998.

Deloria, Vine, Jr., and Clifford Lytle. *The Nations Within: The Past and Future of American Indian Sovereignty.* New York: Pantheon, 1984.

Demos, John. *Entertaining Satan: Witchcraft and the Culture of Early New England.* New Haven, CT: Yale University Press, 1982.

———. *The Unredeemed Captive: A Family Story from Early America.* New York: Vintage, 1994.

Dempsey, David. "A Second Chance—in Paperback." *New York Times Book Review,* 8 Nov. 1970, 6+.

Deutsch, Leonard J. "The Named and the Unnamed." In *Children's Novels and the Movies,* edited by Douglas Street. New York: Frederick Ungar, 1983.

Dittmer, John. *Local People: The Struggle for Civil Rights in Mississippi.* Urbana: University of Illinois Press, 1995.

Dodge, Bernie. "Some Thoughts about WebQuests." 5 May 1997. *webquest.sdsu.edu/about_webquests.html.*

Dorris, Michael. "Native American Literature in an Ethnohistorical Context." *College English* 41 (1979): 147–62.

Dowd, Gregory Evans. *A Spirited Resistance: The North American Indian Struggle for Unity, 1745–1815.* Baltimore: John Hopkins University Press, 1992.

Dresang, Eliza T. "Interview of Joseph Bruchac." Cooperative Children's Book Center, CCBC-Net. 22 Oct. 1999. *www.education.wisc.edu/ccbc/authors/bruchac.asp.*

Drew, Bernard A. *The 100 Most Popular Young Adult Authors: Biographical Sketches and Bibliographies.* Englewood, CO: Libraries Unlimited, 1997.

Drumming Up Resentment: The Anti-Indian Movement in Montana. Helena: Montana Human Rights Network, 2000.

Dunn, Richard. *Puritans and Yankees: The Winthrop Dynasty of New England, 1630–1717.* Princeton, NJ: Princeton University Press, 1962.

Durell, Ann. "If There Is No Happy Ending: Children's Book Publishing—Past, Present, and Future." Parts 1 and 2. *Horn Book Magazine* 58 (1982): 23–30, 145–50.

Eastern Shoshone tribal website. *www.easternshoshone.net* (accessed 15 Jan. 2011).

Edmunds, R. David. "Native Americans, New Voices: American Indian History, 1895–1995." *American Historical Review* 100, 3 (1995): 717–40.

Edwards, Clifford D. *Conrad Richter's Ohio Trilogy: Its Ideas, Themes, and Relationship to Literary Tradition.* The Hague: Mouton, 1970.

Egoff, Sheila. "The Problem Novel." In *Only Connect: Readings on Children's Literature,* 2nd ed., edited by Sheila Egoff, G. T. Stubbs, and L. F. Ashley. New York: Oxford University Press, 1980.

Eisenhart, Margaret, and Lisa Towne. "Contestation and Change in National Policy on 'Scientifically Based' Education Research." *Educational Researcher* 32, 7 (2003): 31–38.

Elizabeth George Speare Collection, Howard Gotlieb Archival Center, Boston University.

Elkins, Stanley. *Slavery: A Problem in American Institutional and Intellectual Life.* Chicago: University of Chicago Press, 1959.

Ellermeyer, Deborah, and Kay A. Chick. *Multicultural American History: Through Children's Literature.* Englewood, CO: Teacher Ideas Press, 2003.

Epstein, Connie C. "Publishing Children's Books." In *Children's Books and Their Creators,* edited by Anita Silvey. Boston: Houghton Mifflin, 1995.

Epstein, Terrie. "Deconstructing Differences in African-American and European-American Adolescents' Perspectives on U.S. History." *Curriculum Inquiry* 28, 4 (1998): 397–423.

Erdrich, Louise. *The Birchbark House.* Reprint, New York: Scholastic, 2000. First published 1999 by Hyperion Books for Children.

Erskine, Margaret. *Esther Forbes.* Worcester, MA: Worcester Bicentennial Collection, 1976.

Farmer, Michelle Latimer. "The Black Experience and the Human Experience: The Two *Sounder* Texts." In *The Antic Art: Enhancing Children's Literary Experience through Film and Video,* edited by Lucy Rollin. Fort Atkinson, WI: Highsmith Press, 1993.

Feldstein, Ruth. *Motherhood in Black and White: Race and Sex in American Liberalism, 1930–1965.* Ithaca, NY: Cornell University Press, 2000.

Fellman, Anita Clair. *Little House, Long Shadow: Laura Ingalls Wilder's Impact on American Culture.* Columbia: University of Missouri Press, 2008.

FitzGerald, Frances. *America Revised: History Schoolbooks in the Twentieth Century.* Boston: Little, Brown, 1979.

Fitzpatrick, Ellen. *History's Memory: Writing America's Past, 1880–1980.* Cambridge, MA: Harvard University Press, 2002.

Fixico, Donald L., ed. *Rethinking American Indian History.* Albuquerque: University of New Mexico Press, 1997.

Flaherty, Julie. "Books: When Religion in Schools Meant Spilled Blood." Education. *New York Times,* 25 Apr. 2004.

Flesch, Rudolf. *Why Johnny Can't Read and What You Can Do About It.* New York: Harper, 1955.

Foner, Eric. *Free Soil, Free Labor, Free Men: The Ideology of the Republican Party before the Civil War.* New York: Oxford University Press, 1970.

———. "Slavery, the Civil War, and Reconstruction." In *The New American History,* revised and expanded ed., edited by Eric Foner. Philadelphia: Temple University Press, 1997.

Forbes, Esther. "Acceptance Paper." In *Newbery Medal Books, 1922–1955, with Their Authors' Acceptance Papers and Related Material Chiefly from the "Horn Book Magazine,"* edited by Bertha Mahony Miller and Elinor Whitney Field. Boston: Horn Book, 1955.

———. *Johnny Tremain.* Reprint, New York: Dell, 1987. First published 1943 by Houghton Mifflin.

———. *Paul Revere and the World He Lived In.* Reprint, New York: Mariner, 1999. First published 1942 by Houghton Mifflin.

Foster, Frances Smith. *Witnessing Slavery: The Development of Ante-bellum Slave Narratives,* 2nd ed. Madison: University of Wisconsin Press, 1979.

Fox, Paula. *Borrowed Finery*. New York: Henry Holt, 1999.

———. "Newbery Award Acceptance." *Horn Book Magazine* 50, 4 (1974): 344–50.

———. *The Slave Dancer*. Reprint, New York: Dell, 1975. First published 1973 by Bradbury Press.

Francis, Lee, and James Bruchac. *Reclaiming the Vision, Past, Present, and Future: Native Voices for the Eighth Generation*. New York: Greenfield Review Press, 1996.

Freedman, Russell. *Lincoln: A Photobiography*. New York: Clarion, 1987.

French, Allen. "*Paul Revere and the World He Lived In*." Book review. *New England Quarterly* 15, 3 (1942): 521–22.

Fritz, Jean. *And Then What Happened, Paul Revere?* New York: J. P. Putnam's Sons, 1973.

———. "For Young Readers." *New York Times Book Review*, 21 Nov. 1976.

Fuhler, Carol J. "Add Spark and Sizzle to Middle School Social Studies: Use Trade Books to Enhance Instruction." *Social Studies* 82, 6 (1991): 234–37.

Gallo, Donald R., and Ellie Barksdale. "Using Fiction in American History." *Social Education* 47, 4 (1983): 286–89.

Gardiner, John Reynolds. *Stone Fox*. New York: Harper Trophy, 2003. First published 1980 by HarperCollins.

Gardner, Howard. *The Disciplined Mind: Beyond Facts and Standardized Tests, the K–12 Education That Every Child Deserves*. New York: Penguin, 2000.

Gardner, Mary. "An Educator's Concerns about the California Reading Initiative." *New Advocate* 1, 4 (1988): 250–53.

Gardner, Susan. "The Education of Joseph Bruchac: Conversation, 1995–1997." *Paintbrush* 24 (1997): 16–44.

Garraty, John, and Mark Carnes. *American Nation*, 8th ed. White Plains, NY: Addison Wesley Longman, 2001.

Garrison, Dee. *Apostles of Culture: The Public Librarian and American Society, 1876–1920*. Madison: University of Wisconsin Press, 1979.

Genovese, Eugene D. *Roll, Jordan, Roll: The World the Slaves Made*. New York: Pantheon, 1974.

George, Marshall A., and Andi Stix. "Using Multilevel Young Adult Literature in Middle School American Studies." *Social Studies* 91, 1 (2000): 25–31.

Gibson, Evelyn Graves. "The Black Image in Children's Fiction: A Content Analysis of Racist Content, Black Experience and Primary Audience in Children's Books Published between 1958–1970 and 1971–1982." *University Microfilms International* #8521083 (1985): 4–5. Cited in Deborah Kutenplon and Ellen Olmstead, *Young Adult Fiction by African American Writers, 1968–1993: A Critical and Annotated Guide*. New York: Garland, 1996.

Giese, Paula. "Native American Books: Middle School (9–14) Books: *Indian in the Cupboard*." Last modified 20 May 1996. *www.kstrom.net/isk/books/middle/mi228.html*.

Gladwell, Malcolm. "The Courthouse Ring: Atticus Finch and the Limits of Southern Liberalism." *New Yorker*, 10 Aug. 2009.

Glancy, Barbara. "The Beautiful People in Children's Books." *Childhood Education* 46, 7 (1970): 365–70.

Gogas, Donna. "*Across Five Aprils*." Classroom website. *www.dscorpio.tripod.com/across_five_aprils.htm* (accessed 15 Jan. 2011).

Graham, Patricia Albjerg. *Schooling America: How the Public Schools Meet the Nation's Changing Needs.* New York: Oxford University Press, 2005.

Gray, William S. *On Their Own in Reading.* Chicago: Scott, Foresman, 1948. Quoted in E. Jennifer Monaghan, "Phonics and Whole Word/Whole Language Controversies, 1948–1998: An Introductory History." *American Reading Forum Yearbook* 18 (1998): 1–24.

Greene, Bette. *Morning Is a Long Time Coming.* Reprint, New York: Puffin, 1999. First published 1978 by Dial Press.

———. *Summer of My German Soldier.* Reprint, New York: Bantam, 1984. First published 1973 by Dial Press.

Greene, Lorenzo Johnston. *The Negro in Colonial New England, 1620–1776.* New York: Columbia University Press, 1942.

Gutiérrez, Ramón A. *When Jesus Came, the Corn Mothers Went Away: Marriage, Sexuality, and Power in New Mexico, 1500–1846.* Stanford, CA: Stanford University Press, 1991.

Hall, Jacquelyn Dowd. "The Long Civil Rights Movement and the Political Uses of the Past." *Journal of American History* 91, 4 (2005): 1233–63.

Hallam, Roy. "Piaget and the Teaching of History." *Educational Research* 12, 1 (1969): 3–12.

Hamilton, Virginia. *M. C. Higgins the Great.* New York: Simon and Schuster, 1974.

Hancock, Marjorie R. "Children's Books in the Classroom: Milestones and Memories of the Literature-Based Revolution." In *Children's Literature Remembered: Issues, Trends, and Favorite Books,* edited by Linda M. Pavonetti. Westport, CT: Libraries Unlimited, 2004.

Handlin, Oscar, and Mary F. Handlin. "Origins of the Southern Labor System." *William and Mary Quarterly* 3, 7 (1950): 199–222.

Harlan, David. "Intellectual History and the Return of Literature." *American Historical Review* 94, 3 (1989): 581–609.

Hartman, Andrew. *Education and the Cold War: The Battle for the American School.* New York: Palgrave Macmillan, 2008.

Heizer, Robert F., and Albert B. Elsasser, eds. "Original Accounts of the Lone Woman of San Nicolas Island." *Reports of the University of California Archaeological Survey #55.* Berkeley: University of California, 1961.

Hendryx, Nancy. "Kindred Spirits." *Concord Monitor,* 20 Oct. 1999.

Hernández-Delgado, Julio L. "Pura Teresa Belpré, Storyteller and Pioneer Puerto Rican Librarian." *Library Quarterly* 62, 4 (1992): 425–40.

Hickman, Janet. "Put the Story into History: How Teachers Can Make Stories of the Past Come to Life in the Present." *Instructor* 100, 4 (1990): 22–24.

Higham, John. *History: Professional Scholarship in America.* Baltimore: Johns Hopkins University Press, 1989.

———. "Multiculturalism and Universalism: A History and Critique." *American Quarterly* 45, 2 (1993): 195–219.

Highsmith, Andrew Robert. "Demolition Means Progress: Race, Class, and the Deconstruction of the American Dream in Flint, Michigan." PhD diss., University of Michigan, 2009.

Hirsch, E. D. *Cultural Literacy: What Every American Needs to Know.* Boston: Houghton Mifflin, 1997.

Hirschfelder, Arlene, Paulette Fairbanks Molin, and Yvonne Walkim. *American*

Indian Stereotypes in the World of Children: A Reader and Bibliography, 2nd ed. Lanham, MD: Scarecrow Press, 1999.

Hoff, Syd. *Danny and the Dinosaur*. New York: Harper, 1958.

Holton, Woody. *Forced Founders: Indians, Debtors, Slaves, and the Making of the American Revolution in Virginia*. Chapel Hill: University of North Carolina Press, 1999.

Honey, Michael K. *Southern Labor and Black Civil Rights: Organizing Memphis Workers*. Urbana: University of Illinois Press, 1993.

Honig, Bill. "The California Reading Initiative." *New Advocate* 1, 4 (1988): 235–40.

Horning, Kathleen. "An Interview with Rudine Sims Bishop." *Horn Book Magazine* 84, 3 (2008): 247–59.

———. "Patriot Games: Yes, Indeed, the British Are Coming! But M. T. Anderson's Revolutionary War Novel Is Unlike Anything You've Ever Read." *School Library Journal* 52, 11 (2006): 40–44.

Howard, Elizabeth F. *America as Story: Historical Fiction for Secondary Schools*. Chicago: American Library Association, 1988.

Hubbard, Dolan, ed. *Recovered Writers/Recovered Texts: Race, Class, and Gender in Black Women's Literature*. Knoxville: University of Tennessee Press, 1997.

Huck, Charlotte S. *Children's Literature in the Elementary School*, 3rd ed. New York: Holt, 1979.

———. "Literature-Based Reading Programs: A Retrospective." *New Advocate* 9, 1 (1996): 23–33.

Hudson, Travis. "An Additional Harrington Note on the 'Lone Woman' of San Nicolas." *Masterkey* 52, 4 (1978): 151–55.

———. "Additional Harrington Notes on the 'Lone Woman' of San Nicolas." *Masterkey* 54, 3 (1980): 109–13.

———. "Recently Discovered Accounts Concerning the 'Lone Woman' of San Nicolas Island." *Journal of California and Great Basin Anthropology* 3, 2 (1981): 187–99.

———. "Some J. P. Harrington Notes on the 'Lone Woman' of San Nicolas." *Masterkey* 52, 1 (1978): 23–29.

Hudson Museum of Maine. "Curriculum Connection: *The Sign of the Beaver*." 27 Jan. 2010. *www.umaine.edu/hudsonmuseum/sigbea.php*.

Hunt, Irene. *Across Five Aprils*. Reprint, New York: Berkley Books, 1964. First published 1964 by Follett.

Hunt, Peter. *Criticism, Theory, and Children's Literature*. Cambridge, MA: Basil Blackwell, 1991.

Hurston, Zora Neale. *Their Eyes Were Watching God*. Reprint, New York: HarperCollins, 1990. First published 1937 by J. B. Lippincott.

Hurtado, Albert L. *Intimate Frontiers: Sex, Gender, and Culture in Old California*. Albuquerque: University of New Mexico Press, 1999.

The Indian in the Cupboard. Directed by Frank Oz. Hollywood, CA: Paramount Pictures, 1995.

Indiana Department of Education. *Indiana Reading List*. Indianapolis: Indiana Department of Education, 2008. *dc.doe.in.gov/Standards/AcademicStandards/PrintLibrary/docs-ReadingLists/2006-ReadingList-AllGrades.pdf*.

Ingersoll, Richard M. "The Problem of Underqualified Teachers in American Secondary Schools." *Educational Researcher* 28, 2 (1999): 26–37.

Interracial Books for Children. Bulletin of the Council on Interracial Books for Children. 1966–1989.

Island of the Blue Dolphins. Directed by James B. Clark. Universal City, CA: MCA Home Video, 1964.

Isserman, Maurice, and Michael Kazin. *America Divided: The Civil War of the 1960s.* New York: Oxford University Press, 2000.

Jackson, Kenneth T. *Crabgrass Frontier: The Suburbanization of the United States.* New York: Oxford University Press, 1985.

Jaenen, Cornelius J. "Thoughts on Early Canadian Contact." In *The American Indian and the Problem of History,* edited by Calvin Martin. New York: Oxford University Press, 1987.

Jennings, Francis. "A Growing Partnership: Historians, Anthropologists, and American Indian History." *Ethnohistory* 29, 1 (1982): 21–34.

Jerald, Craig D. "No Action: Putting an End to Out-of-Field Teaching." Washington, DC: Report of Education Trust, 2002.

Johnny Tremain. Directed by Robert Stevenson. Burbank, CA: Disney, 1957.

Johnson, David R. *A Writer's Life.* University Park: Pennsylvania State University, 2001.

Johnson, Dianne. *Telling Tales: The Pedagogy and Promise of African American Literature for Youth.* New York: Greenwood Press, 1990.

Johnson, Walter. *Soul by Soul: Life Inside the Antebellum Slave Market.* Cambridge, MA: Harvard University Press, 1999.

Johnston, Henry P. *Yale and Her Honor-Roll in the American Revolution, 1775–1783.* New York: Privately published, 1888.

Jordan, June Meyer. "*Sounder.*" Book review. *New York Times Book Review,* 26 Oct. 1969.

Just, Julie. "Bookshelf: *Chains.*" *New York Times Book Review,* 21 Dec. 2008.

Kammen, Michael. *Mystic Chords of Memory: The Transformation of Tradition in American Culture.* New York: Knopf, 1991.

———. *A Season of Youth: The American Revolution and the Historical Imagination.* New York: Knopf, 1978.

Karlsen, Carol F. *The Devil in the Shape of a Woman: Witchcraft in Colonial New England.* New York: W. W. Norton, 1998.

Kauanui, J. Kehaulani. "For the Seventh Generation: American Indians, Youth and Education." Interview with Debbie Reese. *Indigenous Politics: From Native New England and Beyond.* Podcast, 6 July 2009. indigenouspolitics.mypodcast .com/2009/07/For_the_Seventh_Generation_American_Indians_Youth_and_ Education-220483.html.

Keeping the Promise. Based on *The Sign of the Beaver,* by Elizabeth George Speare. Directed by Sheldon Larry. Chicago: Questar, 1997.

Keith, Harold. *Rifles for Watie.* Reprint, New York: Harper Trophy, 1987. First published 1957 by Thomas Y. Crowell.

Keith, Sherry. "Choosing Textbooks: A Study of Instructional Materials Selection Processes for Public Education." *Book Research Quarterly* 1, 2 (1985): 24–37.

Kelly, Timothy, and Bruce VanSledright. "A Journey toward Wiser Practice in the Teaching of American History." In *Wise Social Studies Teaching in an Age of High-Stakes Testing: Essays on Classroom Practices and Possibilities,* edited by

Elizabeth Anne Yeager and O. L. Davis Jr. Greenwich, CT: Information Age, 2005.

Kerber, Linda K. "The Revolutionary Generation: Ideology, Politics, and Culture in the Early Republic." In *The New American History*, revised and expanded ed., edited by Eric Foner. Philadelphia: Temple University Press, 1997.

———. *Women of the Republic: Intellect and Ideology in Revolutionary America.* Chapel Hill: University of North Carolina Press, 1980.

Kerlan Collection of Children's Literature, Children's Literature Research Collections, University of Minnesota Library. Bette Greene Papers. Irene Hunt Papers. James L. Collier Papers. Scott O'Dell Papers. Theodore Taylor Papers. William Armstrong Papers.

Kertész, Judy. "Skeletons in the American Attic: Curiosity, Science, and the Appropriation of the American Indian Past, 1776–1846." PhD diss., Harvard University, in progress.

Kidd, Kenneth. "'Not Censorship but Selection': Censorship and/as Prizing." *Children's Literature in Education* 40, 3 (2009): 197–216.

———. "Prizing Children's Literature: The Case of Newbery Gold." *Children's Literature* 35 (2007): 169–90.

Kirk, Patsy. "Fact or Fiction: An Analysis of Historical Fiction Literature by Elizabeth George Speare." Webquest. *projects.edtech.sandi.net/grant/historicalfiction/t-index .htm* (accessed 19 June 2010).

Kovacs, Deborah. *Meet the Authors: 25 Writers of Upper Elementary and Middle School Books Talk about Their Work.* New York: Scholastic, 1995.

Krammer, Arnold. *Nazi Prisoners of War in America.* New York: Stein and Day, 1979.

Kretch, Shepard. *The Ecological Indian: Myth and History.* New York: W. W. Norton, 1999.

Kupperman, Karen Ordahl. *Indians and English: Facing Off in Early America.* Ithaca, NY: Cornell University Press, 2000.

Kutenplon, Deborah, and Ellen Olmstead. *Young Adult Fiction by African American Writers, 1968–1993: A Critical and Annotated Guide.* New York: Garland, 1996.

Kutzer, M. Daphne. "Thatchers and Thatcherites: Lost and Found Empires in Three British Fantasies." *Lion and the Unicorn* 22, 2 (1998): 196–210.

Kuznets, Lois R. "Sweet and Sour Land: A Critical Comparison of the 'Sounder' Novels." *Illinois English Bulletin* 65, 3 (1978): 23–29.

LaBonty, Jan. "A Demand for Excellence in Books for Children." *Journal of American Indian Education* 34, 2 (1995): 1–9.

LaHood, Marvin J. *Conrad Richter's America.* The Hague: Mouton, 1975.

———. "*The Light in the Forest*: History as Fiction." *English Journal* 55, 3 (1966): 298–304.

Lambert, Peter. *Amos Fortune: The Man and His Legacy.* Jaffrey, NH: Amos Fortune Forum, 2000.

Lamm, Robert. "Betty Evensky Greene." *The Encyclopedia of Arkansas History and Culture.* Central Arkansas Library System. Last modified 5 Apr. 2010. *www.encyclopediaofarkansas.net.*

Larrick, Nancy. "The All-White World of Children's Literature." *Saturday Review of Books,* 11 Sept. 1965.

Lass-Woodfin, Mary Jo, ed. *Books on American Indians and Eskimos: A Selection*

Guide for Children and Young Adults. Chicago: American Library Association, 1978.

"'Last' of 430,353 PW's to Leave U.S." *New York Times*, 8 Aug. 1947.

Lawson, Robert. *Ben and Me: A New and Astonishing Life of Benjamin Franklin as Written by His Good Mouse Amos*. Reprint, Boston: Little, Brown, 1988. First published 1939 by Little, Brown.

Leahey, Christopher R. *Whitewashing War: Historical Myth, Corporate Textbooks, and Possibilities for Democratic Education*. New York: Teachers College Press, 2010.

Lee, Harper. *To Kill a Mockingbird*. Reprint, New York: Warner, 1982. First published 1960 by J. B. Lippincott.

Lee, Peter, and Rosalyn Ashby. "Progression in Historical Understanding among Students Ages 7–14." In *Knowing, Teaching, and Learning History: National and International Perspectives*, edited Peter N. Stearns, Peter Seixas, and Sam Wineburg. New York: New York University Press, 2000.

Lemann, Nicholas. "The Reading Wars." *Atlantic Monthly* 280, 5 (1997): 128–34.

LeMaster, Carolyn Gray. *A Corner of the Tapestry: A History of the Jewish Experience in Arkansas, 1820s–1990s*. Fayetteville: University of Arkansas Press, 1994.

Lenski, Lois. *Indian Captive: The Story of Mary Jemison*. Reprint, New York: Harper Trophy, 1995. First published 1941 by Frederick A. Stokes.

Lepore, Jill. *In the Name of War: King Philip's War and the Origins of American Identity*. New York: Vintage, 1998.

Lester, Julius. "*The Slave Dancer*." Book review. *New York Times Book Review*, 20 Jan. 1974.

Le Sueur, Meridel. *Sparrow Hawk*. Reprint, Stevens Point, WI: Holy Cow! Press, 1987. First published 1950 by Knopf.

Levstik, Linda S. "Historical Narrative and the Young Reader." *Theory into Practice* 18, 2 (1989): 114–19.

———. "'I Wanted to Be There': The Impact of Narrative on Children's Historical Thinking." In *The Story of Ourselves: Teaching History through Children's Literature*, edited by Michael O. Tunnell and Richard Ammon. Portsmouth, NH: Heinemann, 1993.

———. "Narrative as a Primary Act of Mind?" In *Researching History Education: Theory, Method, and Context*, edited by Linda S. Levstik and Keith C. Barton. New York: Routledge, 2008.

———. "The Relationship between Historical Response and Narrative in a Sixth-Grade Classroom." In *Researching History Education: Theory, Method, and Context*, edited by Linda S. Levstik and Keith C. Barton. New York: Routledge, 2008.

Levstik, Linda S., and Keith C. Barton, eds. *Researching History Education: Theory, Method, and Context*. New York: Routledge, 2008.

The Light in the Forest. Directed by Herschel Daugherty. Burbank, CA: Disney, 1958.

Lightfoot, Kent G. *Indians, Missionaries, and Merchants: The Legacy of Colonial Encounters on the California Frontiers*. Berkeley: University of California Press, 2005.

Loewen, James W. *Lies My Teacher Told Me: Everything Your American History Textbook Got Wrong*. New York: New Press, 1995.

Lowenthal, David. *The Past Is a Foreign Country*. Cambridge: Cambridge University Press, 1988.

————. *Possessed by the Past: The Heritage Crusade and the Spoils of History.* New York: Free Press, 1996.

Lundin, Anne H. *Constructing the Canon of Children's Literature: Beyond Library Walls and Ivory Towers.* New York: Routledge, 2004.

MacCann, Donnarae. "Militarism in Juvenile Fiction." *Interracial Books for Children* 13, 6–7 (1982): 18–20.

MacCann, Donnarae, and Gloria Woodard, eds. *The Black American in Books for Children: Readings on Racism,* 2nd ed. Metuchen, NJ: Scarecrow Press, 1985.

MacDougall, Pauleena. *The Penobscot Dance of Resistance: Tradition in the History of a People.* Durham: University of New Hampshire Press, 2004.

MacLachlan, Patricia. *Sarah, Plain and Tall.* New York: HarperCollins, 1985.

Macleod, Anne Scott. "Writing Backwards: Modern Models in Historical Fiction." *Horn Book Magazine* 24, 1 (1998): 26–33.

MacPherson, Karen. "Saturday Diary: Amos Fortune Lives on, an Inspiration to All Free Men and Children." *Pittsburgh Post-Gazette,* 17 Apr. 2004.

Madsen, Valden J. "Classic Americana: Themes and Values in the Tales of Robert Lawson." *Lion and the Unicorn* 3, 1 (1979): 89–106.

Maher, Susan Naramore. "Encountering Others: The Meeting of Cultures in Scott O'Dell's *Island of the Blue Dolphins* and *Sing Down the Moon.*" *Children's Literature in Education* 23, 4 (1992): 215–27.

Main, Jackson Turner. *Society and Economy in Colonial Connecticut.* Princeton, NJ: Princeton University Press, 1985.

March, Tom. "WebQuests 101." *Multimedia Schools* 7, 5 (2000): 55+.

Marcus, Leonard S. *Minders of Make-Believe: Idealists, Entrepreneurs, and the Shaping of American Children's Literature.* Boston: Houghton Mifflin, 2008.

Martel, Erich. "Can 'Social Studies' Standards Prepare History Teachers?" *Perspectives* 37, 7 (1999): 33–36.

Martin, Calvin, ed. *The American Indian and the Problem of History.* New York: Oxford University Press, 1987.

Martin, Michelle H. *Brown Gold: Milestones of African-American Children's Picture Books, 1845–2002.* New York: Routledge, 2004.

Massachusetts Department of Education. *English Language Arts Curriculum Framework.* Malden: Massachusetts Department of Education, 2001.

Matusow, Allen J. *The Unraveling of America: A History of Liberalism in the 1960s.* New York: Harper and Row, 1984.

May, Elaine Tyler. *Homeward Bound: American Families in the Cold War Era.* New York: Basic, 1988.

McCawley, William. *The First Angelinos: The Gabrielino Indians of Los Angeles.* Banning, CA: Malki Museum Press, 1996.

McDiarmid, G. Williamson, and Peter Vinten-Johansen. "A Catwalk across the Great Divide: Redesigning the History Teaching Methods Course." In *Knowing, Teaching, and Learning History: National and International Perspectives,* edited by Peter N. Stearns, Peter Seixas, and Sam Wineburg. New York: New York University Press, 2000.

McDowell, Edwin. "Scott O'Dell, a Children's Author of Historical Fiction, Dies at 91." *New York Times,* 17 Oct. 1989.

McElmeel, Sharron L. *The 100 Most Popular Young Adult Authors: Biographical Sketches and Bibliographies.* Englewood, CO: Libraries Unlimited, 1999.

McGirr, Lisa. *Suburban Warriors: The Origins of the New American Right*. Princeton, NJ: Princeton University Press, 2001.

McGowan, Thomas M. *Children's Fiction as a Source for Social Studies Skill-Building*. ERIC Digest 37. Bloomington, IL: ERIC Clearinghouse for Social Studies/ Science Education, 1987.

McGowan, Thomas M., Lynnette Erickson, and Judith A. Neufeld. "With Reason and Rhetoric: Building the Case for the Literature–Social Studies Connection." *Social Education* 60, 4 (1996): 203–7.

McKeown, Margaret G., et al. "The Contribution of Prior Knowledge and Coherent Text to Comprehension." *Reading Research Quarterly* 27, 1 (1992): 79–93.

McLellan, Dennis. "'Cay' Author Wins Ruling on Sequel." *Los Angeles Times*, 24 Nov. 1994.

McNair, Jonda C. "'I May Be Crackin', but Um Fackin': Racial Humor in *The Watsons Go to Birmingham—1963*." *Children's Literature in Education* 39, 3 (2008): 201–12.

McNeil, Linda M. *Contradictions of School Reform: Educational Costs of Standardized Testing*. New York: Routledge, 2000.

McNulty, Faith. "Children's Books for Christmas." *New Yorker*, 1 Dec. 1980.

Meacham, Jon. "The Revolutionary: He Has the Money and Message to Upend 2008." *Newsweek*, 12 Nov. 2007.

Melish, Joanne Pope. *Disowning Slavery: Gradual Emancipation and "Race" in New England, 1780–1860*. Ithaca, NY: Cornell University Press, 1998.

Merrell, James H. "Some Thoughts on Colonial Historians and American Indians." *William and Mary Quarterly* 46, 1 (1989): 94–119.

Mickenberg, Julia L. "Communist in a Coonskin Hat? Meridel Le Sueur's Books for Children and the Reformulation of America's Cold War Frontier Epic." *Lion and the Unicorn* 21, 1 (1997): 59–85.

———. *Learning from the Left: Children's Literature, the Cold War, and Radical Politics in the United States*. New York: Oxford University Press, 2006.

Miller, Arthur. *The Crucible*. New York: Viking, 1953.

Miller, Wanda J. *U.S. History through Children's Literature: From the Colonial Period to World War II*. Englewood, CO: Teacher Ideas Press, 1997.

Monaghan, E. Jennifer. "Phonics and Whole Word/Whole Language Controversies, 1948–1998: An Introductory History." *American Reading Forum Yearbook* 18 (1998): 1–24.

Moore, Opal, and Donnarae MacCann. "The Ignoble Savage: Amerind Images in the Mainstream Mind." *Children's Literature Association Quarterly* 13, 1 (1988): 26–30.

Moran, Edward. "Dick and Jane Readers." *St. James Encyclopedia of Popular Culture*. Detroit: St. James Press, 2000.

Moreau, Joseph. *Schoolbook Nation: Conflicts over American History Textbooks from the Civil War to the Present*. Ann Arbor: University of Michigan Press, 2003.

Morgan, Peter E. "A Bridge to Whose Future? Young Adult Literature and the Asian American Teenager." *ALAN Review* 25, 3 (1998): 18–20.

———. "History for Our Children: An Interview with Christopher Paul Curtis, a Contemporary Voice in African American Young Adult Fiction." *MELUS* 27, 2 (2002): 197–215.

Morgan, Ron. "An Account of the Discovery of a Whale-Bone House on San Nicolas Island." *Journal of California and Great Basin Anthropology* 1, 1 (1979): 171–77.

Morris, Aldon D. "Birmingham Confrontation Reconsidered: An Analysis of the Dynamics and Tactics of Mobilization." *American Sociological Review* 58, 5 (1993): 621–36.

Morrison, Toni. *Beloved*. New York: Knopf, 1987.

Mosley, Ann. "Signs in Speare's *The Sign of the Beaver*." *ALAN Review* 22, 3 (1995): 19–21.

Moss, Barbara. "Close Up: An Interview with Dr. Richard Vacca." *California Reader* 36 (2002): 54–59.

———. "Making a Case and a Place for Effective Content Area Literacy Instruction in the Elementary Grades." *Reading Teacher* 59, 1 (2005): 46–56.

Moynihan, Daniel Patrick. *The Negro Family: The Case for National Action*. Washington, DC: Office of Policy Planning and Research, U.S. Department of Labor, 1965.

Myers, Walter Dean. *Riot*. New York: Egmont, 2009.

Nagel, Joane. *American Indian Ethnic Renewal: Red Power and the Resurgence of Identity and Culture*. New York: Oxford University Press, 1996.

"Nancy Larrick Succumbs to Pneumonia." *School Library Journal* 51, 1 (2005): 22.

A Narrative of the Captivity of Mrs. Johnson, containing an account of her sufferings, during four years, with the Indians and French. Reprint, New York: n.p., 1841. First published 1796 by David Carlisle Jr., Walpole, NH.

Nash, Gary, Charlotte Crabtree, and Ross Dunn. *History on Trial: Culture Wars and the Teaching of the Past*. New York: Vintage, 2000.

National Center for History in the Schools. *National Standards for United States History: Exploring the American Experience, Grades 5–12*. Los Angeles: National Center for History in Schools, 1996.

National Council for the Social Studies. "About National Council for the Social Studies." *www.socialstudies.org/about* (accessed 15 Jan. 2011).

———. *Expectations of Excellence: Curriculum Standards for Social Studies*. Washington, DC: National Council for the Social Studies, 1994.

———. *National Curriculum Standards for Social Studies: A Framework for Teaching, Learning, and Assessment*. Silver Spring, MD: National Council for the Social Studies, 2010.

———. "Powerful and Purposeful Teaching and Learning in Elementary School Social Studies." Position statement. June 2009.

National Middle School Association. "Middle Level Teacher Certification/Licensure by State." 15 Jan. 2007. *www.nmsa.org*.

———. "Position Statement on Curriculum Integration." Sept. 2002. *www.nmsa.org*.

———. "Position Statement on the Professional Preparation of Middle Level Teachers." Feb. 2006. *www.nmsa.org*.

Nelson, Jacquelyn S. *Indiana Quakers Confront the Civil War*. Indianapolis: Indiana Historical Society, 1991.

New York State Department of Education. *Language Arts Resource Guide: Instructional Materials*. Albany: New York State Education Department, 1996.

Newman, Simon P. "Writing the History of the American Revolution." In *The State of U.S. History*, edited by Melvyn Stokes. New York: Berg, 2002.

Nidever, George. "The Life and Adventures of a Pioneer of California since 1834." In *Reports of the University of California Archaeological Survey #55*, edited by Robert F. Heizer and Albert B. Elsasser. Berkeley: University of California, 1961.

North Carolina Department of Education. "Appendix I: English I Books." In *In the Right Direction: High School English Language Arts*. Raleigh: North Carolina Department of Education, 2002.

Novick, Peter. *That Noble Dream: The "Objectivity Question" and the American Historical Profession*. New York: Cambridge University Press, 1988.

O'Brien, Jean M. *Dispossession by Degrees: Indian Land and Identity in Natick, Massachusetts, 1650–1790*. Lincoln: University of Nebraska Press, 2003.

O'Dell, Scott. "An Adventure with Memory and Words." *Psychology Today* 18 (1968): 40–43.

———. *Island of the Blue Dolphins*. Reprint, New York: Dell Yearling, 1987. First published 1960 by Houghton Mifflin.

———. *Sarah Bishop*. Reprint, New York: Scholastic, 1991. First published 1980 by Houghton Mifflin.

———. *Sing Down the Moon*. Boston: Houghton Mifflin, 1970.

———. *Zia*. Reprint, New York: Bantam Doubleday Dell, 1995. First published 1976 by Houghton Mifflin.

Office of Research and Statistics and Office of Diversity. "Diversity Counts." American Library Association, 2007.

Ortiz, Simon J. "Towards a National Indian Literature: Cultural Authenticity in Nationalism." *MELUS* 8, 2 (1981): 7–12.

Oyate. "Books to Avoid." 1990–2009. *www.oyate.org/books-to-avoid/index.html* (accessed 11 Oct. 2009; no longer available).

Paisano, Edna L. "Population Profile of the United States: The American Indian, Eskimo, and Aleut Population." U.S. Census Bureau, Population Division. *www.census.gov/population/www/pop-profile/amerind.html* (accessed 15 Jan. 2011).

Paris, Leslie. *Children's Nature: The Rise of the American Summer Camp*. New York: New York University Press, 2008.

Paterson, Katherine. *Lyddie*. New York: Lodestar, 1991.

Paxton, Richard J. "'Someone with Like a Life Wrote It': The Effects of a Visible Author on High School History Students." *Journal of Educational Psychology* 89, 2 (1997): 235–50.

Peck, Richard. *The River between Us*. Reprint, New York: Puffin, 2005. First published 2003 by Dial.

Peck, Robert Newton. *A Day No Pigs Would Die*. Reprint, New York: Laurel Leaf, 2005. First published 1972 by Knopf.

Pederson, Patricia Velde. "What Is Measured Is Treasured: The Impact of the No Child Left Behind Act on Nonassessed Subjects." *Clearing House* 80, 6 (2007): 287–91.

Peterson, Robert E. "Teaching How to Read the World and Change It: Critical Pedagogy in the Intermediate Grades." In *The Critical Pedagogy Reader*, edited by Antonia Darder, Marta Baltodano, and Rodolfo D. Torres. New York: RoutledgeFalmer, 2003.

Petry, Ann Lane. *Tituba of Salem Village*. Reprint, New York: HarperCollins, 1991. First published 1964 by Thomas Y. Crowell.

Phillips, Ulrich Bonnell. *American Negro Slavery: A Survey of the Supply, Employ-*

ment and Control of Negro Labor as Determined by the Plantation Regime. New York: D. Appleton, 1918.

Philp, Kenneth R. *Termination Revisited: American Indians on the Trail to Self-Determination, 1933–1953*. Lincoln: University of Nebraska Press, 1999.

Pinkney, Andrea Davis. "Awards That Stand on Solid Ground." *Horn Book Magazine* 77, 5 (2001): 535–39.

Plane, Ann Marie. *Colonial Intimacies: Indian Marriage in Early New England*. Ithaca, NY: Cornell University Press, 2000.

"Pooh and Pals in Paper." *New York Times Book Review*, 13 Feb. 1972.

Prucha, Francis Paul. *The Great Father: The United States Government and the American Indians*. Vols. 1 and 2. Lincoln: University of Nebraska Press, 1984.

Radway, Janice A. *A Feeling for Books: The Book-of-the-Month Club, Literary Taste, and Middle-Class Desire*. Chapel Hill: University of North Carolina Press, 1997.

Ravitch, Diane. "The Educational Backgrounds of History Teachers." In *Knowing, Teaching, and Learning History: National and International Perspectives*, edited by Peter N. Stearns, Peter Seixas, and Sam Wineburg. New York: New York University Press, 2000.

———. *The Language Police: How Pressure Groups Restrict What Students Learn*. New York: Random House, 2003.

———. *Left Back: A Century of Failed School Reforms*. New York: Simon and Schuster, 2000.

———. "Multiculturalism: E Pluribus Plures." In *Debating P.C.: The Controversy over Political Correctness on College Campuses*, edited by Paul Berman. New York: Dell, 1992.

———. "Thin Gruel: How the Language Police Drain the Life and Content from Our Texts." *American Educator* 27, 2 (2003): 6–19.

Reese, Debbie. *American Indians in Children's Literature*. 2006–2010. *americanindiansinchildrensliterature.blogspot.com*.

Rehak, Melanie. "The Life and Death of Paula Fox: An Unexpected Literary Resurrection." *New York Times Magazine*, 4 March 2001.

Renaissance Learning. Website. *www.renlearn.com/default.aspx* (accessed 15 Jan. 2011).

———. *What Kids Are Reading: The Book Reading Habits of Students in American Schools*. Wisconsin Rapids, WI: Renaissance Learning, 2010.

"Report Finds St. Louis Most Dangerous U.S. City." *MSNBC*, 30 Oct. 2006. *www.msnbc.msn.com/id/15475741/ns/us_news-crime_and_courts*.

Rice, Dona Herweck. *A Guide for Using "The Witch of Blackbird Pond" in the Classroom*. Westminster, CA: Teacher Created Resources, 1991.

Richey, Cynthia K., and Doreen S. Hurley. "The Right Stuff: Books That Help Children Develop a Moral Code by Which to Live." *School Library Journal* 42, 6 (1996): 54–55.

Richgels, Donald J., Carl M. Tomlinson, and Michael O. Tunnell. "Comparison of Elementary Students' History Textbooks and Trade Books." *Journal of Educational Research* 86, 3 (1993): 161–72.

Richter, Conrad. *The Light in the Forest*. Reprint, New York: Bantam, 1975. First published 1953 by Knopf.

———. Papers. Manuscript Division, Department of Rare Books and Special Collections, Princeton University Library.

Richter, Harvena. *Writing to Survive: The Private Notebooks of Conrad Richter*. Albuquerque: University of New Mexico Press, 1988.

Roberts, Kenneth. *Northwest Passage*. Reprint, Camden, ME: Down East, 2001. First published 1936 by Doubleday Doran.

Robin, Ron. *The Barbed-Wire College: Reeducating German POWs in the United States during World War II*. Princeton, NJ: Princeton University Press, 1995.

Robinson, Joe. "Adrift in a Sea of Fiction." *Los Angeles Times*, 15 June 2004.

———. "Marooned: 18 Years of Solitude." *Los Angeles Times*, 15 June 2004.

Roediger, David R. *The Wages of Whiteness: Race and the Making of the American Working Class*. New York: Verso Press, 1991.

Rogers, Robert. *Journals of Major Robert Rogers*. Corinth, NY: Corinth Books, 1961.

"*Roll of Thunder, Hear My Cry*." Book review. *Center for Children's Books Bulletin* 30, 3 (1976): 49.

"*Roll of Thunder, Hear My Cry*." Book review. *Horn Book Magazine* 52, 6 (1976): 627.

"*Roll of Thunder, Hear My Cry*." Book review. *Horn Book Magazine* 58, 2 (1982): 174.

Roll of Thunder, Hear My Cry. Directed by Jack Smight Writing. Van Nuys, CA: LIVE Home Video, 1978.

Rollins, Charlemae Hills. *We Build Together: A Reader's Guide to Negro Life and Literature for Elementary and High School Use*. Chicago: National Council of Teachers of English, 1941.

Roorbach, A. O. "The Historical Novel as an Aid to the Teaching of Social Studies." *Historical Outlook* 20, 8 (1929): 396–98.

Rosenblatt, Louise M. *The Reader, the Text, the Poem: The Transactional Theory of the Literary Work*, 2nd ed. Carbondale, IL: Southern Illinois Press, 1994.

Rosenzweig, Roy, and David Thelen. *The Presence of the Past: Popular Uses of History in American Life*. New York: Columbia University Press, 1998.

Royster, Charles. *A Revolutionary People at War: The Continental Army and American Character, 1775–1783*. Chapel Hill: University of North Carolina Press, 1979.

Rubin, Joan Shelley. "Silver Linings: Print and Gentility in the World of Johnny Tremain." *Proceedings of the American Antiquarian Society* 113, 1 (2003): 37–52.

Rushdy, Ashraf H. A. *Neo-Slave Narratives: Studies of Social Logic of a Literary Form*. New York: Oxford University Press, 1999.

Rutherford, Charles S. "A New Dog with an Old Trick: Archetypal Patterns in *Sounder*." In *Movies as Artifacts: Cultural Criticism of Popular Film*, edited by Michael T. Marsden et al. Chicago: Nelson-Hall, 1982.

Ryan, Pam Muñoz. *Esperanza Rising*. New York: Scholastic, 2000.

Santa Barbara Museum of Natural History. "The Lone Woman of San Nicolas Island." *www.sbnature.org/research/anthro/chumash/faq.htm* (accessed 15 Jan. 2011).

Savage, Marsha K., and Tom V. Savage. "Children's Literature in Middle School Social Studies." *Social Studies* 84, 1 (1993): 32–36.

Schmaier, Maurice D. "Conrad Richter's *The Light in the Forest*: An Ethnohistorical Approach to Fiction." *Ethnohistory* 7, 4 (1960): 327–98.

Schneider, Dean. "Talking with Christopher Paul Curtis." *Book Links* 18, 2 (2008): 14–16.

Schon, Isabel. "A Master Storyteller and His Distortions of Pre-Columbian and Hispanic Cultures." *Journal of Reading* 29, 4 (1986): 322–25.

Schwartz, Albert V. "The Black Experience as Backdrop for White Adventure Story." *Interracial Books for Children* 5, 5 (1974): 4+.

———. "'The Cay': An Award Regretted, Not Revoked." *Interracial Books for Children* 6, 5–6 (1975): 19.

———. "'The Cay': Racism Still Rewarded." *Interracial Books for Children* 3, 4 (1971): 7.

———. "Revoking 'The Cay' Award: The Establishment Cries Foul!" *Interracial Books for Children* 6, 3–4 (1975): 7.

———. "*Sounder*: A Black or a White Tale? Flaws in Newbery Award Winner Obscured by Innate White Bias." *Interracial Books for Children* 3, 1 (1970): 3.

Schwebel, Sara L. "Historical Fiction and the Classroom: History and Myth in Elizabeth George Speare's *The Witch of Blackbird Pond*." *Children's Literature in Education: An International Quarterly* 34, 3 (2003): 195–218.

———. "Rewriting the Captivity Narrative for Contemporary Children: Speare, Bruchac, and the French and Indian War." *New England Quarterly* 84, 2 (2011): 318–46.

"Scott O'Dell, Children's Author, Dies." *Washington Post*, 18 Oct. 1989.

Seale, Doris. "*The Sign of the Beaver*." In *Through Indian Eyes: The Native Experience in Books for Children*, edited by Beverly Slapin and Doris Seale. Los Angeles: UCLA American Indian Studies Center, 1998.

Seale, Doris, and Beverly Slapin, eds. *A Broken Flute: The Native Experience in Books for Children*. Walnut Creek, CA: AltaMira Press, 2005.

Seixas, Peter. "*Schweigen! Die Kinder!* Or, Does Postmodern History Have a Place in the Schools?" In *Knowing, Teaching, and Learning History: National and International Perspectives*, edited by Peter N. Stearns, Peter Seixas, and Sam Wineburg. New York: New York University Press, 2000.

Shannon, Patrick. *Broken Promises: Reading Instruction in Twentieth-Century America*. Granby, MA: Bergin and Garvey, 1989.

———. "Commentary: Critique of False Generosity: A Response to Baumann." *Reading Research Quarterly* 28, 1 (1993): 8–14.

Shemilt, Denis. "The Caliph's Coin: The Currency of Narrative Frameworks in History Teaching." In *Knowing, Teaching, and Learning History: National and International Perspectives*, edited by Peter N. Stearns, Peter Seixas, and Sam Wineburg. New York: New York University Press, 2000.

Shulman, Lee S. "Knowledge and Teaching: Foundations for the New Reform." *Harvard Educational Review* 57, 1 (1987): 1–21.

Silver, Linda. "From Baldwin to Singer." *School Library Journal* 25, 6 (1979): 27–29.

Silvey, Anita, ed. *Children's Books and Their Creators*. Boston: Houghton Mifflin, 1995.

———, ed. *The Essential Guide to Children's Books and Their Creators*. Boston: Houghton Mifflin, 2002.

———. "Has the Newbery Lost Its Way?" *School Library Journal* 54, 10 (2008): 38–41.

Simon, Katherine G. *Moral Questions in the Classroom: How to Get Kids to Think Deeply about Real Life and Their Schoolwork*. New Haven, CT: Yale University Press, 2001.

Slapin, Beverly, and Doris Seale, eds. *Through Indian Eyes: The Native Experience in Books for Children*. Los Angeles: UCLA American Indian Studies Center, 1998.

"*The Slave Dancer.*" Book review. *Childhood Education* 50, 6 (1974): 335.

Slotkin, Richard. *Gunfighter Nation: The Myth of the Frontier in Twentieth-Century America.* New York: Atheneum, 1992.

———. *Regeneration through Violence: The Mythology of the American Frontier, 1600–1890.* Norman: University of Oklahoma Press, 1973.

Smith, J. Lea, and Holly A. Johnson. "Dreaming of America: Weaving Literature into Middle-School Social Studies." *Social Studies* 86, 2 (1995): 60–68.

Smith, Marion Jaques. *A History of Maine: From Wilderness to Statehood.* Portland, ME: Falmouth, 1949.

Sonlight Curriculum. "How Literature-Rich Homeschooling Awakens Your Child's Natural Passion for Learning." *www.sonlight.com/literature.html* (accessed 15 Jan. 2011).

"*Sounder.*" Book review. *Center for Children's Books Bulletin* 23, 4 (1969): 54.

"*Sounder.*" Book review. *Commonweal* 91, 8 (1969): 257.

Sounder. Directed by Kevin Hooks. Burbank, CA: Disney, 2003.

Sounder. Directed by Martin Ritt. Hollywood, CA: Paramount, 1972.

SparkNotes. Reading guides for *Across Five Aprils, Island of the Blue Dolphins, Johnny Tremain, The Light in the Forest, My Brother Sam Is Dead, Roll of Thunder, Hear My Cry, Sounder,* and *To Kill a Mockingbird. www.sparknotes.com* (accessed 15 Jan. 2011).

Speare, Elizabeth George. *Calico Captive.* Reprint, Boston: Houghton Mifflin, 2001. First published 1957 by Houghton Mifflin.

———. "Laura Ingalls Wilder Acceptance Speech." *Horn Book Magazine* 65, 4 (1989): 460–64.

———. "On Writing *The Sign of the Beaver.*" *Book Links* 2, 3 (1993): 19.

———. *The Sign of the Beaver.* Reprint, New York: Bantam Doubleday Dell, 1984. First published 1983 by Houghton Mifflin.

———. "The Survival Story." *Horn Book Magazine* 64, 2 (1988): 163–72.

———. *The Witch of Blackbird Pond.* Reprint, New York: Dell, 1971. First published 1958 by Houghton Mifflin.

Speck, Frank Gouldsmith. *Penobscot Man: The Life History of a Forest Tribe in Maine.* Philadelphia: University of Pennsylvania Press, 1940.

Spicer, Mary F. *A Teaching Guide to "Island of the Blue Dolphins."* Eugene, OR: Garlic Press, 1996.

Spigel, Lynn. *Make Room for TV: Television and the Family Ideal in Postwar America.* Chicago: University of Chicago Press, 1992.

Squire, James R. "Textbooks to the Forefront." *Book Research Quarterly* 1, 2 (1985): 12–18.

Stamm, Henry E., IV. *People of the Wind: The Eastern Shoshone, 1825–1900.* Norman: University of Oklahoma Press, 1999.

Stampp, Kenneth M. *The Peculiar Institution: Slavery in the Ante-Bellum South.* New York: Knopf, 1956.

Stauffer, John. *The Black Hearts of Men: Radical Abolitionists and the Transformation of Race.* Cambridge, MA: Harvard University Press, 2002.

Stearns, Peter N., Peter Seixas, and Sam Wineburg, eds. *Knowing, Teaching, and Learning History: National and International Perspectives.* New York: New York University Press, 2000.

Steig, William. *Sylvester and the Magic Pebble.* New York: Windmill, 1969.

Stensland, Anna Lee. *Literature by and about the American Indian: An Annotated Bibliography for Junior and Senior High School Students.* Urbana, IL: National Council of Teachers of English, 1973.

Stewart, Michelle Pagni. "Judging Authors by the Color of Their Skin? Quality Native American Children's Literature." *MELUS* 27, 2 (2002): 179–93.

Stone Fox. Directed by Harvey Hart. n.p.: Worldvision Home Video, 1987.

Stones, Rosemary. "Proud and Prejudiced." *Times (London) Literary Supplement*, 2 Dec. 1977.

Stott, Jon C. "Native American Narratives and the Children's Literature Curriculum." In *Teaching Children's Literature: Issues, Pedagogy, Resources*, edited by Glenn Edward Sadler. New York: Modern Language Association of America, 1992.

Sugrue, Thomas J. *Origins of the Urban Crisis: Race and Inequality in Postwar Detroit.* Princeton, NJ: Princeton University Press, 1996.

Sullivan, Michael. "Robert Peck and Shaker Beliefs: A Day the Truth Would Die." *ALAN Review* 25, 1 (1997): 13–17.

Summer of My German Soldier. Directed by Michael Tuchner. New York: Simon and Schuster Video, 1986.

Sunal, Cynthia Szymanski, and Mary Elizabeth Haas. *Social Studies for the Elementary and Middle Grades: A Constructivist Approach.* Boston: Allyn and Bacon, 2002.

Sunda, Ruth. "Consider the Source: Evaluating Source Reliability through the Study of *The Witch of Blackbird Pond*." Webquest. *www.kyrene.org/schools/brisas/sunda/webquest/considersource.htm* (accessed 15 Jan. 2011).

Superka, Douglas P., Sharryl Hawke, and Irving Morrissett. "The Current and Future Status of the Social Studies." *Social Education* 44, 5 (1980): 362–69.

Symcox, Linda. *Whose History? The Struggle for National Standards in the American Classroom.* New York: Teachers College Press, 2002.

Tait, Leia. *Avi.* New York: Weigl, 2007.

Tarr, C. Anita. "An Unintentional System of Gaps: A Phenomenological Reading of Scott O'Dell's *Island of the Blue Dolphins*." *Children's Literature in Education* 28, 2 (1997): 61–71.

Taxel, Joel. "The Black Experience in Children's Fiction: Controversies Surrounding Award Winning Books." *Curriculum Inquiry* 16, 3 (1986): 246.

Taylor, Alan. *Liberty Men and Great Proprietors: The Revolutionary Settlement on the Maine Frontier, 1760–1820.* Chapel Hill: University of North Carolina Press, 1990.

Taylor, Mildred D. "Acceptance Speech for the 1997 ALAN Award." *ALAN Review* 25, 3 (1998): 2–3.

———. *The Land.* New York: Penguin, 2001.

———. *Let the Circle Be Unbroken.* Reprint, New York: Puffin, 1991. First published 1981 by Dial.

———. "Newbery Medal Acceptance." In *Newbery and Caldecott Medal Books, 1976–1985, with Their Authors' Acceptance Papers and Related Material Chiefly from the "Horn Book Magazine,"* edited by Lee Kingman. Boston: Horn Book, 1986.

———. *The Road to Memphis.* New York: Dial, 1990.

———. *Roll of Thunder, Hear My Cry.* Reprint, New York: Puffin, 1997. First published 1976 by Dial.

————. *Song of the Trees*. New York: Dial Books for Young Readers, 1975.

Taylor, Theodore. *The Cay*. Reprint, New York: Dell Yearling, 2002. First published 1969 by Delacorte Press.

————. "Exploding the Literary Canon." *ALAN Review* 25, 1 (1997): 2–4.

————. Letter to the editor. *Top of the News* (Apr. 1975): 284–88.

————. *Making Love to Typewriters*. Raleigh, NC: Ivy House, 2005.

————. *Timothy of the Cay*. Reprint, New York: Avon, 1994. First published 1993 by Harcourt Brace.

TeachingBooks.net. Interview with Christopher Paul Curtis. 22 Apr. 2002. *www.teachingbooks.net/content/Curtis_qu.pdf*.

Texas Reading Initiative. *Research-Based Content Area Reading Instruction*, rev. ed. Austin: Texas Education Agency, 2002.

Thompson, Katherine F., and Elaine R. Homestead. "Middle School Organization through the 1970s, 1980s, and 1990s." *Middle School Journal* 35, 3 (2004): 56–60.

Thompson, Melissa Kay. "A Sea of Good Intentions: Native Americans in Books for Children." *Lion and the Unicorn* 25, 3 (2001): 353–74.

Thompson, Sally Anne M. "Scott O'Dell—Weaver of Stories." *Catholic Library World* 49, 8 (1978): 340–42.

Thoreau, Henry David. *The Maine Woods*. Reprint, New York: Thomas Y. Crowell, 1909. First published 1864 by Ticknor and Fields, Boston.

Tillman, Lynne. "The Artist's Voice since 1981." *Bomb* 95 (2006). *bombsite.com/issues/95*.

Tjoumas, Renee. "Native American Literature for Young People: A Survey of Collection Development Methods in Public Libraries." *Library Trends* 41, 3 (1993): 493–523.

Tomlinson, Carl M., Michael O. Tunnell, and Donald J. Richgels. "The Content and Writing of History in Textbooks and Trade Books." In *The Story of Ourselves: Teaching History through Children's Literature*, edited by Michael O. Tunnell and Richard Ammon. Portsmouth, NH: Heinemann, 1993.

Toppo, Greg. "See 'Dick and Jane'—Again." *USA Today*, 25 Feb. 2004.

Tremper, Ellen. "Black English in Children's Literature." *Lion and the Unicorn* 3, 2 (1979–1980): 105–24.

Treuer, David. *Native American Fiction: A User's Manual*. St. Paul, MN: Graywolf Press, 2006.

Trites, Roberta Seelinger. *Disturbing the Universe: Power and Repression in Adolescent Literature*. Iowa City: University of Iowa Press, 2000.

Turley, David. "By Way of DuBois: The Question of Black Initiative in the Civil War and Reconstruction." In *The State of U.S. History*, edited by Melvyn Stokes. New York: Berg, 2002.

Uchida, Yoshiko. *Journey to Topaz*. Reprint, Berkeley, CA: Heyday, 2005. First published 1971 by Scribner.

Ulrich, Laurel Thatcher. *The Age of Homespun: Objects and Stories in the Creation of an American Myth*. New York: Knopf, 2001.

U.S. Congress, Ad Hoc Subcommittee on De Facto School Segregation of the Committee on Education and Labor. *Books for Schools and the Treatment of Minorities: Hearings before the Committee on Education and Labor*. 89th Congress, 2nd session. Washington, DC: U.S. GPO, 1966.

Van Kirk, Eileen. "Imagining the Past through Historical Novels." *School Library Journal* 39, 8 (1993): 50–51.

VanSledright, Bruce. *In Search of America's Past: Learning to Read History in Elementary School.* New York: Teachers College Press, 2002.

Vaughan, Alden T. "The Origins Debate: Slavery and Racism in Seventeenth-Century Virginia." *Virginia Magazine of History and Biography* 97, 3 (1989): 311–54.

Villano, Tonia L. "Should Social Studies Textbooks Become History? A Look at Alternative Methods to Activate Schema in the Intermediate Classroom." *Reading Teacher* 59, 2 (2005): 122–31.

Visit with Scott O'Dell, A. Houghton Mifflin Author and Artist Series. Boston: Houghton Mifflin, 1983. Videocassette (VHS).

Vollstadt, Elizabeth Weiss. *Understanding "Johnny Tremain."* San Diego: Lucent, 2001.

Volmann, Tim. "A Survey of Eastern Indian Land Claims, 1970–1979." *Maine Law Review* 31, 1 (1979): 5–16.

Weaver, Jace, Craig S. Womack, and Robert Warrior. *American Indian Literary Nationalism.* Albuquerque: University of New Mexico Press, 2006.

West, Rethel C. *The History of Milo, 1802–1923.* Dover-Foxcroft, ME: Fred D. Barrows, 1923.

White, Haydn. *Tropics of Discourse: Essays in Cultural Criticism.* Baltimore: Johns Hopkins University Press, 1978.

White, Richard. *The Middle Ground: Indians, Empires, and Republics in the Great Lakes Region, 1650–1815.* New York: Cambridge University Press, 1991.

Whitehead, Winifred. "The Mockingbird Encircled." *Use of English* 36, 3 (1985): 31–40.

Wilder, Laura Ingalls. *Little House on the Prairie.* Reprint, New York: HarperCollins, 1981. First published 1935 by Harper and Brothers.

Wilenz, Sean. *Chants Democratic: New York City and the Rise of the American Working Class, 1788–1850.* New York: Oxford University Press, 1984.

Wilkinson, Charles F. *Messages from Frank's Landing: A Story of Salmon, Treaties, and the Indian Way.* Seattle: University of Washington Press, 2000.

Willett, Holly G. "*Rifles for Watie*: Rollins, Riley, and Racism." *Libraries and Culture* 36, 4 (2001): 487–505.

Williams-Myers, A. J. "Slavery, Rebellion, and Revolution in the Americas: A Historiographical Scenario on the Theses of Genovese and Others." *Journal of Black Studies* 26, 4 (1996): 381–400.

Wineburg, Sam. *Historical Thinking and Other Unnatural Acts: Charting the Future of Teaching the Past.* Philadelphia: Temple University Press, 2001.

———. "On the Reading of Historical Texts: Notes on the Breach between School and the Academy." *American Educational Research Journal* 28, 3 (1991): 495–519.

Wintle, Justin, and Emma Fisher, eds. *The Pied Pipers: Interviews with the Influential Creators of Children's Literature.* New York: Paddington Press, 1975.

Womack, Craig S. *Red on Red: Native American Literary Separatism.* Minneapolis: University of Minnesota Press, 1999.

Womack, Craig S., Daniel Heath Justice, and Christopher B. Teuton, eds. *Reasoning Together: The Native Critics Collective.* Norman: University of Oklahoma Press, 2008.

Women on Words and Images. *Dick and Jane as Victims: Sex Stereotyping in Children's Readers.* Princeton, NJ: Women on Words and Images, 1972.

Woodward, Arthur. "Juana María: Sidelights on the Indian Occupation of San Nicolas Island." *Westerners Brand Book, Los Angeles Corral* 7 (1957): 245–70.

Wyile, Andrea Schwenke. "Expanding the View of First-Person Narration." *Children's Literature in Education* 30, 3 (1999): 185–202.

Yates, Elizabeth. "Acceptance Paper: Climbing Some Mountain in the Mind." In *Newbery Medal Books, 1922–1955, with Their Authors' Acceptance Papers and Related Material, Chiefly from the "Horn Book Magazine,"* edited by Bertha Mahony Miller and Elinor Whitney Field. Boston: Horn Book, 1955.

———. *Amos Fortune, Free Man*. Reprint, New York: Dell, 1974. First published 1950 by Aladdin.

———. *My Diary—My World*. Philadelphia: Westminster Press, 1981.

———. *My Widening World*. Philadelphia: Westminster Press, 1983.

Yeager, Elizabeth Anne, and O. L. Davis Jr., eds. *Wise Social Studies Teaching in an Age of High-Stakes Testing: Essays on Classroom Practices and Possibilities*. Greenwich, CT: Information Age, 2005.

Yep, Laurence. *Dragonwings*. New York: HarperCollins, 1975.

York, Neil L. "Son of Liberty: Johnny Tremain and the Art of Making American Patriots." *Early American Studies: An Interdisciplinary Journal* 6, 2 (2008): 422–47.

Zimmerman, Jonathan. *Whose America? Culture Wars in the Public Schools*. Cambridge, MA: Harvard University Press, 2002.

Zimmermann, Susan, and Ellin Oliver Keene. *Mosaic of Thought*. Portsmouth, NH: Heinemann, 1997.

Zinn, Howard. *A People's History of the United States, 1942–Present*. New York: HarperCollins, 1980.

Zipes, Jack. "Taking Political Stock: New Theoretical and Critical Approaches to Anglo-American Children's Literature in the 1980s." *Lion and the Unicorn* 14, 1 (1990): 7–22.

Index

Fictional characters indexed by first name.